SO-BDL-616

FIRST NEGOTIATIONS

A warning bell went off inside Autumn's head when Lloyd Murphy suggested dinner. "Does dinner with you have anything to do with my getting the job?"

His eyes met hers evenly. "Everything. If you take the job, an apartment will go with it. A very nice apartment, and a very nice automobile. I'll coach you, and make you into the best business woman you can possibly be. But it will take time—for both of us."

"Is this something you do often?"

"Only when I see a woman who shows potential. It isn't just sex—although good sex is a great part of it. I like to take beautiful women and mold them into something they wouldn't have been otherwise."

But Autumn had her own evaluation of her potential. As propositions went, Lloyd Murphy's wasn't bad—but it was still only a proposition. . . .

ROSES ARE FOR THE RICH

∅ SIGNET (0451)

SENSATIONAL BESTSELLERS!

☐ **FAME AND FORTUNE by Kate Coscarelli.** Beautiful women . . . glittering Beverly Hills . . . the boutiques . . . the bedrooms . . . the names you drop and the ones you whisper . . . all in the irresistible novel that has everyone reading . . . "From the opening, the reader is off and turning the pages!"—*Los Angeles Times*   (134702—$3.95)

☐ **HER FATHER'S DAUGHTER by William J. Coughlin.** Victoria Van Horn. A beautiful and daring woman in a sizzling novel of money and power. What she wants most is to prove that she's as good as any man in her father's company. When he dies, she gets her chance—only to find herself involved in the high-risk world of a vast corporation where power and corruption are locked in an unholy embrace. "Great entertainment"—*Detroit Free Press*   (400372—$4.50)

☐ **THE TWELVE APOSTLES by William J. Coughlin.** A scorching novel about the ravenous new breed of lawyers . . . big, juicy . . . This portrait of modern life oozes with sex and scandal, glamour and greed . . . and all the other things that go along with the world of money and power. A Literary Guild Alternate Selection.   (136047—$3.95)

☐ **SINS by Judith Gould.** Hélène Junot was the most successful woman in the international fashion world. Hers is the story of a daring but vulnerable woman with the courage to use any means to reach the peaks of money and power, with the heart to give it all up for the love that would make her life whole. . . .   (140249—$3.95)

☐ **LOVE-MAKERS by Judith Gould.** Their glittering hotel chain, sky-high ambitions, and sexual greed crossed all borders. They are four generations of daring, dauntless, desiring Hale women who fight with passion for what they want—love, sex, power, wealth—only to learn that the price of power is far more than they bargained for. . . .

          (140362—$4.50)

Prices slightly higher in Canada

Buy them at your local bookstore or use this convenient coupon for ordering.
NEW AMERICAN LIBRARY,
P.O. Box 999, Bergenfield, New Jersey 07621

Please send me the books I have checked above. I am enclosing $_____ (please add $1.00 to this order to cover postage and handling). Send check or money order—no cash or C.O.D.'s. Prices and numbers subject to change without notice.

Name_____

Address_____

City_____ Zip Code_____
Allow 4-6 weeks for delivery.
This offer is subject to withdrawal without notice.

ROSES ARE FOR THE RICH

JONELL LAWSON

A SIGNET BOOK

NEW AMERICAN LIBRARY

PUBLISHER'S NOTE

This book is a work of fiction. Names, characters, places, and incidents
either are the product of the author's imagination or are used fictitiously,
and any resemblance to actual persons, living or dead, events, or locales
is entirely coincidental.

NAL BOOKS ARE AVAILABLE AT QUANTITY DISCOUNTS WHEN USED
TO PROMOTE PRODUCTS OR SERVICES. FOR INFORMATION PLEASE
WRITE TO PREMIUM MARKETING DIVISION, NEW AMERICAN LIBRARY,
1633 BROADWAY, NEW YORK, NEW YORK 10019.

Copyright © 1986 by Jonell Lawson.

Photo copyright © 1987 Lorimar-Telepictures Productions, Inc. All
rights reserved.

All rights reserved

SIGNET TRADEMARK REG U S PAT OFF AND FOREIGN COUNTRIES
REGISTERED TRADEMARK—MARCA REGISTRADA
HECHO EN CHICAGO, U S A

SIGNET, SIGNET CLASSIC, MENTOR, ONYX, PLUME, MERIDIAN
and NAL BOOKS are published by NAL PENGUIN INC.,
1633 Broadway, New York, New York 10019

First Printing, February, 1986

4   5   6   7   8   9   10   11   12

PRINTED IN THE UNITED STATES OF AMERICA

For the ones I hold most dear,
My husband Chuck,
My sons Charles and Michael,
My daughters Vicki and Carlotta

ACKNOWLEDGMENTS

It is my thought that few books are written without the help and encouragement of friends and family. I would like to take this way to thank the following: Jean Bryant and Cathy Scearce. Also, Dr. Steven Yarnell and Pam Williams.

All my co-writers at Seannache: Kathy Armstrong, Janice Baczewski, Barthe Declements, Bonnie Drury, Beverlye Garka, Norma Johnson, Lorraine Jones, Marilyn Kapp, Muriel Newsome, Irene Pascoe, Helen Passey, Willo Davis Roberts and Pam Toth.

I would like to offer a special thanks to two very special people. Without their help, this novel might never have reached print: my agent Aaron Priest, and my editor Maureen Baron.

For his patience with me and my many questions, I gratefully acknowledge Dr. Frederick P. Moore.

Prologue

Ordinarily she hated funerals, but Autumn had felt untouched by the long, grim ceremony. Earlier, the church on Elm Street had overflowed with townspeople who came to pay their last respects to her husband, Brian Douglas Osborne, or to make sure he was really dead.

She glanced about the graveside and her eyes paused briefly on each member of the family. Standing across from her were Douglas' brothers, Homer and his wife Bea, George and his wife Harriet, and Dale. Their faces were set in the proper grievous expressions, but Autumn knew they were secretly rejoicing that Douglas was finally dead. Each had his or her own reason for wanting the man out of their lives forever.

Tucked at her elbow was Brian Douglas Osborne Jr. No emotion showed on his face as he pulled a soiled handkerchief from his pocket and wiped away trickles of sweat brought by the hot summer day. He was her stepson, four years older than she, an archaeologist, and almost a stranger. They had met ten years before on three separate occasions, twice only briefly. Their third encounter was a bitter memory for her; for Brian the meeting could only be a blur—he was staggering drunk on moonshine.

Autumn had been eighteen with wild, flyaway hair and a face that was still rounded with baby fat. The years had hollowed her cheeks, and hard work had thinned her body. Money had added style and self-possession. It was doubtful he would remember her now. If he should, ten years of hard work could be erased in a matter of moments.

She glanced again at the family, then to the closed satin-lined box that held her husband. A slight breeze rose and danced across her face, lifted the veil, and brought the heavy scent of flowers. To some it was the sickening smell of death. To her it was the sweet smell of success, and she smiled behind her black veil.

"Easy, Mother. Your grief is showing."

She felt Brian at her elbow, heard the whispered words, but turned without a reply and left the fenced area that held four generations of Osbornes. She walked at a fast pace, but with directness and respect for the dead. Pausing in the shade of a tall oak, she stood alone near a small, unimpressive headstone. The grave was off to one side with a patch of wild cornflowers growing at its base. The blooms that had once been a brilliant blue were faded and dull now, the stems bent and hanging like little broken arms. She gazed at the headstone and her eyes dimmed with sorrow. The minister had given her one white rose and bit by bit she tore it apart and scattered the petals over the grave.

"Friend of yours?"

She turned at the sound of his voice, annoyed that he had followed. Like his father, Brian was tall and broad-shouldered. He had the same blond hair as all the Osborne men, heavily streaked from the sun, and uncombed. Clear, wide-set blue eyes smiled with sarcasm over a lush untidy beard. The cut of his suit was strictly Saville Row, but the suit itself was wrinkled. "No," she said. "He wasn't a friend."

"Then why the rose petals?"

"Your father had so many, and this grave looked so bare. I thought it only fair to share with one who has less."

Brian turned toward his father's grave. "Yes, the flowers are plentiful. I wonder how much of it is sincere." He took Autumn by the arm courteously and led her from the cemetery. As they approached the limousine, a uniformed chauffeur stepped forward.

Artie was strikingly handsome, a man with a flawless appearance. Fine shades of gray streaked his dark hair at the temples. His face was sober, a funeral mask, but his blue eyes were as brilliant as the cornflowers, and bore a devil-may-care expression. "Artie," she said, "this is Brian, Douglas' son. He will be your new employer."

Artie acknowledged the introduction by a nod of the head, then opened the door to the Rolls with a slight bow. Autumn smiled to herself in secret amusement. She knew Artie well. His expression seemed to say: How the hell did I get so lucky? If anything, Artie had even more reason than she to despise Douglas Osborne. Unconsciously, Artie's contempt for the father had spread to the son.

Autumn entered the car, followed by Brian. She waited until Artie was behind the wheel and the engine started before raising the panel between the two seats. "How did you know I was your father's widow? I thought you and Douglas weren't in touch."

"The cabbie. Old Will picked me up at the station. He took great delight in telling me all about my new mother. According to Will, Dad married a chick young enough to be his daughter. A woman named Autumn." Brian sprawled in the seat, his long legs arched and spread wide. He sighed and rested his head against the back of the seat. "How did my father die? The telegram didn't say."

"He drowned."

Brian turned to Autumn, his brows arched in surprise. "He drowned? My father drowned? Where did he drown?"

"The pool. If you want details, you'll have to talk to your uncles. I was out of town at the time, so I don't know exactly how it happened."

Brian drew a hand down over his face, as if to wipe away the momentary smile of amazement. "Christ. I always thought it would take a herd of buffalo to bring that old bastard down."

Autumn knew there was a rift between Douglas and his son; still, Brian's attitude surprised her. "You don't seem too broken up."

"Neither do you."

"I'm not, and I won't play the hypocrite and pretend that I am."

"Then why did you marry him?"

"For his money."

Brian threw back his head in wholehearted laughter. "I do like an honest woman." He gazed at her veiled face for a moment, then reached and pulled the hat from her head.

Autumn felt naked without the veil, and unprepared to face him so abruptly. For a moment she felt eighteen again: young, vulnerable. Her first impulse was to turn her face away from him, but slowly and with control she caught his glance and gazed steadily.

Since then, time had made changes, but Autumn asked herself if it had been enough. Her features were fine, her skin fair, almost pale, as if the sun had never touched it. Her deep-set eyes were a soft brown, flecked with gray dots of light that flashed when she was angry, or sparkled when she laughed with pleasure. The one thing that hadn't changed was the hated scattering of freckles across her nose. Short, russet-colored hair with a mind of its own, framed her face in an unruly mass of damp, sweat-soggy curls. Artie had always teased that she was a flawed beauty, assuring her that the freckles and unmanageable hair only added to her appeal. Douglas had both complained and boasted that her manner was the most frustrating blend of lady and whore he had ever encountered.

When there were no signs of recognition from Brian, Autumn smiled, a teasing kind of smile. "Do I get an A?"

"At least. You must have cost Dad a buck or two."

"Several."

"And what miraculous thing did you give him in return?"

"If you have to ask, you've spent too much time with dead mummies."

His whiskers twitched. "Frisky, aren't you, Mother?"

"Don't call me Mother!"

"Yes, ma'am!"

She turned away from Brian and gazed out the window as the Rolls entered the outskirts of town. A sign arching overhead read "EDISONVILLE, KENTUCKY. BIGGEST LITTLE TOWN ON EARTH. HOME OF THE OSBORNE DISTILLERY." It seemed ironic to Autumn that a large number of distilleries were located in Kentucky, a state where many of the counties had elected to remain dry.

It was a clean, homey-looking town. Large maple trees lined the streets. The courthouse sat in the center of town, dividing Main Street and Broadway. The building was surrounded by benches and crowded with elderly men spitting tobacco juice and ogling the passing ladies. Kids screamed playfully, chasing one another around a tall oak. A bored-looking police officer stood on the corner, a cluster of teenagers on the other.

"It's still the same," Brian said with a touch of nostalgia in his voice. "All these years and nothing has changed. It's a good town. A good place to raise kids . . . a good place to grow up."

"You sound as if you missed Edisonville."

"I did. It's home."

"Why did you stay away so long?"

"I had no other choice. As much as I loved Dad, I couldn't live in the same town with him. I wouldn't have lived up to his expectations, no matter what. Everything he did, he did well."

Autumn knew she shouldn't, but the urge to needle him was too great. "Wrong," she said. "He was lousy in bed." She didn't smile, but there was a tantalizing curve at the corner of her mouth. "Are you lousy in bed too?"

He shrugged. "The mummies didn't complain."

She smiled, but rested her head against the back of the seat with a tired sigh. The humidity and heat of the day had eaten away at her vitality, as well as her self-control. Yet, there was still so much to do before she could climb between cool sheets and hide; calls to make, the gathering of the family, and the reading of the will. She wondered how well Brian would manage. Even at the best of times the family could be trying. His walk had been smooth, his stride long and even. He carried himself with the arrogance of an Osborne, but his eyes looked tired and dreamy, as if he hadn't slept for days. She felt herself soften toward him, sorry for a moment that he was going to be caught in the subtle, invisible war she had waged against Douglas and his family. But then the years rolled away and she was alone with Brian again in a stark room, the snow falling outside and the cold winds howling.

Autumn opened her eyes to find him staring at her intently. "Doubtful," she said.

"What's doubtful?"

"What you're thinking. I'm not part of your inheritance."

"What a pity."

She gathered her purse as the car moved slowly through wrought-iron gates and wound its way up the tree-studded drive. The house itself was set on several acres of rolling green hills. It stood majestically on a slight rise, as strongly rooted as the towering oaks that framed the old mansion. The house had been designed to look like a Louisiana plantation home, so much so that when gazing off into the distance one expected to see fields of cotton where weary slaves toiled under the hot sun. It always seemed anachronistic to find only green slopes where horses grazed contentedly.

The Rolls slowed to a stop in front of the house and Brian swung the door wide. Politely he helped Autumn from the car and led her along a stone walkway and between marble columns that had stood since 1905. He hesitated briefly, as if taking a deep breath, then opened the door to the foyer. Autumn swept past him, her heels tap-tapping on the marble floor. She paused at the foot of a winding staircase. "I had your rooms cleaned and aired. I think you'll find everything you need."

"I won't be using them. I'm moving into Dad's quarters."

Autumn felt her composure slipping. She wanted to shout at him, but spoke in a soft, even tone. "Your father and I had connecting rooms. I think you will be much happier in your own quarters."

"No. I think I will be much more comfortable in my father's quarters."

"Whatever!" She turned with a swish of her dresstail, her hips moving in an agitated sway.

"Fascinating," he said.

She paused and glanced back at him. "I beg your pardon."

He grinned. "The house. It feels empty as a tomb. Where is everybody?"

"They all attended the funeral. I would imagine they'll be along shortly. Molly is here. She's my personal maid and tends only to me. When you need something, call for Daisy, Jasper, or one of the others. *Don't* bother Molly."

"Yes, ma'am!"

She moved steadily up the stairs, explaining as she went, "The family has arranged for the reading of the will. Are you up to it, or would you like it postponed until you've had a chance to rest?"

"I'll be fine."

At the door to her room, she paused and spoke quietly. "I'm sorry your father is dead, Brian."

His mouth was hidden by a clump of blond whiskers, but his eyes laughed at her. "Don't go soft on me now, Mother. It doesn't become you."

"Don't call me Mother!" She spun on her heel and slammed the door between them, kicked off her shoes and sent them flying across the room. Molly, a tall woman in her early sixties, rose from a chair near the window where she had been knitting. Her once-blond hair was dove white and wrapped around her head in a braid. Her shoulders curved as if she had known hard work, but her light gray eyes were bright and she moved spryly.

Autumn looked at Molly, her eyes softening into a warm smile. She tossed her purse on the bed, and sent her hat sailing across the room to rest on a white velvet settee. "Would you fill the tub for me, Molly? I want to soak for a while before I have to face the family."

Molly nodded, but she remained in the room. "How'd it go?"

"Fine. Brian is home. He missed the funeral, but he arrived in time for the burial." She gazed at Molly, thoughtful for a moment, then padded in her stocking feet to the dressing room. Autumn returned with clothing appropriate for an evening at the country club. "This should be suitable for the reading of the will."

Molly stared at the black dress, slit at the side and cut low at the neckline to reveal the rise of her breasts. She shook her head in wonder. "You know how straitlaced the family is. If you wear that downstairs today, you'll stir up a hornet's nest."

"Exactly. The family is going to try to oust me now that Douglas is dead. I can't let that happen. I have to stay in Osborne House, for now. If I'm outrageous enough, they'll explode and insist I leave. When they do, Brian will get stubborn. If he's anything like his father, he won't let anybody tell him who can and who can't live in his house."

Molly grumbled, but went into the bathroom and drew Autumn's bath. She returned to stand beside Autumn at the large walnut desk. "I think it's time we went home. Why don't we just pack up and go back to San Francisco? This game you're playing is fine for Artie, but living two lives is wearing on you. The dragon is dead. That oughta end it."

"I can't," Autumn said. "I wish I could, but I can't."

Molly grasped Autumn's hand and shook it hard. A large diamond caught the light and exploded with a million tiny rays. Along with the diamond was a plain gold band that looked strangely out of place. "You've got diamonds on your fingers and furs on your back. You've got more money than you'll ever spend. Can't you be content with that?"

Like everything else about Autumn, the diamonds were a facade, all part of the image she had to maintain. If given a choice, she would far rather be wearing jeans, munching on hot dogs, and making plans to resume her life in San Francisco, which had been put on hold for the last six months. Gently, and with great love, Autumn leaned over and kissed Molly's deeply lined cheek. Molly had raised Autumn, but at some point their roles had reversed and now Autumn felt she had become the parent. "You don't have to stay here, Aunt Molly. Why don't you go to Turtle Ridge? It's nice there this time of year—much cooler."

Molly shook her head. "I'll stay and see you through this thing. You're messing round with dirty folks. They'll find you out one of these days. When they do, you'll be needing me. You're a strong woman, Autumn, but you're brittle, and brittle things can break." Molly had said her piece. She returned to the chair and picked up her knitting.

Autumn pulled gold earrings from her lobes and tossed them in a peanut-butter jar that sat on the desk; the jar was a memento from her past. She unbuttoned her dress and lowered it over firm, well-rounded breasts, and down around long shapely legs. Beneath a slim waist, fine hair began at her navel and grew in a tiny line to the triangle of auburn fur that seemed to flame against her fair skin.

Watching from the chair, Molly arched a quizzical eyebrow. "What's the boy like?"

"He looks like a big cuddly teddy bear, but under all that fuzz I think there's a man that can be as tough as his father if he's pushed." She rolled her panty hose into a ball and tossed them onto the bed. "I didn't think it would bother me so much to see Brian again, but he reminded me . . ." She turned abruptly and walked naked into the bathroom, leaving the words hanging in midair. There were some things even Molly didn't know. Her last meeting with Brian was one of them.

She stepped into her bath and sighed as the hot water embraced her. Leaning her head against the wall of the tub she allowed her thoughts to become muddled and disjointed. Seeing Brian again after so many years had brought it all back, and bits and pieces of the past raced through her mind. There were good times, hard times, and very sad times. Soon, though, it would all be over. She'd be free of the past that had haunted and confined her, driving her toward this day.

Molly was right. The double life she was living was wearing on her. The false front of being both lady and whore was becoming harder and harder to maintain. She thought of the days ahead, and every nerve seemed to snap. She wanted to cry, to scream, to pound her fists against the floor and shout at the unfairness of it all. She had cried once, and screamed, and pounded her fists until they cracked and ran red with blood. And she had vowed that Douglas Osborne would someday fall to his knees as she had fallen to hers.

There had been times when she had felt beaten, the task she had set for herself impossible. Fighting to hold on, she did the one thing that had sustained and strengthened her over the years. She closed her eyes, reached deep into the secret place where she kept them hidden, and took out her bittersweet memories.

I

The Beginning

1

Her name hadn't always been Autumn. She was born Sue Anne McAvan in Turtle Ridge, Kentucky. Turtle Ridge was a small, gossipy town of 2,963 that loafed through the hot summers and hibernated during the long winter months. The town hid from the rest of the world in a valley surrounded by tall, tree-studded hills. The people were simple, slow-moving, and lived by the golden rule, save for her Aunt Molly. Molly lived by her own rules and be damned what the town thought.

Her aunt was a constant source of gossip for the people of Turtle Ridge. She lived five miles from town in a small house on the river's edge. Molly made no bones about the fact that she had better things to do with her time than to sit around clucking like a bunch of hens. They called Molly an odd one because she preferred to live so far from the center of things, and because she preferred the friendship of Tucker, an old moonshiner, over them.

Molly was a pretty woman, unmarried by choice, and thirty-two when she took on the chore of raising Autumn. Uneducated, Molly worked as a cleaning woman for some of the better families in town. Molly often said with a laugh that her life had been quiet, restful, and well-organized until a wee babe was put into her arms. The baby had pink cheeks, a rosebud mouth, big intelligent eyes, and hair the color of maple leaves in autumn. The name Sue Anne never seemed quite right to Molly; twirling an auburn curl around her finger, she decided to call her Autumn.

Autumn's parents were Harry and Sara McAvan. Harry was Molly's younger brother, and a drifter. He had appeared on her doorstep with a woman heavy with child and announced that she was his wife. Molly couldn't tell Autumn very much about her mother. Sara was quiet and spoke little about her life before Harry. Two weeks after they arrived in Turtle Ridge, Sara died in childbirth.

Harry was a dreamer, a happy-go-lucky singer of songs. He played at being a father for a while, then turned Autumn over to Molly. He left Turtle Ridge bragging that he would return within a year, his pockets full of hundred-dollar bills, king of the Grande Ole Opry. Two months later, he was killed while drunk and staggering across a street in Nashville, Tennessee. His legacy to Autumn: a suitcaseful of old clothes, a snapshot of Sara, an old guitar, and $64.38. Molly had the body returned and buried in the valley beside Sara. Then she bought a used crib with the $64.38 and went about the task of raising Autumn.

Life in Turtle Ridge was quiet and uneventful for Autumn. What excitement did arise was usually of her own making, and always brought new waves of gossip. "Ooooh," they would say, shaking their heads with wonder. "I really don't know what we're going to do with that McAvan girl."

Autumn's early memories were foggy and ill-defined. There was a series of kitchens where she was given a pat on the head and told to mind her manners while Molly cleaned. She was always glad when evening came, because they could return to the small house beside the river. Her favorite times were the weekends, when she could roam the hills, swim the river, and watch Tucker making moonshine with his still. And on Saturdays there was always a matinee, and afterwards they stopped at Mart's Diner for a hamburger and a soft drink.

Her aunt wasn't a religious woman, but she thought Autumn should know something about the Almighty, so every Sunday morning they went to the Baptist church in town. Autumn always felt so fancy: dressed in her little white hat with blue flowers on the brim, and her patent-leather shoes. She sat beside Molly with her back straight and proud, listening to Preacher Anderson shout that it wasn't nice to lie, steal, lust after thy neighbor's wife, or fornicate.

Autumn wondered about the words and what it meant to lust after thy neighbor's wife. She was born with an inquisitive mind, Molly said, and often teased her that her first word had been "why." When Autumn asked questions, Molly usually answered in a way that made the young girl think until she found her own answers. When Autumn asked about fornication and lust, Molly sat down and told her outright. Autumn wondered why Preacher Anderson made such a fuss, pounding his fists and shouting damnation. Fornicating seemed like a good thing for folks to do. On the other hand, she didn't want to burn in hell's fire, either. It was something she would have to ponder, much later, when she was a grown-up. For now there were other things, more important things weighing on her mind.

Through television, Autumn had begun to realize there was a world outside Turtle Ridge that was very different from her own. Especially the way people spoke: everybody said "business," not "bidness," and "can't," not "caint," and "mirror," not "mere." "Fill" and "feel," "lack" and "like" sounded the same to Autumn, but the words had a different ring when the folks on the television said them. And not one person said "ya'all," and dinner was eaten at night, not in the middle of the day.

Finally, one day, Autumn went in search of her aunt, her small head crowded with questions. She found Molly hoeing a patch of potatoes, chickens scratching at her feet. Autumn dug her bare toe in the loose dirt and looked at Molly quizzically. "I've been thinking. Folks on the television don't talk like we do here in Turtle Ridge. Are we different, Aunt Molly?"

Molly leaned on the hoe and smiled down at her. "We probably seem a bit odd to some. Folks from the big cities up north have a way of thinking of us hillbillies as dirty, ignorant people who sit around chewing tobacco and peeing in the weeds."

"Are we?" she inquired.

"Not all of us. There's them that is, and them that ain't."

Autumn looked at Molly, her eyes wide with confusion. "Jeb, down at the hardware store, chews tobacco. Is he one of them kind of people?"

"No. Jeb's been out and around. He's a right smart man. He's learned and he's worldly."

Autumn pulled herself to her full height and kicked at a clump of dirt. "Well, I ain't fixing to be no dirty, ignorant pee-in-the-weeds person. I'm gonna be like Jeb. I'll be worldly."

"How're you gonna do that?"

Autumn had to think about the question for a moment. "I'll read," she said, and grinned. "I'll read every book in Turtle Ridge."

Molly nodded in agreement. "I think you're right. You read, and you study your figures real good. Then you'll be worldly like Jeb."

Autumn turned, her head bobbing as she walked off toward the woods. "That's what I'll do," she mumbled. "I'll read and read and read, and I'll study my numbers." She looked back at Molly with a big smile. "I love books, Aunt Molly, but most of all I like doing my numbers."

Molly watched Autumn as she darted off into the trees. "Where you off to?"

"I thought I'd mosey on over and help Tucker with his still." Autumn padded along the path, thinking about Tucker. His clothes were always dirty and his body smelled and he chewed tobacco, letting the juice dribble out of the sides of his mouth. She supposed he was one of them hillbillies, but she loved him anyhow. Several yards along the path, Autumn stepped off into the brush. She had pulled down her cotton panties before remembering that she wasn't to pee in the weeds anymore. Jerking up her drawers, she set out for the house at a run.

Molly had begun to read to Autumn when she was only a few months old. When Autumn was four, Molly had shoved a book into her hand and said, "Read." When Autumn was five, she had tossed her in the river and said,

"Swim." When she was six, Molly took her to school and said, "Learn."

School presented her with a new set of problems. Autumn had been around children before, but never a whole roomful of them. She decided they were wiggly, screaming little monkeys who had not been taught to mind their manners. Bored with the other children, she turned her attention to books, numbers, and watching Miss Ann. The teacher was fat and had the habit of scratching her behind while figuring a problem on the blackboard; a problem Autumn had usually solved long before the chalk was put aside.

Learning was easy for Autumn, but instead of the praises she had always received from Molly, the other children seemed to resent both her quick mind and her quiet reserve. They called her everything from teacher's pet, to carrot top, red-in-the-head, and freckle face. While the girls were calling her names, the boys hid her lunch pail, her coat, and yanked the pigtails Molly braided so neatly every morning.

Autumn had spent so much time alone with Molly that she didn't know how to deal with their childish pranks. She tried laughing at their name-calling, as if she thought it was funny too. And she pretended it was all a big game when the boys took her things and hid them. No one, not even Molly, knew that learning had suddenly become a torture. She studied hard, but woke each morning dreading the day she would have to spend at school, delaying the moment when Molly would drop her in front of the red brick building before going to her own day's work.

Every time Autumn began to hurt inside, or feel tears budding, or anger so raw that she wanted to kick every child within her reach, she would remind herself that Preacher Anderson had said one should turn the other cheek. And Autumn tried. She tolerated the teasing, until the fourth grade. The school year had just begun and the weather was still warm. The children were filing out the door when Bobby Joe Proctor gave her braid a tug and shouldered her aside, causing her to slip and tumble down five steps to the pavement below. Looking at her skinned knee and the rip in her new dress, Autumn flew into a rage.

She jumped to her feet, swinging her lunch box as she rose. The pail struck Bobby Joe alongside the head and knocked him off balance. He stumbled backward, caught his heel on a crack in the pavement, and fell with a thud that left him winded. Autumn saw he had a cut over his eyebrow and was gasping for breath; nonethless, she climbed on top of him and slapped him on the face, screaming that he had torn her new dress.

A shouting crowd of children gathered and teachers came running. Both she and Bobby were taken inside and questioned. Bobby confessed he had knocked Autumn down the steps, but swore it was accidental. When questioned, Autumn only shrugged. Bobby was taken to the doctor for stitches, and Molly was called to the school. The principal explained what had happened and recommended that Molly take Autumn home and blister her bottom.

Autumn and Molly left the school and were several miles down the road before either spoke. Autumn looked at her and mumbled, "Are you going to give me a spanking?"

"Do you think you need one?"

"No. I'm too old for that kind of thing."

"Oh," Molly said, and glanced at Autumn. "Now, ain't that something? The girl's too big to get her butt spanked."

Autumn began to cry, sniffling and wiping at her nose with the back of her hand. "Bobby Joe is the one that needs a whipping. He pulled my hair and he knocked me down on purpose. He made me skin my knee and he tore my new dress."

"Why didn't you tell all that to the principal?"

"It wasn't any of his business."

Molly cleared her throat, snickering as she turned the car into the narrow tree-lined drive that led up the hill to their house. "Has this sort of thing happened before?"

"Yes," she said simply.

Molly frowned, glancing at Autumn from the corner of her eye. She brought the car to a stop and turned in the seat to face her. "Why didn't you tell me the kids have been teasing you?"

Autumn tossed her head and rolled her eyes. "They're just silly children."

"Just children, huh? Whatcha think you are?"

"I may be little, but I don't go 'round pulling people's hair and hiding their things. I mind my manners and I tend to my own business."

"Lord, child. Some times I think you were born thirty years old." Molly shook her head in wonder. "Was it minding your manners to hit Bobby Joe with your lunch pail?"

Autumn slumped down in the seat. One of her braids was loose, her hair tangled, her legs dangling. "I was really mad, Aunt Molly. I didn't know I could get that mad at anybody."

"Are you having second thoughts about what you done?"

Autumn nodded. "What would you have done?"

Molly didn't hesitate. "I'd have cracked the little son of a bitch alongside the head with my lunch pail."

Autumn giggled, swatting at tears on her cheeks. "Then you're not going to spank me?"

"I ain't never spanked you. I don't see any reason to start now."

Autumn followed Molly from the car, trailing along at her heels. "What's for supper? I'm so hungry."

"Hot dogs."

"The special kind?" she asked, licking her lips. "With all the good stuff you put on them?"

"Yeap."

"Hot diggity dog!"

Bobby Joe returned to school with two stitches over his eyebrow, and Autumn returned to school with her dress mended. Bobby glared at her, but neither he nor any of the other children ever teased her again.

Books held a kind of magic for Autumn. They carried her over the hills to worlds where the buildings were taller than the trees, the waters stretched wider than the river, the stores stayed open past six o'clock, and the towns had more than one bank, one hardware store, one diner, one church, one school, one, one one. And to people who had more than one pair of shoes.

It wasn't until the ninth grade that she surfaced long enough to notice the changes that had taken place around her. She had grown taller and thinner each year, with a mass of auburn hair that was beyond her control. She brushed until it hung in long lustrous waves, but fifteen minutes later Autumn looked as if she had been caught in a windstorm. The other girls' breasts were rounded, she noticed, while hers were still flat. Their legs had taken on shapely curves. Her legs were long and straight, and her knees were still knobby.

Autumn watched the girls giggling with the pimple-faced boys, who giggled back, and she felt even more separated from them. She walked along the halls at school, a head taller than even the boys, feeling like a gangly dandelion among a delicate patch of primroses. Again Autumn pretended not to care, but alone at night she wept. After several nights of curling up into a ball, a pillow over her head to muffle her sobbings, she was discovered by Molly. When her aunt asked her why she had been crying night after night, Autumn sobbed that she was ugly and none of the boys liked her.

Molly, her long blond hair hanging loose about her shoulders, drew Autumn into her arms. "Which one of them boys are you pining for?"

Autumn pulled the face of every boy in Turtle Ridge into her mind's eye. She wiped at her tearstained cheeks and grinned sheepishly. "None of them. They're stupid and a damned nuisance most of the time."

"Then why are you crying?"

Autumn shrugged. "I don't know. I guess I thought I was missing out on something."

"You ain't missing, 'less you're wanting. Don't pick a way that ain't yours just 'cause that's the way the other kids are doing it." She touched Autumn on the chest. "Be what's in there. Follow it and you won't go too wrong." Molly pushed her back against the pillows. "Don't you worry none about your looks, either. Your kind of pretty takes time to grow into. Give it a while. It'll come."

Autumn rubbed a finger against her nose. "Will the freckles go away too?"

"I hope not. They give you a kind of sparkle that's awful pretty."

Autumn gazed at Molly and thought back to the time when she had first begun to notice that the other kids had better things in their lunch pails, better clothes, and mommies and daddies. She realized now that she and Molly were the richest people in the valley, because they had each other. "Thank you, Aunt Molly. Thank you for always being here."

"You're mighty welcome."

The memory of that night, and of Molly's gentle under-standing, stayed with Autumn. She had watched over the years as her aunt strove to make ends meet. Now that she had reached sixteen, Autumn wanted to assume at least a small amount of the burden. But work was scarce in the valley. Other than baby-sitting, there weren't many jobs in town.

After talking it over, Molly and Autumn agreed that she would work after school and weekends. Molly asked around and found work for Autumn in three homes. Two of the households she cleaned for were nice, but at one, the woman, Mrs. Baker, was a crab, a nag who paid less than anybody else in town. Autumn scrubbed floors and walls until her knees were callused, her knuckles cracked and bleeding, her nose and eyes smarting from the rising fumes of ammonia. She could handle the ammonia; it was the maggots that turned her stomach upside down. No one else had the repulsive things, but Mrs. Baker's garbage was lined with them and it was her job to clean the container.

Every Monday morning a man came and collected the garbage. Mrs. Baker was too stingy to use plastic bags, so hundreds of maggots were left clinging to the sides of the can. After school Autumn would go to the Bakers', take a pail of boiling water to drown the larvae, then scrub with a brush until they were dead and floating in the water.

Autumn was bent over the can one afternoon, gagging and scrubbing, when she overheard bits of a telephone conversation through an open window. "Her ma was a foreigner and her pa a drifter, so what can you expect?"

Autumn listened absently at first, musing how anyone from the other side of the hills was considered a foreigner in Turtle Ridge. Then she frowned and glanced at the window as Mrs. Baker's voice rose in nasal tones. "I think something should have been done a long time ago. The girl runs wild. 'Course, with that Molly taking care of her, you can't expect much more. A trashy lot if you ask me, but I do what I can for the girl."

The word "trashy" rolled around in Autumn's head and suddenly something snapped. She picked up the garbage can of water and dead maggots, so angry she was trembling, marched into the house, and dumped the mess at Mrs. Baker's feet. "You can say what you want about me, you old biddy, but you keep your rotten mouth shut about my aunt."

Mrs. Baker gazed stupidly at the water as it ran in dirty streams across the clean kitchen floor. "What . . . What . . . Why did you do that?"

Autumn stood with her legs spread wide, hands jammed on her hips. "There is only one kind of person who has maggots in her garbage can. Mrs. Baker, you are a dirty, ignorant, pee-in-the-weeds person."

Her face pink with rage, Mrs. Baker stepped forward, drew back her hand, and slapped Autumn hard across the cheek. "You ungrateful brat. This is the thanks I get for trying to do you a good turn."

Autumn had never been hit before and she stood in shock for a moment. Then her eyes narrowed, her hands curled into fists. "Witch!" She let go with a punch that knocked Mrs. Baker into a spin.

Mrs. Baker stumbled into a kitchen chair, her legs spread at odd angles, her voice quivering with rage. "I'll get you for this, Sue Anne McAvan. I'll get you for this."

Autumn fled the house, little doubt in her mind that word would spread like wildfire and the likely outcome would be no more work for that wild McAvan girl. Still, she climbed on her bike with a feeling of pride and pedaled the five miles home.

Autumn was tense, unsure what Molly's reaction would

be. To keep her mind occupied, she entered the house, picked up her father's old guitar, and returned to the porch. Molly had cringed when Autumn first started picking at the guitar, but then she went out and bought her an instruction book. Now Autumn played competently. She sat on the steps singing and strumming while she waited for her aunt to come home.

It was evening before Molly's old Ford pulled into the driveway. As soon as Autumn saw her face, she knew Mrs. Baker had spread the word. She put aside the guitar as Molly mounted the steps and sat down in the old wooden rocking chair. It made a creaking noise as she rocked to and fro. "I heard about whatcha done. Do you think you're too good to clean other people's dirt?"

"No, but there must be a better way."

"There is, but you might have to handle a lot of garbage before you get it."

Autumn picked nervously at the strings on the guitar. The sound was a dull ping that sent shivers down her spine. "I guess I let my temper get the better of me."

"Yeah, you've got a temper, all right. I've watched it flare, and I've watched you fight to control it. That's a good thing. It takes a lot of control to get where you want to go." Molly paused and looked down at Autumn inquisitively. "Where do you want to go? What are you going to do with this life God saw fit to give you?"

"I've thought a lot about it. I guess what I want most is a man to love, and children to raise, and a home of my own. I don't want a lot of money, but I want enough so the kids will always have shoes that fit, and good food on the table."

"What's happened to the little girl that wanted to be worldly?"

Autumn thought back to that day and smiled. "I've read a lot. I've learned a lot, but worldliness comes from living. You can't do much of that in Turtle Ridge."

"Turtle Ridge ain't the whole world. You've got a good head on your shoulders. You could do fine in the world if you put your mind to it. Everything is there, if you're willing to fight for it. With me it was different. I didn't have no education, and no one ever told me there was any other way. I looked to get married too."

"Why didn't you, Aunt Molly? Was it because of me?"

Molly turned and gazed off into space, a faraway look in her eyes. "I had me a man once, but he died of the pneumonia. I loved that man something awful. After he died, I tried a few others, but they just didn't fill the bill. I decided to go my way alone. I've had my memories of him, and I've had you. I don't feel I've missed anything."

Autumn smiled mirthlessly. "You've still got me, and I'm not going to be bringing in any more money." She reached out and put her hand on Molly's knee. "I'm sorry about Mrs. Baker."

Molly arched a questioning eyebrow. "Are you?"

Autumn licked her lips and a smile broke across her face. "Not really. I haven't had so much fun since the day I beat the stuffing out of Bobby Joe Proctor."

Molly burst into deep-throated laughter. "I'm proud of you, girl. You're honest with yourself, and you got spunk. That'll take you far in this world. It takes a bellyful of guts to survive some of the shit that's dealt ya. I can't promise you the children. It might not be God's way, but I've got a feeling you'll get whatever else you set out for. If it's a man you want, then go after him."

Autumn grinned. "I don't think I'm going to find a man I want here in Turtle Ridge. Bobby Joe and the others in town seem so childish. I want a husband and a family, but I want to get more schooling too. I think that will have to come first." She stroked her fingers against Molly's hand and gazed at her with affection. For sixteen years they had had only each other. The thought of leaving made Autumn ache with loneliness. "It will mean that I'll have to leave Turtle Ridge . . . and you."

Molly nodded, but her eyes dimmed and she drew her hand over Autumn's long hair. "What kind of schooling are you wanting? What do you want to be?"

Autumn shrugged. "I don't know yet. I just want to be something more than I am now."

"I think you're mighty nice the way you are." Molly smiled and rose from the chair. "We've got two years to think about it, to make plans. It's getting late. Let's go fix up some supper."

Autumn rose from the steps and followed Molly, her thin face furrowed in a worried frown. "There'll be talk again. Remember the gossip after the fight with Bobby?"

Molly hiked her dresstail, swished her hips, and kicked her feet in a jig step. "Sticks and stones may break my bones, but words can never hurt me. Be whatcha are, girl, not what the town wants you to be."

Autumn fell into step beside Molly. Her brown eyes glowed as she flipped her skirt and followed her aunt in an Irish dance step.

For the moment the town was forgotten, but by the next morning gossip began to float back to them. "Did you hear what that McAvan girl did to poor Lena Baker? Can you imagine that? Remember that day she almost killed Bobby Joe? Odd one, but then, what can you expect being as how she lives with that crazy Molly McAvan."

By the standards of Turtle Ridge, Autumn grew bolder, more daring, more unconventional each year. They shook their heads even harder. "It's too late now. Molly has let that girl run wild. I hear she even helps Tucker with his still. Come home drunker'n a skunk one day, I'm told. River rat. She swims that river like a catfish, hardly clothed at times. Pretty, though, and getting prettier by the day. Have you noticed she doesn't wear a brassiere? She struts around town wearing jeans so tight they cut right into her crotch. No decency at all—wild as a March hare. But smart, too smart for a woman. Someday it'll get her into deep trouble. You mark my words. That McAvan girl will come to a bad end."

2

Love at first sight! Autumn had thought it a myth, until Lonnie Norton, a stranger in Turtle Ridge. She was eighteen when she met him for the first time. It was the middle of August and the trees along the riverbank were beginning to reflect the first signs of fall. Among the green leaves were tints of dark auburn, with splashes of yellow and gold.

After fighting the currents upstream, she returned home to her special place, the pool in the bend of the river. Lonnie was sitting on a fallen log, a fishing rod propped beside him. His face looked amused as he watched her playing in the water. In his middle twenties, he had a square-set jaw and eyes so deep in color they seemed incandescent against his dark complexion, blue as the cornflowers that grew wild on the hillsides. Smoky black hair gleamed in the afternoon sun.

As Autumn neared the bank, he rose, crossed to the river's edge, and bent to help her from the water. "I saw you playing dangerous games with the currents. That's stupid. Someday the river will get you, sugar, and you'll never come up."

Autumn felt her pulse quicken. She wanted to speak, but her tongue felt suddenly frozen, her legs weak and trembly. His hand was still in midair, waiting. Words refused to come, so she smiled into his eyes and reached her hand to his. Their fingers touched and their minds seemed to become one, each knowing the other intimately.

He pulled her from the water and they stood gazing at one another, until swept into mirthful laughter. "Why are we laughing?" Autumn asked.

"I don't know. I just feel like laughing."

"Me too."

Sharing the same impulse, they crossed and sat on the fallen log. The necessary amenities had to be gotten out of the way, but they seemed intrusive to Autumn, names and ages incidental. She cared only about the man himself. He was tall, with a strong build, but his manner was gentle. She watched his face as he talked. His smile was crooked, and he had a way of arching a brow now and then. What touched her most, though, were his eyes. At odd moments they reflected a deep loneliness, but brightened as if on the edge of laughter when he looked at her.

At such moments, she wanted to reach out, touch him, make the loneliness go away, bring the light back into his eyes. And she wanted to ask why. What has happened in your twenty-five years of living to make you feel so alone at times? And what is it you see in my eyes that brings such a joy to your face? Do they tell you I think I love you, Lonnie Norton?

Night shadows were falling when he rose to leave. Autumn said good-bye, but she knew it was really the beginning. Lonnie returned the next evening, and the next. As they talked, she began to understand the reasons behind the shadows that sometimes touched his eyes. She understood, too, that the strange thing that had bonded them instantly and so completely was the similarity of their backgrounds. Like Autumn, Lonnie had grown up without the benefit of parents. So each had sensed a silent longing in the other. Autumn was luckier, though. She had never felt the loss of her parents, she had had Molly, while Lonnie had had only the state of Illinois.

Lonnie had been ten when his small, safe world suddenly shattered. He and his brother, Artie, were happily playing at a summer camp when their parents were killed in a house fire. There weren't any relatives willing to take on two rowdy boys, so they became wards of the state, to be farmed out to foster homes. Few families wanted to take the two boys, and often they had been separated. But when that happened, after a week or two in their new homes, one or the other would run away to search for his brother. By the time Lonnie had reached eighteen, he had been in six different foster homes. Artie was more rebellious, so he had been in and out of ten. According to Lonnie, the social workers breathed a sigh of relief when they finally became of age.

When he spoke about his past, Lonnie's tone was flippant, but Autumn heard traces of longing for people who were his very own. And when he talked about his brother, his voice became lighter, almost chuckling in tone. Both Lonnie and Artie had drifted from place to place, worked at this and that, until the mines. Artie was still roaming, but Lonnie had found what he wanted to do. He worked as a coal miner in Edisonville at the Black Jewel. The mine was owned by the Osborne family, one of the few mines that hadn't been swallowed by the conglomerate.

More than anything else, she knew, Lonnie wanted to finish college and get an engineering degree, but he was doing it the hard way. He worked a year and saved, then went to college until his money ran out. He had worked the mines from Illinois to Kentucky, the slope mine, the strip, and the shaft. Lonnie had two more years of college, but it would take four to finish if he had to stop and work every other year.

Autumn had always thought of coal mining as a dangerous, thankless kind of work, but it was what he wanted to do, so she kept these thoughts to herself. To Autumn, the most important thing was for Lonnie to be happy—to watch as the lights shone in his eyes when he talked about the future—their future.

They had never been strangers so there was no need for coyness or the traditional courting. They both had known. Hand in hand they walked the woods together, swam the river, sat and watched the sun set from behind the tall hills. And when night shadows fell, they slipped away to the only place where they could be alone, the bend along the river. Autumn had never thought of virginity as something to be guarded until after marriage. It was just a state of being, something to be given to the man of her choice at her choosing, and she had given it freely.

They had been so in tune with each other that Lonnie had never really asked her to marry him, they had simply set the date. They lay together beside the river. "Mrs. Lonnie Norton," she whispered. "Tomorrow I'll be Mrs. Lonnie Norton." She trembled with excitement, curled her body near to his, and pointed across the river to the hills that stood in night shadow. "Since I was a little girl I've looked at those hills and wondered what lay on the other side."

"You'll find it's a lot different than Turtle Ridge."

"In what way?"

"A lot of ways. Turtle Ridge could never be called exciting, but has there ever been a murder here, or a robbery, or a rape? Do you have to worry about walking the streets at night?"

She laughed at the thought. "No."

"You'll find all that, and more, once you cross over the hill."

His voice was serious, but Autumn smiled in the darkness. She wasn't afraid of the world; in fact, she welcomed it. She was, however, apprehensive about Lonnie's occupation, wishing for the time when he would have his degree. As an engineer, he could spend much less time underground. She had some money saved and wanted to help. It wasn't much, not enough for a year of college, but it would have been enough for a year of school for herself, had she worked a job on the side. If not for Jeb, she wouldn't have had any money. He had found the incident with Mrs. Baker funny. When the town whispered behind their hands, he had given her a job in his hardware store. She had worked after school, weekends, and summers for two years. Each week she would give Molly a share to help out; the rest she put away for school.

Autumn wanted Lonnie to have the money, but he was a proud man, so she had waited until the moment seemed right. She rose and gazed at him in the moonlight. "I've been thinking. I have some money saved. Why don't you use it and enroll for at least a quarter?"

He smiled and traced the shadows that played against

her face. "Thanks, sugar, but no thanks. I'll get through college without dipping into a little girl's pocket money. You'll want some things after we're married. Believe me, the house I rented will need some fixing. If you want, you can use your money to patch it up."

Autumn didn't persist. She sighed contentedly and rested her head back against his shoulder, gazing up at the starry night and spinning dreams about their own home, and being there with Lonnie. He had been working at the Black Jewel for only a few weeks, so they would both be strangers in Edisonville.

"Your brother," Autumn said curiously, "what does he look like? Is he dark like you, or fair? Is he older, or younger? Will he be coming to our wedding tomorrow? We've been so wrapped up in ourselves that we've hardly talked about him."

Lonnie chuckled mischievously, as if he had a secret he wasn't yet ready to share with her. "He's dark like me. He's younger, and yes, he'll be coming to our wedding. He lives in Indiana—for now." He paused briefly and his voice became pensive. "Artie is different. He loves excitement and will do just about anything to create it. Basically, he's a great guy. I think you'll like him, once you get to know him. He likes to move around, but he keeps in touch. He's planning to go to San Francisco in a couple of weeks, but he'll be here for the wedding." Lonnie fell silent for a moment, and when he spoke again his voice was filled with pride and affection. "The guy's got magic in his fingers. He can fix anything you throw at him, whether it's a car, a truck, or a toaster."

Lonnie grew quiet. Rising, he gazed down at her in the moonlight. "A family doesn't seem to matter much to Artie, but it means everything to me, maybe because I've never had one. I'll be a good husband, Autumn, and a good father when the time comes." He looked at her with eyes that were warm and expressive. "I want to give you so much. I'd like to slip a diamond on your finger instead of a plain gold band. I'd like to drive you to Edisonville in a limousine instead of an old Ford that leaks oil, and I'd like to move you into a mansion instead of a little old house that looks exactly like the one next door. I can't give you very much, but I'll break my neck to make you as happy as I possibly can. I won't let anything come before you, not college, not my brother.''

Autumn felt a wave of love so strong it made her ache inside. She reached out to him, wanting to feel the warmth of his bare skin against her own, the strength of his arms around her, the firmness of his hips and thighs as they molded against the soft contours of her own. She loved his bold, beautiful body, and thought it fascinating that something so strong could weaken and tremble under the touch of her small hands. "I don't care about diamonds," she whispered, "or fancy cars, or mansions. All I want is Lonnie Norton and a plain gold band." She brushed her fingers across thick chest hair, drew her hand over his belly, touched the velvety skin of his penis and felt it stir beneath her hand. "Would it be indecent if we made love again? I think I'm getting the hang of it now."

"Pervert." He swept his lips over her cheeks, touched her mouth lightly, then kissed her with all the warmth of love. Surrounded by the stillness of the woods and the soft sounds of the moving river, he made love to her with tender words. The gentle touch of his fingers and lips sought all the secret places of her body. Swept along with him, she drifted in and out of reality, moaning softly with pleasure when he penetrated. She closed her eyes and surrendered her mind and body to him.

In a matter of moments she felt lifted, felt herself transcending through time, and space. Eventually she returned to lie on a bed of leaves beneath Lonnie. It was like a sudden crash. Once again the earth was below her, the sky overhead. The quiet night sounds and the moving river echoed alarmingly in her ears. Autumn wanted to escape back into that strange new world where there were no thoughts or sounds, only her and Lonnie, feeling and reacting.

She buried her face in the damp hollow of his throat. "Better and better," she whispered. "It gets better and better."

"Wait," he said. "It will get even better."

She groaned. "I hope not. If it does, I'll die from it." His face was still, but he spoke with a chuckle in his voice. "I love you, Autumn McAvan. I just hope that crazy mixed-up world out there doesn't ever change you."

A smile broke across her face and she sat upright with sudden laughter. "This town has been trying to change me since the day I belted Bobby Joe Proctor with my lunch pail. I've been Turtle Ridge's cross to bear since I was eight years old. At eighteen, I'm still considered their most troublesome child." She leaned close to him and whispered, "It's been said that I actually go swimming with hardly any clothes on."

"Nooo! You wouldn't?"

"Yeees! This is the way the story goes. If you slip down to the river very quietly on a warm, moonlight night, you'll see that McAvan girl leap into the water like a frog with nothing but her panties on." Autumn laughed and jumped to her feet. "Come on. Last one in's a rotten egg." She set out for the river's edge at a run, arched her arms, and gave a leap, diving into the rippling water. She surfaced near the middle of the river and looked for Lonnie. He was within a foot of her, grinning his crooked grin. "Devil." She dived again, her bare bottom shining in the moonlight as she arched and disappeared.

Autumn knew all the deep pools and tried to play hide and seek, but Lonnie was always there when she surfaced. He took her hand and they drifted lazily with the currents, pausing to embrace, the feathery water touching their skin as softly as a whisper.

With Lonnie, Autumn wanted to drift forever, but he turned in the water and urged her upstream. She smiled when he held her away from the middle where the dangerous currents flowed. They worked their way back to the clearing beside the pool, walked hand in hand from the water, and dropped down on the grassy bank.

She gathered her long auburn hair and squeezed the water from its thick strands. Lonnie stretched out beside her, his eyes luminescent in the moonlight. They sat together and listened to the night sounds, the slap of the water against the bank, the breeze as it whispered through the leaves. Tomorrow Autumn knew she would be leaving the river, and the little house among the trees, and Molly.

Molly hadn't been happy about Autumn's marriage to Lonnie. Her aunt had thought them too young.

After making love to Lonnie for the first time, Autumn had entered the house, her back stiff with false courage. Molly was knitting, her feet propped on a stool. "I have something to tell you," Autumn said. "I hope you won't fight me about it."

Molly put her knitting aside and looked at Autumn quizzically. "Whatcha got nipping at your mind now?"

"Lonnie," she said bluntly. "I'm going to marry him in September."

Molly jerked upright and slammed her feet to the floor. "You're fixing to marry a stranger?"

Autumn frowned. "I thought you liked Lonnie."

"Yeah, I like him just fine, but you've only known him a spell. You're only eighteen, Autumn, and a hayseed at that. You don't know about men and their slick ways. You're like a blackberry that's all juicy and ready to be picked by the first sweet-talking man who comes along. You'd best think about what you're doing."

"Lonnie isn't a sweet-talker, and I have thought about it. He's what I want."

"What about school? Have you thought about what you'll be giving up?"

"I won't give it up. I can still go to school, after Lonnie gets his degree. Marriage doesn't mean a woman has to give up everything like it once did."

Molly grimaced. "You want it all, don't you? You want the husband, the kids, the home of your own, and the schooling. Mighty few are lucky enough to get it all. Most have to sacrifice something. You've read your books, and you've got yourself a dab of sophistication, but you ain't got no real-world learning behind you. There's time. Wait and grow up some first. Get some of that learning you've been wanting."

"I'll do my learning with Lonnie. You told me once that if I found the man I wanted, I should go after him. Lonnie is the man I want."

Molly grew quiet. She picked a leaf from Autumn's tangled hair and gazed at it softly, remembering a special time in her own life. "There was a time when I had leaves in my hair too. And there was a time when my face glowed with the same kind of light I see shining on your face now. It's the kind of light that only comes from long hours spent in a man's arms. I've always told you to stand up and fight for whatcha wanted, even against me. I don't reckon there's cause for you to change now.''

Autumn squealed and wrapped her arms around Molly, but she wondered how her aunt had known. Did the first time really show on a woman's face? She drew away and looked at Molly closely. "I've been wondering. Are you still a virgin, Aunt Molly?''

Molly grinned and rumpled her hair. "Lord no. I can't think of anything worse than dying poor, 'less it's dying a virgin.'' She rose from the chair. "If there's going to be a wedding, and it seems there is, I reckon we'd best get busy. I can't have you going off with that boy with ragged underwear. And we have to get you to a dentist and make sure you ain't got no rotten teeth. No man needs to marry up with a girl needing a lot of money put in her mouth.''

Autumn sat cross-legged on the floor. "He's marrying me, not a horse.''

"Same difference. Both have to be shod and fed. It takes a lot to get by these days. That boy will have enough trouble just getting himself through college.''

"He isn't a boy, Aunt Molly. He's twenty-five.''

Molly smiled and shook her head in wonder. "You kids. Ya'll think you know what life's all about. You think you got it all figured out, but you ain't. I don't want to dampen your spirits, or take away the shine, but life's a hard row to hoe. I just hope it don't deliver you too many bad surprises.''

3

Autumn moved about her room, touching, remembering all the years of her life. It was a little girl's room and reflected her childhood, all pink and white and ruffled. Faded and time-worn, now, but it was still the nicest room in the house and shouted of Molly's love. Everything had been stitched and painted by Molly's nimble fingers. Autumn realized now how much her aunt had had to scrimp and save to buy her a few of the things every girl wants.

Stuffed animals were propped here and there, one wall lined with books and record albums. There weren't any banners, or posters, or snapshots of friends. Autumn had always preferred to spend her time with Molly because everybody her own age seemed too young.

She paused in front of the mirror, recalling the day she had first seen her image through different eyes. The changes seemed to have taken place without her awareness. Somewhere between *Gone With the Wind* and *The Godfather*, everything had shifted and found its rightful place. She remembered leaving her room and announcing to Molly: "I'm kind of pretty."

"Yeah," Molly had said. "I've been wondering how long it would take you to notice. I could have told you, but I figured it was something you had to learn for yourself. It's been a wondrous thing to see." Molly hesitated and looked at Autumn with wise gray eyes. "There's something extra about you, too. I guess folks call it sex appeal.

You have a look about you that'll draw the men like bees to honey. It could get you in a lot of trouble if you're not careful how you use it.''

"If I'm so gorgeous, why aren't the boys in Turtle Ridge swarming over me like bees?''

"What chance have you give 'em? Besides, they're just boys. Your stiff back and uppity ways scare 'em off. It'll be different once you meet a few full-growed men. They'll know what they want, and they'll know how to get it.''

The conversation with Molly had taken place almost a year ago. Since then, she had met her "full-growed" man. In a few hours, she would be his wife.

Autumn turned from the mirror and walked toward the door, casting a last look about the room. For a moment she could see a little girl with pigtails curled in a chair with a book, a deep frown on her face as she struggled to understand the big words, a little girl bent over a guitar, trying to play along with one of her favorite records and failing miserably. As she had grown, the big words had become clear and the music had begun to flow smoothly. A part of Autumn wanted to stay in the safety of the pink-and-white room, but another part told her it was time to go.

Quietly she said a good-bye to the little girl, gathered her memories, and went down the hall to Lonnie. She entered the room with a nervous smile, but stopped short and stared in astonishment. Molly grinned from ear to ear and motioned toward the two men who were waiting there. "They bear a faint resemblance, don'tcha think?''

Lonnie and Artie stood side by side. Both men were dressed in blue suits; each was holding a small box with a corsage. They had identical blue eyes. The same dark hair and the same mischievous smiles on their faces. Lonnie had failed to mention his brother was also his twin.

They were so alike that Autumn wondered for a moment which man she was marrying, but only for a moment. The eyes were the same color and shape, but the expressions were different. Artie was probably one of the sweet-talkers Molly had warned her about—a rogue. His glance was audacious, flickering hot and cold. Lonnie's eyes were warm and looked at her with love.

Choking back a bubble of laughter, Autumn went to

Artie and kissed him on the cheek. "Hi, honey." She slipped her arm around his waist and gazed at Lonnie with a "get-acquainted' smile.

Lonnie looked crestfallen. "You have the wrong man, Autumn!" His voice had a bite to it.

"Serves you right." She left Artie and slid into Lonnie's arms. "What's the big idea?"

He shrugged. "It's a game we've been playing since we were kids. We couldn't resist." He frowned down at her. "I bet him ten bucks you would know which man was which."

She winked. "You win." Autumn held her hand out to Artie. "I'm Sue Anne, alias Autumn, and soon to be your sister-in-law."

Autumn twisted the gold band Lonnie had slipped on her finger and turned in the seat as the car crested a hill. They had intended to have a quiet wedding with only the family, but when they got to the church, half of Turtle Ridge was there with jars of jelly, jam, pickles, patchwork quilts, and crocheted doilies. Even Mrs. Baker had come, rice in hand. Autumn had whispered to Molly that they were there to make danged sure their problem child didn't change her mind.

She gazed out the rear car window and watched as the town of Turtle Ridge grew smaller and smaller, the stores and houses becoming mere dots in the valley. The people were gossips, all of them, but Autumn loved every busy mouth. Deep down, she knew they loved her, too. That was the way of things in Turtle Ridge

Autumn sniffled, gazing at Artie. He had left his car in Edisonville and driven to Turtle Ridge with Lonnie. She sat between the two men. "I'm glad you could come to our wedding."

He grinned. "A team of horses couldn't have kept me away."

Autumn wiped at her cheeks. What little sophistication she possessed had slipped and tears started shortly after Preacher Anderson pronounced them man and wife. When they returned to the house beside the river, she had sat with her aunt and wept openly while the men packed her belongings in Lonnie's car. Saying good-bye to Molly had been the hardest.

She smiled ruefully at Artie. "I've never been away from Turtle Ridge before, or my Aunt Molly."

Artie returned her smile and nodded toward the guitar in the backseat. "Do you play that thing?"

"She sure does," Lonnie said, "and sings like an angel."

Artie pulled the guitar from the backseat and shoved it onto her lap. "Play us a tune, little sister."

She kicked off her shoes, turned slightly in the seat, and settled the guitar under her arm. At first her fingers felt stiff and wooden, the notes stilted and discordant. But slowly she relaxed, her voice, growing soft and whispery as she sang old folk tunes Molly had taught her. When she switched to modern songs Artie and Lonnie sang along.

Their voices rose higher and higher as the miles sped past. By the time they reached Edisonville, Autumn was laughing wildly at the two men. They had identical voices, too. Both sang off-key, in a deep, raspy tone.

She looked up at the arching sign overhead as they arrived. "EDISONVILLE, KENTUCKY. BIGGEST LITTLE TOWN ON EARTH. HEART OF THE COALFIELD." She returned the guitar to the backseat and gazed around her as they entered the city limits. There seemed to be very little difference between Edisonville and Turtle Ridge. Edisonville was much larger, but it was still just another hick town. "Is there murder and robbery and rape in Edisonville?" She joked.

"No," Lonnie said. "It's a safe town. Douglas Osborne sees to it."

She looked at him oddly. "What does he have to do with it?"

"He owns it, sugar. He owns the town, and he owns the people who live here."

"That's ridiculous. One person can't own other people."

"They can if they have enough money." Lonnie cut the car sharply and took a right. "There's something I want you to see." After a few blocks, he turned onto a road that became wider, smoother, quieter, and shadier. A couple of miles out of town, he pulled the car into a clump of trees and gestured for them to get out. He pushed aside thick shrubbery and nodded his head at the opening. "Take a look at that."

Autumn stepped between the two men and looked through the gap Lonnie had made amid the shrubs. "Jesus! That house is bigger than all of Turtle Ridge." To Autumn, Osborne House looked like the pictures she had seen of the White House. It gleamed like polished marble in the sun, set on grounds that looked as if each blade of grass had been clipped individually.

In the distance a man on horseback rode at full gallop. Blond strands of hair whipped in the wind. He leaned forward and rose slightly in the saddle as the horse bunched and leapt a four-foot fence with easy grace. As he neared the stable, the rider slowed the horse and patted it on the neck. "Who is that?" she asked.

"Brian Osborne," Lonnie said. "He's home from college for the summer. I've seen him at the mine a couple of times."

"Digging coal?" Artie asked sarcastically.

"No, but he has. The men tell me he worked right along with them when he was sixteen or so."

Autumn turned to Artie and grinned. She thrust her nose in the air and held her fingers out in a delicate manner. "I've seen enough. You'd best take me away from all this poverty before I faint." With hips swaying, she tiptoed in her stocking feet to the car. "Home, James!"

Lonnie bowed with an exaggerated flair. "Yes, madam." He took her hand and helped her into the car. "Would you like to see what paid for that big white mansion?"

"The mine?" she asked.

He nodded. "It's on the way."

"Sure. I'd love to see where you work."

Lonnie's job as a miner had been a distant thing, a little worry that flickered in and out of Autumn's mind, but seeing the mine brought reality into sharp focus. Fear nagged at the base of her spine as Lonnie pointed out a long line of steel buildings for electrical and hydraulic, a machine shop, welding and automotive works. He explained how the coal was brought from the mine on a conveyor belt to the tipple, where it was sent through a shaker screen, culled and graded, washed, sorted, and then loaded into cars to be transported. He went into detail about the room-and-pillar method used in the Black Jewel, the blow down of a coal face, overburden and the different methods used in supporting roofs. He had talked for half an hour when Artie began to shift in the seat.

Lonnie laughed and started the engine. "I forget some people aren't as interested in mining as I am."

Autumn forced a stiff smile. "I thought it was fascinating."

"You would," Lonnie said. "You're faithful." He pulled the car away from the mine and onto Maple Road. "It's an old mine. It's almost mined out. The equipment has seen better days, too. We have a lot of breakdowns. Last week it was the conveyor belt. Once before, the blower system went out and they had to clear the mine until it had been repaired."

"Why don't they buy new stuff?" Autumn asked.

Lonnie glanced from Autumn to Artie and grinned. "Because it wouldn't be worthwhile to buy new stuff. At the rate they're going, the Black Jewel will be mined out in a couple of years. They're running three shifts, and unusually large crews." He paused and frowned. "It's a gassy mine."

"Gassy?" Autumn asked. "What does that . . .?" She fell silent when he turned the car onto a graveled road and she saw houses that were little more than hovels crammed one next to the other. It looked like desert country. Nothing enclosed the area but dirt and the sky overhead. "What is this?"

"Miners' Row." He pulled the car into a driveway in front of one of the houses and cut the engine. Lonnie smiled mirthlessly and gestured with his hands. "Be it ever so humble. Sugar, this is your new home."

Autumn stared at the house he indicated—in comparison, Molly's was a palace. "Wellll. It's near the mine. That will be convenient."

Artie shook his head and laughed. "She *is* faithful."

Autumn left the car with the men, but waited while they carried her things inside. She stood near the car and stared at her new home. The house, a cracker box with a peaked roof, was a dim gray and showed signs of rot. Rickety-looking steps led to a postage-stamp-size porch, where a front door sagged and squeaked every time it was moved. After the mansion on the hill, it looked like a dirty little outhouse.

She crossed the yard, but paused on the porch when the men walked through the doorway. Artie was grinning. "I hope you have magic in your fingers. You're going to need it." He leaned and kissed her on the cheek. "You're a doll. I wish I had seen you first."

Autumn grinned. "Thanks for helping Lonnie move my stuff, big brother."

"No problem, little sister." He turned to Lonnie. "I'm going to head back to Indiana now so you and Autumn can do whatever it is newlyweds do. I'll drop by before I leave for San Francisco."

"Wish you'd stick around," Lonnie said in a wistful voice.

"I can't. Itchy feet."

"Why San Francisco?"

He shrugged. "I've seen Indiana. I haven't seen San Francisco."

"Yeah, but you've got a good job in Indiana. It seems a shame to give it up."

"I'll get another. There's always a spot for a good mechanic." He grinned. "I'm the best."

Lonnie laughed then. "Modest, too." He hooked his arm over Artie's shoulder and walked with him to his car. They talked for a moment, then Artie climbed behind the wheel. He flashed a grin at Autumn, winked, and then he was gone. Lonnie walked back to the house with eyes downcast, mumbling. "That's my brother, always looking for greener pastures." As he neared the porch, he looked at Autumn and a wide grin lit up his face. "Hello, Mrs. Norton."

"Hello, Mr. Norton. When are you going to show me my new home?"

He laughed, took both steps in one stride, and scooped her up in his arms. The sagging door squeaked as he carried her over the threshold. "I'll fix that damned door," he mumbled.

The linoleum floor was so worn there wasn't any color

left in the pattern. It groaned when Lonnie walked across it. A sofa leaned against one wall, a chair against another— both were dirty and tattered—along with a couple of heavily scarred tables. The room was heated by a small gas stove. "Did you buy this furniture," she asked cautiously, "or was it already here?"

"We lucked out. It was here when I rented the place."

She looked at him to see if he was teasing. He wasn't. "Really? I can't imagine why anyone would go off and leave all this good stuff." As she followed him, Autumn began to plan how she would use her school money to upgrade the furniture a little.

The kitchen was an even greater disaster. Grease ran in caked streams down the front of the range, and the burners were charred black. Three unmatched chairs sat beside a table. The sink was gray and covered with pot marks. Cabinets made of some kind of rough boarding were painted a bright orange. The odor of years and years of hamhocks and beans penetrated every inch of the room. Cockroaches peeped at her in broad daylight, unafraid. They made little scratching sounds as they scurried from crack to crack. "We'll have to get rid of the local inhabitants," she said.

Lonnie nodded. "I know it's not much, but we can fix it up. Can't we?" Before Autumn could reply, he led her toward the bedrooms. "These houses were built years ago for the miners, but there aren't many living here now. Most are old folks who live on fixed incomes, or people like you and me who are trying to save money." He paused beside a bedroom with a desk, chair, and makeshift bookcase. "I'll need to study, or I'll get behind. I figure we can add a couple of chairs and a television and have a nice den." Still holding her hand, he led her into their bedroom, a sheepish expression on his face.

Autumn drew in her breath with surprise. The walls had been painted an eggshell white. The bed was new and covered in a spread printed with bold, fall-colored flowers. Two nightstands on either side of the bed held glass-based lamps. The old floor was hidden beneath a hooked rug, and snowy white curtains hung at the windows. "It's beautiful," she whispered.

"I wanted you to have at least one nice thing." He

picked her up, carried her to the bed, and stretched out beside her.

She rubbed her hand against the spread. "Did you do this? It has a woman's touch."

"I did the work. Ella picked out the stuff and told me what to do."

"Who is Ella?"

"She lives next door."

"Yes, but who is she?"

Lonnie cleared his throat. "This is a safe town, but it's a hot little town with a treat for everybody. We have the country club for the elite. The Elks for the middle class, and we have the bootleg joints for the workers. It's a dry town, but right outside the city limits it jumps. We can offer you bootleg whiskey, gambling, and a little relaxation of the feminine kind. Ella works at one of the joints. She's a hooker, but she's an all-right gal."

Autumn's eyes were wide and staring. "She's a whore?"

"No. Ella isn't a whore."

"Any woman who sells her tail is a whore, Lonnie. Even I know that much."

"There's whores, and then there are whores. Ella isn't a whore. Wait until you meet her, you'll see."

Autumn's eyes narrowed inquisitively. "How did you meet her?"

"At the joint where she works, but that was before I met you."

Autumn understood and sat upright in bed, her mouth falling open in disbelief. "You paid good money for . . . for . . . a woman . . . a whore?"

"Nah," he said, and looked off to the far wall.

She took his chin and forced him to look at her. "You did, didn't you?"

"What if I did?"

"I don't know." She looked perplexed, shrugging. "I guess I thought only ugly men had to pay money for it."

He laughed at her simplicity, grasped her head beween his hands, and kissed her on the mouth. Her lips were warm, but still and unresponsive. He drew away and looked at her oddly. "What is it? What's wrong?"

"I don't think I'll like living next door to a woman you've . . . you know."

"Ella? I didn't."

"You didn't?"

"No. I met her at one of the joints, but I didn't have sex with her."

"But you did with the other women?"

"Once, or maybe twice. It doesn't have anything to do with us, Autumn. I love you. I didn't love them. They were bodies, someone a man goes to when he's lonely, or needs to bury his prick in something warm, or when he's simply had too much to drink. Ella is a good person, but if it bothers you to live next door to her, we'll move."

Her eyes shone with teasing. "Move . . . and leave this splendid house? What are you trying to do to me, Lonnie?"

Their eyes met in understanding. He gathered her close for a long, deep kiss that ended on a note of laughter. She rolled from the bed, tugging at his hand. "Come on. Let's go kill cockroaches."

In the kitchen, Autumn remembered Lonnie's earlier remark, and asked him now, "What does 'gassy' mean?"

"It means you've had too much hamhocks and beans."

"Be serious, Lonnie. What does it mean?"

"Methane."

4

Lonnie had been right about Ella, but there was still too much of Turtle Ridge in Autumn for her to feel at ease with the woman. She was, however, curious and intrigued. Prostitution was something you read about in books or saw in movies. It didn't concern someone you knew, and certainly not the woman next door.

After meeting Ella, Autumn reminded herself that Molly had taught her not to be judgmental and to accept people for what they were, not what you would like them to be. Still, Autumn kept a tiny space between herself and Ella.

During the day Ella had a fresh-scrubbed look, but when evening came her face reflected all the colors of the rainbow. She was ten years older than Autumn, with honey-colored hair that reached her shoulders, large expressive green eyes, and an easy, outgoing manner that was irresistible. Autumn could not imagine anyone disliking Ella. She was warm and honest, with a generous nature, which forced Autumn to admit that her own thoughts were those of a snob, something she had always hated. Autumn tried to accept Ella as she was, but each time they met, old Preacher Anderson and his pounding fists echoed in her thoughts, shouting hell and damnation to those that lusted and fornicated.

Autumn didn't avoid Ella. She enjoyed talking to her neighbor, and they often went shopping together. Ella showed her around town, pointed out the best places to go for a good buy, and taught her how to haggle with used-furniture dealers. During one such trip, Ella mentioned that her father was a Holy Roller minister in Indiana. The contrast between Ella's life and her father's seemed so incredible that Autumn burst into riotous laughter. Autumn looked at Ella and suddenly the barrier she had built between herself and the other woman was unexpectedly and completely shattered.

Ella laughed too, as the space between the two women snapped closed. Over the weeks an enduring friendship grew that was as tight a bond as the love between two sisters. Autumn felt Ella had in some small way filled the gap left by Molly's absence.

As the two women grew closer, Ella talked about her life before she came to Edisonville. She had been shy as a child, and felt herself plain. Repressed by and terrified of her father, Ella was eighteen before she had even been inside a movie theater. Makeup was a sin against God, an evil device sent up from the devil to tease and tempt men to stray from the ways of the Lord.

Her father had kept a tight rein on Ella until Jack came along and freed her. Jack was a tall, handsome devil, a stranger passing through town. They met innocently, at a corner drugstore. He was aggressive, and knew the right things to say to a timid girl like Ella. Within days she was hopelessly in love, and thought Jack was in love with her, too. When he wanted her to leave town with him, she didn't hesitate.

Jack never wanted to stay in one place for very long, so they were always on the move. At each new town, Ella would work as a waitress or clerk while Jack loafed. They had been together for two years when they moved to Edisonville and Jack discovered the card rooms. He didn't care for work, but he loved to gamble.

After four months in Edisonville, Jack got in so deep that he couldn't get out. He went to Ella, and in a half-cooing, half-fearful voice, he tried to coax her into working off his debt at Rex's place. Ella was so afraid of losing him that she had finally agreed.

The first time she had felt like a piece of meat stretched on a rack. The next time had been easier, the next easier still. By the time Jack's debts were paid, whoring had become a way of life for her. Bit by bit Ella had changed. She was no longer shy or afraid. Her life was under her control now, not her father's, not Jack's. When he was ready to move on, she smiled and waved good-bye. "You know," Ella said one day, "I still wonder sometimes if I ran away with that jerk because of love, or just to escape old pops."

Ella freely admitted that a man had led her into prostitution, but she had stayed with it because it filled a need. She was fighting desperately to get out now, though. She joked about looking in the mirror one morning, suddenly aware of the lines gathering at her eyes, then decided a whorehouse wasn't a fit place for a woman pushing thirty. She wanted more: respect, dignity, perhaps a family, if she could find a man who would have an ex-hooker for a wife.

When Autumn suggested that it might be easier if she moved away from Edisonville, Ella explained that her clients were also her friends. For what she had planned, Ella would need their patronage. She had moved from a nice apartment to Miners' Row to save money. There was a diner on Fifth Street that would be up for lease in a few months, and she wanted to take it over. Most of the money she made went straight into the bank, and she drove an old car that barely made it around town.

Over the weeks the two women had opened their minds to one another. There were no secrets, save for one that Autumn had to share with Lonnie before she could tell anyone else. It began as a suspicion, which soon grew into a reality. Autumn was pregnant, and her stomach was doing all the normal, expected flip-flops.

Every morning was the same. Wave after sickening wave gripped her middle, until it felt twisted into a hard, churning knot. She lay in bed swallowing, trying to push back the acid bile that rose in her throat. Choking back a moan, she eased from beside a sleeping Lonnie and set out for the bathroom at a run. Her feet firmly planted, Autumn leaned over the toilet while her stomach did rapid crescendos as she gagged with the dry heaves.

She hadn't told Lonnie, and wasn't sure how to tell him.

Maybe: Lonnie, do you remember the first time beside the river? . . . Well, I'm going to have a baby. . . . No, that wasn't what she wanted to say. Lonnie, how would you feel about a son or a daughter? . . . Lonnie, I love you—I'm going to have a baby. . . . Lonnie, where are we going to get the money for a child? . . .

Shortly after moving to Edisonville, she had seen a doctor. When he learned there was the possibility that she could be pregnant already, he had fitted her with a diaphragm instead of prescribing the pill—closing the barn door after the horses are out, as Molly would have said. After the first time, Lonnie had taken precautions, and then came the diaphragm, so Autumn knew the baby must have been conceived the first time they made love.

Autumn thought back to that night beside the river and smiled. Lonnie had plunged boldly, not expecting to find a virgin even in Turtle Ridge. Then he'd looked guilty, as if he had just robbed the Turtle Ridge National Bank. "You didn't act like a virgin," he had said.

"How is a virgin supposed to act?"

"Shy, nervous, awkward."

"How many virgins have you had?"

"None, until now."

"Then how do you know?"

Their eyes met and they had laughed together. "Don't worry," he said. "Women seldom get pregnant the first time."

That was the end of August. It was now the early part of October, so Autumn knew she had to be six weeks pregnant, give or take a day or two. She straightened, looked in the mirror, and blinked at her reflection, her pale, pregnant reflection, and asked, "Lonnie, will you still love me when I'm all fat and swollen?"

She returned to the bedroom, slipped into a robe, and was bending over Lonnie when she saw he was awake and gazing through the dim light at the ceiling. " 'Morning," she said.

" 'Morning, yourself. You're up early."

"I woke early."

"Why? The alarm hasn't even gone off yet."

"Just woke." Hurrying from the room, she went to the

kitchen and made coffee. While the coffee was perking, she fried bacon and eggs for Lonnie. She sat down at the table and was nibbling on a piece of toast and sipping black coffee when he entered the room.

He took a chair across from her and motioned toward the rest of the food. "Aren't you eating?"

"I'm not hungry."

"You haven't been hungry for the last week or so. You're usually ravenous in the mornings." He took a sip of coffee and his eyes sought hers over the rim. "The diaphragm was a waste of time, wasn't it?"

She blinked with surprise. "How did you know?"

"It's a dead giveaway when a woman hangs over the toilet every morning. I've been waiting for you to tell me. What were you going to do, wait until it was born and hope I didn't notice you getting fat?"

"You've known," she said sharply, "and you didn't tell me? I've been trying to think of the right way to tell you for days, and you've known all along. That's dirty, Lonnie. Really dirty."

He grinned. "What did you think I would do, send you back to Molly? I wouldn't do that. I like your cooking."

She watched as he plowed eagerly into his breakfast. If he was bothered by her pregnancy, he wasn't letting it interfere with his appetite. He paused now and then to smile at her, otherwise he ate as if it were just another morning. She waited until he had put his fork aside and was sipping coffee before asking, "How do you feel about the baby?"

"It's a toss-up. I'd like a good coonhound, but I guess I'll have to settle for a snotty-nosed kid instead."

"Thanks! Thanks a lot. I'm puking and you're making jokes. Lonnie Norton . . . I love you. But right now . . . I hate you." She leapt from the chair, drew back, and threw her toast at him.

He laughed and grasped her around the waist and pulled her onto his lap. "I think it's great, sugar."

She backed off from him with a worried frown. "It sounds great, but have you thought about what it could mean?"

"Yeah. College can wait another year."

"No it can't. I've been thinking."

He groaned. "Heaven help us. When you think, we usually end up in trouble."

"No. Be quiet and listen. We can make it if I go to work. I'm healthy, and I'm only sick for a little while in the mornings. I can work right up until the baby is born. And later I can get a baby-sitter. The most important thing is your degree."

"Hey," he said, and frowned, annoyed. "I didn't marry you so you could put me through college."

"I know you didn't. What I'm doing is for both of us. I want good things for my children as much as you do. I don't want them to ever have to go to school wearing shoes that pinch, or to feed them hamhocks and beans every night because that's all we can afford. Besides," she said, and grinned. "I don't want a dirty-faced miner for a husband. I want a fancy engineer."

He smiled too. "I can't say no to you. If it's working you want, go to work." He eased her from his lap and stood. "You see a good doctor, you hear. If we're going to have a kid, I want it to be healthy, and I want you taken care of. Talk to Ella. She should know the best doctor for you to see." He picked up his lunch pail, grinned and winked. "Love ya, sugar."

She smacked him a kiss, but frowned as the door closed behind him. It wasn't going to be as easy as she had pretended. Without telling him, she had already gone to every hardware store in town, only to learn they had all the help they needed. She had gone to several other places too, but the results were the same. Work at the mine hadn't been going well either. During the last month there had been numerous shutdowns because of the faulty equipment. Lonnie had had only three full weeks of work since they were married.

She gathered the dishes and took them to the sink, ran water, and added detergent. Autumn wished now she hadn't spent all her school money on furniture. She had planned to spend only a little, but the new-used sofa made the chair look even worse, so she bought a new-used chair, which made the tables look like junk, and soon she had refurnished the place.

Still, the house was livable now. Ella had helped her paint it. Lonnie had spent weeks with hammer and nails. Molly had brought her sewing machine and made drapes and slipcovers. Lonnie had his den now. The living room was put together with used furniture, but it was clean and comfortable. The kitchen was warm and cozy, a soft yellow and white. They had taken a dirty shack and turned it into a home.

Autumn went back to the dishes, but the worry stayed with her. She finished the kitchen, gathered up the throw rugs, and took them outside to be shaken free of dust. Ella was standing on her porch, drinking a cup of coffee, smoking a cigarette, and gazing off into space. Usually she slept until noon, so Autumn was surprised and pleased to see her up and about so early. She needed to hear the sound of a cheerful voice.

Autumn tossed the throw rugs on the porch and ran down the steps. She was barefoot and stones dug into her feet. She did a hopping little dance across the yard to Ella's porch, her robe flapping carelessly about her legs. "Guess who's going to have a baby?"

Ella's green eyes widened playfully. "Who—Lonnie?"

"No. We drew straws and I lost." Autumn slid onto the porch and tucked her bare feet under the tail of the robe. "I need a doctor. Do you know a good one?"

"Are you kidding? I know every money-grubbing bastard in Edisonville. I've never used him, but Dr. Albright is thought to be the best. I'm going into town shortly. Why don't you come along and I'll show you where his office is. We'll stop and you can make an appointment."

"Sure. What time do you want to go?"

"Five minutes ago. I'm making a big deposit in my account today. I'm almost there. A couple of months and the diner will be mine, and so will my body." Ella tossed the cigarette butt to the ground and emptied what coffee was left from the cup over the porch rail. "You know, now that I've decided to get out, I feel damned greedy about my bones and who hops them." She bent and gave Autumn a nudge. "Hurry and get dressed. And for Pete's sake, don't forget your shoes again."

*   *   *

They made a quick stop at the bank and a side trip to the market, then Ella drove across town to Dr. Albright's office. Autumn frowned as they neared a large, sprawling brick building. The parked cars were all late models and ranged from sports cars to Cadillacs. "I can't afford this place, Ella."

"Nonsense. Any quack can give you a diaphragm, but you're having a baby. You should have the best."

Ella parked beside a red convertible. The sun had driven away the early-morning chill and the top was down. The driver sat behind the wheel and Autumn recognized him as Brian Osborne, the man she had seen on horseback. When she left her car, he gave her an off-the-shoulder glance, then turned and stared. He smiled. "You're new in town, aren't you?"

She nodded and hurried after Ella. In the doctor's waiting room, they were told that Dr. Albright wasn't taking any new patients. "That figures," Ella said, and urged Autumn toward the door. "Dr. Albright treats the elite in Edisonville. Dr. Carlson is the next best. We'll check him out."

Autumn agreed and followed along with Ella to the car. The convertible was still parked at the curb, but now there was a blond woman with Osborne. She was talking to Brian and he was nodding, but his eyes were following Autumn as she slid into the seat beside Ella.

Ella laughed as she started the engine and pulled away from the curb. "I think Brian likes you."

"I thought he went to college. Why would he be home now?"

"Who knows?" Ella cut the wheel and turned onto Main Street. "The woman is Lisa Albright. She's the doc's daughter, and spoiled rotten from what I've heard. Rumor has it Brian and Lisa are slated to marry. It's been planned since they were kids. Brian and Lisa are the leaders of the country-club set. They do most of their playing at the club, but sometimes they feel like slumming and hit the joints. When they do, they really raise hell."

Autumn only half-listened as Ella rambled on. She didn't care about Brian Osborne, or Lisa Albright, or the country-club set. She had too many other things on her mind. She lowered her hand to her stomach and thought of the life growing there; a son, a daughter. Autumn didn't care which. She wanted the baby, but it certainly complicated things. Glancing at Ella, she asked, "Do you know where I can get a job?"

Ella looked blank for a moment. "That's a good question. There aren't many jobs in town. What can you do?"

"Clean dirty houses. I'm a real whiz with garbage cans."

Ella grinned wickedly. "You could try Osborne House. They use a lot of people."

"Sure, and have Junior ogling me. No thanks. I used to clean houses in Turtle Ridge. If I did it again, it would be like taking a step backward."

"Well . . . there's always the garment factory. They make jackets. You could try there. It's owned by Douglas Osborne."

"What isn't?"

"Not much."

"I don't think I want to work for him."

"It pays better than anything else in town, and I understand they'll train you."

"On second thought, I think I'd like to work for Douglas Osborne."

"I thought you'd change your mind. We'll go to the factory first, and then see Dr. Carlson."

Autumn gazed out the window as they drove down Broadway. Every other building had the name Osborne across the front. "I don't understand this town. Everybody acts as if the Osbornes are some kind of gods. I get the chilly feeling sometimes that the town is afraid of them."

"The town depends on them. They look to the Osbornes for survival. To the town, the Osbornes *are* God . . . Especially Douglas."

"Oh," Autumn said, a fine eyebrow arched. "And does the great man walk on water, too?"

"You betcha. And when things really get bad, he brings forth wines from the heavens and bushes heaped with . . . stale bread."

*   *   *

Autumn could hear the steady hum of the power machines from behind the wall at her back. Facing her was a receptionist in front of a door that was ajar, marked "Manager—Mr. Martin." She had almost completed the application when male voices rose in anger from behind the door. She glanced at Ella inquiringly.

"It sounds like Douglas and Brian. From what I've heard, they fight like cats and dogs."

"We just left him. How did he get here so fast?"

"He drives faster than me." Ella grinned and rolled her eyes. "Boy, does he ever. It isn't at all unusual to see his red car flying down Main Street with old Chief Hadley in hot pursuit."

Autumn grinned and turned back to the application, but jerked her head up when the voices grew louder.

"You won't," she heard a gruff voice say.

"I already have, Dad. Archaeology is what I want to do."

"You're an Osborne. Someday this town will be yours, and you have to be ready to handle the responsibility. Changing your major to archaeology is stupid, asinine, and I won't have it."

"There's nothing you can do about it."

"The hell there isn't. I'll pull your ass out of college and bring you home. You're not going to waste your life playing with a bunch of fucking mummies."

"Like hell, you will. I'm twenty-two and the money Mom left me will take care of college or anything else I want."

"Sure." Disgusted. "You have a couple hundred thou, and you think you're rich. The way you like to play, it won't even keep you in booze and women."

Autumn looked at Ella and clucked her tongue. "Only a couple hundred thou," she whispered. "Poor little boy."

Ella grinned and looked back at the door as the voices became shouts. "You're just being stubborn."

"So are you, Dad."

"Is it too much to ask that my only son work along with me?"

"We can't work together. I'm not your kind of man. You give with one hand, while you take away with the other. I've seen you pull a man out of a hole, only to kick the poor bastard in the teeth before he's hardly off his feet. Over the years I've watched you whip my uncles into well-performing robots. That isn't going to happen to me. I have a life, and I'm going to live it my way.''

It sounded to Autumn as if a chair had been overturned, and then Douglas' voice boomed, wild and furious. ''I've had enough of this bullshit. You get your ass back to college and take care of things. I want to hear within a week that you've changed your major. That's an order.''

''Stick your order. I'll be home for the holidays. We can talk again then.''

''Come back here, Brian. I'm not through yet.''

''Yes, you are.''

Autumn glanced at Brian as he entered the waiting room. His young face was red with anger, but his eyes looked troubled and just a little sad. She felt sorry for him, and smiled faintly. Recognition flickered in his eyes and he gazed at her steadily for a moment. Then his jaw twitched as he turned on his heel, darted around the receptionist, and disappeared down a long hallway.

Autumn rose with the application and approached the woman at the desk. The receptionist took her application and smiled. ''We don't have any openings now, but we'll call you if something comes up.''

''Do you think I can expect to hear soon?''

The woman glanced toward the office door, and then at Autumn. ''No. Our policies have changed. We are accepting applications, but Mr. Osborne has ordered that we hire only the skilled. It takes six weeks to train a woman, and we lose money if she doesn't work out. You understand.''

A sharp reply was on the tip of Autumn's tongue, but common sense told her the receptionist wasn't at fault. Douglas Osborne was the one who gave the orders, the one who decided who would work in Edisonville and who wouldn't. ''Yes,'' Autumn said dully, ''I think I'm beginning to.''

5

The sound cut through the night, a thunderous noise that grew with high-keyed intensity. It was a keening, wailing sound that rose higher and higher until it became ear-shattering. Autumn jerked awake with a start and sat upright in bed. The air felt charged, as if a lightning storm was crackling around her head. She felt inexplicably frightened and reached for Lonnie. He was already out of bed, across the room, and hurrying into his pants, his frame a large shadow in the moonlight. She leaned and groped for the lamp switch beside the bed. "What is it?" she cried. "What is that god-awful noise?"

"The alarm." His voice was tense, his face pale. "There's trouble at the mine."

"Trouble? What kind of trouble?"

"I don't know. It could be a cave-in."

She gasped and slapped her hand over her mouth. The thing she'd kept pushed to the back of her mind had happened, but Lonnie was with her. He was safe. "Do you think it's bad?"

"I don't know." He turned toward the door, grabbing his coat as he half-ran from the room.

"Where are you going?" she called.

"To the mine. Men could be in trouble. We have to get to them."

"No!" Autumn leapt from the bed. She chased after him, her long gown whipping about her legs as she ran through to the living room. He was nearing the door when she caught him by the arm. "Don't go. Let someone else do it."

"Autumn . . ." he said in a disappointed voice.

She felt ashamed and looked away from him. Her first and only thought had been for Lonnie. He was right. There could be men caught deep in the bowels of the mine. Their wives would be alone, their hearts leaping in fear. She nodded and opened the door for him, watching as he left the house at an all-out run.

She put her hands over her ears as the sound of the alarm whirled and reverberated around her. It was the same sound she heard every day at noon, but coming in the middle of the night, it was like a death call. The cold December wind howled and beat at the eaves of the little house, adding an eerie note to the turmoil that disrupted the quiet.

Autumn didn't know if it came from the chill in the room or from the sounds around her, but a hard shiver began at her neck and raced along her spine. She hugged her arms tight across her breasts, padded barefoot to the bedroom, and dressed in a thick robe and slippers. The bed looked warm, soft, and inviting, but sleep, even if it came, would have seemed sinful somehow. She left the room, reflecting that it had been only a few minutes since she had leapt from the bed, yet it seemed like a distant and faraway time.

Wandering aimlessly through the house, looking but not seeing the things around her, she forced herself into the living room and sat on the sofa to wait for Lonnie. She picked up a book from the end table, but stared dazedly at the blue-and-orange flames as they flickered in the little gas heater.

Autumn was still huddled in the corner of the sofa when dawn streaked the sky. She watched as the sun burst from the east, bringing with it a clear, cold day. The wind had calmed, and the house was silent now. It seemed like just another morning, except that Lonnie wasn't with her. Ordinarily she would be cooking breakfast about this time, making his lunch and chattering to him about Ella or their baby that was growing so rapidly in her belly. Her clothes were too tight now, and soon she would be forced into maternity clothes, clothes they couldn't afford. The weeks had slipped into December and she was still without work.

She touched the mound of her stomach and suddenly felt the need to see Lonnie, to assure herself that he was all right. Rising from the sofa, she went into the bedroom and dressed in warm clothes. If Lonnie couldn't come to her, she would go to him.

The scene at the mine was almost more than she could comprehend. It was mass confusion, and Autumn stood transfixed. The air hummed with an excitement that gripped and distorted reasoning. Tempers were hot, men shouted. As she watched the crowd around her, goose bumps rose on her arms and a tingling sensation curled around her head.

The area was roped off and guarded by the police, but an unruly mob pushed and shouted loudly. One man stood a head taller than the rest. He wore a woolen jacket, a red stocking cap and had sandy-colored hair that bushed out around the edges of the hat. He shouted "motherfucker" in a deep gravelly tone, and shook his fist in the air while stamping his feet against the frozen ground. He paused long enough to take a handkerchief from his pocket and blow his nose, then shouted and waved his fist again.

A shorter, heavyset man edged by him and pushed against the ropes until he was threatened by a police officer waving a billy club. Mumbling angrily, he disappeared into the crowd, only to be replaced by another, and still another shouting, angry man. The police raced frantically as they fought to control the mob. They called again and again for everybody to go home, but the men were past hearing, past caring.

Autumn knew it was foolish, but she wanted to see what was beyond the roped-off area and entered the crowd. Within minutes she was fighting to keep her balance. When the crowd moved, she was swept along with it. Flying elbows jabbed her in the ribs and breasts. Hard masculine shoulders shoved her roughly from side to side. At one point she squealed and kicked a man who stood with his heel grinding on her toes. He turned as if ready to strike out, but lowered his fist when he saw a woman. He gazed at her condescendingly. She wrinkled her nose at him, pushed between the men, and inched her way forward until she could see into the roped-off area.

Limousines that had to belong to the Osbornes were parked there along with four ambulances. To her left was a news van. Reporters hovered about like vultures. Men black with coal dust appeared and disappeared. She heard bits and pieces of conversation that tightened her stomach into a hard ball. "Cave-in . . . explosion. Worst mine disaster in recent history." She didn't want to hear more, but the words kept whirling around her. "Fifty-three men trapped . . . some thought dead . . . hours before they'll be reached." And there were a lot of questions: Why? . . . What was the cause?

It was a nightmare, a crazy disjointed nightmare, and she was caught in the middle. The churning, pressing crowds made her feel claustrophobic. Her ears were buzzing from the shouting and her nostrils burned from the strong fumes of sulfur. She was going to faint—or throw up. She shoved against the man in front of her and screamed, "Let me out of here. I'm pregnant and I'm going to throw up."

Among the maddening clamor, Autumn felt an odd moment of humor when heads jerked around to stare; then it was like the parting of the Red Sea as the men moved aside to let her pass. She knew now that it had been a mistake to come to the mine looking for Lonnie. She wanted the warmth and quiet of her little house, but to give her head time to clear, she slid onto the fender of a car and gazed off at the rolling hills in the distance. All the signs of fall had faded. The naked trees looked cold and empty, and the quiet of the hills evoked a feeling of serenity. A startling contrast against the insanity that raged around her.

As her eyes swept over the bobbing heads, she saw the women for the first time. Unlike the men, the women stood quietly off to one side. They were huddled in small groups, some with their arms locked together in support. There was a tense, waiting feel about them that reached out and grasped at Autumn. Their ages varied, but each face was stretched taut with strain. They were strong, silent women with tired, hollowed eyes.

Autumn didn't know any of them, but she had seen one or two around town. A tall, thin woman worked in a diner where she and Lonnie sometimes went for a hamburger. Janie, as her name tag read, worked as a checker at the market where she shopped. Autumn had spoken to her a few times. She was vivacious, full of laughter. Everything was funny to Janie, but Janie wasn't laughing now. Her small face was drawn and her pink cheeks were wet with silent tears.

Autumn swallowed the lump in her throat and looked back at the crowd of men. The silly man in the stocking cap was still shaking his fist. She slid from the fender, wondering why. Why were they angry? Who were they angry at? As she turned to leave, a man rushed past her. He was covered in coal dust and looked tired and haggard. She ran after him and caught his arm as he reached for the handle on his car. "My husband," she said in an anxious tone. "Lonnie Norton. Do you know him? Have you seen him? Is he all right?"

The man gazed at her with a blank, weary look as if it were too much effort to think. "Yeah," he said, nodding his head. "I know Lonnie. I saw him in the pit a few hours ago. He's okay."

She felt weak with relief. "Thanks."

He turned from Autumn and was climbing in his car when a reporter appeared and shoved a microphone into his face. The man turned on him in a rage. "Get the hell away from me."

"All I want are a few facts. Is it as bad as they say? How many dead? What was the cause?"

The man's broad, coal-smudged face twisted into a frown of irritation. His brown eyes darkened and he spoke in a low, derisive tone. "Fuck yes, it's bad. If you want facts, ask the Osbornes."

"I can't get to them."

"That ain't my fault."

"What was the cause?" the reporter asked. "Why is everyone being so hush-hush?"

"Look, bloodsucker. I ain't got a thing to say. I'm tired and I'm gonna go home and get some rest." He climbed into his car, started the engine, and was gone with a ragged grinding of the gears.

The reporter quirked an eyebrow, then turned to Autumn with a shrug. "What about you, miss? Do you have somebody in the mine? Maybe a husband . . . father . . . brother? What are you feeling now?"

She looked at the mike and then at his backside. "I don't think you really want to know." She stalked off, wondering if outsiders would ever understand the minds of small-town Kentuckians. They might fight among themselves, but grief was a private thing, not something to be turned into a three-ring circus by overeager reporters.

Turning up the collar of her coat and shoving her hands deep into her pockets, she hurried through the empty streets. Even the wind seemed disturbed and at odds with itself. It was a bitingly cold day, but when Autumn had walked to the mine earlier, there was hardly a breeze stirring. Now the wind came again suddenly. It ripped through the trees, sending fallen leaves tumbling end over end, whipping her hair until it spread around her face like an auburn fan. Her cheeks were soon burning from the sting of its bite, her nose rosy red. Wisps of steam escaped with every breath. Feeling the wind whistle against her legs, she burrowed deeper into the warmth of her coat, her head bent against the cold air. She entered Miners' Row at last, moving at a fast jog.

The cracker-box house had never looked so good to Autumn. Beyond its weather-beaten door were warmth and sanity. At that moment it seemed to her the whole world had turned topsy-turvy. She burst into the house, tossed her coat on the sofa, and was going to the gas heater when she stopped in surprise as Molly walked out of the kitchen. Autumn had been so deep in thought that she had passed her aunt's car without even seeing it. For a moment Autumn wanted to run to her as she had as a child, feel the soft touch of her hand, tell her where it hurt. "I'm glad you're here," she said simply.

Molly nodded. "I heard about the trouble on the television early this morning, so I hurried on over. I thought y'all might be needing me, but your face kind of tells me Lonnie is all right."

Autumn turned her back to the heater and arched toward its warmth. "He's fine—I guess. I can't help but worry. He was home when it happened, but he's at the mine now. I was there a while ago. I couldn't believe it, Aunt Molly. It's crazy. Sane, easygoing people are acting like wild animals. They're pushing and shoving and shouting obscenities at the same people they were drinking moonshine with yesterday."

Molly eased down on the sofa. "It's the shock," she said. "They'll simmer down. Then's when the hurt'll really come. The shouting and the nasty words help drive the hurt away. Anger is man's best defense against hurting."

"It all happened so quickly," Autumn said. "We had no warning. They haven't even had a breakdown since October." She turned away from Molly and held her hands toward the heater. "It's hard to believe. I feel like I'm living a bad dream and I'm waiting for Lonnie to walk in the door any moment and tell me it isn't true." She turned back to Molly with a frightened expression. "The thing that scares me is, it could have happened on Lonnie's shift. I could be one of the women standing and waiting. I'd die if anything happened to Lonnie."

"No you wouldn't. You might want to, but you wouldn't." Molly rose from the sofa. "I made some coffee. I think we'd best cook up some food. Lonnie's gonna be coming home. When he does, he's gonna want a smile and a soft touch from his wife. He ain't gonna wanta see your face all puckered and afraid. I reckon he's seen plenty of that today."

Autumn knew Molly, in her subtle way, had told her to grow up. She followed Molly and they moved about the kitchen automatically. Molly wasn't one to chatter, but she kept up a steady stream of conversation. "Bobby Joe Proctor has gone away to college. He hopes to be a big-city lawyer someday. . . . The lockers at school were searched and pot was found, which caused a big stink in Turtle Ridge. . . . Tucker's still was raided—he thought by the kids. . . . Jeb said the hardware store would never be the same without you, honey. . . . Folks still remember the day you flew into a temper and dumped a can of maggots on Mrs. Baker's floor."

Autumn thought back and laughed, but she was unable to dispel the underlying current of tension. They fried chicken, which grew soggy in the oven as noon came and went without Lonnie. Autumn worked around the house with Molly, but the day-to-day routine that usually calmed her only led to frustration. By late afternoon she was pacing the floor and watching the clock.

Lonnie had been gone for twenty-two hours. Autumn looked at the clock. Ten P.M. She turned on her toes, swinging her hips angrily, and cursed, "Damn the mines. Damn that dirty hole in the ground. And damn the Osbornes."

"Why?" Molly asked. "Because they own the mine?"

"They not only own the mine, but they own and control everything in Edisonville. That old pisser sits in his big white house and reigns over the town like God Almighty. It's unfair. No one should have that much control over anyone else. It makes me want to kick and scratch and claw." She kicked at a throw rug and sent it flying across the room.

Molly looked at her with a placating nod. "Why don't you go make some coffee? There's time enough to fret about the mines and the Osbornes later."

Autumn looked at her oddly. "I just made some coffee a little while ago."

"It's stale. Pour it out and make some fresh. Lonnie'll be coming home anytime now. He'll be wanting some fresh coffee."

Autumn knew the coffee wasn't stale. It was Molly's way of keeping her busy. She went to the kitchen, pausing briefly to straighten the rug she had kicked into a ball. She crossed to the window and gazed at the shadowy frame of Ella's house. It stood in darkness and the drapes were drawn. Ella was in Lexington making arrangements to lease the diner on Fifth Street. She had finally made it. A few more weeks, two months at the most, and Ella would be respectable by the narrow-minded standards of Edisonville.

Drawing her hand over the smooth surface of the counter, Autumn picked up the coffeepot and stared at it dully. She plopped it down and went into the living room, where

Molly sat with her eyes half-closed. "We may as well drink the stale coffee. And we may as well eat that old dead bird in the oven. Lonnie won't be home for hours yet."

"Who says?"

Autumn turned at the sound of his voice and her heart stepped up its pace. He stood tall and strong, this man who was the center of her universe, his broad shoulders almost filling the doorway. His smiling cornflower-blue eyes always seemed to bring a touch of spring when he looked at her. Now, however, they were clouded with fatigue; the brilliance was lacking and there was no quick, crooked grin.

"What would you like first?" she asked. "A shower, or hot but soggy chicken?"

It was crooked, and it came slowly, but he smiled and said, "You."

6

The debacle of the last two days ended as abruptly as it had begun. One moment they were pulling bodies from the mine, and then suddenly it was over, bringing a strange kind of silence that engulfed the town. In the length of two days, twenty-six men had suffered serious injuries, thirteen had minor injuries, and fourteen were dead. The mine had been closed, putting many men out of work.

Autumn had moved through the days in a haze of waiting and confusion. Lonnie was home, then he was gone. He slept short hours and ate on the run. Deep lines of fatigue creased his face, his eyes dulled with remorse over the loss of his coworkers. There had been times when she caught a glimpse of something more. *Anger, confusion?* Autumn couldn't define the momentary expression that flickered in his eyes.

During the brief periods when he had been home, she stayed at his side. When he showered, she waited with a towel. When he ate, she handed him the food. When he slept, she lay curled in his arms. And when he was gone, she waited with Molly. As Molly had predicted, the hostility which first gripped the town was gone now, leaving them sealed in a wall of gloom.

Autumn entered the bathroom as Lonnie stepped from the shower. She pulled a towel from the rack and drew it over his chest, shoulders, and down the length of his body. "We're out of bread," she said. "I sent Molly to the store. Artie called. I told him everything was fine. I haven't seen her, but Ella's car is in the driveway. I think she got back from Lexington sometime last night." Idle chatter, she thought. Why am I making idle chatter when there is so much I want to say? She slid into his arms and he gathered her close, as if to draw some of her softness into him, and she did the same, hoping to absorb some of his strength.

She pulled away suddenly and looked up at Lonnie. "I don't understand. How can one explosion cause so much havoc?"

He frowned, and worry lines crinkled at his eyes. "Being inside a mine shaft when there's a methane-gas explosion is like being inside the barrel of a cannon when it explodes. The stuff can be hell."

She felt tiredness spread over her and spoke in a weary voice. "What's going to happen now?"

"I'm not sure." He slipped his arm around her waist and led her down the hall to their bedroom.

She stretched out on the bed and watched as he dressed. His movements were jerky, his face preoccupied, as if there was something weighing heavily on his mind. His work had gone fairly well the last month and they had managed to save a little, but the old Ford had quit and refused to go, so they had had to use what money they had. "What is it?" she asked. "Are you worried about being out of work?"

"No. I'll find work."

"Then what is it?"

He shoved his wallet into a back pocket and sat down on the bed beside her. "Something happened at the mine. I'm not sure if I should tell you. I don't want you to get upset."

"I'm not a fragile flower, Lonnie. We Irish are made of strong stuff. We may crack a little now and then, but we don't break easily."

He smiled faintly and spoke in an Irish brogue. "Ahh, 'tis said well, me love." He turned on the bed until he was facing her directly, and spoke in a tight voice. "It happened yesterday. I'd been at the mine for about twelve hours, and I was getting a little punchy. I'd pulled ten, fifteen men out, some dead. I found what I thought was another body. The man was off to one side, away from the others. He was foreman on the swing swift.''

''*Was?* Then he's dead?''

''He is now, but he was alive when I found him. He died, but he talked to me first.'' Lonnie rose to his feet, pacing the room and curling his hands into fists. ''None of this should have happened. There was a problem with the blower system, and Osborne knew it.''

''Which Osborne?''

''It has to be Douglas. He's head of the family and in charge of the mine. The foreman was in bad shape. He wasn't speaking too clearly, but I put the pieces together.'' Lonnie sat down on the bed beside her. ''A section of the blower system broke down again. The foreman called Maintenance. They did come, but it was going to take hours before they could have it repaired. The foreman called Osborne and asked permission to pull his crew. Osborne refused. He said the blower system would keep the air clear even with the section down.''

Lonnie sat with his wide shoulders slumped and drew his hand down wearily over his face. ''In some mines it might have worked, but not in a mine as gassy as the Black Jewel. There's a constant seepage of methane in all mines, but there's little danger of an explosion if the ventilation system is working properly.'' Lonnie frowned and shook his head in wonder. ''Methane is funny stuff. It gathers in pockets. The slightest spark can cause an explosion.''

''What caused this one?''

He shrugged. ''Who knows? It could have been any number of things. Maybe some wiseass decided to sneak a quick smoke. The point is, Osborne knows his mine. He knows it's a gassy bitch, but he kept it open. The air is monitored often. Within a couple of hours the methane had risen to a dangerous level. The foreman called Osborne again. Osborne said to hang tight. He said Maintenance would have the section rolling shortly. The foreman returned to his area intending to pull his crew on his own. He didn't get the chance. He got caught in the explosion.''

''It's negligence, isn't it?''

His eyes sparked with anger. "Damn right, it's negligence. Methane explosions aren't uncommon, and machinery does break down. Osborne was negligent when he refused to pull the crew. He killed them as surely as if he put a gun to their heads."

"There will be an investigation, won't there?"

"Yes, but it won't amount to much. The report will read: 'BLAST TRIGGERED WHEN MINERS HIT A POCKET OF METHANE GAS.' Case closed. It's as simple as that."

"What are you doing to do?"

"I'm going into town and ask around. It's doubtful, but maybe someone else knows about the calls to Osborne and can back me up."

"What if you can't find anybody?"

"Then I'll go to the mining officials alone. I'm going to make so much damned noise, they'll have to take a closer look. Osborne isn't going to get away with this—not if I can help it. If I have to, I'll stand in the courthouse square and tell what I know to anybody who will listen."

"Why did he close the mine for good?"

"The mine would have been closed during the investigation anyhow, but it wouldn't have been closed permanently like he's planning. Now Osborne claims the mine has shown a low profit for the last five years and has been working at a near-loss for the last year." Lonnie rose from the bed, pulling Autumn along with him. "I would have sworn the mine was good for another couple of years." He walked with his arm around Autumn to the front room and paused at the door. "I don't want you to mention this to anyone. Okay?"

"No," she said, "I won't."

He kissed her lightly and had turned to leave when Molly pulled her old Ford in alongside his. He ran down the steps when she climbed from the seat with a bag of groceries. "Hi, Molly. Need some help?"

"No. I've just got one bag." She nodded toward the sack. "Brought some nice fresh hamhocks. I thought they might taste good with some pinto beans and cornbread and a sweet white onion."

"Sounds great." Looking back at Autumn, he grinned and waved. "Love ya, sugar."

A strange feeling of misgiving gripped Autumn and she had to fight to keep from chasing after him, begging him not to go. She trembled violently, but told herself it was the result of the last two anxiety-ridden days. She smiled, lifted her hand, and waved as he drove away.

Molly looked at her closely. "What's wrong? You've gone pale as a ghost."

"I think someone just walked across my grave." She turned to go into the house, but paused as Ella dashed across the yard.

Ella spanned the steps in one jump, waving a paper in her hand. "It's done. The diner will be mine February 16. I feel guilty being so happy after what has happened, but damn, I'm happy."

Autumn smiled. "Great. Come inside and tell me about it." She steered the two women into the house, took their coats, and led them into the kitchen. Ella took a chair at the table and Molly went to the sink and put the beans on to soak.

Autumn pulled three cups from the cabinet, poured the coffee, and setting the cups on the table, slid into a chair across from Ella. "Are you going to keep working, or do you plan to take a long vacation until you open the diner?"

"I wish I could, but I'm flat broke. I'm going to have to really hustle to put together enough money to stock the place. And I want something in the kitty in case business falls off now that the mine is closed."

Molly turned from the sink. "What kind of work do you do? I don't think I've heard anybody say."

Ella looked at Autumn with a question in her eyes. Autumn grinned and shrugged. "I'm a hooker," Ella said.

The expression on Molly's face didn't change. "I hear it pays good." She dried her hands on a towel, crossed to the table, and picked up a cup. "I think I'll take my coffee into Lonnie's den and watch a little television. There's a soap opera comes on about now I try not to miss. I got caught up in the silly thing while I was working 'round the homes in Turtle Ridge." She trotted off toward the rear of the house, mumbling, "Them folks on the television have got so many danged problems, I feel like I'm shitting in tall cotton just to have a roof over my head and beans in the pot.''

Autumn grinned and watched her aunt until she had disappeared into Lonnie's den. She turned back to Ella. ''What do you know about the Osbornes?''

''Not much,'' Ella said. ''All I know is what I hear around town.'' She took a cigarette from her purse and lighted it with a package of book matches. ''The four brothers own the mine jointly. There's Douglas, Homer, George, and Dale. Everything else in town is owned by Douglas. From what I've heard, he started wheeling and dealing fresh out of college. He's a shrewd businessman and tough as nails. The distillery was first owned by the Wellingtons. He got control somehow. It's the same with everything else he owns.'' She took a drag on the cigarette and smiled with a hint of satisfaction. ''I won't be the only one affected if the mine stays closed. Douglas will hardly notice it, but the brothers will be hurting. The mines are their only source of income—except for the joints.''

''The joints? You're kidding. Why would the Osbornes bother with bootleg whiskey when they have so much?''

''Because they pull in a whale of a lot of money. Whiskey, slots, women—and all tax-free. And a damned cheap investment. All they need is an old farmhouse on a quiet country road. A few chairs and tables, a jukebox, a makeshift bar, and a few rooms in back for the women.'' She leaned and jabbed her cigarette out in an ashtray. ''It isn't commonly known, and could never be proved, but Douglas permits it all.''

''What about the police?'' Autumn asked.

''Douglas eased Homer in as mayor years ago. The police are taken care of. There's a raid now and then, but a call is sent out and and the place is clean by the time they get there. Amos Patterson manages the feed store for the Osbornes. He acts as a front. Those that even stop to wonder, think he's behind it all.''

''How did you find out?''

''I was there late one morning when Amos Patterson came in to talk to Rex. Rex Carter manages one of the joints. He runs the house where I work. The door to his office was ajar and I overheard Amos talking to Douglas on the phone. From the tone of the conversation, I knew they weren't talking about the feed store, so I listened. Amos was getting his orders from Douglas."

Autumn laughed quietly. "Even with all their big white houses, the Osbornes are still nothing but dirty, ignorant, pee-in-the-weeds people."

Ella looked at her oddly, but grinned. "Let's go in the diner and get a hamburger. I'm going to pretend everything is fine. Maybe you can come up with some good ideas for poshing up the place."

The two women left the house in high spirits, but they had hardly reached town before their moods took a downward plunge. The events of the last two days hung heavily in the air. The town seemed unusually quiet, all movements slow. Faces were long and set with remorse, shoulders slumped. Autumn felt the gloom creeping over her, as thick as sticky mud. "God! When will it end?"

"You know," Ella said, "I've been with half the miners at the Black Jewel. Some were married. I know the names of their wives, kids, and what they like best for supper. That does something to a person." She pulled the car up in front of the diner and cut the engine. "It's crazy what comes to mind at a time like this. I keep seeing their dicks and funny tails. Some had little dicks, some big, some short and fat, some long and skinny. They all treated me good, though. There'll be a freebie waiting for any man that wants it."

Autumn grinned to herself. "You're all heart, Ella."

Ella looked at Autumn, her eyes full of wonder. "I don't believe myself. Did I just say what I think I said? I'll start a run on the whorehouse with that kind of talk." She opened the car door and jumped out. "No more. This is a big day for me. I'm not going to let anything spoil it."

The diner was a long room with a counter at one end and eight tables, each with a vase of dusty plastic flowers. Yellowed curtains hung limply at three small windows.

The room was empty except for the counterman, a large fellow with a belly that bulged over a soiled white apron. His gray shirt had a rip in the pocket, and he looked at them through small eyes that appeared almost lost in his fat, flushed face. His expression was enough to bring back the gloom permanently.

"You want posh," Autumn said, turning quickly to Ella. "I'll give you posh. We'll start with the floors. Something from Persia, I think. And for the windows, I suggest something in red—velvet maybe." She walked about the room, drawing her fingers over the scarred tables. "These will have to go. We'll pick up some Chippendale. We'll want embossed linen for the tables, real flowers, and fine vases—Ming dynasty."

"What's a Chippendale?"

"Furniture named for a cabinetmaker in England."

"I thought it was a dog."

Autumn grinned. "With the Chippendale, a crystal chandelier is a must."

"Naturally," Ella said. "No diner should be without Chippendale and a chandelier."

The counterman stood with his chubby hands on his thick waist. "What do you screwy broads want?"

Ella slid onto a stool and slapped her hand against the counter. "I want two hamburgers with all the works for me and my friend, and hurry it up. This is the new owner you're looking at."

Autumn took a stool beside her, propped her elbows on the counter, grinned up at him. "Hold the onions, sweetface."

They spent the afternoon planning, teasing the sour counterman until his heavy middle shook with hard chuckles. Evening shadows were falling when the two women left the diner, the counterman's laughter echoing behind them.

"Brrr," Ella said. "It's cold enough to freeze the balls off a brass monkey."

Autumn shivered in a silent agreement and switched on the radio, which issued a lively version of "Deck the Halls." It was the tenth of December and the store windows were aflame with Christmas lights, despite the town's prevailing mood. The air was crisp and invigorating. A few people hurried along the streets, their collars pulled high against the cold.

Ella drove slowly while they admired the decorations.

Once they reached the outskirts of town, Ella joined Autumn and they sang "Jingle Bells" in harmony, laughing when they couldn't remember the words.

"What are you doing for Christmas?" Ella asked.

"We're going to Aunt Molly's. I can't think of anywhere in the world I'd rather be for Christmas than Turtle Ridge. It's like another world, Ella. When I lived there, I thought of it as a dead little town. Now I realize we had something rare. Those people are at peace with themselves, and with the world."

She leaned her head back against the seat and listened as Ella hummed along with the radio, her head full of Turtle Ridge, her aunt, and Lonnie. This Christmas was special. It would be their first together. And next year there would be toys under the tree. She hugged herself, sudddenly so full of joy she felt ready to burst.

The car had traveled several yards on the graveled road of Miners' Row when she heard Ella gasp. She opened her eyes and looked around for something out of the ordinary, but everything seemed to be going on as usual. Lights were begnning to come on in the little houses, and children were being called in from play. Twinkle lights blinked on some of the peaked roofs. "What is it?" she asked.

Ella pointed ahead as the car dipped and the headlights picked up a patrol car parked in front of Autumn's house. "Don't worry. It's probably nothing."

Icy fear rushed through Autumn. "Lonnie!" She jumped from the moving car, stumbled, regained her balance, raced for the house and up the steps, bursting through the doorway. Two officers turned toward her. Molly, her face stricken, looked at her anxiously.

"What is it?" Autumn gasped, her voice trembling with emotion. "What is it? What's wrong?"

A silence that seemed to stretch into forever gripped the room. Her hands trembling, Molly stepped forward and pulled Autumn into her arms. "There's no easy way to tell you, child. Lonnie is dead."

"No!" Autumn pushed away from Molly. Her skin felt tingly, her body buoyant. She had the sensation of speaking too loudly, too quickly. "No, No. Lonnie isn't dead. It's a mistake. You're all wrong."

"It's no mistake, ma'am." An officer spoke in a kind voice and looked at her with understanding. "We wouldn't be here if we weren't sure."

Autumn felt caught in a world of make-believe, a crazy surrealistic world. Lonnie wasn't dead. She couldn't have been so happy only a few moments before if Lonnie were dead. She loved him too deeply. She would have sensed if he were even in danger. She couldn't have laughed and joked away the hours with Ella if Lonnie were dead. She would have known. Yes, Lonnie was a part of her, and she would know if a part of her died. "You're wrong, officer. You've made a terrible mistake. My husband isn't dead. He'll be coming home anytime now. You'll see. You'll all see."

The older of the two officers looked at her with eyes filled with pity. "There's no mistake. I wish there was, but there isn't. Your husband was killed when his car went over an embankment in an area the kids call the High Banks. It's about twenty miles outside of town." His face softened and he spoke in a low, consoling tone. "His neck was broken. If it's any consolation, he died instantly."

Autumn was smiling. She twisted the wedding band around and around on her finger and looked from one officer to the other. "See? I told you he wasn't dead. There was no reason for Lonnie to be at the High Banks. I know where he went. He wouldn't have left town. He had important things to do here." She turned as Ella entered the room. "They're trying to tell me Lonnie is dead. It's crazy, Ella."

Ella sucked in her breath and looked at Molly for an answer. Molly nodded and went to Autumn, tears gathering in her eyes. "You have to be strong, child. And you have to face the truth." She pointed to the coffee table. "They found them things on his body."

Autumn looked down at Lonnie's old battered wallet, a gold wedding band that matched her own, and an old watch that didn't keep good time. Her life had begun the day she met Lonnie, and now it was ending. She was disintegrating, crumbling, and she screamed against the pain that ripped through her chest. And she ran, screaming down the creaky steps, through the streets of Miners'

Row, plunging into the night that was a deep, dark pool, gobbling her, pressing in on her.

Harder and faster she ran, her feet slapping against the frozen ground. Running away from the ugly hurting words, running away from the crazy screaming woman, stumbling, running, falling. Pain, though unreal, cut across her chest and stabbed at her middle. Tears, blinding hot tears burned against her cheeks. Blood, crimson red, stuck to her fingers, her knees, and trickled down her legs. Voices called to her: Autumn . . . Sue Anne.

Amid the calling voices were soft whispers, "Love ya, sugar," and images swirling in and out of focus: a crooked grin, blue eyes smiling. "Love ya, sugar." From far away she heard an anguished scream: "Lonnie, Lonnie . . ." Then lights that flashed red, spinning around and around, a pricking pain, then darkness.

A blinding whiteness, and the voice screamed again— "Lonnie, Lonnie!"—and then the pricking pain that sent her into darkness. She was caught, trapped in a maze of stark white and spinning blackness. She felt herself slipping away, sinking deeper and deeper into a dark pool without light, sound, or movement, only blessed stillness.

7

Autumn fought her way out of darkness, conscious only of rage. Her eyes darted wildly. Everything was stark white. A small sign on a door read "Patients Only." A steady hum of meaningless voices came from outside the room. She lifted her head and gazed at the needle in her arm, her eyes following the tube to an IV bottle that dripped steadily.

Awareness brought a wave of scattered memories. Bright lights glaring against her eyes. Men and women in white who spoke in impersonal voices: "She's bleeding. She's aborted the baby." The words seemed unrelated, distant. "Hysterical . . . amnesia." She heard screams. The light, and then the sting of needles that again forced her into darkness.

Autumn pressed her hand against her mouth, knowing that if she screamed they would come with the needle again. Moaning, she whispered Lonnie's name, feeling as though she had been dragged through the pits of hell.

Molly, who sat near the bed with her head in her hand, dozing, jerked at the low, hollow sound of Autumn's voice. She rushed to the bed and reached for the call button, but Autumn shoved at her hand. "Don't. There's no need. I'm fine." She lowered her hands to her stomach, knowing, but having to ask, "My baby? It's dead, isn't it?"

Her face drawn, Molly nodded and took Autumn by the

hand. "I've been so worried about you. I blame myself for all this. I should have told you more easy-like. I was in a bad way. I wasn't thinking."

"How?" Autumn asked in a voice tinged with bitterness. "How could you have made it easy, Aunt Molly? What magic words could you have used?" She pulled her hand away and touched her flat stomach again. "Gone, all gone. He took them both. That bastard took them both."

"He? Who?" Molly's voice cracked with fear and emotion. "What are you talking about?"

"Nothing. Nothing." She cast a glance about the room. "How long have I been here?"

"Two weeks. Dr. Gordon said you'd be snapping out of it anytime now. He thought it would be good for you to find me here."

"Two weeks," Autumn whispered. Somewhere between the dark and the light she had lost two weeks of her life. She turned and looked at Molly. "Who is Dr. Gordon?"

"He's the 'head' doctor they called in to take care of you."

Autumn sat upright in bed. "A *head* doctor? They called in a psychiatrist? Why?"

"You've been out of your mind for two weeks. I don't really hold with head doctors, but he looked after you real good. Since Dr. Carlson was already taking care of you when you lost the baby, they called him in too. Your hands and knees were stove-up pretty bad and you had to have a D-and-C. There's no need to fret, though. The bleeding stopped a long time ago. Dr. Carlson said you healed real good."

Autumn threw back the sheet, swung her legs over the edge of the bed, and sat upright with a strange kind of calm. "Where is he? Where is Lonnie?"

Molly hesitated. "I wish I did, but I ain't got no magic words. Lonnie's at Oak Hills Cemetery. I found Artie's phone number in your little book and called him. He come and saw to everything. He couldn't stay, though. He had to get back to work. I'm to call him if you need anything."

Autumn eased from the bed and stood. Her legs felt rubbery, her head woozy, and she grasped the pole of the IV for support. Her hand clasped tightly, she rolled the pole along with her as she inched about the room. She went to the sink, ran cold water into a basin, and splashed it over her face. After drying herself with a small towel, she walked the length of the room, then turned and retraced her steps.

Molly watched her with a worried frown. "Don't you think you better stay in bed until you're stronger?"

"I'll never get stronger if I stay in bed." With an uneven but determined stride, she walked back and forth, back and forth, feeling cold and withered inside, full of hate. She felt weighted down, her limbs a heavy burden to be tugged and pushed around the room. When attacked by weakness, she paused, breathed deeply, and then began again, pacing slowly until her head had stopped its spinning and her legs had stopped their trembling. Abruptly Autumn looked down at her wrist, grasped the needle, and gave a quick jerk.

"Lord!" Molly hurried to her side, took her hand, and stared at the tiny drop of blood. "Why did you do that?"

"I wanted the damned thing out of my arm." She gave the pole a shove and crossed to the narrow closet. "Are my clothes in here?"

"Clothes . . ." Molly repeated in alarm. "What do you want with clothes? Just where do you think you're going?"

"To Lonnie. I'm going to Lonnie."

"You can't, child. They won't let you leave here."

The rage Autumn held in tight control burst forth and her cheeks flamed in angry red. She spun on her toes, hands on her hips and chin held high. "No one is keeping me from going to Lonnie. No one."

Molly touched her with a calming hand. "Simmer down. There's no need to get yourself all worked up." Molly turned toward the door. "I'll see if I can get you out of here. Seems to me I saw Dr. Gordon in the hall a little earlier. Maybe he's still here."

Autumn went to the closet and pulled her clothes out piece by piece. She stared at them in awe. The knees in her jeans were ripped, her shoes badly scuffed; her jacket coated with dirt and blood. She ached with sorrow, surrounded by the truth, the thing she had known since awakening. Lonnie hadn't gone over an embankment. He had been sent over. The High Banks were in an area twenty miles from town where the kids went to park and neck, nothing but woods and a curving road with a deep ravine that ran along the edge.

Lonnie had been angry, angrier than she had ever known him to be. He'd told her about a talk he had with a crew foreman. The foreman had called Osborne to ask that the men be pulled until the blower system could be repaired, but Osborne had refused. Lonnie had gone to town to try to find someone else who knew about the calls to Osborne, calls that would have proved negligence.

Lonnie wouldn't have gone to the High Banks alone. There was no reason for it; someone had taken him there. The only one who had anything to gain was Douglas Osborne. With the foreman dead and Lonnie gone, there wouldn't be anyone to stand against him. He would be free, free to sit in his big white house, to reign over the town, the people, life and death.

The truth lay inside Autumn like a heavy stone. She felt choked by it, enraged by it. Jerking her feet into the jeans, she pulled her sweater over her head in a twisting motion. She was putting on her shoes when Molly returned with a man in a dark suit. Vaguely, through the haze of the past two weeks, Autumn remembered having seen his face. "I'm leaving," she said curtly.

He was a beanpole of a man, with dark hair, graying slightly at the temples. His face was half-hidden by a distinguishing beard. Kind blue eyes looked at her with understanding, and when he spoke, his voice was soothing, almost musical. "Where are you going, Sue Anne?"

"To my husband."

"Could we talk first?"

Autumn nodded and sat down on the bed, fighting for control. He was a psychiatrist. If she screamed, if he could see the turmoil that raged inside, he would keep her from going to Lonnie.

He took a chair and gazed at her analytically. "You're angry. Why?"

She shook her head.

"You don't want to tell me?"

She shook her head again.

"Where is your husband?" he asked abruptly.

Autumn was thrown off guard for a moment. She knotted her hands into fists. Remembering her resolve, she rested them in her lap. "He's gone."

"Where is he gone?"

"He's at Oak Hills Cemetery. I have to go to him."

"Yes," he said in a soft tone. "I understand. Could we talk about the baby?"

"It's dead," she said, finality in her voice. "I don't want to talk about it."

"Your baby is dead, but Lonnie is only gone. Why is that, Sue Anne?"

Autumn was suddenly aware that she was digging her nails into her thigh. She again rested her hands in her lap. "How should I know? You're the doctor. You tell me."

He was quiet while writing in a manila folder. "Tell me everything you can remember about the last two weeks."

She sat with her back stiff and gazed at him evenly. "They said Lonnie was dead. I didn't believe them. They had some of his things. When I saw them, I knew Lonnie was gone. I don't remember very much after that. I remember running from the house and falling. I remember bright lights that hurt my eyes, nurses, the sting of needles, and food I couldn't eat. I remember being forced from the bed and made to walk, when all I wanted was to die. I remember you talking to me, but it's like a dream now."

"Do you still want to die?"

"No," she said with truth in her voice.

He smiled and nodded with understanding. "Good. You're doing well, Sue Anne. You've been through a very bad time, but you're going to be fine. I'd like to keep you here under mild sedation for a while longer. However," he added when she jerked forward. "I'll give you a pass to leave the hospital. It is sometimes hard for the mind to accept death when there isn't a body in repose. I hope a visit to your husband's grave will help you." He gave her hand a light squeeze. "You have to bury him, Sue Anne. If you don't, you'll never find peace of mind. I think we should talk further about this anger I sense in you, too."

His voice trailed off as he rose. "We'll talk again later."

She smiled, a smile that didn't quite reach her eyes. "Thank you, Dr. Gordon. Thank you for taking care of me."

Autumn gazed at the small mound of dirt, surrounded by many other impersonal headstones. She knelt beside the mound, trying to feel connected to Lonnie. In sweeping waves she smoothed her hand over the earth, gathering loose soil and letting it filter slowly through her fingers. The scent of fresh-turned soil mixed with the scent of withered flowers permeated the air. The ground was damp against her bare knees, jutting through rips in her jeans. Her mind repeated over and over that Lonnie was sleeping beneath the mound, but it was unreal, part of the long, long dream.

His name and his birth and death dates were typed neatly and enclosed in a flimsy metal plaque that was hammered into the soil at an angle. She straightened the plaque and stood, gazed up at the naked tree limbs overhead, held out her hand, and caught icy raindrops. "It's beginning to rain." She looked back at the plaque. "I'll have to get a headstone."

A look of fear and uncertainty flickered across Molly's face. She took Autumn by the arm. "Come away," she pleaded. "It's cold here."

Glancing back briefly, Autumn followed without argument. They weaved around the headstones, frozen leaves cracking beneath their feet. Cold drizzling rain mixed with sleet soaked their heads and shoulders. They were passing an area enclosed by a wrought-iron fence when Autumn paused and stared with contempt at the enormous headstone that stood in the center. Strong, violent emotions struggled inside her as she read the name Osborne. Her head began to throb and she pressed her hands hard against her temples.

Molly reached out and took her by the shoulders. "You're scaring me, girl. I'm getting you out of this awful place." She led Autumn from the cemetery and urged her into the car. "I'm taking you back to the hospital right now. It was bad, your coming here."

"No," Autumn shouted. "I'm not going back there. I want to go home." She turned her head toward the window and placed her hand over her stomach, rubbing as she rocked to and fro. "Just take me home, Aunt Molly."

Molly pleaded, but Autumn shook her head, never speaking, just shaking her head. After a while Molly grew quiet, as if resigned. Autumn gazed out the window as they drove through town. The Christmas decorations were still up, but the glitter was gone. The town looked tired and worn.

"When was Christmas?" Autumn asked suddenly.

"Yesterday." Molly glanced at her with a thoughtful frown. "I think we should pack up and go home to Turtle Ridge."

"No. I'm staying here."

"How?" Molly asked. "The town's in a mess. There's no work for you here. How will you get along?"

"I'll find a way." She turned in the seat and looked at Molly with affection. "I love you, Aunt Molly. I'll never forget all you've done for me, but it's time for me to be on my own. I want you to go home. I need time alone to think things out and to decide what to do. What I can do. Ella's here. I can go to her if I need help with anything."

Molly remained silent until she had parked her car in the driveway beside the house. She cut the engine, turned to Autumn, and looked at her long and hard. "I don't like leaving you alone, but I've always let you decide what was best for you, and it's worked out good. You're a fine girl, and you're strong. You'll find the way. It might take you a while, but I know in my gut you'll come out at the head of the line. I've always known it." Molly swept an auburn strand from Autumn's forehead. "Love, death, it's all part of living, and we have to find our own way of dealing. You loved your Lonnie, but he's gone now. You loved your coming baby, but it's gone too. It won't be easy, but you'll have to find a way to fill the empty hole. I'll leave you be, but I'll always be here if you ever need me."

*　　*　　*

The house was so silent that the sleet sounded like raining bullets striking against the tin roof. The sound followed her as she walked from room to room. Lonnie was everywhere. His work jacket hung on the peg in the kitchen. A pair of worn and dirty boots sat on the floor near the door. A book on mining lay open on his desk, as if he had only stepped away for a moment. Cigarettes lay on the nightstand in their bedroom. She brushed her hand against the spread, and tears misted her eyes. For a moment he was there, smiling up at her. "Love ya, sugar."

She stumbled from the room, half-blinded by tears. Lonnie was gone. There would be no more love in the sweet morning twilight. She paused and stared down at Lonnie's things on the coffee table, picked up his wedding band, and slipped it on her thumb. It was as though a horror movie were being rerun. Molly was there, Ella, and the officers, all looking at her in pity, and telling her Lonnie was dead. So gentle, so full of love. Lonnie hadn't asked much from life, just her, their child, and a college degree.

Alone now, she was free to release her rage. She spun, screaming hate against Douglas Osborne. She dropped to her knees and beat her fists against the floor. Her angry screams echoed in the hollowness of the empty house. A numbness began to spread over her, dulling the pain that stabbed her knuckles, the cuts that ran red with blood. She cried for Lonnie, and for the son or daughter she would never know. And she vowed before God to destroy the man who had taken them away from her.

8

The night was cold and starry. Autumn closed the door and walked woodenly, untouched by the big yellow moon that smiled down at her. For two days she had encased herself in the house where she had lived with Lonnie. His battered wallet contained fifty-three dollars and she had clasped it in her hand as she sat in the brown rocker, rocking and thinking.

She had thought of one plan, only to discard it for another. What could an eighteen-year-old girl with fifty-three dollars do against a man like Douglas Osborne? The police would laugh at her story, the mining authorities would think her deranged. But there was no doubt in her mind that Douglas had taken Lonnie from her. Every word, every gesture from Lonnie the day he told her about Douglas' refusal to pull the crew still lay inside her like a stone. *Douglas killed Lonnie to cover his own guilt.* It would take time, maybe years, but somehow, someday, she would bring the mighty Douglas Osborne to his knees as she had fallen to hers. He would feel her pain, and he would feel her loss. Autumn promised herself that much.

Her thoughts were clear and decisive as she stepped onto Ella's porch. She opened the door without knocking and crossed to where Ella sat on the sofa. "I need a job," Autumn said, her voice oddly quiet. "I need one now, and I need one that pays good. I want money and I don't care

what I have to do to get it. I want out of this town, and I
want out fast.''

Ella half-rose, her eyes scrutinizing. She smiled with
admiration and eased back to the sofa. "You're a real
trooper, kid.''

Autumn took a chair next to Ella. "About the job?''

Ella shook her head. "It's not for you, Autumn. Hook-
ing's the shits. The johns put a few dollars in your hand
and from that point on you're nothing but a piece of meat.
Why do you think I'm getting out?''

"Can you think of a way I can make more money?''

Ella didn't hesitate. "No, but can you handle the word
'whore'? Can you handle being a whore?''

"I can handle it. I can handle anything that will get me
what I want. What I have to have. Whoring is a means to
an end. It will get me out of town where I can find a way
to do the things I have to do.'' She spoke softly, but
clasped and unclasped her hands nervously as she related
to Ella all that Lonnie had told her about the explosion, the
foreman who talked to Lonnie before he died, how Lonnie
had gone into town to try to find someone other than
himself who knew about the calls to Douglas.

Talking about it brought it all back, and Autumn left the
chair and began to pace around the room. As she talked,
Ella's face stiffened and her eyes grew wide, then narrowed as she began to understand. Autunn paused in front
of her. "Money begets money. Power begets power. I
need money and power for what I have to do. I have to be
in a position to meet Douglas on his own terms.'' Autumn
spun and began to pace again. "When Douglas learned
that Lonnie knew about the calls, he got rid of him.
Another accident. Like the explosion.'' She paused, her
eyes flashing cold anger. "He killed Lonnie. He made me
lose my baby. I hate him, Ella. I hate that man with every
breath I draw.''

Ella nodded. "I wish there was something I could say,
kid, but there isn't. It's a waste—a damned waste.''

"You believe me, then?''

"From what I've heard, the man is capable.''

Autumn threw herself down in the chair. "As soon as I
get some money, I'm leaving, but I'll be coming back.

When I do, I'm going to turn this town upside down. I'm going to prove that Lonnie was murdered.''

Ella smiled mirthlessly. "That might not be so easy. The other thing you want to do might not be so easy either. Fucking for money isn't for every woman. There's only a few that can, or will.''

"I can and I will, if you'll help me.'' Autumn saw the look of indecision on Ella's face. "Please, don't say no. This is my decision to make, Ella, not yours.''

Ella sighed, resigned. "Okay, hon. I'll talk to my boss. In the meantime, you think about it good and hard. You can always change your mind if you want.''

"It will only be for a short while.'' Autumn chewed her lip for a moment. "Aunt Molly. I couldn't stand for her to know.''

"We'll think up a new name for you.'' Ella motioned toward Autumn's middle. "What about the miscarriage? Do you think your body is ready?''

"It's been almost three weeks. That's time enough.'' Autumn rose from the chair. "I want to see Aunt Molly. I'll take a bus to Turtle Ridge, but I'll be back in a couple of days, by New Year's Eve. I'd like to start work then. Can you fix it with Rex?''

Ella nodded, but stared intently. "About Douglas. Tread easy, Autumn. He's tough, and a real bastard from what I've heard. He'll step on you as if you were no more than a bug.''

Autumn said tiredly, "He can't hurt me, Ella. I don't have anything left to lose.''

A stranger stared at Autumn from the cracked and smudgy mirror. Her eyelids were coated with blue eye shadow, her cheeks pink with blush, her lips flamed a brilliant red. Mascara darkened her lashes. Ella had given Autumn a red satin robe that fit so snugly it looked painted on.

She turned from the mirror and gazed at Ella, her brows drawn together in a frown. "I look like a . . .''

"Whore?'' Ella interjected. "No you don't. That's the problem.'' She loosened the wrap at Autumn's throat. "Don't stand so prissy. The men who come here aren't looking for a lady. If they were, they'd stay home with their wives.'' She stroked her hand against Autumn's hair. ''Are you sure you want to do this?''

''I'm sure.''

''Okay, kid, but don't say I didn't warn you.'' She stepped back and looked at Autumn. ''With your hair, face, and body, you'll have the jerks knocking down the door. Leave them feeling great and you'll have a following that will help you out of town fast. You might leave with a sore pussy but you'll have money in your purse. Lots of it.''

''How do I leave them feeling great?''

''You hump and you bump and you huff and you puff, and you make them think it's all for them. If he walks away feeling like a superstud, he'll be back for more tomorrow night.'' She patted Autumn on the shoulder. ''It's about that time. A man will be sent back here to you. If there's any trouble, bang on the wall. I'll get Rex. He doesn't let anyone mistreat his girls. Good luck.''

Autumn watched Ella leave and sank down in a chair. The room wasn't great, but it was neat. The bed had clean sheets and warm blankets. A lamp from the nightstand cast a rosy glow. Two overstuffed chairs sat facing each other as if for idle chatter between two friends. A gas heater warmed the room, and it was almost cozy.

Ella had coached her on what to do and what to expect. Smile, always smile, and give them what they want. Wear only a robe. It saves time, and time is money. Insist on being paid first. If he passes out, call for Rex and have the room cleared for the next one.

She closed her eyes and tried to shut out the noise that came from the front of the house. It was New Year's Eve, and the men were celebrating at the top of their lungs with drunken whoops and hollers. Slot machines were clanking, the jukebox blasting Glen Campbell.

Surprisingly, she didn't feel nervous or regretful about her actions. She felt detached. She had closed her mind to the men, what she would be doing with them, and thought only of the money. It was a job, she told herself, just a job. A week, maybe two, and she'd be gone . . . free of this town that had brought her so much pain.

Autumn closed her eyes and felt the warmth of the

heater swirl around her. She had drifted into a light sleep when an uproar from the hallway jolted her awake. Startled, and feeling groggy from the heat, she leapt up without thinking and half-staggered to the door.

The noise had brought Ella and the other women from their rooms and they were grinning and watching while one man laughed and poured beer over the head of another. Autumn frowned and hurried to Ella. "What's going on?"

"Young Osborne. He and some of his buddies are celebrating the new year. We'll have a lively time tonight."

One of the two men sat on the floor and laughed crazily while beer ran down his face. Brian Osborne supported himself against the wall, an empty beer bottle in his hand. He was dressed in dark trousers and a heavy leather coat. His blond hair was tousled and fell across his forehead. He was looking at Autumn, with a silly grin on his face. She waited for some sign of recognition, but if he remembered her, it was lost in the haze of liquor. Autumn eased closer to Ella and whispered in a voice filled with apprehension, "Does he come here for sex?"

"Only when he's drunk on his ass."

"Is he drunk enough now?"

"Yeah, and he's singled you out."

The grin had left his face and he was staring at Autumn with an appraising eye. "Oooh, no," she said, her voice a whispered moan. "I can't. Not with him."

Ella slipped her arm around Autumn's waist and gave a light squeeze. "You have to, hon. You can't pick and choose. Besides, he's an Osborne. The people in this town don't say no to Douglas or his son. If you turn Brian away, Rex will toss you out of here on your ear." Ella looked at her with understanding. "You don't have to love them. Hell, you don't even have to like them. Just think of the money and where it will take you."

"I'll do it," Autumn said, "but only if I have to." She made a dash for her door, but laughing, Brian crossed the hall in two long strides and caught her by the arm. She pulled free and looked up at him with a cold stare. "I'm sorry, Mr. Osborne, but I'm busy. You'll have to pick someone else. I have a man in my room. He paid for the night."

"So get rid of him."

"I can't do that. It would be bad for business."

"Then I'll do it for you." He opened the door and looked about, then back at her, confused. "There's no one there. You lied." He took her arm and shoved her into the room, kicking the door closed behind him.

The strength, the force of him, made her feel trapped and dizzy. His face swam in and out of focus like rippling waves of heat. She rubbed her hand against her eyes. "Please. Pick someone else."

"I don't want someone else."

"Why me? There are four other women, and they're all prettier than me."

"Maybe, but they don't have red hair. I'm hung up on redheads."

"My hair isn't red. It's auburn, or are you too drunk to see the difference?"

"It looks red from where I stand."

She could feel the anger churning, growing, bubbling up inside her. Autumn didn't feel trapped anymore, but burning with rage. All the hate she felt for his father was now directed at Brian. "Stupid. You're stupid, and you're drunk. I don't want you near me, and most of all I don't want to get in that bed with you. You make me sick."

Brian laughed at her, crossed the room, and grasped the bedpost. "Where in the hell did they find you? I think somebody had better tell you where you are and what you are. Like it or not, this is nothing but a dirty whorehouse, and you're nothing but a cheap little whore."

Her eyes met his in a level gaze. "Whore? Not yet, Mr. Osborne. This is my first night, and you're the first man, so you can't call me a *whore* until I take your money and climb into bed with you. I don't think you'll find me cheap, either. If you want me, it will cost you two hundred dollars . . . in advance."

He blinked with surprise. "Two hundred . . . in this dump? You have to be crazy."

She shrugged. "It's my price. Take it or leave it."

He swayed against the bedpost, his eyes filled with

mischief. "Okay, Miss Prim and Proper. You'll get your two hundred, but first I want to see what I'm buying. Show me what's under the robe. You could be bowlegged. I wouldn't pay two hundred for a bowlegged whore."

Her hands felt sweaty and she rubbed them against her thighs, fumbled with the sash for a moment, then eased the robe from her shoulders and tossed it onto a chair. She turned to face him and understood what Ella had meant. He looked her over from head to toe as if she were a choice piece of steak. He motioned toward her legs. "What happened to your knees?"

She looked down at the raw skin left from where the scabs had fallen off and spoke in a voice that was barely audible. "Jack fell down and Jill came tumbling after."

"Riddles?" He reached in his back pocket, pulled out a wallet, and removed two hundred dollars.

She took the bills and fingered them for a moment. "It must be nice to have enough money to buy anything or anybody you want."

"Is that what you think?"

"It doesn't matter what I think." She put the money in her purse. At the same time she wondered if he was as drunk as she had thought. He spoke clearly and intelligently; however, he was hanging onto the bedpost, and having trouble getting out of his trousers. When he began to lower his shorts, she picked a spot on his chest and stared at blond fur, trying to remember everything Ella had said. Smile, give them what they want, and . . . A sudden fear burst into her thoughts. "Do you have . . . you wouldn't have a social disease, would you?"

"No, do you?"

"Me! No. I wouldn't have . . ." Autumn paused and stared back at him, confused as to what to do next. Did men kiss whores first, or did they just hop on? Did she go to him, or did she wait for him to come to her?

Naked, he came to her, pressed his thumb against her lips, and smeared. "Go wash your face. You look like a clown."

She jerked, her hand shot out by reflex, and she laced

him a stinging blow across the cheek. "You take me the way I am, rich boy, or you don't take me at all."

A muscle twitched in his jaw and for a moment he looked as if he were going to strike her back. "Brat!" He shoved her down on the bed, threw himself on top of her, and shifted until he was between her legs. "You're a bitch, a real bitch. You've got your money, so start whoring." He thrust into her.

Autumn stared over his shoulder at the cracks in the ceiling. One large crack spanned the length of the room, with many smaller ones spreading aimlessly in every direction. She studied the pattern. Somehow it seemed symbolic, but she couldn't think why. Was there a crack in her? Would bits of her leave and wander aimlessly? No. She had direction. Maybe there would be bits of her left along the way, but someday she would return. And she promised herself that when the day came, the man above her would treat her with respect.

She lay rigid, her arms at her sides, and waited for him to finish. She didn't hump or bump as Ella had said, but stared at the cracks and counted his strokes; some fast, some slow, and oddly enough, always gentle. His heart pounded against her breasts as he rubbed back and forth. His breath came fast, then faster. She felt him tense, whisper inaudibly, and then the heat of his semen.

It was over, and she sighed, pushed hard against his chest. "Now you can call me a whore, Mr. Osborne."

He seemed as eager to leave her as she was to have him gone. He rolled to his back and glanced at her from the corner of his eye. "That was the lousiest lay I've ever had."

"Same here," she said dryly.

He leaned on his elbow, his eyes confused as he gazed down at her. "It's crazy. You're mouthy, cold as hell, an independent bitch, but I'd still like to fuck you again."

"It will cost you another two hundred. In advance."

"If I got out of this bed, I'd fall flat on my face."

"I'll get your wallet for you."

"Crazy about me, aren't you?"

"No, just your money."

He drew his hand over her breasts, stomach, and inner

flesh of her thighs, brushed his fingers against her cheek. "You're going to be a very beautiful woman someday. If this place doesn't break you first. What's your name?"

"Mary," she said. "Mary Lou."

"Mary Lou what?"

"It doesn't matter. You'll never see me again. I don't intend to be here long."

"I'll see you. I'm buying you for my vacation. Call it a late Christmas present to myself. For the next week you will belong to me. I'll set it up with Rex. Before the week is over, I'm going to make you come if it kills the both of us."

Autumn folded her arms over her breasts and stared at the ceiling. "I'm numb from the neck down, Mr. Osborne. If you can make me come, I'll give *you* the two hundred dollars."

"It's a deal." He tipped her face and kissed her on the mouth. At first his lips were firm, but then they became weak, the kiss sluggish. He moaned and fell back against the pillows. "I think I should let *you* rest awhile first."

Shortly, quiet snores echoed from the bed. Autumn slipped away, padded barefoot to the bathroom, stepped into the shower, and scrubbed until her skin glowed bright pink. The rooms had grown chilly and she left the bathroom shivering, grabbed her robe, and crossed to the window.

The temperature had dropped and it was beginning to snow; the first snow of winter. She leaned against the windowframe and watched the flakes as they swirled and drifted; big white cotton balls running, chasing, and playing in the wind. She listened to the snow whistling around the eaves, her thoughts wandering.

The house had grown quiet and the ground was covered in white when she turned away from the window. Always before she had loved the snow, but now it brought a strange feeling of sadness. Perhaps it was because she would never look at the white scene through the eyes of a child again. She touched her stomach and felt the loss. Her child, Lonnie's child, would never see the snow, never run and play in its downy softness. It wasn't a conscious decision, just a realization that there wouldn't be more

babies, ever, because there wouldn't be love again. Like
her aunt, Autumn would go her way alone.

She turned and looked at the bed. Brian was sprawled
naked, his arms and legs outflung, the blankets kicked into
a ball. The chill in the room wasn't bothering him; he had
enough antifreeze rushing through his blood to keep him
warm on the coldest of nights.

Autumn didn't want to wake him and have him reach
for her again, so she decided against climbing into bed and
turned toward the chair, giving his trousers a hard kick that
sent them sailing. They hit against the far wall and his
wallet fell free. She stared mesmerized at all the green
bills that spilled over the floor. Then she inched across the
room and bent to her knees. She touched the money
gingerly, sat cross-legged on the floor, and played with it,
arranging it in neat stacks, counting it again and again. It
added up to three thousand and ten dollars, more money
than she had seen at one time in her entire life . . . more
than enough to get her out of Edisonville. And indirectly,
it would be a small stab against Douglas Osborne.

For a moment Preacher Anderson and his teachings
came to mind, but she pushed the guilt aside and gathered
up the money. She began to plan how to get out of town
without being caught. She'd have to tell Ella, borrow her
car, go home and pack a few things, and drive to Indiana.
From there she could take a plane. Except for Ella, no one
would know or care where Sue Anne Norton went.

She dressed quickly, gathered her coat, and was turning
to leave when she paused and looked down at Brian.
Lonnie's face had begun to show tiny crinkle lines around
the eyes, but Brian's twenty-two-year-old face was youth-
fully smooth. She recalled the argument she had overheard
between Brian and his father. In a sense, Brian was a
victim of Douglas Osborne too.

She pulled the blanket up to his chin and brushed the
tumbled hair from his forehead. "Good-bye, Brian Osborne. Sleep well."

II

San Francisco

9

In the midst of a noisy New Year's Eve party, Autumn stood alone, gazing out at the lights of the city. *How ironic that she should again be surrounded by hills.* If dropped in the center of San Francisco, Turtle Ridge would span maybe three blocks. At first she had felt choked, swallowed by the enormity of the city, but over the past year she had carved a niche and built her own private world among the thousands of cold, indifferent strangers.

A week after arriving in San Francisco, she had gone to work at Murphy's, one in a large chain of department stores. Autumn thought it was a good place to begin, because the chain's headquarters were in her building. The top floors at Murphy's were filled with executives—and executive positions. She could start at the ground floor of the store, and work her way upward. From the beginning she had tried to make herself invaluable. Whenever someone needed help, she always volunteered, even if it meant working overtime. She had had four raises and was spending more and more time on the fourth floor, assisting the assistant buyer.

She had taken on the job without title or increased pay, only more work. However, the buyer was being transferred and the assistant was moving up, which left a spot for her. She was to have an interview in two weeks. If the job came through, it would mean a large raise, and her first official step upward.

Autumn thought back to her "debut" at Murphy's and smiled. It hadn't been funny then, nothing had been funny at that time, but now she could look back and laugh. She had been at Murphy's less than a week when the sprinkler system in ladies' apparel went haywire, spewing out water and sending everybody into squeals. Maintenance was called and the water shut off, but not before everything and everyone was soaked, including herself. The VIPs from the top floor came running.

One man, with an air of power and authority stood out from the rest. He looked in his early forties, with an oval face and strong chin marked by a deep cleft. His green eyes narrowed as he looked around, assessing the damage. With an annoyed gesture he ran fingers through thick sandy-colored hair. He conferred with another executive for a moment, then turned abruptly to leave.

Autumn walked up the aisle toward him, her clothes soaked and clinging, her hair hanging in wet strands. She stepped to one side, but he paused directly in front of her. His glance moved over her in an up-and-down sweep. The frown left his face and he began to smile, a slow, easy kind of smile. She brushed aside a curl that clung to her cheek and gazed up at him. His eyes meet hers and his face sobered, as if he had looked past the brown in her eyes and caught a glimpse of the pain that lay inside.

Autumn felt nervous under his scrutiny, and spoke absently. "A mess, isn't it?"

"A mess," he echoed. He waved a hand, gesturing for her manager. "See that this young lady has dry clothes—if you can find any." He turned quickly, walking at a fast pace.

In time, Autumn learned that the man was Lloyd Murphy himself, owner of the chain. She had seen him a few times over the last year, passing in the halls, or he would walk through women's apparel with other men. He had never spoken to her, but he always glanced into her eyes with the same scrutinizing gaze. She sometimes wondered what he could possibly see there that could interest him so.

Autumn turned from the window, leaned against the frame, and gazed at the people scattered around the room. They wore silly hats, joked and laughed while waiting to greet the new year. Artie was smiling down at Julie Swanson, the latest in a long line of women. He had the same expression she had seen on Lonnie's face so many times. Autumn understood now the strong pull she had felt when leaving Edisonville, the strange force that had drawn her toward San Francisco. Artie was the closest thing to Lonnie she had left.

She had intended to stay with Artie for only a short time, but the days had slipped into weeks, and the weeks into months. When Autumn first arrived, Artie had looked so stricken that she had hardly mentioned Lonnie, nor did she tell him the truth about Lonnie's death. It wouldn't have served any purpose, only added more pain. She had called Ella and learned that Brian had left the next morning with a hangover. He hadn't mentioned Autumn or the three thousand dollars she had stolen. Perhaps he had felt foolish for allowing himself to be rolled by an eighteen-year-old girl in his father's own whorehouse.

The girls came and went, so Ella's boss only inquired casually as to what had happened to the redhead. Ella put him off with a shrug, laughing wildly when she saw the large black spot where Autumn's house had once sat. The officials were equally mystified as to what had happened to Mrs. Lonnie Norton. Again, Ella only shrugged.

Autumn hadn't planned the fire. It was a spur-of-the-moment thought. After stuffing what clothes she could into her one suitcase, she gathered a few personal things of Lonnie's—his wallet, wedding band, watch, and a pearl-handled pistol he had kept carefully oiled and polished. She paused for a moment and glanced about the house they had spent so much time and money turning into a home. It made her stomach hurt to know Douglas Osborne would profit by moving someone else into their house.

Autumn was at the front door when she stopped and stared at the open flame on the gas heater. It was so easy. She simply placed the corner of a towel in the flames and dropped the other end onto a throw rug, waited, and watched until the fire had spread. The wood floor was so old it ignited as if it were soaked in gasoline. She left town that night with one suitcase, her father's old guitar, and the house in Miners' Row a billowing flame behind her. One small strike against Douglas Osborne.

The party, the noise from the crowd, pulled Autumn back to San Francisco with a start. She jerked her head up, frowning, when a woman squealed in a high-pitched voice. Someone had shoved ice down her back and the woman was squirming and bouncing in the chair, her long brown hair fanning and falling onto her face. Autumn sighed and turned back to the window. The last thing she wanted tonight was to be in the midst of a New Year's Eve party, but living with Artie had turned out to be one long fiesta.

At first Autumn had thought of Artie as complex. Over the months, she had come to realize that he was the most uncomplicated person she had ever known. With Artie, there was no pretense. What you see is what you get. Artie had a good mind. He could do or be anything he wanted. But Artie didn't want, at least not in the typical sense. The only thing he needed was a life filled with spontaneity, new places, new faces.

To enable him to live an unplanned life, he rented a furnished apartment. Material possessions were a handicap, not an asset. If he suddenly decided to move on, what would he do with a table and chairs? Artie knew himself well; he didn't want to have to worry about anybody's happiness but his own. He cared enough about people to stay far away from entanglements. A wife and children were like the table and chairs. What would he do with them when he decided it was time to move on? He was capable of loving, but his need to feel free and unencumbered was stronger than any need he might feel to have a special woman of his own.

Once, Autumn had questioned him about his wanderlust. He'd laughed. "The world is a big place, with big doings. Why be content with one small corner, when you can have it all?" He shrugged. "It's just the way I am. Lonnie was quiet, settled, content with the norm. From the time I learned to walk, I was off looking for new horizons to explore."

"Gypsy, hobo," she had called him.

For now Artie was content, or relatively so. He worked as a mechanic, specializing in foreign sports cars. He made good money and insisted on paying most of the expenses. She bought the food, cooked, and kept the apartment. It was a comfortable arrangement for both, but lately she had felt the urge to move out. When the subject came up, there was always an argument with Artie. Having Autumn there was his way of protecting his brother's widow. Still, there was something in the air between them she didn't understand, and it gave her a feeling of uneasiness.

She turned now and her eyes sought his. He smiled and crossed to where she stood. "Why the bewildered look, little sister?"

She shrugged. "I don't know. Maybe it's the time of year."

He nodded, slipped his arm around her waist, and urged her away from the window. Artie treated most women with indifference, but he was always gentle and thoughtful with her. Insisting she sit beside Julie on the sofa, Artie shoved a drink in her hand and said, "Smile . . . make merry. A new and better year is only a couple of hours away."

She watched his broad shoulders as he turned and circled the room, mingling with his guests. Lifting the glass to her lips, she took a sip, glancing at Julie.

A friendship between the two women had sprung up, and Autumn wondered why. If Julie had a serious thought, Autumn had yet to hear it. Perhaps it was their differences that drew them together. Julie was twenty-four, but Autumn thought of her as a child who had to be humored at times. Julie had her own apartment, but she slept over at Artie's more nights than she slept at home.

Julie was mellowed out on grass and rolled her head toward Autumn. Her deep green eyes peeped out from beneath a halo of shimmering blond hair that hung loose to her shoulders. A petite, cute, and cuddly woman—the kind one would least expect to find working as a barmaid. She looked too soft and innocent to handle rowdy drunks, but according to Artie, she could gentle the roughest. Evidently Julie approached her job at the Doghouse Bar in the same trusting and carefree way that she approached life in general.

Julie smiled at Autumn. "Do you know what I was

doing this time last year? I was crying my eyes out over my ex-husband. What were you doing?''

Selling my body for two hundred dollars, she thought, but said, ''Making arrangements to move here.''

Julie held the joint out to Autumn, but quickly withdrew her hand. ''I forgot. You never touch the stuff. It destroys motivation.'' Julie leaned until her nose was almost touching Autumn's. ''Why do you want to be motivated?''

Autumn laughed good-naturedly. She had tried dope a few times and hated it. All it did for her was to put her to sleep. ''I came to the big city in search of fame and fortune. I won't find it if I'm laid back on grass half the time.''

''Why do you want a fortune?''

''It's been my lifelong dream to be rich.''

''That's sick.''

Autumn smiled at her again and reached to the coffee table for a cigarette. She toyed with it for a moment before lighting it, then let the smoke roll around in her mouth. It tasted terrible. Julie, who was watching her, asked, ''When did you start smoking?''

''Just now.''

''You don't do it right. You're supposed to inhale.''

''Who cares? You do it your way, and I'll do it mine.''

''Are you kidding? I wouldn't touch that stuff. It rots your lungs.'' Julie looked ready to fall asleep as she slid farther down on the sofa, turning to gaze at Autumn. ''Do you think Artie cares for me?''

''I don't know, Julie. Do you care for him?''

''I care for every man I sleep with.''

''Do you sleep with every man you care for?''

''Yeah, except black men. Do you suppose I'm a racist?''

''I don't know. Have you ever slept with a Chinese?''

She shrugged. ''No Chinese ever asked me.'' Julie passed the joint to the woman next to her and squinted at Autumn through lidded eyes. ''What about you? How many men have you slept with?''

''Two.''

Julie backed away and looked at her in horror. ''Two? That's awful. Christ, don't you get horny?''

''No,'' Autumn said flatly. ''I don't have the time.''

Which was true. In addition to working at Murphy's, she was attending school two nights a week, squeezing in economics and marketing on Tuesday nights, and management and motivation classes on Thursday nights. The overtime she worked, school, studying, and the apartment kept her so busy she was too tired to notice that the bed was empty when she climbed exhausted between the sheets.

After another puff on the cigarette, she grimaced and dabbed it out in the ashtray. Julie was a clown, but Autumn suspected there was something deeper simmering below the surface and felt protective of her. "I wouldn't get too hung up on Artie," Autumn said. "He's different. He isn't looking for a wife and the homey scene."

"Are you trying to tell me something?"

"Only that Artie isn't the kind to settle down and raise a batch of kids. He likes fun and excitement."

"No man is ready to settle down until the right woman comes along."

Autumn groaned inwardly at Julie's naïveté. She had moved to San Francisco from New Mexico after her divorce, and thought all men were just like the cowboy next door: wanting nothing more than a fast horse, a good pickup truck, and a woman to cook and warm his bed. Autumn knew warning her was useless; Julie heard only what she wanted to hear.

She finished her drink and left the sofa to Julie. Through Artie she had been both exposed to and protected from the various elements of West Coast living. He had a wide range of friends, but Autumn had made a point of remaining on the outer edge of the circle. She joked now, mingled and played hostess, kept the ashtrays empty, the glasses filled, the room from becoming a total disaster, but she also kept everybody at arm's length.

Julie had fallen asleep, and Artie was smiling down at a brunette with heavily rouged cheeks. There had been a gentleness in Lonnie that was lacking in his twin brother. Artie walked and moved quickly, with a reckless grace. Even now, when he was surrounded by people, there was a hint of boredom in his manner, which seemed to appeal to women. The woman was now gazing at him with an "ask-me-and-I'll-say-yes" expression.

Autumn was heading for the kitchen for more ice when she was suddenly jerked off her feet and onto a man's lap. Caught by surprise, she stared dumbstruck at a man she thought was called Bill. He had long stringy hair that hung in his face, a shaggy beard, and he smelled of sweat. She didn't want to make a scene, so she said quietly, "Be nice and let me go."

"Ya'll be good," he said in a voice mimicking her accent. He gripped her waist and ran his hand under her dress. "I've heard you little hillbillies are really hot stuff." He wiggled his fingers against the mound between her legs. "Mmm-hmmm."

"Bastard," she shouted, and grabbed at his hand.

He laughed and was bending his head over hers when Artie's hand came down hard against his shoulder. "I wouldn't do that, unless you want your face bent until it's looking at your ass." He took Autumn's hand and pulled her from Bill's lap and into his arms. The expression on Artie's face sent Bill out of the chair, then out of the apartment.

"Are you all right?" Artie asked.

"I'm fine, but I don't care much for your friend."

"He isn't my friend. I thought he was yours."

"I heard him called Bill, but I don't know him." Their eyes met and they laughed together at their party crasher.

Artie shrugged. "At least he added a little excitement."

"Are you bored?"

"A little."

Autumn knew something that would excite him—going after Osborne—but she couldn't tell him until the time was right. "I think I'll go to my room and call Aunt Molly and wish her a happy new year."

Artie nodded. "Wish her one for me."

She left him and walked down the hall toward her bedroom. Breaking away from Edisonville had been easy, but leaving Molly was much harder than she had thought. She missed Molly and the closeness they had shared, a closeness few mothers and daughters ever had. Autumn and Artie had gone to Turtle Ridge for Christmas. Ella came for Christmas Day, and there was turkey with cornbread dressing and all the trimmings, Molly had strung the tree with colored popcorn the way she had when Autumn was a child. Autumn had tried to enjoy it all, but the memories of Lonnie were still too strong.

Autumn knew Molly would be sitting in front of the television watching the crowd in Times Square bring in the new year. She answered the phone on the second ring and Autumn shouted into the receiver, "Happy New Year, Aunt Molly."

"Well, I'll be," Molly said happily. "I didn't expect to hear from you so soon. I was sitting and knitting and thinking about you being way out there on the coast. I wish you'd come home. Them folks out there ain't our kind."

Autumn thought of Bill and his sweaty body and silently agreed. It would be a few years before Turtle Ridge could accept some of the things going on in their living room, if ever. "I can't, Aunt Molly. I just learned I might move up to assistant buyer. That's a lot more than I could expect back home."

"Yeah, there ain't much here. I ran into Bobby Joe the other day. He's in a hurry to get through college so he can be rid of Turtle Ridge too. He asked about you. I think he's still sweet on you."

Autumn smiled and listened as Molly rambled on. It was out of character and she knew it was her aunt's way of hanging onto the sound of Autumn's voice. Molly was lonely and it showed in the way she spoke, low and with longing to have her little girl home again.

"Well," Molly said, "I know this is long distance and it's costing you money. I'll hang up now. You be careful and write, you hear."

"I will, Aunt Molly, and you be careful too." Autumn worried about Molly. If her aunt should fall and hurt herself, she could lie there for days before anybody found her. Autumn didn't like her being alone in the country, but there wasn't anything she could do about it at the moment. Maybe later Molly could come and stay in San Francisco. If Autumn could ever get her to leave Turtle Ridge.

She broke the connection and put through a call to Ella. Ella's voice boomed so loudly that Autumn had to hold the receiver away from her ear. "Have I got news for you!" Ella shouted. "You're going to love this."

"So tell me."

"The shit really hit the fan at Osborne House. Brian and his father had a fight to end all fights. The old man laid down the law, told Brian either he conformed or he was out, and I mean out!"

"Out?" Autumn asked. "Like how?"

"Out of the family, cut off—no dough."

"What did Brian do?"

"He told his father to stick it and left the house."

"How do you know all this?"

"Their gardener. He loves my hamburgers. He got it from Daisy, their housekeeper. She makes a point of knowing everything that goes on in that house. And she loves to gossip. She told the gardener and he told me and everybody else that wanted to listen. It's all over town."

"How is Douglas taking it?"

"From what has been passed on to me, he's mad as hell and kicking everything in his path. Everybody is waiting to see who will give in first."

"Is Brian still in town?"

"No. He packed up and went back to college."

Autumn smiled with pleasure. It had to be a hard blow for Douglas to lose his only son and heir.

Ten minutes later, Autumn hung up the phone on a note of laughter. Going to the chest of drawers, she dug under a stack of sweaters, pulled out a scrapbook, and opened it to a special page.

She had bought the scrapbook shortly after coming to San Francisco, and through Ella she was slowly filling the book with clippings cut from the Edisonville *Times*. They were small, unimportant news items, but they enabled her to learn more about the Osborne family. The most impressive article had a picture of Douglas with a big contented smile spread across his face. According to the article, the investigators of the explosion had concluded that the accident had happened when miners hit a pocket of methane gas, and absolved Douglas Osborne of any responsibility.

In the clipping Osborne announced proudly that the Black Jewel had been in the family for generations and was part of the family's heritage. The mine would remain as it was on the day of the explosion—as a monument to the family and to the men who had died there.

She had other clippings, but that one was her favorite, and over the months she had reread it until it was dog-eared. Thinking about Brian, she smiled down at the face in the clipping. "Hello, Douglas Osborne. How does it feel to lose someone you love?" It made her feel good inside to know that Douglas was now suffering too. Slapping the book closed, she hid it beneath her sweaters and returned to the living room.

Artie glanced at her and smiled as she came toward him. "I thought you had gone to bed."

She laughed and shook her head. "I feel too good to go to bed. It's a new year, so let's celebrate."

Suddenly the room exploded with noisemakers and shouts of laughter as the hour reached twelve. Artie grinned and pulled Autumn into his arms. "Happy New Year, little sister." He bent and pecked her on the mouth.

Autumn pulled away and smiled up at him, but the uneasiness was back. "Happy New Year, yourself, big brother."

10

❧

A steady, irritating clank-clank-clank roused Autumn from a drugged sleep. She sat upright in bed with a roaring head and a mouth that felt stuffed with dry cornbread. With a grimace she rolled her tongue around her mouth, the clanking whirling and banging against the inside of her head. The sound seemed to be coming from the direction of the kitchen, and she climbed gingerly from the bed, holding her head with both hands. Whatever it was, she was going to find it, and then she was going to kill it.

She stumbled into her robe and went down the hall and through the shambles of the living room to the kitchen. Artie stood in his robe with a cup of coffee. Beside him was a carelessly loaded dishwasher that was rattling and going clank-clank-clank. Autumn bolted across the room and slammed her hand against the button, then stood and listened to the beautiful silence. "I hurt." She groaned, and dropped down at the table.

Artie grinned and poured her a cup of coffee. Digging a bottle of aspirin from a cabinet, he set them in front of her, along with a glass of water. "What's the matter, little sister, got a hangover?"

"Have I ever. There's a hundred little evil men with spurs on their heels and hammers in their hands, kicking and beating the shit out of my brain."

"I can't remember you ever drinking so much before."

"I was celebrating."

"Celebrating what?"

She shook her head, took a sip of coffee, and frowned. "I grew up on moonshine strong enough to knock a two-hundred-pound man on his butt. Old Tucker had a still, and I used to sip at the stuff. It got me once when I was fifteen, and that taught me when to stop. I don't know what happened last night." She rubbed her temples, stroking in small circles. "What about you? Do you have a hangover too?"

"No. I had to stay straight to look after you."

"Why? What did I do? The night's a little foggy."

"For one thing, you gave me a lecture on the way I treat women, especially Julie. According to you, she's tender and I'll break her heart."

"I didn't."

"You did. Then you sat in the middle of the floor with a couple of guys and chugalugged whiskey. You boasted you could outdrink any man in the room."

"Did I?"

"You tried. Afterward, you hopped on the coffee table and danced an Irish jig."

"Jesus!"

"Yep. Then you passed out and I put you to bed."

"About time." She fingered the rim of the coffee cup. "I was naked when I woke. Who did that?"

"I did. I've seen naked women before." He went to the counter and poured another cup of coffee. When he looked back at her, his face was still. "You woke while I was undressing you and got things mixed up. You had me confused with Lonnie." He paused and took a quick sip of coffee. "You owe me a medal, little sister. I wanted to stay. God, how I wanted to stay." Then he walked out of the kitchen, saying over his shoulder, "I left your room wishing to hell I had a face of my own."

Suddenly she understood the strange uneasiness she had begun to feel, and wondered why it had taken her so long to realize what had happened over the months. There were personality differences, but Artie was still the living image of Lonnie. Slowly she was drawing closer to him in her need for Lonnie. Only last night she had flown naturally into the safety of his arms over the unpleasant incident with Bill.

A year ago she would have given Bill a sharp jab in the ribs with her elbow and wrenched herself free of him. Over the months, in her vulnerability, she had grown dependent on Artie. In the back of her mind she had known Artie was there and would protect her. Artie was a virile man with strong desires. Someday in her loneliness she would reach out for him. Caught off guard, he wouldn't walk away. She'd be trapped in a hopeless situation with no way out, clinging tightly to one man because he was the image of another.

It could be disastrous for her, and so unfair to Artie. The only solution was to put distance between them. It would be a small but safe distance. She wouldn't go far away from Artie, just far enough to keep perspective. He could live his life as he wanted, but as long as he was near, she'd always have a small part of Lonnie. Through the one man, the other lived on.

The coffee had grown cold and she shoved away from the table. A turkey sat on the counter waiting to be stuffed, but Autumn couldn't force herself to face the naked old bird. She turned toward the living room, where Artie sat with Julie. His eyes met hers in a steady gaze; then the moment passed and he looked at her with a quick grin. "The little men back again?"

She rubbed her temples. "Yes, and I think they brought their sisters and brothers and a carload of cousins." She glanced at Julie, who looked fresh as a daisy in a pale yellow robe. Her skin glowed and her cheeks were flushed. Autumn had caught a glimpse of herself in the living-room mirror. Her hair hung to her waist in a tangled mass. Her skin wasn't dewy, but clammy, and her cheeks weren't pink, but pale. "I hate you, Julie."

Julie's eyes widened and she spoke in a small voice. "What did I do?"

"You're too beautiful!" Autumn laughed, then pleaded, "It's getting late. Will you stuff the turkey and shove it in the oven for me? I'll take care of the rest later."

"Stuff the turkey? I don't know how to stuff a turkey."

Autumn wasn't in the mood to play mother and frowned

in annoyance. "For Pete's sake. Just shove the stuffing up its butt and stick it in the oven."

"I don't know how to make stuffing."

Autumn glanced at Artie, who was grinning at them, then at Julie. "Learn fast. Otherwise you can eat a bologna sandwich for dinner. This chief cook and bottle washer is taking her miserable head back to bed." She walked down the hall to her room and burrowed under the blankets on her bed. A tightness caught in her throat, but she knew it wasn't the whiskey. It was the tears. They were always there, tiny bubbles of tears trapped in her throat. She couldn't cough them up, and she couldn't choke them down. They lay waiting for the right time to come to the surface. When that time came, Autumn knew it would be like a dam bursting.

Several days had passed before Autumn could bring herself to talk to Artie about moving out. She didn't have a definite plan, only that she had to put distance between the two of them. He was leafing through a copy of *Mechanix Illustrated* when she broached the subject. "Don't be ridiculous," he said. "For one thing, you can't afford to move out."

Autumn turned away from him. She could afford to move into a place of her own, but she couldn't tell him why, and cursed the money she had stolen from Brian. The mere mention of the three thousand dollars would be like opening Pandora's box. Everyone knew she and Lonnie didn't have any money; she would have to explain where it had come from. The night with Brian was a secret she shared only with Ella.

She had put the money that remained after she got settled in San Francisco in the bank, but when she heard some of the people at work discussing a new stock that was being offered to the public, she invested it, almost hoping to lose the money. She bought in at $10.25 a share. The stock shot up to $21.75 and she sold. After the rush of buying, the stock began to drop. When it hit $12 dollars a share, she bought back in. It had since risen to $16 and was steadily climbing. It was as if the money was blessed with the Midas touch because it had once belonged to the Osbornes.

She rose from the chair and stood in front of Artie. "If I get the promotion, it will mean a good raise. I can afford a small place of my own."

"It isn't just the money, Autumn. A nineteen-year-old girl from the sticks shouldn't be living alone in this city. You're not in Turtle Ridge now, and the men here aren't wet-behind-the-ears boys."

"I can take care of myself."

He raised an amused eyebrow. "Like you did the other night with our party crasher?"

"That's another reason I have to move out. I'm leaning on you too much. I have to learn how to handle myself with men like Bill. I won't, if you're always around to fight my battles for me. Besides, I'll be twenty in April, and Molly always said I was born thirty years old."

Artie took her hand and pulled her down on the sofa beside him. "Does this sudden desire to move have anything to do with what I said the other morning?"

She nodded, but remained silent.

"I thought so," he said. "Look, honey. No man could undress and put you to bed without wanting to make love to you, sister-in-law or not. That doesn't mean I'd ever take advantage of you." He put a finger under her chin, tipped her face, and looked at her studiously. "Your head seems to be on a different plane than most women's. You breeze in and around men and seem totally unaware of the impact you have on them." His hand fell from her chin and he grinned impishly. "You bring out the man in men. That damned untouchable air you have is a challenge to them. Living here with me, you've been more or less protected. I'm just trying to keep you in one place until you're old enough to see this, and have learned to handle it."

"There are things I see that you don't. What if I should reach out for you again, and catch you in a weak moment? A time when you couldn't walk away like you did the night you were putting me to bed?"

"Would that be so terrible, Autumn?"

"Yes. It would be terrible for me, and for you. When I

look at you, I see Lonnie. I'd never know if it were really you I wanted, or Lonnie. Worse, you'd never know either. Would you want that?"

"Hell, no. My ego couldn't handle it."

She smiled and shrugged. "Me girl, you boy. Sooner or later we'll end up in the same bed if I stay here. I don't think that would be good for either of us, do you?"

"No," he agreed, and shook his head. "Julie has an extra room. You can move in with her."

"Julie!" Autumn sprang to her feet. "I can't live with Julie. She'd drive me crazy."

"Coming from me, this will sound phony as hell. I'm irresponsible and I know it, but you have to be sensible and think of the money. I know what you make at Murphy's. Even if you do get the job, it would still take everything you make to live alone. Not to mention the fact that you could use the protection of another woman living with you. Wacky as she is, Julie is a great gal, and she could use your share of the rent. She's been having trouble paying her bills since her roommate moved out."

Sighing, Autumn nodded. It was the simplest solution for the moment. "You call Julie and tell her she has a new roommate. I'll start packing."

Autumn fingered the fringe on a jacket, then stepped back to admire her display of leather goods. A small department featuring the latest fads had been her idea, so she thought of this private corner of the store as her own. Murphy's was a family business, and its merchandise was middle-class and dull. They had never made it a point to carry the most current, occasionally outlandish styles.

Autumn had fought for the idea for several months, stressing the point that young people were the nation's biggest buyers. She pointed out too that the teenagers of today had much more money to spend than in the past, and that more and more attention was devoted to style—their own, maybe, but style nonetheless, or at least what the other kids were wearing. If Murphy's was to capture their attention, it would have to carry what they wanted to wear, not what Murphy's expected them to wear.

A small corner had finally been partitioned off, posters

put up, and the top rock music played, maybe not as loud as the teenagers would have liked, but it was a place where they felt comfortable. It was advertised as the Mod Shop. Her idea had proved to be very profitable. And to Autumn, good ideas were the key to success. In time, she was sure, they would take her from the ground floor to the top.

She left the small department and crossed to lingerie, where Maggie stood arranging gowns on a table, part of a new line the store was now offering. Maggie was in her thirties. She had been at the store for five years and knew all the ins and outs. They never saw one another outside the store, but they sometimes had lunch in the coffee shop together.

Autumn paused beside her to help arrange the gowns. Maggie smiled. "How about lunch today?"

"I can't," Autumn said. "I'm going upstairs shortly to help Ruth."

"Isn't she the buyer that's being transferred?"

"No. That's Colette. Ruth will be taking over her job."

"Which leaves an opening for you, right?"

"I hope so."

Maggie had been lounging against the table. She nudged Autumn and quickly turned back to the work at hand. "Look busy. Here come the VIP's." She leaned closer and whispered, "I wonder what my husband would say if he knew I broke out in a hot sweat every time that man walks past."

"What man?"

"Lloyd Murphy. A sexy beast, don't you think?"

Autumn shrugged. "I suppose." She hadn't thought of Lloyd Murphy as anything more than the owner of the chain, a man she saw maybe once a month in passing, a man who gazed at her with scrutinizing eyes. She pulled a bundle of gowns from a box, musing how the VIP's walked through and completely ignored the staff. They paused, they talked, they gestured, looking through the people as if they didn't exist. She glanced at Lloyd Murphy as the three men walked down the aisle toward her table.

Lloyd Murphy's eyes weren't scrutinizing now; instead, they smiled into her own. "Hello, Sue Anne."

"Hello, Mr. Murphy."

Maggie waited until the men were out of earshot, watching their backs as they walked down the aisle. "Now, how do you like that. I've been here five years and he doesn't know my name. You've been here one year, and already he's calling you Sue Anne."

"The Mod Shop," she said. "The new department had to be cleared through him. My name was probably mentioned." She turned back to the gowns, smiling. Lloyd Murphy knowing her name could mean only one thing. Finally her name was being known in high places.

Living with Julie wasn't as bad as Autumn had feared. Julie was lighthearted and kept Autumn laughing at her crazy antics. Actually, they had little time to get into each other's hair. Julie worked most nights, and Autumn worked days and attended business college two nights a week. When they did meet, it was usually on the run.

The apartment was small and pleasant and in a good neighborhood with a bus stop a block away. Across the hall from them was an elderly man named Landers who walked his dog every morning and stopped to chat with Autumn while she waited for a bus. In some strange way, he made her feel in touch with Molly. She found herself watching for him and his little dog, named Puddles.

The first week, she had stayed so busy with work, school, and moving into the apartment that she'd hardly had time to think of her upcoming interview. But Monday morning she woke with a knot in her stomach and a light shivering of nerves. She took special care in dressing and chose a black suit and rust-colored blouse that enhanced her hair. After a light touch of makeup, she brushed her hair until it snapped and crackled. She tried to pull strands back from her face, but wayward curls fell forward and lay against her cheeks. Annoyed, she slapped at the curls, grabbed her shoulder purse, and headed toward the kitchen and the enticing smell of bacon and eggs.

Julie usually slept late, but it was her day off and she sat at the table with pen and paper. She looked up and scowled when Autumn entered the room. "My paycheck never seems to go as far as it should. There's a blouse at Murphy's I'd like to have. Oh, well. Next week."

"I'll loan you the money. Better still, come to the store and show me which one and I'll buy it for you. We'll take advantage of my discount."

Julie nodded and pointed at the table. "Surprise. I cooked breakfast this morning."

Autumn took a chair across from Julie and picked at the eggs, which were scrambled into hard balls. "Didn't your mother ever teach you to cook?"

"Sure, that's the way she made them." Julie grinned and shrugged. "Cooking isn't my thing. I think I was meant to be some rich man's doodad."

"I thought you weren't interested in money."

"I'm not. I just want to be taken care of."

"You had a husband. What happened to him?"

"He was an asshole, but then, I always pick assholes." She leaned her elbows on the table and gazed at Autumn pensively. "I've been thinking."

"Since when do you think?"

"Shut up and listen. You're wanting fame and fortune. I've thought of a way you can pick up a few bucks if you're game."

Autumn scraped burned edges from the toast and looked at her with skepticism. "How?"

"You're great with the guitar, sexy-looking, and your voice isn't bad. You could play and sing at the Doghouse. Everett can't afford to pay you, but you'd make tips. I don't know what the problem is. We do a fairly good business, but Everett's always in trouble. I feel sorry for him. He's kind of sickly and he isn't really a businessman."

"Why does he own a tavern?"

"It belonged to his parents." She paused and snickered. "I think the place has been in the family since the gold-rush days."

"You said he was sickly. What's wrong with him?"

"Some kind of heart thing." Julie gazed across at her. "Well, what do you think?"

"I'm underage, remember? Besides, I have school twice a week, and I'm not giving that up for anything or anyone."

"Your age doesn't matter. We can't serve you drinks,

but you can get a permit from the state and perform there on your free nights.''

Autumn put aside the toast she had been nibbling on and rose from the table. ''I'll think about it. I have to go now. I certainly don't want to be late today.'' She stood before Julie and smoothed the skirt over her hips. ''How do I look?''

''Great. For a hick, you've got good taste. What's the big occasion?''

''I go in for my interview today. God—I'm nervous.''

''Don't be. You'll do great. I'm so sure, I'm going to plan a celebration. I have the night off. I'll call Artie and some of the gang and we'll have a get-together. I'll even cook dinner.''

''Forget the dinner. If I don't get the job, I won't feel like eating. If I do, we'll go out.'' She turned, but paused in the doorway. ''I have to get this job, Julie. I just have to.''

''Why? You're doing all right.''

''I don't want to do just all right. I want to climb. I want to climb higher and higher until there is nothing between me and the moon.''

Julie looked at her with a perplexed frown. ''What is it with you, Autumn? What drives you?''

''Memories.'' She smiled faintly. ''Wish me luck.''

''For what it's worth—you've got it.''

11

The offices in the Murphy Building took up several floors, all filled with executives who handled small matters such as promotions of assistant buyers. To Autumn's knowledge the chairman of the board and major stockholder didn't interview anyone at her level. Why, then, was she sitting across the desk from Lloyd Murphy?

She watched him as he leafed through her folder. He was dressed in an expensive but sober gray suit that fit his broad shoulders so well it had to have been tailored only for him. He couldn't have picked it off a rack at Murphy's. His oval face was thoughtful, and now and then he absently fingered the deep cleft in his chin. His blond-flecked sandy-colored hair was combed neatly.

To Autumn, the office looked more like a living room in somebody's home than a place of business. A leather sofa curved in front of a fireplace where orange-and-yellow flames lapped around charred logs. The crackle of the fire changed the atmosphere in the room from formal to cozy. Heavy oak tables rested on deep oriental rugs. A bar with sparkling crystal sat in a far corner. A large oak desk almost surrounded Murphy; his chair was cavernous. Directly behind him, floor-to-ceiling windows, with sheer drapes drawn against the glare, provided an impressively majestic frame. The room held the faint sweet odor of pipe tobacco.

Autumn wiggled her toes and wished she could kick off

her shoes. It was easier to think clearly when her feet were bare. She shifted uncomfortably. "There must be some mistake, Mr. Murphy. I don't think I should be here."

He smiled and flipped the folder closed. "There's no mistake." From the desk he picked up a gold cigarette box and held it out to her. She hesitated at first, but then thought it might help her to relax, so she accepted a cigarette and leaned forward to use the flame from his proffered lighter.

Settling back in his chair to observe her, Murphy asked, "You don't inhale?"

"No. I only smoke so my fingers will have something to do."

He smiled again, a slow, easy smile. "Are you nervous?"

"Some."

"Are you afraid of me?"

"No, just nervous."

He motioned toward the bar. "Would you like a drink?"

"No, I'm not that nervous."

Another faint smile; then: "Why did you come to work at Murphy's?"

"Murphy. It's a good Irish name. I was a McAvan before I married. Besides, you were running an ad for a salesperson."

He picked up a pencil and toyed with it idly. "You're a widow?"

"Yes. My husband's been dead a year now."

"I'm sorry. Were you in love with him?"

She blinked at his sudden and unexpected question. "Well . . . yes. *Very much.*"

He nodded. "You've had four raises in the time you've been here. That's unusual."

"I work hard. I feel I earned them."

He tossed the pencil onto the desk and was quiet while she put her cigarette out in an ashtray. "I understand you're taking business administration at a night college. Are you interested in becoming a manager?"

She smiled a little and motioned toward the folder. "Does that folder tell you what I have for breakfast, too?"

"You have one boiled egg, half a grapefruit, one piece

of wheat toast with butter and honey, alternated with a bowl of cream of wheat.''

Autumn was confused and rubbed nervous, sweaty hands against her skirt. ''Are you always so thorough?''

''Only in special cases.''

''Am I a special case?''

''Definitely. Now for my question. Are you interested in becoming a manager?''

''Yes. I want to know everything about the inner workings of big business. I want to know how to build one up, or how to tear one down.''

He smiled faintly. ''Where would you like to go with this company?''

''I think I could be content with your job.''

He leaned back in his chair with a hearty laugh. ''So . . . you want to run a department-store chain, do you? Are you going to be a future competitor? Should I be frightened?''

She felt young, foolish, and shifted in her chair. ''You're laughing at me.''

''No. I'd never do that. I like ambitious women. I don't feel frightened of them, or threatened by them. I find them interesting and very exciting. Before my wife died, God rest her soul, she liked to putter in the kitchen. She was great with Irish stew and stuffed a mean turkey, but she was boring, damned boring.''

Autumn tried to hold it back, but burst into laughter at his unexpected candor. ''I'm sorry,'' she said quickly. ''I didn't mean to laugh.''

''That's fine. You have a good honest laugh, and you don't giggle. I like it. I want to hear more of it.'' He pushed back from the desk and glanced at his watch. ''We'll go into detail about your job over dinner tonight in my apartment. I'll send a car for you.''

A warning bell went off inside Autumn's head and she tensed. Watch your temper, she warned herself, watch your rotten temper. ''Does dinner with you have anything to do with my getting the job?''

His eyes met hers evenly and when he spoke his voice was unemotional. ''Everything. If you take the job, an apartment will go with it. A very nice apartment, and a very nice automobile. And a damned nice expense account. I'll coach you and build you into the best business-woman you can possibly be. It will take time, and it will mean hard work for both of us."

"Is this something you do often?"

"Only when I see a woman that interests me, and shows potential. It isn't just sex, although good sex is a great part of it. I like to take beautiful women and mold them into something they wouldn't have been otherwise. I would, of course, give you time to get to know me. When I was younger, I was like a rank bull, but time has mellowed me. I've watched you for a year, but I've waited. Even when you smiled, you looked so sad. I wanted to give your heart time to heal." He tapped his finger against the folder. "You're young and inexperienced. I'll wait until you're ready."

"Aren't you putting the cart before the horse? Aren't you supposed to wine and dine me first, and then make the offer?"

"Normally. But then, most women aren't so blunt. They don't ask what my intentions are when I invite them to a simple dinner. You asked me a question, and I gave you an honest answer."

Autumn fingered the leather on the arm of the chair and felt the very life draining from her. She thought of Brian and the night she had sold her body for two hundred dollars. At the time she had thought it was the only way. But now she wasn't so sure. After the night with Brian, she had felt dirty and ashamed.

The present surroundings were different and luxurious, but it amounted to the same thing. It would be at a higher price, but she'd still be selling her body. "I have to feel free and unencumbered, Mr. Murphy. I don't think I would like to be any man's mistress."

He fingered the cleft on his chin and looked amused. "I'm not entirely sure, but I think I've just been rejected."

She nodded.

"That's too bad. I can't make you a buyer, Sue Anne. You're not ready, and without my help you'd fall on your face." He uncurled his robust frame from the chair and held out his hand. "It will take you longer, but I think you'll get what you want eventually."

His hand was warm against hers, his grip firm. "Do I still have a job?"

"Oh yes. I've yet to fire a woman for rejecting me." He gave her hand a light squeeze. "I like and admire you, Sue Anne. If you ever need anything or have a problem, you can come to me."

"Autumn," she said. "Some call me Autumn."

"Yes. I know."

"Naturally." She rose from the chair and gazed across at him. He was leaning against the front of his desk, his arms folded over a burly chest. His face was still, his gaze intent. All pretense was gone, and his eyes showed open desire. Suddenly she was acutely aware of being a woman. She felt alive with it, heady, and realized the control she could have over the big powerful Irishman. If she walked across the room to him, countless doors would open for her—until he found a new interest.

Sex, she decided was a game men and women played. Me Tarzan, you Jane. Come swing on my vine with me. After I bed you down in my hut, I'll bring you the best bananas in the jungle. And Jane giggles and wiggles and squeals with delight. Until there aren't any more bananas, and on and on.

Autumn wasn't intimidated by Lloyd Murphy now, or his position. At the moment he was at his weakest and she had the upper hand. "Good-bye," she said. "Even though I didn't get the job, it has been an enlightening experience. Thank you."

He uncurled his arms and straightened to full height. "With your hair you should never wear anything but black."

"Ahhhh, the Irish. They're all so full of blarney."

The mask quickly slipped over his face and he was again the cool businessman trying to swing a deal. "Think about it, Autumn. All the money you can possibly need. Anything you want. And I promise, the sex will be great."

"I have no doubt of that, Mr. Murphy. No doubt at all. Your offer is very generous, but I really don't care for bananas. They're just too fattening." She turned, leaving him gazing after her with a perplexed, open-mouthed expression.

Once free of his suite of offices, she raced to the elevator, paced as it lowered her to the first floor, bolted from the small cage, and weaved her way through the shoppers to women's apparel. When Maggie looked at her questioningly, Autumn shook her head and tore into her work with a frenzy. She said a silent thanks that Maggie didn't press her for details. What could she say? *The job is mine if I want to fuck Lloyd Murphy.*

She worked through the afternoon with growing bitterness and a feeling of desperation. Bitterness at Lloyd Murphy because he had the power to pull strings at will, and desperation because she saw the last year as wasted. She hadn't moved ahead; she was still just a clerk. Four raises ahead of when she started, but still just a clerk waiting for a pat on the head and her next piddling raise.

She was on the verge of quitting. She was angry enough to quit, but where would she go? She had a year invested at Murphy's. To leave would mean starting at the bottom again. She jerked a skirt from a rack, wanting to tear it to shreds because it belonged to Lloyd Murphy. "It isn't fair!"

"What isn't fair?"

Autumn had thought herself alone, and whirled, startled. She almost fell against Julie. "God, you scared me. What are you doing here, anyhow?"

"I came to pick out the blouse, remember?"

"Blouse, blouse, blouse." Autumn mouthed the word and tried to sort her thoughts. Her breakfast conversation with Julie seemed to have taken place weeks ago. She glanced at the pink blouse Julie was holding. "Is this the one?"

"Yeah, except it's the wrong color. Do you have it in blue?"

Autumn grabbed the blouse from Julie and tossed it on the counter. "I need to get out of here. Let's go upstairs to the coffee shop. I have a story to tell you. Farfetched, but true."

*   *   *

"He what?"

Autumn nodded and circled the rim of her cup with a finger. "Yes. I can have the job, if I want to become his live-in protégé. I have to admit it's tempting. I don't know if I have the patience to do it the hard way. After a year, I'm nowhere. Through him, I'd jump from the first floor to the fourth. It would be a start. A damned good start. That's all I need, Julie. Give me a toehold, and I'll climb. I know I will. I have to."

Julie exhaled deeply. "Wellll, is he the kind of man you could cuddle up to without puking?"

Autumn smiled for the first time since the interview. "I love you, Julie. You have a way of making the sun shine even when it's raining."

Julie shrugged. "That's something you have to think about. Nothing is worth climbing into bed with someone who's repulsive."

"There's nothing repulsive about him. He isn't Artie's kind of handsome. Few men are, but he has a kind of vitality that could be exciting."

"What do you know about him?"

"Only the few things I've heard. He's always been a leader, even at college. At Harvard, he was captain of everything. He married young. His wife died three years ago in a car accident. He has a daughter that jets around in his plane. She's mentioned in the gossip columns about once a month or so."

"What kind of man is he? A swinger?"

Autumn laughed quietly. "I don't know. He keeps his personal life private. He's a tough businessman, from what I've heard. After his father died, he took over and built Murphy's into what it is today." She fell silent and looked down at her cup. "He could do a lot for me, give me the break I need."

"It sounds as if you're trying to talk yourself into it."

"I don't know. At first, I didn't want any part of it. Now I'm not so sure. I'll have to think about it. The only other offer I've had is to sing at the Doghouse."

"Don't knock it. There are a lot of restless men who come to the place. All you'd have to do is show a little leg and sing pretty. I think you'd do great."

Autumn shook her head. "My voice is fine, but my projection is weak."

"Use a mike."

"I'm not an entertainer, Julie."

"It doesn't matter. All you have to do is show leg, wiggle your behind, jiggle your boobs, and the men will come running."

"Bananas," Autumn whispered. "Play the game and you'll get your banana." She glanced at her watch, and then quickly rose. "I have to go. Do you want the blouse? We don't have it in blue."

"Nah." Julie followed and they left the coffee shop, weaving through the crowd. On the escalator Julie looked down at Autumn. "I don't suppose you want that celebration tonight?"

"Celebrate what?"

"I'll think of something." Julie shrugged and grinned. "What are you going to do about Murphy?"

"Who knows? See you later." Autumn left Julie and returned to her area. She worked through the afternoon, but in a better frame of mind. One thing was certain. Lloyd Murphy wouldn't be getting any extra work out of her, unless it showed up on her paycheck in terms of dollars.

She was gathering her coat to leave for the day when an unfamiliar woman appeared, handed her an envelope, and hurried away. Confused, Autumn opened the envelope and pulled out a note written in a scrawling hand.

Your stock has done well until now. I suggest you sell it, and buy Murphy's. I think you will have a nice surprise in a few months. Bananas?

Normally Autumn didn't dream, but that night she woke trembling, bathed in sweat from a crazy, disjointed, but very real nightmare. She was standing on an auctioneer's block, naked and in chains while a man with a gavel auctioned her to the highest bidder. Brian Osborne and Lloyd Murphy were in the dream. They were shouting and each was waving a banana. The whole of Turtle Ridge stood behind the two men, shaking their heads and clucking.

She crouched on her knees to try to hide her nudity. Then, out of the fog Douglas Osborne appeared. His face slowly changed into the shape of a dragon spitting flames of fire at her. Terrified, she screamed and tried to run, but the chains kept her riveted. The dragon inched closer and closer. The heat of the flames grew hotter and hotter, until her tender skin felt seared. She was being engulfed, sucked into the flames, when she fought her way back to awareness. "Jesus!"

Tense, she leapt from the bed. Going into the bathroom, she turned on the faucet and splashed her face with cold water until it tingled. She pulled a towel from the rack, then paused to stare at her reflection, trying to see herself through a man's eyes. What was it Artie had said? "An untouchable air men found challenging." Sex appeal, Molly had called it. Molly had said she would draw men like bees to honey. She had thought her aunt biased. Lonnie had thought her beautiful. She had thought him blinded by love. And Brian. He had singled her out of a group of four women, some much prettier than she. He had called her beautiful too. She had thought it must be the booze. And now Lloyd Murphy. He wasn't biased, or in love with her, and he hadn't been drunk. Yet he wanted her enough to offer anything.

She peered more closely at her reflection. All she saw was a fairly well-proportioned woman with curly hair that was a bitch to manage and freckles on her nose. She couldn't see it, but if nature had endowed her with something special, she would use it. She'd play the game, but she'd play it her way. She would get her banana, but she'd get it without compromising herself.

Autumn went to Julie's room, sat on the bed, and shook her awake. "I know I'm not beautiful, but they don't know I'm not beautiful. If we don't tell them, they'll never know for sure."

Julie blinked sleepily. "What's the matter with you?"

"I think it's called bats in the belfry." She grabbed Julie's hand and pulled her up from the bed. "We have to talk, make plans. I had a dream and now I know what to do. I'm going to use my untouchable, sexy air and get myself a big fat banana."

12

Julie was right. The Doghouse Bar *did* look as if it had been around since the gold-rush days. The bar was in a funny-looking building shaped like a wedge of pie and surrounded on all sides by gray cement. Behind the bar was a shoe store. The rest of the space was empty, with a "For Rent" sign on the door. The inside was typical. A bar ran the length of one wall, and twenty or so tables sat facing a small stage. Old gas lamps, no longer in use, were still on the walls. Even in the dim light the equipment looked old and worn; still, there was something comfortable about the place.

If somebody asked her to describe Everett Corbett, Autumn would say he was a neat-appearing man with sad puppy-dog eyes that followed her everywhere she went. He was quiet and soft-spoken, a shy man. When she talked to him about working there, he simply smiled and nodded. She knew from Julie that he was forty-nine, married once, and divorced. He had owned a stationery store with his wife, but the store had been sold and the profits split. His mother had died when he was in his twenties. Shortly after his divorce, his father died and he had taken over the Doghouse. From that point on the bar had gone steadily downhill. Julie thought it was because Everett had just stopped caring.

Autumn used the hours before she started working at the bar to rehearse. The place was quiet in the early evening.

During those hours she became better acquainted with Everett. He lived in an apartment over the bar. The rest of the upper floor was also empty, with a "For Rent" sign in the window. He worked during the quiet part of the evening. Wally, the bartender, and Julie came in later. Usually Everett sat in a corner with friends, chain-smoking and sipping Bloody Marys, or he retired to his apartment overhead. He seemed to like to talk to Autumn, or debate. He tossed out odd and unexpected questions that she had to fight to find answers for.

She caught him alone one evening and decided to turn the tables. "Are you still grieving over your divorce?"

He looked at her with a direct gaze. "Does one hurt less over the loss by divorce than over a loss by death?"

Autumn winced, wanting to kick herself. "I'm sorry. That was thoughtless of me."

"Can you answer my question?"

"No. I've lost, but not by divorce."

"I'm sorry too. We've both been thoughtless. Julie told me about your husband's death. You've been hurt. We've both been hurt. Life does that to you."

"Are you bitter?"

"No, I'm not bitter. It wouldn't help me, and it wouldn't change the facts. My wife turned to another man because she wanted someone more exciting."

"Will you marry again, or would you be afraid?"

He shook his head. "I wouldn't be afraid, but I would want to know the woman well. I would want her to know me well."

"In what way?"

He only smiled, turned, and walked away.

Once Autumn received the permits she needed they set the date for her to begin singing. Wally rigged the stage with a mike, a stool, and a flood of pink lights. The night she opened—the word made her throat flutter—she weaved her way through the tables crowded with laughing customers and stepped onto the small stage, wearing a long-sleeved black satin blouse and black slacks. She turned and faced the crowd with a hesitant smile.

"My name is Sue Anne, and I'm going to play and sing

for you." She tapped the jar that sat on the floor beside her stool with a toe. "Most entertainers use a brandy snifter, but I couldn't afford one, so I'm using a peanut-butter jar. If you have any requests, I'd be happy to play them for you."

She slid onto the stool, hooked the heel of her boot onto a rung, and pulled the strap of the guitar over her head. Her fingers strummed automatically, but she looked down at her knee as it twitched nervously, and knew if she opened her mouth to sing she would sound like one of the frogs from the river at Turtle Ridge.

She lowered the guitar to her lap and looked at the crowd of faces, who looked back at her with watchful, expectant eyes. "I learned to play and sing on the front porch of a little house in Kentucky. My only audience were friendly fireflies, a couple of owls, and maybe a bird with insomnia. I've played for folks before, but they were friends, or drunk. I can either wait until you're all drunk, or we can become friends."

The next moment Autumn discovered how wonderful people can be, even a room full of strangers. There was a sudden explosion of clapping, and friendly hoots of encouragement. A large man in a leather jacket stepped forward, shoved a bill in the jar, and called out a request. She smiled her thanks and arranged the guitar under her arm, leaned toward the mike, and pretended the faces were friendly fireflies.

When she finished the song there was another round of appreciative clapping. Before she lost their attention, Autumn quickly went into another song. Bit by bit the jar grew full, but she could feel the strain on her throat. To leave would mean the dollars would stop, but finally she was forced to escape to the back room to give her throat a rest. She grabbed a Coke at the bar. Wally, the bartender, winked and made a circle with his thumb and index finger.

She had liked Wally right away. His hair was snowy white and thinning at the temples. He wore heavy horn-rimmed glasses and looked more like an accountant than a bartender. She threw him a grin and hurried to the room behind the bar, where Everett had insisted she stay when not onstage. Minor trouble, he called her.

The room was filled with cases of liquor, a hot plate for quick heat-ups, a counter, a sink, and a refrigerator. A recliner with broken springs sat in a corner. She dropped down with a sigh and propped her feet on a case of vodka. She had been there for only a moment when Wally poked his head through the doorway.

"How're you doing?"

"My throat hurts. I don't know if my voice will last till closing time."

Julie popped in behind him. "I cleaned out your jar. You have thirty-two dollars."

Autumn sat upright in the chair. "You're kidding."

"Nope."

"That's over ten dollars an hour. I'll finish the night if it kills me."

"Don't count your dollars before they're in the jar," Wally said. "The place starts to clear out about twelve. There'll only be a few here at closing time."

Autumn left the chair and crossed to the sink. She poured out the sticky Coke and drew a glass of water. "As long as they're here, I'll sing. Every time a man puts a dollar in my jar, I feel like kissing him. That money is going to buy me more stock in Murphy's."

"Stock?" Julie asked. "Why are you buying stock in Murphy's?"

"I had a tip by way of a note from Mr. Murphy. He opened a store on the east coast. It's doing well from what I've heard. If he should suddenly announce an east-coast chain, the stock will jump, maybe even split. If it does, I want to be in on it. At any rate, I'm going to take his advice. He knows more than I do." She returned to the chair, sipping at the water and looking from Wally to Julie. "Who's minding the store?"

They looked at one another and laughed, then turned and left the room arm and arm. Autumn rested her head against the back of the chair, her feet up. The evening had gone better than she had expected and thirty dollars was more than she had hoped to make. There was only one thing missing: Artie.

Why hadn't he come? When she had called and told him what they were planning, he was against it, but when he saw she was determined, he wished her luck and promised to be there for moral support. She had hardly seen him since she had moved in with Julie, and she missed him. There were times when right in the middle of a conversation, his face would come into her mind's eye; or was it Lonnie? She felt the familiar stab inside and leapt to her feet, then turned hurriedly for the door and bumped into Everett.

He smiled, took her hand, and urged her back to the chair. "You haven't taken a long enough break. Rest a little longer." He sat down on the case in front of her. "I've been watching you. You're doing very well."

"Yes, I know. Everybody is watching me. I'm beautiful."

"Did I say you were beautiful?"

Autumn felt foolish and turned her face away. "I'm sorry. I was being sarcastic. I've had a lot of decisions to make lately, and behind it all seems to be the word 'beautiful.' I'm confused. What *is* beautiful? What makes one woman beautiful, and another only pretty? What is the dividing line?"

"It's a reflection, Autumn. Beauty is something a woman projects. Handsomeness is something a man projects. Pearl Bailey is beautiful. Sophia Loren is beautiful, but they are two entirely different women. Yet the image they project is beauty. This is true of you, Autumn. It's something that comes from within."

"There's nothing beautiful coming from within me." She rose from the chair and kicked the case he was sitting on. "The vodka in that case was distilled in a town where I once lived. It was sold by a man I detest. I'm in San Francisco, and he's in Kentucky, but one way or another he reaches out and reminds me. I couldn't escape from him if I wanted."

"What is this man to you—an ex-lover?"

She laughed with rancor. "I call him a dragon. Does a woman make love to a dragon?"

His legs were spread and he dropped his arms so that they were dangling between them. "Is he the dragon, or is the dragon something inside you?"

"I don't know. I've never thought of it in that way. The two are intermingled."

"Like the conscious and the subconscious?" he asked.

"Yes. Once I rid myself of the one, I'll rid myself of the other."

"Not necessarily. Suppose this man were to die tomorrow? Would this free you of the dragon?"

She thought of Douglas Osborne being dead and buried behind the wrought-iron fence, but it brought no peace. "No. I don't think it would."

"Then the dragon is inside you, not the man himself."

"You don't understand, Everett. I have to be the one to destroy the dragon. Then I'll be free."

"How are you planning to do this? Murder him?"

"No, of course not. That's his way, not mine."

"Then how do you propose to rid yourself of this man you call a dragon?"

"The only way there is, money and power."

"There are other ways, less childish ways."

"How?"

"Forgiveness. Once you forgive this man, you'll be free. It's really the only way."

"No. I can't forgive him, but you've made me understand what the word 'beautiful' really means." She leaned and kissed him on the forehead. "You're beautiful, and you have a beautiful heart. The most that can be said for me is that I'm pretty, or sexy."

She left Everett and dashed through the room filled with droning voices, sudden hoots of laughter, and random puffs of curling smoke. Women sat here and there, but eighty percent of the audience were men, with dollars in their pockets. She stepped gracefully onto the stage and stood with her hands on hips, long legs spread. The pink lights caught her auburn hair and cast a coppery glow that seemed to float about her face. She felt an unnatural excitement building and grew more daring, her voice filled with vibrancy. "Hi, everybody. I'm back, and my peanut-butter jar is empty."

A man called out from the back of the room, then half-staggered his way between the tables to the stage. He took a wad of money from his pocket and tucked a ten-dollar bill in the jar. "Bet this will make the pretty lady sing."

Autumn looked down at the money and thought: God

bless drunks—but said, "Loud and clear. What would you like me to sing?"

" 'San Antonio Rose.' "

"Oh no." She laughed and rested her hand on his shoulder. "I know the tune, but I can't remember the words. Can you think of another you like?"

"Nope," he said, and wobbled a little, his eyes dull and lidded. "I want 'San Antonio Rose.' "

She picked up the guitar and settled herself onto the stool. "All right. You sing, and I'll play."

He didn't hesitate. The stage was raised slightly and he pulled the mike to his mouth and his deep baritone filled the room. Another voice joined his, and another, and still another. He remained onstage and the peanut-butter jar filled over and over as he and Autumn went from song to song. The baritone half-stood, half-leaned against the stage. At one point he rested his hand on her thigh. She was ready to swat him as she would an annoying fly, when Wally came forth and signaled: Hands off.

Before the evening was over, she was poked, patted, pinched, and propositioned. The offers ranged from a trip to Reno to a hotel down the street. One man caught her after a break and was telling her what he could do for her in bed. She smiled and said, "I've found that people who talk a lot are already doing what they do best."

Everett disappeared sometime after midnight, but the crowd didn't thin out as Wally had predicted. Her voice was all but gone by closing time. When Wally finally locked the door on the last customer, she collapsed at a table next to Julie and began counting the last batch of bills.

"What a night," Julie said. She removed her shoes and rubbed the bottom of her feet. "We haven't had a night like this since I came to work here. If this keeps up, Everett will have to hire another girl to help out."

Wally sat down at the table with them and flipped his fingers through the stack of bills. "How much did you make?"

Autumn leaned forward and whispered hoarsely, "You're not going to believe this. I made ninety-eight dollars. If I work here five nights a week, I'll make five hundred dollars.''

''I don't want to dampen your spirits,'' Wally said, ''but the same crowd comes here every night. They had fun singing along with you, but you were new. A novelty. I think the dollars will slowly taper off until you're only making a little pin money.''

''He's right,'' Julie said. ''This is a gathering place for the neighborhood crowd. They come here and have a few drinks and bullshit with their friends. We get some new faces now and then, but they drift on, looking for something a little more exciting.''

''Has Everett thought to try to make this place a little more exciting?'' Autumn asked. ''I hate the thought, but when the crowd has had it with me, he should get something else in here. A small band would liven things up.''

''He doesn't care,'' Julie said. ''He knows his heart isn't going to keep ticking much longer. According to his doctor, he'll be dead within a year if he doesn't shape up. He's been told to stop drinking and to give up cigarettes. He's had two heart attacks. He knows a third will kill him, but he ignores the doctor's warnings.''

Autumn frowned and looked around the barroom. It wasn't fancy, but the land it sat on had to be worth a small fortune. ''I don't understand,'' she said. ''Why doesn't he sell this place and take it easy?''

''This is his home,'' Wally said. ''He knows every shopkeeper for miles around. This place and his friends are all he has. Everett likes to drink, and he likes to smoke. Take the things he enjoys out of life, and he wouldn't be living anyhow. He'd only be existing. At least that's his philosophy.''

''What will happen to this place?''

''He has a cousin back east. It will go to him.''

Autumn thought of Everett and his sad puppy-dog eyes that looked at her so adoringly. It was one way, but she would have to think long and hard before she made that kind of decision.

13

San Francisco was a magnificent city, a fairyland of spiraling streets and scaling hills, but it had a wet kind of cold that seemed to sneak in with the fog and nip at you until you were chilled to the bone. Autumn shivered as she stepped from a streetcar, pulled up the collar on her coat, and walked briskly toward the Doghouse. It was Saturday and she had spent the afternoon at Fisherman's Wharf. She loved the pier, the milling people, the smells, and watching the boats slip through water that seemed to stretch into forever. Bit by bit, San Francisco was becoming home.

She paused in front of the Doghouse and laughed quietly at the face that smiled up at her from a marquee. It was new, and no doubt meant as a surprise. Below her photograph was the heading "SING ALONG WITH SUE ANNE." She wrinkled her nose at the russet-haired woman who grinned back at her, then turned and entered the bar. She smiled at Wally. "And what is that outside?"

Wally grinned broadly. "Does it make you feel famous?"

"Notorious. I wondered why you had that guy in here taking my picture. It's great, Wally. Thanks." She looked through the crowd for Julie. Her blond friend was talking with one of the customers and counting out change. Julie wasn't as naive as Autumn had thought. When Artie had finally stopped calling altogether, Julie had moped for a while, then found a new man. Several, in fact.

Autumn glanced at the stage and then at Wally. "My stool awaits. Time to get my famous butt in gear."

Wally motioned toward the back room. "Artie is here. He's waiting for you."

Artie seldom came to the Doghouse, and Autumn was surprised. "Why is he hiding in the back room?"

Wally shrugged.

Autumn circled the bar and entered the room frowning. "Why aren't you out front drinking, laughing, and making merry?"

His face was sober. "I have to talk to you, Autumn."

She was confused by his tone and manner, and looked at him oddly. "What's wrong?"

"Nothing's wrong. I just need to talk to you about something."

She nodded, hung her coat on a rack, then sat down on a case across from him. "What's on your mind?"

"I'm going to Alaska."

"What!"

"I'm going to Alaska."

Four little words, but they slapped against her brain like rocket fire. Artie was her anchor, her link to Lonnie. "No," she said. "You can't."

"Why can't I, little sister?"

Autumn waved her hands, groping for words. "I need you . . . I need you here—in San Francisco."

"For what? You're doing fine on your own."

"No. I depend on you. I'd be lost without you here. I wouldn't know what to do. Just knowing you're here in town keeps me on an even keel."

"Me, or my face?"

Autumn stood abruptly, turning away, trying to escape his eyes, the truth in his words.

Artie rose and took her by the shoulders, forcing her to look at him. "I'll admit I'm bored and want to move on, but the main reason I'm leaving is you. You can't keep Lonnie alive by feeding on me, Autumn. I'm Artie, not Lonnie. Lonnie is dead. He's been dead over a year now, and running to me every time you feel the need to see his face in the flesh is only keeping you from accepting his death. I've accepted it. It's time you accepted it too."

"I know Lonnie is dead. I *have* accepted it."

"Yes, but you haven't really *buried* him. I've seen you look at me, reach out to touch me, and then jerk your hand away as if suddenly remembering who I am. What I'm doing is for you." He paused and his voice softened. "I don't intend to stay away forever. I'll be back, little sister."

She frowned, puzzled. "Why Alaska?"

"New horizons."

"It's cold, snowy, an awful place. What will you do there?"

"Prospect." He grinned. "Haven't you heard? There's gold in them there hills. I've always wanted to try prospecting. I'll get a job to pay for bread and bed. When I'm not working, I'll pack up my gold pan and head for the hills. Who knows? I might strike it rich."

"Is that what you want—to strike it rich?"

"No! Hell no. If I found the stuff, I'd have to do something with it. It isn't the gold, Autumn, it's the thrill, the excitement of looking for it."

She smiled, gazed at his face, and wanted to reach out and stroke the features that were so like Lonnie's. And she wondered why the word "beautiful" was reserved only for women. She stretched to tiptoe and kissed him on the cheek. "I have to go to work now—take care." Autumn picked up her guitar and the peanut-butter jar and walked toward the doorway. She paused to look back at him. "Don't stay away too long."

Autumn moved between the tables to the stage and climbed onto her stool. She smiled out at the people, but her eyes watched as Artie's large frame circled the bar and disappeared out the doorway. *Stupid woman.* Did you really think you could put a man like Artie in a cage and take him out whenever you felt the need to see Lonnie's face?

She pulled her gaze away from the empty doorway, tucked the guitar under her arm, and began to strum. Autumn looked out at the people with what she had come to think of as her phony barroom smile.

The evening seemed endless, the crowd more boisterous and demanding than ever. She felt like a wind-up toy sitting on her stool, plunking her father's old guitar, and singing along with them, or pretending to. She took more breaks than usual, sneaked a couple of drinks, and found it helped her to smile and made the evening slip past a little more easily.

The room began to clear at about one-thirty. They left in pairs and groups till there were only a couple of stragglers. Autumn turned them over to Wally and Julie and escaped to the back room. She had maybe ten minutes to kick back and stare at the wall before Julie and Wally descended on her, or so it seemed. Her feet had hardly touched the packing case before Julie entered, a question in her eyes. "You look awful. Is there anything wrong?"

"No, I'm just tired. Having two jobs is wearing me down."

"Are you sure that's all?"

"I'm sure."

"Okay." Julie grabbed her coat from the rack. "I've got a date. I'll see you in the morning." She grinned. "Then again, maybe I won't. If I don't come home, don't worry about me."

Autumn nodded and looked past her as Wally entered the room. Please, she thought. Don't tell me I look awful. And don't ask me what's wrong. As if he had read her thoughts, Wally gathered his coat and turned toward the rear door. "Don't forget to lock up," was all he said.

Autumn rested her head against the back of the seat and listened to the silence. She hadn't exactly lied to Julie. The late hours, school, and working two jobs were wearing her down. Some mornings she had to fight to get her body out of bed and off to Murphy's. She had seen Lloyd once since the day in his office. He had walked past without speaking to her, but he had nodded and smiled faintly.

Thinking back, Autumn realized his smile had been arrogant, as if to say: I know you, girl. You're hungry. You'll be back.

She felt a sudden rush of anger. Anger at Lloyd Murphy, anger at Artie, and anger at the power both men held over her. One because of his face, the other because of his money. "The hell I will," she said, and leapt to her feet.

"The hell you will what?"

She spun, startled by the sound of Everett's voice. "I thought you had gone to bed."

He shook his head. "What kind of dragon are you fighting tonight?"

"Dragons, dragons," she said. "Dragons everywhere." She flopped back into the chair, gazing at Everett and wondering why no one but her had been aware of his feelings. Feelings that had grown stronger and stronger, displayed in his eyes when he looked at her, reflected on his face when he smiled. Were people blind?

Everett sat on a case and gazed at her intently. "You're upset."

Autumn didn't bother to deny it. "Artie is leaving. He's going to Alaska."

"And you feel alone?"

She nodded. "Artie is like family. I have so little, I cherish what I have."

He looked down at his hands, and then at her with a nervousness she had never seen in him before, his voice shy and hesitant when he spoke. "If . . . if you married me, you wouldn't be alone. You'd have family. We'd both have family."

Autumn wasn't surprised. "I thought you weren't going to get married, unless you knew the woman well."

"I know you, Autumn. I know you better than any other man ever will, and you know me. You know I'm forty-nine. You know I'm anything but exciting. You know I'm ill. You know I'm not going to live too many more years. And you know I own this bar." He reached and took her hand in his. "I know you have a goal. And I know you're tormented because of this goal. I know you want power and money. This tavern isn't much, but it's yours. It will start you on your path, whatever that may be. It would make me feel good to know I had in some way helped ease you closer to whatever it is you want so badly."

"And what do you want in return?"

"Just you as my wife."

Autumn had thought of this very thing many times. It was against everything she had always believed in. She had been within an inch of discarding the idea altogether. Now she looked into his soft brown eyes and wondered:

Why not? What am I saving myself for, love and babies? Maybe if she had never loved so intently, there could have been someone else. As it was, sweet memories of Lonnie beat constantly against her brain. And always in the background was Douglas Osborne, guiding her path, driving her on and on.

Autumn drew Everett's hand to her lips, nodding. She couldn't bring the kind of love to the marriage that she had had for Lonnie, but she felt a deep affection for this man. In that moment, she made a silent pledge: in return for his trust and generosity, she would never do anything to hurt or disappoint this gentle, tender man.

14

Autumn had been married just short of a month when she was pulled away from a customer by her department manager and sent to Mr. Murphy's office. The summons was unexpected, and as she took the executive elevator to the top floor, she spent the time speculating as to why. The position for assistant buyer had been filled, so Murphy couldn't have changed his mind. There seemed no reason for them to meet again; nonetheless, he wanted to see her right away. Someone had said that Murphy had been out of the country for several weeks, and had only returned the day before.

The office was the same, flames crackled in the fireplace, crystal sparkled on the bar, but the atmosphere didn't feel cozy anymore. And the man himself was different. Murphy smiled, but the smile didn't quite reach his eyes, and when he motioned for her to be seated, it was with an agitated wave of his hand. Autumn didn't know why, but she felt provoked by his attitude. She wanted to turn and walk out the door. Common sense told her, however, that if you were smart, you wouldn't show Lloyd Murphy your backside. Not if you wanted to keep your job. She crossed and stood in front of his desk.

He spoke softly but with a bite to his words. "Sit down, Mrs. Corbett."

Autumn smiled to herself, understanding now. Murphy said *Corbett* as if the name brought a bitter taste to his mouth. He had expected her to wait, to think, and then return to him. Instead Autumn had married an older man with much less to offer, and it touched a sore spot in Murphy's strong Irish pride. She sat down across from him, her gaze direct. "What did you want to see me about?"

He was toying with the pencil and it made a rapid tapping sound as it slid back and forth between his fingers and struck against the desk. "I just learned that you married Everett Corbett. A bar owner."

"That's right."

He gave a pencil a twirling toss. "Why?"

"Women do marry, Mr. Murphy."

He leaned with arms folded on the desk, his voice critical. "Women marry for love or money. I can't believe you married this man for love, and he doesn't have any money. You're bright, ambitious, grasping. You have everything it takes to become a fine businesswoman. With me behind you, the heights you could have reached were unlimited. Why marry him, when I offered you much more?"

"He offered me the security of marriage. That wasn't what you had in mind."

Frowning, Murphy left his chair, circled the desk, and half-sat on the edge, gazing at her with perplexity. "You're puzzling, Autumn, very puzzling." His arms crossed, he rubbed a finger against the cleft in his chin. "I wouldn't have thought marriage was that important to you."

"Marriage for the sake of marriage is not at all important. If I were in love with you, I would be with you. But I like being married," she said with some surprise. "I like belonging to someone, and having someone who belongs to me. Everett offered me his name and everything that goes with it. You only wanted to buy me for a while. I'm not for sale, Mr. Murphy."

"Would you have accepted marriage if I had offered?"

"No. You're too healthy. I have things to do, and you'd get in my way."

"Hmm," he said, a smile curling the rim of his mouth. "Too healthy, am I? Suppose I told you I have a fatal illness? Would you marry me then?"

Autumn smiled too. "You're not ready to drop dead, and you didn't ask me, so the question is irrelevant."

"No, I'm not ready to drop dead, and I didn't ask you—and I wouldn't. You're too young. It's doubtful, but if I should marry again, it will be to another woman that stuffs a mean turkey but bores the hell out of me. I don't want to wonder where my wife is, and what she is doing. With you I wouldn't know, and I'd be eaten with jealousy. Jealousy is a destructive emotion, and one I avoid. It weakens a man."

"What you're saying is that I'm the kind of woman a man wants but doesn't marry?"

"Not if he's in his right mind."

"Everett married me."

"That's his problem, not mine."

Autumn rose from the chair. "I'd like to go back to work now—if I still have a job."

He smiled. "Of course."

She turned and walked toward the door, was reaching for the knob when he called her name. Autumn paused, frowning. "What is it now?" Laughing, he held her shoes up by the narrow heels. Autumn felt the heat of embarrassment against her cheeks. In her stocking feet she crossed to where he stood. "I do that sometimes when I get nervous."

He grinned, a strand of sandy hair falling onto his forehead. "I do like you, Autumn. You've got a poker face that will bluff you through just about anything." When she went to take her shoes, he teased and held them out of reach, caught her around the waist, and pulled her into the close circle of his arm.

Surprised by his unexpected show of playfulness, Autumn was caught off guard by the sudden touch of his body against hers. The strength of his arm around her felt reassuring. She wanted to sigh, to relax and rest her cheek against the roughness of his jacket, to breathe deeply of the spicy scents that were the essence of maleness. She wanted to say: Yes. You take over. You be the leader. Stand tall and strong between me and Douglas Osborne. Fight my war, Lloyd Murphy, so I can be soft again.

She felt his lips brush against her forehead, heard his

words, harsh in meaning, but spoken in a whispered caress. "It's not too late. Divorce is easy. All you have to do is sign a paper. My attorneys will take care of the rest."

Autumn realized that unconsciously she had begun to enact her fantasy. Her cheek was pressed against Lloyd Murphy's chest, her arms were circling his waist. She pushed him away, feeling guilty, and angry at her own softness. Was she going to try to lean on every man that passed through her life—flop her head on every strong shoulder that was offered?

Autumn grabbed her shoes, stumbling as she shoved her feet into the leather. When Murphy reached to steady her, she slapped at his hand. "Go away!" Once balanced, she stood and gazed at him directly. "You're wrong about me. Everett doesn't have to wonder where I am or what I'm doing. There won't be a divorce—ever. He's a good, gentle man, and he's ill. I won't leave him, and I won't do anything that will hurt him—ever."

"Ill?" Murphy quirked an eyebrow. "How ill?"

"He has a serious heart problem. He could die in a year, maybe two."

Lloyd nodded, a knowing smile breaking across his face. "I see. You married him for the bar, didn't you?"

"Yes," she said bluntly.

He smiled again with pleasure. "I was right about you. You're hungry, damned hungry. I like it. Hunger makes a woman sexy." Crossing to his desk he picked up a pipe and chewed the stem for a moment. "You're smart, Autumn, but you're jumping now, making moves without thought and direction."

"No," she said. "I have direction. Someday the Doghouse will be mine. It's my first step backward." She smiled at his look of confusion. "It's really very simple, Mr. Murphy. In order to get what I want, I have to work my way backward. Along the way, I have to become very, very rich."

He shook his head in wonder. "You're building castles in the air, Autumn. That run-down bar isn't going to make you rich."

"You're wrong. I was taught that anything is possible if you're willing to fight for it. I'm a fighter, and I'll fight for what I want." Murphy leaned against his desk, chewing on the stem of the pipe, laughter in his eyes. "Laugh if you want, but while you're laughing, you wait and you watch."

"I'll wait," he said, "and I'll watch. You're too much of a woman to waste yourself wet-nursing a dying man. You'll get fed up. When you do, you can come to me. I'll be here."

A sarcastic remark was on the tip of her tongue, but instinct told her to tread softly. Someday she might need the big Irishman. "Maybe," she said. "Then again, maybe not."

Darkness had fallen over the Doghouse, but Lloyd Murphy and his laughter still floated in and out of Autumn's thoughts as she dressed for her evening downstairs. His laughter had made her angry and she had lashed out at him. "Wait and watch," she had shouted, mostly to cover her own doubts. The Doghouse didn't seem like much when she looked at it through his eyes. Perhaps she *was* building castles in the air.

She finished dressing and went into the living room, where Everett sat reading. The sounds of Beethoven's *Waldstein Sonata* filled the room. Neither she nor Everett had wanted any fanfare, so they had slipped away and married quietly. She had waited until the last moment to remove Lonnie's ring, and then hesitated. Everett had looked at her with understanding and added his ring to Lonnie's.

The living quarters over the bar were comfortable and reflected Everett's quiet personality. The rooms were neat, sedately furnished. An entire wall was lined with books on every topic, a stereo, and a large selection of classical records. The living room was situated above the front of the bar, the bedrooms were in the rear, and the kitchen faced east, capturing the morning sun. Off the kitchen, Everett's office reflected his lack of interest in the Doghouse. Deeds, bills, and insurance papers were stuffed at random in drawers. Unpaid bar tabs that dated back six months were shoved in with utility bills. All of which told Autumn the Doghouse was rapidly sliding downhill.

She crossed the room to where Everett sat and brushed her hand against his thick hair. His eyes weren't sad anymore, but bright and expressive when he looked at her. He was drinking less and taking his medicine without having to be reminded. Bottles with complex labels lined the cabinet beside the sink. There was Peritrate to prevent angina. Digoxin to strengthen the heart. Nitroglycerin for sudden sharp pain. Lasix for circulation.

Despite his illness, Everett was a passionate, but shy and gentle man. Autumn felt regretful and guilty at times, because all she had to give in return was deep affection.

Smoke curled up from his cigarette, and she pulled it from his nicotine-stained fingers to tap it out in the ashtray. "You smoke too much."

He smiled and motioned her to the ottoman. "I saw an attorney today."

"Really? Are you divorcing me already?"

"My wife makes a funny joke. I'm having a will drawn up that will leave you all my incidentals. I want you to have the Doghouse, but I don't see any reason for you to have to pay capital gains or any kind of inheritance tax. If some distasteful event should take place, I want it to be as easy for you as possible. And I want you to have as much as possible. I'm making arrangements to sell you the Doghouse at a very reasonable price. This will include the entire building."

"Are you sure?" she asked. "You're putting a lot of trust in me. I could take the bar and then kick you out."

He laughed quietly. "I know you, Autumn. Better, I think, than you know yourself. I don't have any fears or misgivings about what I'm doing. This is best for me, and you, and the Doghouse."

She folded her arms and rested them against his knees. "There are some things I've been wanting to talk to you about. The books are a mess. I think we should turn them over to an accountant. And the bar tabs. Some of the people who come here haven't paid their tab in months. I don't understand how you've even stayed in business. And it's impossible to lease the rest of the building when it's in such rotten shape. If you want to lease, you're going to have to make repairs. And—"

He laughed and placed a finger against her lips. "I love to watch your eyes light with excitement when you talk about this place. The Doghouse is yours. You do whatever you want."

"I have some plans," she said.

"I've turned the place over to you. You don't have to check with me before making changes. You're the owner now. Do what you think is needed."

"What about you? What will you do with your time? It isn't good for you to be idle."

"I won't be idle. I've been making plans too. I haven't told anybody before, but I used to write a little. I've even had a few articles and short stories published. I'd like to try to write a novel."

She smiled at the excitement in his voice. "That's wonderful," she said sincerely. "What will you write about?"

"Maybe I'll write about a woman named Autumn."

She groaned playfully. "Please, anyone but me. I don't think I would like to see myself in print." She rose, smiling down at him. "I have to go downstairs now, but we'll talk later—make plans. A writer needs quiet, and a place to think." She bent and kissed him lightly on the mouth, checked his shirt pocket for the pillbox he was supposed to carry at all times, but constantly forgot. "Don't forget your stroll. It's important."

Autumn left Everett and took the stairs that led to the back room. There was no denying she loved the idea of ownership. It meant freedom to call the shots as she saw them, to make changes without having to ask a by-your-leave of anybody. She would be "the owner." Proprietress of the Doghouse Bar, slipping under, but still afloat. During the weeks she had worked there, she had come to understand why Everett was always in trouble financially. At least fifty percent of the customers did more bullshitting than drinking. If money was put into the bar, and it was managed differently, it could become a profitable business. Everett had been too soft, but she wasn't.

Going to the doorway, she motioned for Wally. He entered the room in good humor, but when she explained that Everett was turning the bar over to her, his eyes darkened in disapproval. "What's the matter?" she asked.

"You sing pretty, Autumn, but you're a woman, and a kid. Everett was a fool to turn this place over to you."

"Shit!" She sagged with disappointment. Dropping onto the lumpy recliner, she said, "Not you too. I had thought you were above such male foolishness. I stopped being a kid when I was eighteen, and I can't help being a woman."

"I've never worked for a woman, Autumn. I don't think I can."

"Don't think of me as a woman. Think of me as Autumn. I need you here, Wally. I can't handle this place without you. Julie is fine, but she's scatterbrained. If you leave, I'm in trouble."

"I won't leave you in a bind. I'll give you time to find someone else."

"I don't want someone else. I want you."

He shook his head.

"Please. Give it a try. One month. If you don't like working for me, then go."

Wally shook his head.

"I'm planning on making some changes—big, exciting changes."

He shook his head again.

"What do I have to do, Wally, beat you at Indian wrestling? If that's the case, then I'll lose."

His face slid into a slow, reluctant smile. "What kind of changes are you planning?"

"First, I want to hire someone to take over for Everett in the afternoon. He wants to try to write, and I'd like him to have the chance. Next, I want every customer who hasn't paid his tab cut off until he does."

"You'll lose a lot of customers if you do that."

"So what? If they aren't paying, they aren't any good to us anyhow."

"Okay," he said. "I'll agree to that."

"I won't know what kind of shape the place is in until an accountant has gone over the books, but I have a little money of my own. I'll sing and play during the week, but I want to get a small band in here on the weekends. I'd like to try to draw a different kind of crowd. One that drinks instead of just bullshitting.''

He nodded. "I agree. What else?"

"Once we get this place hopping, I'm going to try for a loan so I can knock out the walls and turn this pie-shaped pile of bricks into the hottest boogie palace in San Francisco.'' She leaned forward, her eyes bright with excitement. "Well? What do you think?"

"You know"—Wally grinned—"with me behind you, you just might make it.''

She squealed and leapt into his arms. "Look out, San Francisco, here we come.'' She kissed Wally on the cheek with an echoing smack, turned, and danced about the room. Wally, shaking his head and laughing at her, ducked through the doorway.

She jumped high and clicked her heels, danced a jig to the refrigerator, grabbed a frankfurter, and flopped into the old recliner. Biting into the weiner, she gazed up at the ceiling and began to imagine what the new Doghouse would be like—alive with a million flashing lights, the music hot and blasting, the dance floor jammed with twisting figures. And the cash register steadily clinking.

She was twitching her foot and humming along to the imaginary music when Julie entered the room. Autumn had always turned to Julie for some laughs when she was moody, but lately her blond friend had grown distant, abrupt, almost rude. It was out of character for Julie, and Autumn had wondered why. Several times she had tried to talk to her, but Julie had put her off with a wave of the hand. Trying to be casual now, Autumn shook the hot dog at Julie. "My aunt makes the best hot dogs I've ever eaten. She tops them with a lot of good stuff of her own making. I've tried to get her to tell me what she puts on them, but she says it's her secret.''

"Why don't you flash one of your famous smiles, Autumn? That should do it.''

Autumn's mouth dropped open. "What was that crack about?"

"You," Julie said. "Wally just told me that Everett is turning the bar over to you. Everett is the kindest man alive, and you're using him. You don't care about him. All you care about is his money."

"Julie! That's not true."

"The hell it isn't. Ambition is fine, Autumn, but you've become a cold, scheming bitch. When you get what you want from Everett, you'll move on to something or some*one* else." She paused and her gaze raked over Autumn. "I envied you. I thought you were wonderful, but now you make me sick. And the thought that makes me the sickest is knowing I brought you here. I turned you loose on that lonely, vulnerable man, and you moved right in."

"No," Autumn said, and reached out to her. "I would never do anything to hurt Everett. As long as he needs me, I'll be here for him, Julie. You can count on that."

"Are you trying to tell me you married him for love?"

"No. I married him for the Doghouse, but that doesn't mean I don't care for him. I don't love him in the same way I loved Lonnie, but I have very special feelings for him. There are many kinds of love, Julie. That's something I don't think you've learned yet."

With a swish of her blond hair, Julie turned toward the door. "For Everett's sake, I'll stay until you can find someone to replace me, then I'm quitting. I don't want to be anywhere around you. What you have might be catching."

Autumn sat feeling the joy slipping away, her throat lumpy with tears. She looked at the bit of hot dog, swore, and threw it hard against the wall. A long night stretched before her, and she grabbed the guitar and the peanut-butter jar and entered the barroom. She glanced at Julie, but crossed to where Wally stood wiping a counter. "You better run an ad for two people. Julie is quitting."

"Julie? Why?"

"Me. She's angry with me for marrying Everett. She thinks I'm a cold, scheming bitch. Do you feel the same, Wally? *Am* I a cold, scheming bitch?"

He smiled. "Maybe, but what a way to go! If I were dying and owned a bar, I'd trade it for a broad like you." He patted her hand. "I'll admit I was skeptical when you first married Everett, but whatever the reason, you've been good for him. You've got my vote."

"Thanks. It's good to know I've got at least one friend." She turned for the stage, but paused. "One more thing. I don't want any more liquor from the Osborne distillery sold in my bar." She stepped onto the stage, gazed out at the crowd, and wondered how in front of a room full of people she could still feel so alone. It had been even worse since Artie left. At times she found herself looking through the crowd for his familiar face. She had had two postcards, each from a different town. Artie was moving, drifting from place to place, job to job, from creek bank to creek bank, searching for shiny yellow dust that he didn't even want.

As she slid onto the stool, Autumn longed for the house among the trees, longed to walk the riverbank, to listen to the quiet night sounds. And she missed Molly. "I'm going home," she whispered. "As soon as possible, I'm going home."

15

Over the next three months Autumn moved at a hard pace. Her trip to Turtle Ridge was delayed, pushed aside to when she would have more time. Response to the band was even greater than she had anticipated. The old crowd drifted away and new faces appeared, ones that liked to drink and play, not sip and chat. Business had grown— doubled, tripled. They had hired another man to relieve Wally, and another girl. The shoe store had moved to a new building, leaving that area vacant and ready for use. The bar was packed every night, bursting at the seams. It was time to expand.

The Doghouse was hers now, but because of her age and the nature of the business, Everett acted as trustee. All decisions had to be approved by him. When Autumn went to Everett with her plans, he refused. There would be no loans, no mortgages against the Doghouse.

Frowning, he sat down in a chair across from Autumn. "Are you angry?"

"Yes . . . No. I don't know." Autumn gazed at him, confused. His denial was contrary to everything she knew about the man. He didn't pry, or interfere, or question. Anything she wanted had been fine with him, until now. "I'm not sure what I am," she said. "I'm surprised, and very disappointed."

"I wish you had told me what you were planning."

"I wanted to wait until I was sure. The place is packed

every night, and overcrowded on weekends. If we enlarged, we could double the business we're doing now."

"You're new at this, Autumn. I know the business and I know the bar crowd. They're fickle. They'll come to the bar for a year, or maybe even two, then they'll find another favorite spot. If we enlarged, we would end up with empty space and a mortgage hanging over our heads. That's not what I want for you."

"I can wait until I'm twenty-one," she said stubbornly. "Go against you."

He looked at her as one would a wayward child. "You can, but you won't."

Everett was right. As long as he lived, she would have to do as he wanted. Autumn didn't know if it was because of her or his writing, but Everett was living his life with new incentive. He was relaxed, happy, not at all the sad man she had married. He had stopped smoking completely, and limited his drinking to one glass of wine at dinner. His many cups of coffee had become herbal tea. Everett was fighting for his life, and she did admire a fighter; nonetheless, she couldn't just stand still and wait. "If I can get the money without a mortgage, will you then agree?"

He nodded, placation in his voice. "I'll agree."

Autumn left her chair, crossed to the window, and gazed down at the people walking toward the Doghouse. There was a way she could get the money, *maybe*. Lloyd Murphy had said to come to him if she ever needed anything. Would he lend her the money? If so, *what would he expect in return*? And what would she be willing to pay?

Autumn spun on her toe. "To hell with it. To hell with everything. I'm going home."

Everett smiled. "You're such a child, Autumn. Every time you feel hurt, or angry, or disappointed, you storm through the apartment shouting that you're going home. You've been going home for three months and you haven't made it yet."

"Then I think it's time I did." She tossed her head of long auburn hair, marched to the phone, and dialed the airport. She glanced at Everett. "Shall I make the reservations for one or two?"

"Are you asking if I'd like to come with you?"

"If you don't mind being left with Aunt Molly. I'll be busy. There are things I have to do. And I want to see Ella."

He nodded. "Make it for two. I'd like to meet Molly."

Ella had made a lot of changes in the diner. The place was neat and clean, with red-and-white-checkered curtains at the windows and bright red tablecloths. Customers filled several tables. A waitress in white stood taking an order. Ella had made other changes, too. She was getting married to a man named Cliff Johnson, a truck driver with two children.

Ella was standing in the kitchen with her back to the door. Autumn smiled, recalling the afternoon they had first come to the diner and the fat, grumpy cook. "One hamburger," she said, "and hold the onions, sweetface."

Ella turned at the sound of her voice. The two women fell into an affectionate hug. Ella pushed away and gazed at Autumn. "Ohh, you get prettier and prettier. God, could you rake in the bucks at Rex's place." She led Autumn into an office at the rear of the diner and mixed two drinks from a bottle of moonshine. Ella held the glass out to her. "Betcha ain't got nothing like this in San Francisco."

Autumn took a sip and wrinkled her nose at its bite. "Raw."

"Hot off the still."

Autumn relaxed back in the chair, gazing at Ella. What a pair, she thought. Me, a hayseed grasping for wealth. Ella, an ex-hooker grasping for the comfortable family life. Still, there was a strong bond between them. Ella knew it all. With Ella, Autumn didn't have to pretend. "What's new in town?"

Ella smiled. "You mean, what's new with the Osbornes?"

Autumn only nodded.

"Not much. Harriet, George's wife, just returned from a trip to Paris. Bea, Homer's wife, is churchy. She and several other women have opened a kind of foundling home for kids. Homer is mayoring, George is in and out of town running errands for big brother. I don't hear much about Dale. He's odd, a recluse."

"Humanitarians," Autumn said. "They all sound so lily white. Isn't there any dirt connected to the family?"

"None that I've heard. Douglas keeps some woman set up in town, but that's nothing. He's a man, and a widower. It's expected."

"What about Brian? Did he come home for the summer?"

"No. I heard he spent the summer on the Riviera. He lost his girl, though. Lisa Albright married a man from Louisville."

Autumn didn't care about Lisa or whom she had married, but it gave her a moment of satisfaction to know the rift between father and son was broadening. She smiled. "How sad."

Ella grinned too. "What does Molly think about your marriage to Everett? Has she questioned you?"

"Not a word. She probably guessed I married Everett for the bar. Aunt Molly has a way of looking at a brick wall and seeing what's on the other side." She paused and smiled. "It took some fast talking, but Aunt Molly is coming back with us to spend a couple of weeks. I'm hoping I can convince her to stay longer." Autumn glanced at her watch, rose from the chair, and set her half-finished drink on the desk. "I'd like to stay and talk, Ella, but there are some things I want to do here before the stores close. I'll be in Kentucky for a couple more days. Why don't you bring Cliff out tomorrow night? We'll have a barbecue. Later we'll slip away for a long talk. You can tell me all about your truck driver."

Ella nodded and smiled broadly. "Sounds good. We'll be there."

They walked together through the diner. Autumn smiled a good-bye, then hurried outside to her car. The engine started with a hum and she pulled away from the curb. Her face became quiet, sober, as she turned the car toward the outskirts of town.

Autumn knelt beside Lonnie's grave. On impulse, she had gone into the woods at Molly's house and found a clump of cornflowers. The blossoms were dead now, but they would bloom again come spring, bright blue, the color of Lonnie's eyes. Digging a hole with a tablespoon she had brought from Molly's, Autumn planted the wildflowers at the base of the grave.

The mound had settled and grass covered the site. The small, insignificant plaque lay flat, the print faded by the sun. She gazed at the space where Lonnie rested and felt nothing, drew her hand against the earth, but still felt nothing. They said he was dead, buried beneath the soft green grass, but they were wrong. Lonnie wasn't dead. All the things he was, still lived on, locked tightly in her secret place.

Autumn rose and left the cemetery without a backward glance. She drove into town to a monument works and ordered a headstone to be set on Lonnie's grave. Once the arrangements had been made, she headed the car back toward the outskirts of town. After several blocks she turned the car into Miners' Row. The houses, crammed one against the other, looked even smaller and dirtier than she remembered, the air filled with the stink of poverty.

All that remained of Autumn's house was a pile of burned timbers, but Lonnie was there, whistling in the shower, hammering on the weather-beaten door that never did stop squeaking, poring over textbooks, grabbing her for a quick kiss that became long and sweet, whispering, "Love ya, sugar." Her lips quivered and she pressed her foot against the accelerator, speeding away from Miners' Row, the poverty, and the death.

Autumn didn't slow down until she reached the center of town. She brought the car to a stop at a light, glancing absently at the buildings, the courthouse, the drugstore, the bank. People were coming and going, but one figure stood out among all the rest. She stared, her heart suddenly pounding. The man was tall, blond, and walked with self-assurance. His body was firm and lean, his shoulders broad. He left the bank entrance and paused at the curb, less than ten feet away from her car.

She had seen his face only in a clipping, and it had been blurred. Autumn had always thought of him as old, but he looked younger than Everett. He had clear blue eyes, a jutting chin, and a face only lightly etched with lines; a healthy, fit man, an older version of his son, Brian. ''Not fair, not fair,'' she half-moaned. He was walking, talking to a blond man beside him, while Lonnie lay sleeping.

She shoved her foot hard against the accelerator, turning against the light, against the traffic. Tires squealed and horns blasted, but Autumn didn't slow down. She sped away from town, knowing now that she would go to Lloyd Murphy. *She would go to the devil himself if he would get her what she wanted, what she had to have.*

16

Molly had never been far from Turtle Ridge, and Autumn wanted to show her some of the wonders of San Francisco. She took a week off from Murphy's and tried to cram as much sightseeing as possible into seven short days. Molly had her first lobster at Fisherman's Wharf, her first chow yok in Chinatown, a ride across the Golden Gate Bridge, a glimpse of the Bay Bridge at sundown, a picnic at Lincoln Park, and a crooked ride down Lombard. They were in and out of museums, rode cable cars, and toured Nob Hill. An elevator ride to the top of Coit Tower ended their tour, and Autumn went back to work.

One week slid into two, and then three, and Molly stayed on. When she mentioned leaving, Autumn found some excuse for her to stay a few days longer. Bit by bit Molly had taken over the kitchen and was beginning to take over the running of the apartment. Autumn felt her aunt was taking on the role of a maid, and it bothered her. At the same time she realized that Molly had missed having someone who depended on her alone. Autumn felt it was her turn to take care of Molly now, but she would have to make her aunt feel needed. There was more than enough room in the apartment, and Everett reveled in having two women fussing over him.

Autumn sat down with Molly and asked her point-blank to stay on and help out with the apartment. Molly agreed, but only until the income from the Doghouse was such that

Autumn could quit her job at Murphy's. Autumn had no intention of telling Molly that the bar more than paid its way now, and that she was going to squeeze every dollar possible from Murphy's until she was either fired or collapsed from the exhausting schedule she had set for herself. In addition to working at Murphy's, she had added to her college load. Several hours a week were spent on paperwork for the Doghouse. Usually she didn't get to bed until long after midnight.

August had slipped into September when Autumn finally called Lloyd's office and made an appointment to see him. Once she had decided to go to Lloyd, there hadn't been any hurry. Now that Molly was settled in, Autumn felt the time was right.

While waiting for her appointment, she rehearsed her speech over and over. But when she walked into his office, her mind went blank. She smiled tentatively, squeezed a manila envelope tight against her breasts, and took the chair he indicated.

He sat relaxed, a question in his eyes. "What can I do for you, Mrs. Corbett?"

"You once told me that if I ever needed anything, I could come to you."

He nodded. "What is it you need?"

"Forty," she blurted, "maybe fifty thousand dollars."

Lloyd Murphy didn't flinch. "For what?"

"I want to expand the Doghouse."

He smiled and stretched back in his chair. "What am I going to get in return for my money?"

"I can't offer you a mortgage against the Doghouse, but I'll give you one percent over the prime interest rate."

"I can get a better return for my money elsewhere."

"Well," she said, and shifted nervously in the chair, "one and a half percent."

He motioned toward the packet. "We'll talk terms later. Why don't you show me what you have in the envelope?"

Autumn rose and spread her papers over his desk. At first she spoke slowly, but then the words began to tumble one over the other. A film of nervous perspiration appeared on her face. She wiped her upper lip with a fingertip and glanced at him closely. His face was still, but his eyes told her he was laughing at her. "Damn you, Lloyd Murphy. Damn you to hell." She tried to run and gather papers at the same time. "You have no intention of lending me money. You want me to fail. You think I'll get tired of waiting and come to you. It isn't going to happen. You can buy your tail somewhere else."

Lloyd sprang from the chair and leaned with hands propped on his desk. "What the hell makes you think your ass is so special? I don't have to pay to get fucked. I have greedy women throwing themselves at me six times a day, and a dozen on Sundays. If, and I say if, I should ever help you, it would be for your wits, not your ass."

"Go to hell, you . . . fucker!" She ran from the room and slammed the door with a bang that sent the startled secretary half out of her chair. Autumn had reached the hallway when she turned and raced back into his office. She banged the door again and shouted, "Am I fired?"

"No," he shouted back at her. "But I might wash your mouth out with soap. For a nice little girl from Turtle Ridge, you've got a real nasty mouth."

"Try working around a bar and see what it does to your mouth."

"I can afford it. You can't. It shows lack of control."

"You were laughing at me."

"Yes, I was laughing at you. I let you off easy, Autumn. If a man had walked in here to make a pitch as unprepared as you, I would have thrown him out in the first five minutes."

"What do you mean?"

"This." He took the envelope, tossed it in the wastebasket, and motioned her toward a chair. "First, you wanted to borrow money. Forty, maybe fifty thousand dollars. You have no idea how much it will cost to enlarge the Doghouse. Next, you show me plans. Neat ones, but drawn by you, and not to scale. What you're planning is a complete overhaul. You want to open up and knock down walls. What will keep the ceiling from collapsing? Maybe it can be done. I don't know, but neither do you. Then there's the parking. The basement parking area won't handle the crowd you're planning. Or do you plan to cater to the elite who drive up in their limos, and send their cars away until later? If you are, you can forget it. The Dog-house will never attract anything but the middle class. Last, but in no way least. Have you checked with the city? There are codes, zoning. You don't even know if the city will let you expand. This isn't my area, so I don't know either, but I would expect the person putting a package together to have these facts for me." He paused and frowned. "These are only a few points, Autumn. If I wanted to get really picky, I could go on and on."

Embarrassment burned against her cheeks. "I feel so stupid."

"Don't. Stupid is one thing, inexperienced is something else." He motioned toward the sofa. "Let's forget busi-ness for a while and have a drink."

"Yes," she said quickly. "Whiskey. Straight."

"Straight?"

"You can add some ice." Autumn left the chair and sank into the soft leather on the sofa. She watched as he went to the bar and mixed the drinks. His stride was even, his steps measured, as if to move himself carefully from one point to another without an awkward pause. She glanced at him as he returned to the sofa, promising herself never to let her emotions cloud her judgment again. "Which was worst," she asked, "the beginning, the middle, or the end?"

"The beginning. Always tell a man how much money you're going to make for him before telling him how much it's going to cost." He relaxed against the sofa and took a sip of the drink. "There's something I would like you to understand, Autumn. If I should ever finance you in a business venture, it will be because you've picked a win-ner. If I ever make love to you, it will be because you want it too."

Autumn heard both statements, but the one that clicked in her brain was the first. She looked at him from the corner of her eye. "Would you really? I mean—finance me after the fool I made of myself today?"

"Sure. I don't have anything against making money. If you come up with something I think is a winner, I'll stand behind you."

"What do you think of the Doghouse in terms of growth?"

"It can provide a fair income. If you are able to expand, you could increase your profits, but there isn't enough there for a second party, or high interest rates. If I lent you the money, it would be as a favor. I don't do favors. Or I could give you the money and let you use your ass to pay me back. A deal like that wouldn't be any good for either of us. If that was all I wanted, I'd go to a hooker." He paused and smiled. "Besides, I don't think your Aunt Molly would approve."

Autumn shook her head in wonder. "Isn't there anything you don't know about me?"

"Very little."

"I can understand how you learn most things, but how did you find out what I like for breakfast?"

"Simple. It was done by a telephone survey with your roommate. I believe her name was Julie?"

"Yes," she said, and thought of her old friend. The last she had heard, Julie had moved to Los Angeles with some man she had met. "Julie left after I married Everett. She didn't approve."

"I know," he said absently.

Autumn turned on the sofa and looked at him quizzically. "Why are you doing this? Why are you keeping tabs on me?"

He shrugged. "I like you, Autumn. You're complex. A puzzle. A crazy mixture that is both fascinating and frustrating. One minute you're a cute kid kicking off your shoes because you're nervous. The next you're a mature, sensible, and very sensuous woman. The two make an intriguing combination. I expect great things from you. It's going to be interesting to see how you pull it off."

Autumn set her glass on the coffee table. She stood and looked down at Lloyd. "In case you don't know it, Lloyd Murphy, you have just pulled the rug out from under my feet. I don't have anywhere left to go. If you know how I'm going to perform this great feat, I wish you'd let me in on it. This cute kid is fresh out of ideas. When I came here—" She paused and turned, startled, when the door burst open as if hit by a high wind. A young woman with long sandy-colored hair rushed into the room. Autumn had seen her face in the newspapers often enough to know it was Lloyd's daughter, Lindy. She had her father's green eyes, but her features were too much like his to be pretty. She had a pleasant face, though, and moved with his vitality.

Lindy, wearing faded jeans and a pullover, swept across the room and wrapped herself in Lloyd's arms. "Hi, Daddy." She turned and looked at Autumn. "Are you one of Daddy's protégées? He likes to make women into all the things he can't make me."

There was no malice in her voice, and Autumn smiled. "No. I'm one of your daddy's salespeople."

"Really? I tried working as a salesgirl. I was going to work my way to the top, but I'm too much like my mother, I suppose. I don't have a head for business."

It was obvious to Autumn that Lindy was the apple of her daddy's eye, and she looked at Lloyd and grinned. "Does she stuff a mean turkey too?"

"No." He gazed at Lindy with an affectionate scowl. "Her specialty is traffic tickets and getting kicked out of colleges."

Lindy poked him in the ribs. "You love it, and you know it." She smiled at Autumn. "To Daddy, a woman without spirit is worthless, as stimulating as a limp dishrag." She motioned toward Lloyd. "It's his fault I'm such a brat. He taught me to live by his own three slogans: If it's a gift, take it. If it can be bought, it isn't worth having. If it's not for sale, find another way to get it. Poor Mother. What a time she must have had with this wicked devil."

"Be quiet," he said in a chuckling voice. He turned with Lindy in the curve of his arm and introduced her to Autumn.

"What a pretty name," Lindy said. "I wish it were mine. Lindy—dull . . . dull." She frowned as if weighted by a heavy burden. "I stopped by to tell you that I'll be late for the party tonight, but I will be there. I had to have my new dress altered and it won't be ready until after six."

"Awww," he said. "Poor Lindy. She doesn't have a thing to wear."

"I have things to wear, but you wouldn't approve. This dress is the first sensible thing I've bought in years. And I did it all for you." She turned in his arms and looked at Autumn. "It's my twenty-first birthday and Daddy is having my godparents and other friends who trotted me on their knee over for cocktails. Obligation parties are the pits." She paused and looked at Autumn closely. "You look like fun. Why don't you come?"

Autumn thought of mingling with their Nob Hill friends and almost laughed. "I can't, Lindy, but thanks."

"Sure you can. Daddy will send a car for you." She kissed Lloyd on the cheek, turned, and left the room as abruptly as she had entered.

"Is she always so energetic?"

"Always. And she even has a good idea now and then. I'll send a car for you at eight."

"I really can't."

"Afraid?"

"Why should I be afraid?"

"Perhaps to see what you could have had. I think you should come. Then go home and compare the evening with me against an evening at the Doghouse. You might want to change your mind."

"And if I refuse?"

"Then it will prove to me that you're afraid to take a chance. I don't admire cowards."

"If I come and then refuse?"

"Then I would have taken my best shot and lost." He took her by the shoulders and gazed intently. "You're a hungry woman, and in a hurry. If I persisted, I could probably ease you into a spotted affair. Unfortunately, I'm a hungry man, too, and possessive. I want you rid of Corbett and all other entanglements, so that your mind is free to mold as I see fit. Come tonight, and then decide."

She nodded. "I'll accept your challenge, Mr. Murphy. I'll be ready at eight."

Lloyd's apartment was no less than Autumn had anticipated. His home was pretentious and reflected his wealth. Even the air felt rich. Jewels winked their brilliance from throats and fluttering fingers. Servants in stiff uniforms moved about inconspicuously on thick carpeting with silver trays of sparkling champagne and luscious-looking canapes. Huge chandeliers cast mellow lights that caught against the varying shades of blond, brunette, and her own auburn hair.

They stood in groups and spoke in titillating voices. The men wore well-cut suits, and the wives, originals. Autumn had pulled her one good dress from the back of the closet, last worn on New Year's Eve. Soft mint-green silk, crisscrossed over her breasts, molded over shapely hips and fell to floor length. Her jewelry, only the two wedding bands on the same finger.

Lloyd had graciously introduced her to everybody, but then he'd drifted away and now she stood with Lindy and a group of women who were discussing the best colleges, the best hairdresser, a new restaurant they had discovered, where they had spent the summer, where they planned to spend the winter, and other ways of spending money in general.

A woman with dark hair swept back in a French roll smiled at Autumn, diamonds twinkling at her ears. "Where did you spend the summer, dear?"

"Here. I did get away and spend a few days on the left bank."

"Paris? How nice."

"No. Turtle Ridge."

"Turtle Ridge? I don't believe I know the place. Is it new?"

"No. It's been around for years. Since the 1800's at least. It's small—hidden—very exclusive. You have to belong before they will let you in."

The woman's eyes sparked with curiosity and she turned to the woman beside her. "Have you heard of this place, Jean?"

"No." Jean looked at Autumn with new interest. "What are the amusements?"

Autumn shrugged. "Anything you want."

"It sounds fascinating."

"It is. There isn't another place like it in the world."

Her interest piqued, Jean moved closer to Autumn. "I must know. Where is this marvelous place, darling?"

"Well," Autumn said hesitantly, "you take a jet to Louisville, then a bus to Edisonville. Then another bus to the fork on Route Six. From there you have to walk."

"Walk? Don't they have limousine service?"

"Oh no! Not in Turtle Ridge. They don't like the fumes." She looked from one to the other. "If you decide to go, just tell them Sue Anne sent you. They'll let you in." She turned, Lindy at her side, and grabbed another glass of champagne from a passing tray. "The rich are so gullible."

Lindy snickered. "What and where is Turtle Ridge?"

"My hometown. I grew up there."

"You're as full of blarney as my father. Speaking of Daddy . . ." She grabbed Autumn and pulled her to where Lloyd stood with a group of men. Lindy tucked her arm in his and urged him off to one side. "My duty is done. Fun and laughter await me." She grinned at Autumn. "My real birthday party is just beginning. Yachting. Want to come?"

Lloyd slipped his arm around Autumn's waist. "I give you permission to go outside and play, but Autumn is staying with me."

Lindy stepped back and saluted. "Farewell. I'm off to the wars."

Autumn watched her leave and wondered why Lindy had latched on to her, a stranger, so furiously. "Your daughter is different."

"The rich are different." He motioned toward the room. "How does it compare with the Doghouse?"

"It doesn't."

"Are you impressed?"

"Lordy yes. I'm here to tell you. Ya'll rich folks shore know how to live good."

He grinned, smeared caviar on black toast, added a drop of lemon, and aimed it at her mouth. She backed away, wrinkling her nose and waving off the toast. "No way. I've gutted catfish. I didn't see anything in there I would eat."

"This isn't catfish."

"Catfish or sturgeon—a fish is a fish."

"Caviar goes with being rich. You have to cultivate a taste for both."

"I'll wait until I'm rich."

Autumn didn't see him gesture, but he popped the caviar in his mouth, then led her to the terrace, where they were met by a servant who draped a fur cape over her bare shoulders. "It's cool tonight" was all he said.

They crossed and stood together near the edge of the terrace. It seemed to Autumn that all of San Francisco lay at her feet, symbolic of what he could offer. Lights of every color spanned earth and sky, capped by a gold-and-yellow moon, a spectacular private exhibit held only for the rich to gaze upon. "The rich are different," she said. "At least the women are. They're like spoiled children."

"They *are* children. There is a lot of old money in there. The women haven't had to work, or be concerned with anything other than parties, where to have their hair done, or whether or not their husbands are too interested in their latest mistresses. I was new money and not accepted until I married my late wife. She was old money."

"Is that why you married her?"

"Mostly."

"Were you faithful to her?"

"Never."

"Was she faithful to you?"

"Always." He slipped his hands inside the cape and pulled her into his arms. "I don't want to think about her, only you."

Here, wrapped in mink, surrounded by the glitter of wealth, she felt far away from the Doghouse and Everett. She gazed at his face in the moonlight, the firm set of his mouth, felt the strength of his hands, hot against the skin on her back, and wanted to be held, kissed by the big Irishman. She swayed forward, her lips reaching for his.

The cape fell from her shoulders, but the heat of his body warmed her. She pressed into him, wanting to feel again that sweet abandonment of self. For a moment her body complied, responding to the night and the man. But perched at the base of her mind, intruding, accusing, were Everett and her own self-imposed promise. Her body went tense in his arms.

"Don't," he whispered. "You're holding back. Let go, Autumn."

She buried her face in the curve of his throat so tightly she could feel the rapid pace of his heartbeat. "I like being in your arms. I like you touching me, but I feel uncomfortable."

"It's the people. Once we're alone, everything will be fine—great."

"No. It's Everett. I feel guilty."

"You will at first, but only at first. Once you're away from him, everything will be different. Stay here tonight. I can make you want me, if you'll let me."

She pushed away from him, shaking her head. "If I stayed tonight, I might never leave."

"That's what I had in mind."

She shook her head again. "I can't. Everett is ill, and he's tender. He's like my child, a sick child."

He groaned with exasperation. "I'm beginning to hate that son of a bitch." He gripped her arms and forced her to look at him. "Get rid of him, Autumn. He can only hold you back." He turned her to face the lighted room from where soft music and the hum of voices drifted to them. "It can all be yours, but only if you get rid of that deadweight you're carrying."

She pulled her glance from the room and looked at Lloyd. "I don't want anything in there. The dress I'm wearing is from a rack at your store, but I'm happy with it. My apartment doesn't have knee-deep carpeting or chandeliers, but I'm content. All I want is money, Mr. Murphy. Cold hard cash."

"Cold hard cash, or diamonds. You can have it all, but first Everett has to go."

"I can't." She offered him her hand. "You challenged me, and I accepted. I hope you'll do the same for me someday."

"Stubborn Irish. I'm not going to give up on you."

She smiled and gray dots of light danced in her eyes.

"God, I hope not. I wasn't lying when I said I liked you holding me. When I'm free, I'd like you to hold me again, but not for just a moment."

"I'll wait," he said. "That bastard has to die before me."

17

Autumn stepped behind the bar and mixed her first legal drink. It was April 28, her day. She tipped her glass to Wally. "Cheers!"

"What are you going to do to celebrate your big one?"

"I am going to sit on a bar stool tonight and drink with the big kids. I'm going to dance, and I'm going to sing with the band." She tipped her glass, glancing about the bar. Without Lloyd's help, enlarging the Doghouse had been impossible, but restoring the empty portion had been very possible. She had called in a contractor to make the necessary repairs, then turned the space over to a real-estate broker for leasing. Painters were called in to give the bar area a new look. She interviewed and hired a band that had a more *in* sound. The atmosphere at the Doghouse had taken on a more exciting tone. A new and younger crowd filled the bar nightly.

Laughter drew Autumn's attention and she glanced to where Lindy sat with some of her friends. She hadn't seen Lloyd since the night on the terrace, not even in passing, but in late October his daughter Lindy began to come to the Doghouse with invitations to go nightclubing, parties, quick trips to Reno or Mexico in her daddy's jet. Autumn thanked her, but refused.

Lindy usually came to the bar with friends, but sometimes she came alone. For the most part, the conversation between them was idle, but now and then Lindy would talk about herself. Through Lindy, Autumn began to form a stronger image of Lloyd. He was a man totally independent of women. He didn't need them in the usual sense, only to provide gratification in one form or another. He had helped many women to fulfill their ambitions, but only because he found it amusing, and always on his terms. He loved Lindy, but Autumn wondered if it was only because she was an extension of himself.

At first she thought Lindy came to the bar because it was quaint and different from her own world, but when her visits became more frequent, Autumn began to look for a different reason. Lindy bursting into Lloyd's office, the party, the sudden invitation, all seemed too coincidental now. Lloyd had said he wouldn't give up. When the party failed, he had turned to Lindy and used her to dangle other treats. Autumn thought his tactics sly but funny. She laughed secretly for days, playing the game with Lindy.

Lindy came less often now, but when she did come, there were always invitations meant to tease and tempt. Autumn gazed at Lindy and suddenly felt tired of their little game. She crossed to her table, chatted for a moment, then separated Lindy from her friends and led her to the back room, which was now an office. When Autumn confronted Lindy with what she suspected, Lindy smiled and nodded. "The party was already planned. Daddy called that morning and asked me to drop by his office and casually ask you to the party. A couple of weeks later, he asked me to come here with another invitation. When you kept refusing, it became a challenge even for me."

"Did you ever ask your father why?"

"I didn't have to. I know Daddy, and I know how his mind works. He wants you, and he's trying to make you discontented with your life here."

"Doesn't it bother you?"

She shrugged. "Daddy and I have an understanding. I don't interfere in his life, and he doesn't interfere in mine. As a father, he's the greatest, but he's a devil of a manipulator, a plotter. He puts as much thought and care into winning over a stubborn woman as he puts into opening a new store. Daddy is a harsh businessman. He runs his private life just as harshly. I would imagine he's very much the same in bed.''

Autumn smiled and silently agreed. She'd been in his arms for only a few moments, but his fingers moved with expertise. He knew how to get the most from a touch, or a whisper, or a mere glance. ''I'm not sure I understand,'' Autumn said. ''What exactly are you trying to tell me?''

''Only that Daddy doesn't give up on something he wants. Don't leave any cracks he can slip through, or you'll find yourself wrapped up nice and tight. Dependent on him.''

''I think you're wrong in this case. I tried to borrow money from your father, and he refused. A loan to me would have given him a kind of hold.''

''You *are* naive, Autumn. Why should Daddy lend you money? It would only make you more comfortable here with your husband. As long as you need money, you'll need him.'' She smiled and turned toward the door. ''Remember. If there are cracks, Daddy will find them. Keep them closed.''

Autumn looked at her oddly. ''Why are you telling me this?''

''I like you. And with Daddy, you'll need all the leverage you can get.''

''I doubt I'll even see him again.''

''Don't count on it.'' Lindy waved her fingers and then she was gone.

Autumn left her office and half-skipped up the stairs to her apartment, feeling lighter, less weighted than she had in months. She had left her job at Murphy's and spent the last week doing nothing but sleeping and reading. Now that her days were free, she planned to go to college full-time. Nights she would work in the bar. She would have the tips, and save the wage paid for a serving girl.

From the kitchen came the sounds of Molly and Everett talking, along with good smells. When she entered the room, Everett smiled and held out a gift wrapped in gold paper. ''Happy birthday, Autumn.''

Autumn laughed, tearing at the paper. ''Ohh,'' she said, hugging a stuffed animal. ''Isn't that cute? Look at this, Aunt Molly. The puppy has crossed eyes.''

Molly smiled and turned from the counter, holding a plate out to Autumn. "Happy birthday."

Autumn looked at the hot dog and shouted, "Hot diggity dog!" She took the plate and sat down at the table, took a big bite, and purred. "Mmmm, that is soooo good. No one in this world makes a doggy like you, Aunt Molly."

Chewing slowly, Autumn stared at the hot dog. She frowned thoughtfully, picking with her finger to try to see what Molly had topped it off with. "What's in here?"

"Lots of good stuff."

Autumn licked her finger, her eyes bright with silent laughter.

Molly stood with hands propped on hips, scrutinizing. "What are you up to now?"

"It was here," she said, shouting. "It was here all the time!"

"What was here?"

"A way to get rich!"

18

Lloyd sat behind his desk, kicked back with a leg propped across a knee, the bowl of his pipe cupped in his large hand. He wore a relaxed, indifferent expression, but his eyes told her he was pleased to see her. Even though she had left the store, Autumn had still felt a strong sense of his presence. Like the sea: you don't have to touch the water to know it's there.

Autumn shifted the brown paper bag she held on her lap. "It was good of you to see me."

He nibbled on the pipe stem. "It's been a while."

She nodded. "Since Lindy's party—six months."

He smiled, as if remembering. "You're looking good."

"Thank you."

"How was your birthday?"

"Great. I got a little drunk, worked behind the bar, sang with the band, and danced a jig with the guys." She drew a deep breath, gathering courage. "Did you know fast food is the third-largest industry in the country, grossing billions a year?"

"Yeah," he said, perplexed. "I think I heard that somewhere." He pointed the stem of his pipe toward the brown paper bag. "What do you have there?"

"Your lunch. And it's going to get cold if we don't get down to business." She rose and placed the bag on his desk, removed a place mat and napkin and spread them in front of him. From the bag she pulled a foil-wrapped package from among hot-water bottles and carefully un-wrapped a foot-long hot dog topped with Molly's special slaw, chili, minced onions, grated cheese, and a hearty heaping of sour cream.

Lloyd stared down at the hot dog. "What is that thing?"

"What does it look like?"

"I'm not sure, but it bears a faint resemblance to a hot dog."

"It's a 'Hotdiggitydog.' "

"Does it bite?"

She glared. "Shut up and eat, unless you're afraid."

Lloyd looked skeptical, but picked up the hot dog and took a big bite, Tasting, chewing, he nodded his head slowly, sour cream ringing his upper lip. "Not bad. For a hot dog, it's not half bad."

"Mr. Murphy, that hot dog is going to make you millions." She picked up a thick envelope and for the next hour shoved facts and figures at him. "We will be featuring the hot dog, but to keep everybody happy, I think we should sell hamburgers, too. One person can manage four stands. Me, in the beginning." She placed a sheet of figures in front of him. "I worked on this with my aunt. It will tell you to the second how long it takes to make and wrap a hot-dog sandwich. A foot-long sandwich can be made in the same length of time as a regular size, and we can charge much more. However, because of small children, I suggest we sell both. Otherwise parents will buy one hot dog and break it in half, costing us the sale of two at the regular price. In the time allowed, three people at minimum wage can operate one stand—in the beginning." She placed more papers in front of him. "I checked all the wholesalers. This will tell you cost per hot dog, hamburger, fries, soft drinks, and ice cream—and profit, which, as you can see, is good. Everything we need can be bought, except the slaw. We'll need to have a small processing plant, and one driver to deliver. I checked an outlet and priced the fixtures we will need for the stands and the plant. The costs are listed."

Autumn paused and watched as he frowned over the papers she had given him; then she began again. "I've been in touch with a real-estate agent. He has found us five locations. One for the processing plant and four for the stands. All are near schools and shopping centers and within a short distance of residential areas. The buildings will need some changes. I had a contractor in to look them over. Here are the costs.'' She added sheets of figures to the growing stack. "I had an attorney look into the legal end. All sites are zoned commercial, so we won't have any problem there. All we have to do is lease the space and apply for the required permits. The attorney I hired doesn't foresee any problems, but I'm sure you will want your own attorney to look into this. I also have a list of insurances we will need, and the costs.'' She gave him a moment, then placed the remaining papers in front of him. "I sold my stock in Murphy's and hired a research team. Their findings are on your desk, along with their projections for the future of Hotdiggitydog.''

Autumn walked to the window and stood quietly, waiting while he looked over the papers. This time Autumn had moved slowly before she came to Lloyd. She had called her accountant, and he had put her in touch with one of his clients who owned a restaurant. Once she learned what was needed, and where to go, the rest fell into place. It had been expensive, but the results were well worth the cost.

She left the window and returned to Lloyd's chair, gazing down at his bent head. "Any questions?''

"Not at the moment.''

"Then the only thing we have to discuss is financing.'' She smiled when he fingered the cleft in his chin, something she had learned he did when stalling for time to think. She crossed her arms over her breasts and moved closer to his chair. "You've boasted that you're not prejudiced against women. Any new business is a risk, but I've put together a good package. One you wouldn't refuse if I were a man. You challenged me, Mr. Murphy, and I accepted. Now I'm challenging you.''

He looked at her with open admiration, and then down at her bare feet. "Nervous?''

"Terrified!''

*   *   *

Lloyd agreed to finance the business in return for forty-five percent of the company. Autumn retained controlling interest, fifty-five percent. She had used the Doghouse for collateral, but with a clause: if the business failed, Lloyd couldn't touch the bar as long as Everett lived.

Autumn watched the buildings being prepared for the opening. Each one had a drive-in window for takeout, plus tables outside with peppermint-striped awnings. For their grand opening they gave out balloons and candy canes. Autumn wanted to be part of the action, but until she had gained some experience, Lloyd refused to allow her to do more than assist. He hired a top-notch manager and turned the business over to him.

The first six months were slow, as predicted, but then it was as if San Francisco had suddenly discovered hot dogs. Lloyd had been more or less indifferent, waiting, watching, but once they began plans to add another four stands, he made good his promise to instruct Autumn in the ways of the business world. He was tireless, a harsh teacher. He took her to business lunches in restaurants or on his yacht that stretched long into the afternoon. Everyone seemed relaxed, chatty, but subtle points were made.

On a moment's notice, he would call her to his office. She sat quietly and listened, sometimes through four or five meetings. Afterward he would question her, insisting on every detail, asking for her impressions. If she guessed wrong, it meant twice as many meetings the following week. "Watch the eyes," he would scold, "watch the eyes, Autumn. And listen. Are they speaking hesitantly, too quickly, evasively, are they smiling too much?"

By the end of a year, Autumn had begun to feel like a piece of clay to be molded into another Lloyd Murphy. Only once had there been any indication that he even remembered she was a woman. He had called her to his office, then chewed the stem of his pipe as he walked, circling her, his eyes narrowing in thought. "The hair," he said. "It's pretty, but it has to go."

Autumn grabbed at her long hair, feeling suddenly exposed. "My hair? Why? What does my hair have to do with selling hot dogs?"

"It makes you look too young. Men, important men, bankers, aren't going to feel comfortable doing business with a woman who looks like a teeny-bopper. We need to put some age on you. The clothes will have to change, too."

"I've been told I have good taste."

"Your taste is fine for a twenty-two-year-old. We're going to try to stretch it to . . . at least twenty-eight." He paused in front of her, his head cocked to one side. "Tailored." With a proprietary gesture, he cupped his hand under a breast, bouncing it.

"Well . . . Lloyd!"

He grinned. "Tailored to show off your figure, but to conceal it at the same time. We want to emphasize your brain, not your bust. I want you ready in two weeks with a complete new wardrobe, and buy the best. It's called: Hold your head high, and spit in their eye." He winked. "Now, get out of here. A hot blond is waiting for me . . . at least I hope she's hot."

She laughed quietly. "You're incorrigible."

"Wrong word. Try 'horny.' " He gazed at Autumn and his face went still. "If a redhead I know wasn't so damned . . . stubborn." He picked up a strand of her hair and held it against his lips. "Your hair always smells so sweet, like flowers."

Autumn didn't think it was planned, but he pulled her into his arms. When he kissed her, she forced the image of Everett into her mind's eye, her body stiff against his.

He pushed her away, his eyes angry and confused. "You won't let yourself feel, will you, Autumn? Why? What is it with Everett that has you so tied in knots?"

"It isn't Everett. It's the paper that says I'm his wife. You and I are business partners, but that's all. There can't be anything more."

He spun and stalked toward the door, then paused, and shook his pipe at her. "You've slapped me in the face for the last time, Autumn. It's going to happen, but when it does, it will come from you. I won't touch your dammed oh-so-precious body again." The door slammed behind him.

*   *   *

Autumn began to take control of the business more and more. When she was twenty-four, Lloyd turned the reins over to her completely. After saturating California, they had moved their operation to Arizona, and then came Nevada, Utah, north to Idaho, Oregon, and Washington. By the time Autumn was twenty-seven, Hotdiggitydog stands were tucked on every corner and in every shopping mall along the west coast and a good part of the Midwest, with future plans to branch out to the east coast.

When Artie returned to San Francisco, Autumn had used every means possible to keep him there. He worked for the corporation as a field manager. Not only did she pay him a top salary, but the job kept him moving, and happy.

It was a closed corporation, with a board of directors. Lloyd was chairman of the board. He had eased Autumn into a seat on the board at Murphy's with the pretense that a feminine point of view was needed: someone young with corporate experience and a feel for fashion and trend. He paid her a huge salary and in exchange, he was assured of her vote. There had been times when Autumn had felt nauseated by the things people did in the name of business. When she felt like running, thoughts of Lonnie and of Douglas Osborne had given her the push to do what had to be done.

For appearances, she had gone along with the wardrobe and bought the finest, but she had worn costume jewelry until one night at a dinner party. Lloyd's eyes had narrowed as he stared at the fake diamonds flashing on her fingers. He was quiet until the drive home. Gripping her hand, he had pulled the rings from her finger and tossed them out the window. When she refused to spend good money on glitter, he called her miserly, but several pieces had been delivered to her office within a week.

After an article in a women's magazine referred to Autumn as the beautiful but eccentric millionairess who lived over a bar, went to her office at times wearing jeans, and drove a beat-up 1970 Ford, he'd relaxed and promoted the image.

Autumn had allowed herself only one extravagance. She had a new house built for Molly in Turtle Ridge beside the river, a Swiss chalet, complete with balconies and over-hanging eaves. The furnishings were all new, and posh, with carpets so thick one sank to the ankles. A stone fireplace sat against one wall. Large windows faced the river. The grounds were landscaped, with a flagstone path leading to the clearing beside the river. The clearing had been left as it was. The fallen log where Lonnie had sat was rotting, but it was there, exactly as when she had first seen him.

Autumn had left the frame house standing and moved Tucker in as caretaker. The chalet was kept ready and waiting for them at all times. Molly needed only to pack her knitting and other treasures she carried from place to place. Her aunt spent the entire time cleaning a house that was already spotless. When Autumn teased her, Molly grinned. "Cleaning a fancy house like this ain't work, it's fun." Nonetheless, when it came time for them to leave, Molly was so tired she climbed into the jet, dropped into her seat, and slept until the plane sat down in San Francisco.

Lloyd was a grandfather now, but the man himself was still the same. A bit of gray that twined among his sandy hair had been added, and a few lines around his eyes. Often his name had been linked with the names of various other women, but he and Autumn had remained the choice topic in his tight circle of friends; gossips had put them in a torrid sex triangle for the last five years.

He had wanted her to meet all the right people, so over the years he had escorted her to a long line of gatherings. She had mingled with new money, old money, bankers, politicians, industrialists, even oil tycooons from Texas. She had sat down with some of the best, and she had sat down with some of the worst.

Autumn had accepted this as all part of the game, or so she thought. After a weekend spent with some of Lloyd's out-of-town business associates, she felt ready to run again. The weather was unexpectedly warm for fall, so they had spent the weekend cruising in Lloyd's yacht. When Sunday finally came, she walked along beside him to his car, grumbling as they climbed into the backseat of the limousine. "In what pile of manure did you find Claymore?"

Lloyd took a seat beside her. "Don't knock him. He

pulls a lot of weight on the east coast. When we move in, he'll be needed.''

She nodded. ''I think I'll pack up Molly and go to Turtle Ridge for a few days. I'm tired of kissing up to morons.''

''You—kiss up? That will be the day. Your mouth is going to be your downfall yet. I heard what you said to Claymore. 'Creepy bastard' isn't going to win you any points, Autumn.''

She looked across at him and glared. ''He pinched me on the tit.''

Lloyd chuckled, but gazed at her at length. ''You've grown into a real beauty over the years, Autumn. Sometimes when you turn your head a certain way, or look at me with a certain expression, I find myself staring. Then I pick your face apart to see why.'' He shrugged. ''It isn't any one thing. It's a look, a quality that makes men want to touch you. Claymore is no exception.''

She looked at him with an annoyed frown. ''Why do men always take the side of another man? The jerk pinched me on the boob. This is my body. It's my right to say who touches me and who does not.''

''I wasn't taking his side, Autumn. I was simply explaining.''

''What you're saying is that he had a right to pinch me. Because I have a certain look, men should feel free to touch me whenever they want. Isn't that what you're saying?''

''No . . . Shit, why don't you stop being so damned female?''

''I am a female, Lloyd, or have you forgotten?''

''Not likely!''

''What is that supposed to mean?''

''It means I'm well aware that you're a woman. You're the one that seems to forget.'' His face wrinkled into a frown. ''When you're in one of these hairy moods, I can't decide if you need to be thrown on the floor and have all hell screwed out of you, or should be turned over a knee and spanked.''

Autumn turned away quickly and gazed out the window at the gathering night, confused by her hostile mood. Was he right? Was she simply being female, or was there an underlying motive? Over the years she had refused to let herself think of Lloyd as anything but her partner and benefactor. But the last few months she had felt edgy, more conscious of him as a man than ever before. Even thoughts of Everett couldn't push the feeling away. Once, late at night, the pull had been so great that she had almost left her bed to go to Murphy. She had gone to her office instead, burying herself in work.

She turned from the window and looked at Lloyd, aware of a waiting kind of tension that had risen between them. Or had it been there from the beginning—subtle, coming to the surface only now that her life had slowed down somewhat.

Lloyd was still frowning, a little puzzled now. "What do you want from me, Autumn? Jealousy? Am I supposed to be jealous because you were pinched on the boob? You've been pinched before. You'll be pinched again. If I were going to be jealous, it would be of Everett. He's the one you go to bed with every night."

She looked at him with a stiff smile. "I'm sorry. I'm being a bitch. What I need is some time in Turtle Ridge to relax—get things back into perspective. I'm going home for a while."

He nodded in quick agreement. "Yeah. Why don't you do that?"

19

ea

After a quiet week at the chalet, Autumn returned to San Francisco and stepped back into her role as president of the Corbett Corporation. For the most part, she ran the business without any help from Lloyd. He was there for any meeting of importance, but the day-to-day running of the company was hers. Lloyd was equally busy, so it wasn't unusual for a week or more to pass without any communication between them. She had decided after her last stay in Turtle Ridge that the best solution would be to avoid Lloyd. She saw him at meetings, but refused any business dinners or lunches whenever possible.

She tried to spend more time at home with Everett, but found it difficult. He had his life and she had hers. If he was already asleep when she came home from a late night, she slept in a separate room in order not to disturb him. Most mornings they had breakfast together, but some days he was already working at his desk when she rose, so Autumn left the apartment without doing more than casting a quick glance into his office.

It wasn't unusual for him to be preoccupied, his thoughts far away in some fictional world, but lately she had caught him gazing at her as if trying to puzzle out a problem that was very real. She remained silent, knowing that when he worked it out in his own mind, he would come to her.

Autumn knew a resolution had been reached when she came home from the office one evening to find Everett waiting for her on the sofa. Molly was out shopping. He motioned for her to sit beside him. "There's something I've been wanting to say to you for a long time."

Autumn tossed her coat and briefcase on a chair and sat down beside him. "What has made you so serious?"

"I wanted to tell you that I'm sorry. I'm sorry I've taken up so much of your life. It wasn't what I had intended."

"That's silly," she said, frowning. "You have nothing to be sorry for. I wasn't forced to marry you."

"No, but things didn't go the way we both expected. I fooled everybody and lived longer than I should have. I've kept you from fulfilling a very important role in every woman's life. If I hadn't married you, you might have found someone else. In the time we've been married, you could have had a child, or even two."

"Is that what this is all about? Children?"

"In part. I've been selfish. Having you has made everything good for me, and everything not so good for you. You need someone young, someone you can build a life with, not an old man who has to baby his heart."

Autumn smiled. "Are you asking me for a divorce?"

"No." He grinned and picked up her hand. "I just wanted to thank you for being my wife, for giving me these years."

"No thanks are needed. You haven't taken anything away from me. When Lonnie died, I gave up all thoughts of a family. I don't want love. I don't want children, either."

"Then you won't marry again—not even when you're free?"

"No—I won't marry again."

He was quiet for a moment, gazing at her intently. "What happens, Autumn, when the dragons are dead? What will you do then? How will you fill your life?"

"Nothing will happen. I'll just go on as I am." She smiled. "Maybe I'll give McDonald's a run for their money."

"Yes," he said, rising from the sofa. "I'll bet you could at that." He touched her cheek with his fingertips. "I think I'll turn in now. I'm tired tonight."

She nodded, rose and went to him. "Don't ever feel that you've taken something away from me. I seldom stop to think, but when I do, I feel richer just from having known you."

He looked at her with a quiet smile. "Good night, Autumn." He turned toward the door, but paused. "If you don't mind, I'd like to sleep alone tonight."

Everett had never made a point of asking to sleep alone, and she thought it odd, but nodded. "Good night, Everett."

Autumn woke the next morning with a sense of dread. The feeling stayed with her, a heaviness in the pit of her stomach, while she showered and dressed for the office, followed as she left the room. She turned for the kitchen, then paused and looked back at Everett's closed door. *Wrong—something was wrong.* As she hurried to his room, the short distance between their doors seemed to grow longer and longer. The drapes were still drawn, the room dim. His form lay still under blankets. She called his name quietly, crossed to the bed, touched his cheek—cold. . . lifeless.

She moaned softly, her thoughts racing. Molly—should she call for Molly . . . . the doctor? No—there was no need for a doctor. Her husband was dead. She picked up the receiver from the nightstand beside the bed and dialed. Her hands were trembling so badly that she dialed the number twice before the call was completed. First there was a servant, then Lloyd. "I need you," she said.

His voice rose in response to the quiver in her own. "What is it, Autumn? What's wrong?"

"It's Everett. I don't know what I'm supposed to do."

"Is he . . . what's wrong with him?"

"He's dead. He's cold—so cold, Lloyd."

"Where are you now?"

"Here. With him."

"Is Molly with you?"

"No. I haven't told her yet."

"Leave the room. Go to Molly. I'll be there shortly."

Autumn hung up the phone, but she couldn't leave Everett alone. She sat on the edge of the bed beside his still body, this gentle man who had been her husband for eight years. Somehow, Everett had known. Last night had been his way of saying good-bye. He hadn't wanted her to wake and find him dead beside her, so he had asked to sleep alone.

His hair was always so neat, but now it was tousled. She smoothed the strands into place, took his cold hand, and held it against the warmth of her own. In the dim light, she sat beside Everett, holding his hand and waiting for Lloyd to arrive.

The funeral had been small: just Molly, Lloyd, Artie, a few friends, and employees from the Doghouse. Autumn had removed her wedding ring, burying it in the wreath of flowers that covered the casket, then said a silent good-bye to the gentle man with the sad brown eyes.

She removed her hat and combed slender fingers through short auburn hair, glancing at Lloyd as the limousine pulled away from the cemetery. "I want you to call a board meeting for tomorrow afternoon."

Lloyd shook his head. "That won't be necessary. Everett's death won't have any effect on the corporation."

"This has nothing to do with Everett. I'm mothballing the east-coast project for a few months."

He arched a brow in startled surprise. "You're what?"

"I'm pulling back."

"No, you're not. I won't let you."

She smiled. "I outrank you, darling. Your forty-five percent doesn't buy you that big a vote. Chairman or no, if I want to stop the project, I can."

His body tensed beside her. He glanced across at Molly, and then to Autumn. "We've put one hell of a lot of time and money into this for you to just abandon it on a whim."

"It's not a whim, and I'm not abandoning it. I'm only delaying it for a while. I'll have other announcements to make tomorrow at the meeting."

"What announcements?"

"Tomorrow, Lloyd."

He looked at her, scowling angrily. "I don't like surprises, Autumn. I want to know what's in that head of yours before I walk into a meeting."

Autumn spoke slowly, forcing patience into her voice. "I have to get my thoughts in order. You'll learn tomorrow along with the others. I promise. It won't hurt the company. We'll pick up the coast in a few months. In a way, it's for the best. The economy is cockeyed right now. I don't want to take a chance on losing everything I've worked for. You can afford to ride out a depression, but I can't.''

"I wouldn't let you go under. I think you know that."

She glanced into his eyes and laughed quietly. "No, I don't suppose you would, not when your forty-five percent would be going under too."

He shook his head, grinning. "You're a hard woman, Autumn."

The tension eased and they talked idly until the Doghouse came into view. She gathered her hat and purse as the car pulled into the basement parking area. Lloyd hated her living over the Doghouse, almost as much as he hated the old car she drove to some of the fanciest places in San Francisco.

She glanced at Lloyd with jest in her eyes. "If you will go along with me tomorrow, I'll get rid of the old Ford." She rested a hand on his arm. "Think about it. The fender is dented, the paint is scratched and faded, all but gone, and the carpet is shot. It's a bad reflection on you as my partner. Can you imagine how it must look when I—"

"Enough, enough," he interjected, giving her a push toward the door. "I'll call the meeting, but I won't make any promises beyond that."

Autumn followed Molly from the car, then stood for a moment watching as the big black limousine eased from the parking area. Her purse clutched under her arm, she turned and mounted the stairs with Molly to the office— Wally's office now.

The bar was closed and she was met with a harsh silence that seemed to ring against her ears. She hurried to the apartment upstairs, only to be faced with rooms that seemed to shout of Everett's absence. She turned to Molly then, wanting to hear a voice, even if it were only her own. "You've been awfully quiet. You usually talk up a storm to Lloyd, but I don't think I heard you say a word during the entire ride home. Is something wrong?''

''Yeah, there's something wrong. Your man is dead, but all you could talk about was business and making more money. I don't reckon I like what's become of you the last few years.''

''I don't reckon I like it either, but it's the way of things, Aunt Molly.''

''Don't you feel, Autumn? Can't you feel something for that man you lived with for years? Can't you allow him even one tear?''

Autumn turned away, swallowing against the lump that had been stuck in her throat for three long days. Her face felt stiff, and she rubbed her hands against her cheeks. ''I feel,'' she whispered. ''I feel for that kind man until I ache with it, but I can't let it out. If I did, I'd break.'' She turned and faced her aunt. ''You cry for Everett. If you can, cry a little for me too.''

Molly looked at her with worried eyes. ''I'll cry for your man, and I'll cry for that pretty young girl from Turtle Ridge. Money didn't matter to her. All she wanted was a home of her own, and children to raise.''

Autumn's smile was mirthless. ''She's gone, Aunt Molly, but maybe someday she'll be back. Maybe then she can sit down and cry. She'll cry for Lonnie, and her baby, and she'll cry for Everett. But for now, she's got no time for tears.''

20

Artie had loved his twin brother and Autumn felt he had a right to know the truth about Lonnie's death. She had been reluctant to tell him until a time when she could be in a position to control his impulsive nature. He could go straight to Douglas Osborne, and that would be disastrous. Artie had mellowed some, but he was still headstrong, happiest when living on the edge of excitement. He worked at mundane jobs, but during the years she had known him he had become bored with skin diving, mountain climbing, demolition racing, and parachuting. He didn't seem to need anyone. If he had ever felt anything deeper for a woman than physical attraction, he'd never mentioed it to her. Over the years, they had come to accept and understand the deep affection they felt for one another.

Autumn gazed across her desk and watched Artie's face as he struggled to comprehend all she had told him. "It was murder, Artie. Pure and simple. There was a foreman who died, but he talked to Lonnie first. A section of the blower system broke down. The foreman called Osborne. He wanted to pull his crew, but Douglas refused. When the methane level rose, he made another call to Osborne and asked again to pull his men. Osborne still refused. He said he'd been in touch with Maintenance and they would have the system repaired shortly. The foreman returned to his section intending to pull his crew anyhow, but it was too late. He was caught in the explosion."

Artie looked confused. "What does this have to do with Lonnie?"

"Lonnie was going to take what he knew to the Federal Mine Safety and Health Administration, but first he wanted to try to find somebody that might know about the calls. He had started asking questions around town. He must have asked the right question of the wrong person. A few hours later his car went over the embankment." She frowned and rubbed her fingertips against her forehead. "There wasn't any reason for Lonnie to go to the High Banks. It's a stretch of curvy road with a deep ravine running along the edge. It's a wooded area where the kids go to park and neck. Lonnie wouldn't have gone there on his own."

Artie's face had gone pale as she spoke. He rose and stood over her. "Why the hell didn't you tell me before?"

"I wanted to wait until the time was right. I have money now, and I'm going back. I'll need your help."

"You've got it. How do we do it?"

"I don't know. I didn't know how I was going to make a million dollars then, but I did." Her voice lowered in thought. "Several years ago I hired a private investigator and sent him back to Edisonville. I wanted to get the names of all the maintenance men who worked at the mine. There were four. Three relocated, but one stayed in Edisonville and opened a fairly good-sized machine shop. This told me one thing. He had to be the man Osborne called that night. He opened the shop with payoff money. At that time, I didn't have enough money even to think about going back, so I waited." She made a hopeless gesture with her hands. "The man died a few years ago. Now we can't learn anything from him."

She motioned him back to the chair. "The years have taught me something you're going to have to learn, Artie: patience. We'll have to move very slowly, step by step. There can't be any racing in and confronting the man. What we do will have to be subtle. I don't want to draw any attention to either of us. It began at the mine. I think that's a good place to start. I want to know why the mine was closed when there were still two years of work left. And I want experts to look at the blower system. To do this, I'll have to gain control of the Black Jewel. It will have to be done through the other Osborne brothers, though. Douglas has too much money. I can't fight him on that level."

"How do you plan to work through the brothers?"

"Any way I can. I've tried, but I haven't learned anything that can be used against them. I'll have to get to know Douglas and find out some family secrets." Her eyes narrowed and she spoke the words firmly. "But in my own time, and in my own way."

Artie smiled a little at her hidden meaning. "How?"

"From what I understand, he really likes the ladies. I think I qualify."

"Won't you be recognized?"

"It's doubtful. I was only there for a short time and Lonnie and I were so wrapped up in each other that we hadn't bothered to make any friends. There's Ella, but she's on our side. I met the son, Brian, but he won't be a problem. He and his father had a fight and according to Ella, haven't been in touch for years. Brian is out of the country."

"What about my face? It's Lonnie's."

She shrugged. "Grow a beard. It's been ten years. They wouldn't remember Lonnie's face clearly, if at all. He was just another miner with coal dust under his fingernails. It would be a good idea to change your name, though. I plan to. If I'm known at all, it would be as Sue Anne Norton. I'm known here to most as Sue Anne Corbett. I'm going back as Autumn McAvan."

He nodded. "You've put a lot of planning into this."

"I've thought of little else." She waved her hand in gesture about the office. "The Doghouse . . . this—it was all just a way to send me back."

Artie rose from the chair again, his eyes bright with excitement. "When do we start?"

"As soon as possible. I don't want Douglas to die before I can get to him." She paused in thought. "I'll go first and find some excuse to settle there. When the time is right, I'll send for you." She leaned back in her chair and stretched. "That's about all I can tell you for now. Finish whatever it is you're doing, and then take a vacation and have some fun. But keep in touch."

"Sounds good, little sister."

She watched him leave and wondered if she would be able to control him. Edisonville wasn't a stimulating town. Artie might decide to create a little excitement of his own, drawing attention to himself, and then to her. Autumn knew she would have to wait until it was absolutely necessary before calling him in.

She pressed her intercom. "Grace."

"Yes, Mrs. Corbett."

"I'm going to grab a few minutes on the sofa. Don't let me sleep too long. I want to be wide-awake for the board meeting at two."

The board had six members other than herself, all chosen by Lloyd. There was Murphy himself, plus an investment counselor, a banker, an attorney, a real-estate broker, and the owner of another fast-food chain. All were men, which was fine with Autumn. Her officers were all men, too, and chosen by her. She had made a point of surrounding herself with men, but retained her woman's instincts. She knew when to give, to be soft, and when to be rigid and unyielding. And she knew when to take advantage of her femininity.

Autumn glanced at Lloyd as he opened the meeting. Now was the time for her to be soft but *un*yielding. She waited until Lloyd had finished speaking, then, choosing her words carefully, looked around the table at the six men, two dark, two fair, one black, and one bald. She spoke softly but with strength in her voice. "In the past I have gone along with the decisions of this board, even when I disagreed. Consequently, I will ask you to go along with me now."

She paused and glanced at each member. "I am well aware of the time and money that have gone into organizing the east coast. For several reasons, I am asking you to delay the project."

No one spoke, but there were the sounds of shifting in chairs, the shuffling of feet. She carried on in the same tone. "Not only am I concerned about the economy, but I have to be out of town for an undetermined length of time on personal business. This is something I've been planning for years. It's very important to me. I don't feel I can go on with our plans until it's taken care of."

She glanced at Lloyd and tried to reassure him with her eyes. "I'll be in touch with Mr. Murphy. He'll be able to reach me at any time. And I'll return for board meetings or anything else that requires my attention. You all know and respect Edward Goodman as a businessman. I have already spoken to him. He has agreed to step in and take over for me. I have good officers under me. I'm sure this company can function quite nicely without its president until I return." She looked about the table. "Any comments?"

Glenn, the real-estate agent, frowned. "We've selected several sites. If we don't go ahead, we could lose our options."

She smiled and shook a finger at him. "You haven't done your homework, Glenn. The options are good for two more years." She gazed at the shiny head of the bald man for a moment. "I'm aware of the possible losses, and that the project could continue without me. This is my company. My child. I want to be here to guide it along. The wait could be a good thing. A few months will give us some idea of what the economy is going to do."

Glenn spoke again. "I don't think we have to concern ourselves about the economy. We sell a cheap product, and women hate to cook. They hate to clean-up afterward. They'll settle for a hot dog, if they can't afford a steak."

Chuckles around the table.

Lloyd wasn't chuckling. He spoke in a dry tone. "It would seem Mrs. Corbett has made her decision. I know the lady well. Any further discussion on this matter would be a waste of time. For the record, I suggest we give the lady our affirmative vote."

Autumn smiled. "Thank you, Mr. Chairman." Even though he wore a faint smile, the color was rising in his face. While she talked, he had lit up his pipe, drawing deep, angry puffs. The big Irishman was on the verge of losing his cool. Autumn waited until the rest of the men had left the room, and then pretended to rise from the chair as if all was settled.

He grasped her arm. "What the hell is going on?"

"You heard. I have to be out of town for a few months."

"You don't have any personal business that could hold you out of town—not for months." He shook the pipe stem under her nose. "You're forgetting something, Autumn. I know everything about you, personal and otherwise."

Autumn stared at the pipe, remembering the many times he had used it to point at her, to gesture, to scold her as if she were a child of ten. "No more!" she shouted, grabbing the pipe from his hand. "No more! For seven years you have shaken this fucking thing in my face. You won't do it again." She gripped the pipe with both hands, trying to snap it in half. When it wouldn't break, she banged it against the edge of the table. Again and again she banged, but the pipe refused to break. Autumn glared. "What's this fucker made of—steel?" She heaved it against the far wall.

Lloyd stood as if mesmerized. Coming out of his trance, he stamped his foot against the ashes that smoldered on the carpet. "You crazy . . . What the hell are you trying to do, set the place on fire?"

Autumn had burned the palm of her hand; she stood rubbing the sting against her leg. "You think you know so much about me. You don't know even a tenth."

"I know I've put a lot of time into you and your damned hot dog. I'm not letting you walk away now."

"It's your hot dog too, or don't you care?"

"Yeah, I care. Now." He looked at her with derision. "When you came to me, I didn't give a rat's ass about your wiener. I didn't expect it to go any further than four stands, but I invested—time and money."

Autumn gazed at him narrowly, understanding now. Lloyd had been Lloyd: If it can't be bought, find another way to get it. When she had left the store, he had felt her slipping away. He had invested because it brought her back under his control. She had walked right smack into the crack Lindy had warned her against.

The crack, however, was still open. When the business became successful, it had won her an even greater independence. Autumn thought it was funny, and laughed out loud at the realization. "Backfired, didn't it?"

The anger left his face and he grinned too. "No. I can't say I'm sorry. Over the last seven years I've had more fun with you and your damned hot dog than I've had in my entire life.''

"You make it sound as if it's all over. I'm only going away for a while.'' She rested a hand on his arm. "You know how much I love this business. If what I have to do wasn't so important, I wouldn't be going.''

He nodded and eased her into a chair, sitting beside her. "It would help if you told me why. What is it that's pulling you away, Autumn? Will you tell me?''

She nodded, and then slowly began. She told him about Lonnie's death and about Douglas Osborne. "The shock put me in the hospital for two weeks. It killed my unborn baby. I was so desperate afterward that I sold my ass in a dirty whorehouse for two hundred dollars, to the son of the man responsible.'' Her hand was still stinging and she rubbed at the palm with her fingers. "What would you do to a man who did this to Lindy—cost you your grandson? Would you simply forget about him?''

His face showed many things, one of which was a new understanding of Autumn. "I'd pin that bastard's cock to the wall.''

"Exactly. That's what I intend to do.'' She looked down at the red spot on her hand, avoiding his eyes. "About the whorehouse—it was only the once.'' She looked at him now. "How do you feel about that?''

Lloyd grinned a little. "Envious. What I offered a bundle for, he got for two hundred.''

"Not quite. I rolled him for three thousand dollars. I felt the old fucker owed me, not to mention his son. Brian's being out of the country will make it easier for me. On the other hand, I would love the chance to shove that night down his rich little throat.''

"Who knows about this?''

"Only you, a friend in Edisonville, and Artie. He's going back with me.''

He nodded a smile. "Good.''

The relief on his face was so great that Autumn thought of her earlier outburst and felt guilty. "I'm sorry about the fight. It was silly of me.''

"My pipe,'' he said, and rose quickly. He crossed the room and picked up the pipe, mumbling, "The bowl is cracked.'' He returned to Autumn, frowning, still mumbling. "Damn, this was my favorite pipe, too.''

"I'll buy you another. One that's not all gooky.''

"You don't know anything about pipes, do you?''

"No.''

He smiled down at her. "Like women, they need a little seasoning before they're any good.'' He picked up her hand, looked at the burn, then touched his lips against her palm. His eyes were still now, gazing into hers.

Until that moment, Autumn hadn't realized the full significance of the last few days. Now she was free, really free. The waiting was over.

She pulled her hand from his and touched the cleft in his chin with a fingertip. One thing was certain. When Lloyd made a strong statement, he stood behind it. Autumn knew it would have to be she who went to him. He wouldn't ask her again.

After deciding to leave for Turtle Ridge in two weeks, Autumn crammed the hours with meetings that overlapped. She wanted things to go smoothly while she was away. She met with her banker and arranged for large sums of money to be deposited in their branch in Indiana under the name of Sue Anne Corbett. She spent the evenings shopping for a new wardrobe that would fit her new identity and station in life. And she ordered a car under the name of Autumn McAvan to be delivered to Turtle Ridge. Artie and some of his less-than-respectable friends arranged for the other necessary identification, driver's license, and credit cards, all under the name of Autumn McAvan. She wouldn't dare use them, but they would pass an untrained eye.

She waited until the day before they were to leave, and then told her aunt, saying only that Molly would be staying in Turtle Ridge while Autumn took care of some business in Edisonville.

Molly, who was always happy to go home, began gathering her knitting. Autumn went into the bedroom and packed an overnight bag. When Molly asked where she was off to, Autumn only smiled. "A little R-and-R. I'll see you tomorrow.''

* * *

Lloyd's apartment door was opened by a sober-faced butler named Arnold, who looked through Autumn rather than at her. He spoke in a haughty tone. "Mr. Murphy isn't here, Mrs. Corbett."

"I know Mr. Murphy isn't here, Arnold. I plan to wait for him."

"Is Mr. Murphy expecting you?"

"No, Mr. Murphy isn't expecting me." Swinging her overnight bag, Autumn ducked through the doorway. She had been in and out of Lloyd's apartment for years now, but Arnold still looked at her as if it were the first time. She paused and looked back at him, her brown eyes teasing. "Put a bottle of champagne on ice and have a cold supper prepared. Then scat. Mr. Murphy and I are going to have an orgy."

Arnold arched his chest and stiffened his back. "I can't do that, Mrs. Corbett."

"Okay. Stay and watch."

"Mrs. Corbett!"

She smiled. "Chill a bottle of champagne—make that two—and have supper waiting for when Mr. Murphy comes home. I'll wait for him in the bedroom."

She watched as he scurried off toward the rear of the apartment, his back ramrod straight. Lloyd's bedroom was larger than her entire apartment, and ultra-grand, but she wasn't impressed by his wealth anymore. His bed was low to the floor and covered in a royal-blue spread that lay in folds over white carpeting. One wall was covered with sliders that led to the same terrace where they had kissed on the night of the party.

Carrying her overnight bag to the bathroom, she turned on the water, then dropped her clothes and slid into the round Jacuzzi. She let her mind drift, but there amidst the foamy water she pulled the pieces together. Autumn now knew how to settle in Edisonville and how to make contact with Douglas Osborne.

Her skin tingling, she left the tub and pulled a tissue-thin black negligee from her bag. She slipped it over her head, then dabbed perfume on lightly. According to Lloyd, men hated heavy perfume—which meant Lloyd Murphy hated heavy perfume. After brushing her short curls, she added a touch of blush to her cheeks, but only a touch.

Taking a novel from her bag, she crossed to the bedroom and sat on a chaise longue to wait. Arnold checked in a couple of times to ask her about dinner and to tell her the wine was chilling. Otherwise the afternoon was quiet and restful. By the time Lloyd arrived, Arnold had brought the champagne and it was sitting near her in a basket.

Lloyd entered the room without surprise. But his eyes deepened in color when she rose from the longue, her body a shadowy form of soft lines beneath the folds of chiffon. He crossed the room and took her hand. "Lady, you are an unpredictable delight."

Autumn eased the jacket from his shoulders and removed his tie. "The champagne is chilled, and dinner is waiting. Or I can offer you a redhead. She isn't chilled, and she's been waiting a long time."

Lloyd didn't hesitate. He pulled her into his arms, and his lips sought hers. She had come to him aggressively, but the moment his lips touched her, the big Irishman dominated her mind and her limbs. She felt weak, only half-aware as he led her toward the bed, her arms a tight coil about him as he dropped clothes and kicked off shoes.

He made love to her slowly, skillfully, touching her in all her most sensitive places, some that had never been touched by any man. Large hands that were meant to crush, grasped her gently, and long, thick fingers left her body trembling.

His mouth played games with her lips, traced patterns over her bare skin until her senses screamed inside with wanting. She murmured softly, groping as she circled his erection with her hand, directing him to her opening. She arched to receive him, and then moved her body in pace with his, slow and then fast, and then faster.

She could feel her body begging to be released after its long sleep, but among the haze a tiny voice whispered, "It isn't happening." Autumn had thought it was because of Everett, but it was her. She grasped at Lloyd frantically, urging him on until his body hammered into hers. He strained over her, his face bathed in sweat, using his penis as an instrument to coax her to a climax. But it didn't happen. Frigid, frigid, she screamed inside, but moaned aloud.

Lloyd understood her whimpers for passion and drove into her, allowing his own fervor to be released. She felt the warmth of his strong Irish juices and smiled inside. Finally she had put one over on the big Irishman.

Autumn woke tangled in sheets with a hard lump pressing against her hip. She wiggled and pulled a champagne bottle from beneath her. There were other bottles scattered about the room. Bits of their supper were still on the table.

She yawned and stretched lazily, glancing at Lloyd. In the books she had read, the woman woke and gazed at the man beside her and mused how boyish and innocent he appeared while in sleep. Lloyd didn't look boyish and innocent. He looked like what he was: a big, sexy Irishman sleeping off an orgy.

Autumn wondered about herself. Was she frigid? She understood the definition to mean coldness, without sexual desire. Over the years, she had denied her own feelings, but now she freely admitted that she had never stopped wanting to make love with Lloyd since the night on the terrace. Many times she had found herself watching him during board meetings, wanting him until she had had to give her mind a nudge to concentrate on the people around her. Her body had been alive with wanting last night, but something kept the key from turning.

Lightly she touched the thick mat of sandy hair on his chest, drew a fingertip around a nipple. He didn't realize it, but she knew he wanted her only because she had been unattainable. Now that she was free, his interest would wane, which was good. She didn't want to be loved, only wanted.

She felt a strong attachment for the man: gratitude, physical attraction, and just plain need. Autumn didn't want to, but had to admit that she was very dependent on Lloyd. She looked to him for strength and guidance. He couldn't hurt her, though, and she couldn't hurt him. After her, Autumn knew there would be another young, pretty protégée.

Autumn had to go to the bathroom and tried to ease

away from Lloyd, but his eyes flew open and she was caught in a grasp of powerful arms and robust laughter. He pulled her half on top of him, gazing at her with a sleepy-looking smile. "Do you know how long I've waited to hold you without your eyes crossing with guilt?"

She grinned playfully. "You can take the girl out of Turtle Ridge, but you can't take Turtle Ridge out of the girl."

He gathered her close, burying his face in her hair. "I can't let you leave and go head-hunting for Douglas Osborne—not now."

She pulled away, folding her arms over his chest. "Nothing will change. We're both so busy that we don't have a lot of time to be together anyhow. We'll see each other almost as often as we did before. Edisonville isn't on the moon. You can fly down and we'll hide out at the chalet. Even with all your loot, you'll have to admit it's a beautiful place. I'll be flying back, and if you get the urge, you can send the plane for me." She paused and smiled. "There's an airstrip in Edisonville, but I don't think you'll be using it. It belongs to Douglas Osborne. About five years ago he had it put in and bought a Cessna. Evidently the Cessna was too slow, because he had the strip enlarged and bought a small Lear, complete with private pilot. He named the plane the *Donkey Cart*."

"*Donkey Cart?* Why?"

"I don't know."

His eyes narrowed in thought. "I've been doing some checking up on Douglas Osborne. He's not the kind of man you should be fucking around with."

"I'm not planning to fuck him."

He laughed and tousled her hair. "You know what I mean. You be careful how you handle him. I don't want you hurt." He swept auburn hair back from her face, touched her lips with a fingertip. "About last night . . ."

"No, no," she said, her eyes teasing. "I'm the one that's supposed to ask that."

"What are you supposed to ask?"

"I'm supposed to ask if last night was as beautiful for you as it was for me. I'm also supposed to ask if you still respect me."

"Yes, and yes." He took her face between his hands and forced her to look at him. "About last night," he said again. "Was it an obligation fuck?"

"What do you think?"

His face spread into an enormous smile. "If it was, you gave me the best present I've ever had. You throw yourself into sex as wholeheartedly as you do your damned hot dogs. I love that in a woman."

"You would." She moved away from him, laughing, brushing a teasing nipple against his nose as she got up. He came after her with laughter, cupped a breast with his large hand, and brought his lips over the swell to a pink nipple. She frowned when her body responded to his mouth.

Lifting his head away, she bent and gave him a smacking kiss on the mouth. "I have to go pee, and we stink. Let's take a shower. Then you can feed me breakfast, and then we can orgy some more." Autumn bounced off the bed and was almost to the bathroom when he called out to her. She turned and stood with legs crossed.

Lloyd lay with his arms folded beneath his head, his gaze direct. When he spoke, his voice was cold, demanding. "You go, and you do your head-hunting. But don't you ever forget who you belong to."

III

The Return

21

Autumn stood beside the river, surrounded by the ghosts of a young girl and a dark-haired man. Both were so young, so full of plans for the future, making love, laughing foolishly, sure there would be a million tomorrows for them. Death was a distant shadow, something that happened only to the old, to the unfortunate someone else. They were going to have it all. They did have it all, until the night her world suddenly stopped turning.

She glanced at the fallen log and then turned and strode along the flagstone path leading to the Swiss chalet that was Autumn's gift to her Aunt Molly. Time had dulled the pain, but the memories were keen, edged by the ugliness in which Lonnie had been taken, his strong, virile body sent over an embankment, twisted and torn. Officers looking at her with pity. "His neck was broken. If it's any consolation, he didn't suffer." Autumn knew that every road comes to the same end, but Lonnie's road had come to an end far too quickly, chosen by a man who sat comfortably in a big white house.

She entered the chalet and smiled at Molly, who stood loading the dishwasher. Autumn had spent a lazy week there, but now her bags were packed and loaded in the car, along with a few of her own treasures. On impulse, she had brought the peanut-butter jar with her, along with Lonnie's wedding ring and his pearl-handled pistol.

She picked up her purse from the counter. "I'll give you

a call as soon as I know where I'll be staying. Tucker is here, and he'll be looking in on you.''

Concern wrinkled Molly's forehead. "I've got a funny feeling about you traipsing off to Edisonville—kind of spooky. I get a tingling along my spine every time I think about it.''

"I think you've picked up a case of the hill superstitions. You used to laugh at such nonsense.''

"Yeah," Molly said, and grinned. "I reckon I did." She frowned. "You be careful just the same.''

"I always am." She leaned forward and kissed Molly on the cheek. "I love you, old lady. Love you with all my heart.''

"I'll take the love, but I ain't no old lady, and I don't need no moonshiner looking after me. Lord, that's like the blind leading the blind.''

Autumn had to agree with Molly. Tucker was older than her aunt, and did a lot of nipping at the jug, but the house was isolated and she wanted to know someone would check up on Molly. "Humor me," Autumn said, and hurried away from the house before her intuitive aunt could press her further. Autumn had to guard her words, as well as the tone of her voice, lest Molly learn too much; she wanted her aunt's life to be free of worry.

She slid behind the wheel of a four-year-old very ugly blue Honda, started the engine, and pulled away from the house. The day was bright and sunny, a treat after the fog and cooler weather of San Francisco. She rolled the window down and felt the warm breeze against her cheeks. Spring was making the countryside come alive. The tall trees were budding, and dotted the hills with splashes of color. It would be so easy to drift into the indolence that surrounded Turtle Ridge, if she allowed herself.

Autumn closed her mind to the quiet hills and went over the story she had fabricated for herself—based on half-lies, half-truths. The car was registered under the name of Autumn McAvan, with California plates. She would open an account in Edisonville under the same name and deposit thirty thousand, a sum to fit her story. Cliff, Ella's husband, had agreed to rig her car for a breakdown, her reason for being stuck in Edisonville. While her car was being repaired, she would look for a vacant piece of property owned by Douglas Osborne, an excuse to bring them together. The rest would take care of itself.

She checked into the town's new Holiday Inn, staying in her room only long enough to drop off her luggage. Out-of-town calls that went through the switchboard could be traced, so she found a phone booth and called Molly to let her know where she would be staying, picked up a newspaper, and drove to Ella's as planned.

The house was neat and modest, with climbing rosebushes along the porch rails. Ella, who still ran the diner, had taken the afternoon off. She stood in the doorway, her face spread in a welcoming smile. Her trim figure had rounded and there was silver showing amid her brown hair. Billy Ray, Ella's five-year-old, stood at her side, grinning up at Autumn. Christmas and other gatherings at the chalet had become a habit, so she had known the boy since his birth, and adored him. She whipped a package out from behind her back. "Guess what I have?"

His green eyes, so like Ella's, widened. "Is it for me?"

"Is your name Billy Ray?"

He nodded rapidly, his brown curly locks dancing around his ears.

"Then I bet it's for you, but first I get a big hug and a juicy kiss." She pulled him into her arms and breathed in deeply of his sweet innocence. Much too quickly, he became impatient and wiggled free. He raced into the living room with his package, pulling excitedly at the wrappings.

Ella directed Autumn toward a kitchen that smelled of freshly baked cookies. "Well," Ella said, "you did it. You're back. I hope you know what you're going up against."

"I have a fair idea. I'm nervous, and I'm scared, but I'm here, and I'm staying."

"Cliff left on a run this morning. He'll be gone for two days. When he gets back, he'll screw up the car for you." She pulled two cups from a rack on the wall. "Coffee?"

Autumn nodded and sat down at the table, picked a cookie from the stack, and nibbled. "How much have you told Cliff?"

"Everything."

"Does he believe me?"

"He thinks it's likely."

Aware of the quiet, Autumn glanced around the room. "Where are Cliff's boys? I have presents for them in the car, too."

"They're in school." Ella set the coffee cups on the table and took a chair across from Autumn. "When this is over, you should find a good man and have a bunch of kids of your own."

Autumn shook her head. "Children need a mummy and a daddy to love them and each other. I can't give that to a child."

"Bull. I've watched you with my kids. You love them to pieces. You have a lot to give, Autumn. Any kid would be lucky to have you for a ma."

"I could love a child very much, but marriage without love is no good. Children know when they're loved and they know when their parents love each other. It would be cheating and selfish of me to have a child when I know this about myself."

"I don't mean to speak against the dead, but Everett was older, and sickly. Don't you think it could be different with someone else?"

"No," she said bluntly.

"I thought maybe Lloyd?"

"Lloyd's wonderful. If I could love anyone, it would be him. He's exciting, thoughtful. He puts a lot into pleasing a woman. I love being with him, but I'm not in love with him."

"Maybe you're afraid, Autumn. Or maybe you're refusing to see what's there. Could you be so hung-up on getting Douglas Osborne that it's blinded you to everything else, even love?"

Autumn shrugged. "I don't know."

"What about Lloyd? Is he in love with you?"

Autumn hesitated and recalled Lloyd's proprietary remark, the chill in his eyes, the warning in his voice: "Don't you ever forget who you belong to." It had bothered her then, and it bothered her now. She had kept pushing the words to the back of her mind, only to take them out to reexamine them, telling herself it was just a meaningless remark. A temporary feeling of possessiveness. She had felt the same way, until she had reasoned it out. Sex brought her closer to a man. Couldn't a man like Lloyd also be possessive without love? They had spoken over the phone several times since, but there was nothing to indicate that he had attached any significance to their lovemaking. Probably he had already forgotten that he had made the remark.

Autumn smiled to herself. Lloyd Murphy was too smart to fall in love, especially with her. He wanted a woman that stuffed a mean turkey. If he grew bored, he would find excitement elsewhere. "No," she said. "I'm sure he isn't."

"It took you long enough to answer."

"I had to give it some thought."

Ella looked at her narrowly. "What about when all this is over? What will you do then? You're going to be damned lonely."

"No, I don't think so. When this is over, I'm going back to build my company into the biggest fast-food chain in the country. That ought to keep me busy." She took a sip of coffee, then opened the paper to the ad section. "How hard is it going to be to find a furnished apartment? I'd like to get out of that tiny hotel room as soon as possible. I need a private phone line too."

"I don't know," Ella said. "Let's have a look at the paper."

Autumn slipped through the night, angry that she had to hide behind darkness to visit Lonnie's grave. Since she'd left town, she had been to the cemetery only once, and then her hair had been covered by a scarf and she had worn dark glasses. Now she was in Edisonville to stay. If she were seen near Lonnie's grave and remembered, it could create a lot of problems.

The Kentucky moon spilled a bright pathway as she walked between the headstones to the tall oak that sheltered Lonnie's sleeping place. She knelt beside the grave and brushed her fingers over the engraving on the headstone. "I'm tired, Lonnie, and I want this to be over. I stand tall, and I talk big, but I'm so confused. The truth is in this town, but how can I find it? He's on one side of the fence, and I'm on the other. Should I climb over the wall, or should I wait until I find the gate? When I find the gate, will it open? So many questions, my darling. Where can I go for the answers?''

22

The place Autumn rented was small, a one-bedroom apartment behind a once grand old house, the chauffeur's quarters over the garage. It was adequate, furnished in Danish modern, and private. The apartment was closed off from the main house by a maze of unkept hedge. Since Autumn was supposed to be a stranger in town, she had to avoid Ella and her family until she had lived there a reasonable length of time. She went to the diner to eat. If the place was empty, she and Ella had a few drinks and talked.

By the end of two weeks, Autumn had shaped the apartment into a comfortable nest. Her car had been in and out of the garage, a breakdown and repair on record, should it be checked, and money had been deposited in the bank under the name of Autumn McAvan. She was now a resident of Edisonville, Kentucky. The biggest little town on earth. Home of the Osborne distillery.

She had found a building owned by Osborne, but his real-estate dealings were handled by his attorney. The building needed some repairs, which she used as an excuse to go straight to Osborne. His office was near the center of town, a large brick building that stood six stories tall. She had expected to be nervous and apprehensive. Surprisingly, she felt an unnatural calm as she walked down the hall to his office. His secretary was middle-aged and smiled pleasantly. "May I help you?"

"Yes, I would like to see Mr. Osborne. He has a building I would like to rent."

"Mr. Osborne's real-estate matters are handled by his attorney. You'll have to see Mr. Allison."

"I had hoped to save time by dealing with Mr. Osborne directly."

"I'm sorry, but Mr. Osborne doesn't like to be bothered with small matters such as this. You'll have to take it up with Mr. Allison."

Tough, Autumn thought. "The building needs quite a few repairs. I feel it necessary to talk with Mr. Osborne."

The secretary smiled, but she wasn't relenting. "Mr. Allison will handle any repairs that are needed."

Autumn glanced toward the door the secretary guarded so furiously. "Is Mr. Osborne in?"

"No. He's out of the office for the day."

Of course, Autumn thought. After two weeks of moving at a snail's pace, what else could be expected? Autumn was impatient now with slow-moving, never-get-in-a-hurry Kentuckians. "Where is Mr. Allison located?"

"His office is on Main Street, across from the bank. If you'd like, I'll make an appointment for you."

"No. I can make my own appointments." She turned and stalked outside to her car, drove the few blocks to Mr. Allison's office, and parked near the entrance. She slammed the car door with a hard thud. Autumn hated the damned Honda. Once this was over, she was going to drive the little sucker into the river and buy the biggest gas hog on the road, which no doubt would please Lloyd immensely.

She entered another brick building and approached another middle-aged secretary. "I'd like to see Mr. Allison, please."

"Do you have an appointment?"

"No," she said, and her voice rose, "I do not have an appointment. However, it is very important that I see him as soon as possible."

"I'm sorry, but Mr. Allison is out of the office. Can this be handled by another member of our firm?"

"I suppose. There's a piece of real estate owned by Mr. Osborne that I would like to lease. I was told to come here."

"Oh . . . well," she said, and smiled. "Mr. Proctor can handle it for you. He's the junior member of our firm."

"I don't care if he's in diapers. If he can put me in touch with Mr. Osborne, I'll be more than happy to see him. I'll even burp the little son of a gun."

The secretary grinned and spoke into the intercom with a slow, lazy tone. "Mr. Proctor. There's a lady here to see you about leasing a piece of property owned by Mr. Osborne. Are you free to see her?"

A deep male voice came through the intercom. "Yes, Marge. You can send her in."

Marge motioned toward a door. "You'll find Mr. Proctor at the end of the hall."

"Thank you." Autumn walked impatiently down a wide corridor. She paused in front of a door marked "Proctor" and then entered a cubbyhole of an office. A young man sat with his head bent over a paper, his glossy black hair shining in the afternoon light.

Autumn felt her heart pounding against her chest. The black hair belonged to Bobby Joe Proctor, the boy she had hammered over the head with her lunch pail. She knew that Bobby had become an attorney, but never imagined that he would be here.

Bobby was something she hadn't counted on. He could ruin everything, and her brain was already shouting: Run, run, run. But Bobby would have to be faced eventually. She needed time to think, and turned toward the door—too late.

"Sue Anne," he called. "Sue Anne McAvan." He rose quickly and circled his desk. "God, it's good to see you. What brings you to Edisonville? What brings you to my office?"

Autumn drew a deep breath and tried to gather her wits. She had one thing in her favor. They were both hill people, and hill people stuck together, regardless. She placed a finger over her lips. "I'm Autumn McAvan. I don't know a Sue Anne McAvan, do you?"

His dark eyes smiled at her and he shook his head. "I won't tell on you, if you won't tell about knocking me cuckoo with your lunch pail."

She nodded and grinned. Bobby was rough-featured, but he wasn't pimple-faced anymore, and stood a head taller than she. College had smoothed out the rough edges and added polish. He had asked her to the senior prom, but going to a dance with a boy she had licked in school hadn't appealed to her.

She crossed the room and held out her hand. "It's good to see you again, Bobby."

"Please—make it Bob."

"Bob it is."

He led her to a chair and slid onto the edge of his desk. "Why are you trying to lease property in Edisonville? From what I've heard, you're a hotshot businesswoman in San Francisco."

Autumn hesitated. She had been careful. The town knew only that she had moved up in the world of business. They didn't know about the Corbett Corporation or the Doghouse. She needed time to think, time to find out what was in Bobby's head. "I don't want to talk about me. I want to know about you. Are you married? Do you have a family?"

"No to both."

"Why not?"

He shrugged. "I'm still in love with you."

"Charmer. You've come a long way since knocking a little girl down a flight of stairs."

"You won't believe this, but it really was an accident. I was crazy about you even then, but I didn't know how to do anything but pull hair. Later, in high school, I was scared to death of you. It took all my nerve to ask you to the senior prom, and then you said no." He paused and looked at her closely. "I think I'm still in awe of you. You're even more beautiful than I remembered."

Autumn smiled sweetly. No one could have been crazy about her freckled face. Later, she had been tall and skinny. It wasn't until the last year of school that she had developed enough curves to resemble a girl. Bobby was after something. She smiled again and glanced at her watch. "I missed breakfast and I'm famished. Are you free for lunch?"

He grinned and nodded. "The food at the club is about the best in town. Would you like to go there?"

"My, my. Moving up, aren't you?"

"No. A membership in the country club goes with the job. I'm not moving. I'm sitting still."

She linked her arm in his. "Tell me about it over lunch?"

The country club was a stately old building. Perched on a hill, it was grand and imposing, with everything to keep the fancy folks of Edisonville happy. There were tennis courts, a golf course, swimming, dining, and dancing. The dining room was elegance itself: mahogany tables with stiff, high-backed chairs were arranged to allow for privacy, upholding the old Kentucky tradition.

Autumn sipped at her drink cautiously. She had lost her Southern accent, but give her a few drinks and her speech became down-home hillbilly. Her story of being from San Francisco wouldn't be very believable if she slipped into a Kentucky accent.

After lunch, she watched, listened, and coaxed Bobby into talking about himself, realizing quickly that she had found a gold mine in him. They were the same age, but unlike Autumn, he hadn't been kicked around enough to have learned subtlety. Eyes, voice, movement, all shouted repressed ambitions and open discontent. On the minus side, Bobby could destroy everything with one word. On the plus side, it wouldn't hurt to have an attorney who knew the right people in town. He was in a direct line with Douglas Osborne, and pushing hard.

"Okay," she said. "Let's dicker. You've been coming on to me since I walked into your office. Most men I meet are after sex. You're greedy. You're after money *and* sex. That's fine. There's nothing wrong with grabbing all you can get. Money in reason, you can have. Sex is out. I have someone in San Francisco." She paused and frowned. "I'm spoiled. When I pick up a phone in San Francisco, things happen. When I pick up a phone here, I'm put on hold—figuratively speaking. You're in a position to pave the way and make things easier for me. In return, I'll try to give you what you want. First, though, you're going to have to tell me what it is you're after."

His face reddened, giving him a boyish look. "Given a

chance, I can be a damned good attorney. I'm not getting that chance where I am now. I want my own law practice, and I want you for a client. You're here, and you're here for a reason. I can handle anything you need as well as my work for Allison.''

She opened her purse and took out a checkbook. "I can agree to that. In fact, you now have two clients. Sue Anne Corbett and Autumn McAvan.'' She pulled a figure out of the air, an amount she thought would cover several months' rent on an office, furnishings, and a little extra to sweeten the pot. "The check is drawn against a bank in Indiana. I would prefer you cashed it out of town for the time being.'' She passed the check to him. "Your retainer. I believe this buys me confidentiality.''

He nodded and shoved the check into his pocket. "What can I help you with, Autumn McAvan?''

"Douglas Osborne. Tell me everything you can about him and his brothers.''

Bob looked surprised, but he didn't question her. He relaxed back in the chair and frowned thoughtfully, pulling everything he knew about the Osbornes to mind. "The Osbornes are an old and respected family that dates back four generations. Coal made the family rich, but years and the lessening demand have eaten the hell out of what was once a vast fortune. Douglas planned ahead for the inevitable. While the brothers were spending like there was no tomorrow, he was building more and more. Once the mine closed, the brothers became dependent on Douglas.''

Bob leaned forward and reached for his drink, smiling a little. "Old Doug gives them enough to keep them happy, but not enough to make them independent. He wants them under his control. Homer is mayor, but Doug runs this town and everybody knows it. George works for Douglas, a gofer. Dale hasn't worked since the mine closed. He lives simply and quietly. He shows up at the club about once a month with one of the women from around town. That's the only time I see him. Douglas is a widower, with a string of mistresses. Some don't last very long, but they all leave with a healthy bank account. He isn't cheap when it comes to paying off his women.''

"What about weaknesses?''

"If he has any, it's obstinacy. He'll go to any lengths to get what he wants. He's intrigued with the impossible. Tell him he can't, and he will."

"You've given me only surface stuff, Bob. What about the side an attorney sees?"

He shook his head. "I can't help you there, Autumn. Our firm represents them, but Allison handles all their affairs personally. I sometimes handle small matters like the building you want to lease, which you haven't explained."

"It's a sham," she said. "I'll tell you about it later. The brothers. What about vices, women, drinking, anything like that?"

"If there is anything, they keep it well hidden. They would have to. Douglas goes crazy if even a hint of gossip touches the family. The brothers seem like regular guys. It's Douglas that's peculiar."

"Peculiar?" Autumn asked. "In what way?"

"In the way he runs this town and his companies. He wants this place to remain exactly as it is. No new business opens here unless he gives his okay. He's got the town locked up tight, and he intends to keep it that way." Bob paused and grinned. "Old Doug sits at his desk and runs his empire like a monarch. He has been obsessed with rebuilding the family fortune to what it once was, which he has done. He has holdings that spread across the country, but he seldom leaves town. He makes everyone else come to him, or he sends John Allison or one of his other gofers." Bob hesitated and laughed outright. "Douglas allowed the Holiday Inn to come into town for the sole purpose of having someplace to stow his out-of-town business associates. When he wants to do business with someone, he sends the *Donkey Cart* and they come here."

"Why did he name it the *Donkey Cart?*"

"Because that's what he thinks of his business associates. Jackasses."

She smiled, her eyes sparkling. "That's beautiful. You know, the man sounds fascinating." She folded her arms on the table. "There are a few things I want from you that might seem odd. First, I want you to cart me around town and introduce me to people who might know something about the Osbornes that isn't common knowledge. A woman can sometimes learn things an attorney can't.''

"Easy. It will be my pleasure."

"This one might not be so easy. I want you to find out where the records from the mine are kept. It's been ten years, so they could have been destroyed."

"Another easy one. The records are kept in the basement at Osborne House. That's something else peculiar. Douglas reveres the Black Jewel like it was something God-given. He's kept every ledger, every invoice."

"How do you know?" she asked.

"Some legal documents on the old mine were tucked away at the back of a filing cabinet. I found them while I was rearranging the files a few months ago. I asked Allison if I should just throw them away, and he almost fainted. He sent me to Osborne House with them. I would assume they're in the basement with the rest now."

"Great. That's like trying to break into Fort Knox." She took a small sip of her drink and gazed steadily at Bob. "There's one more thing I need from you. I want you to put me in touch with Douglas Osborne. Tomorrow."

"Not so easy. That's a tall order. Allison is the only one who has contact with Douglas. Osborne doesn't even come to our office. Allison goes to him."

She smiled, her voice silken. "You tell me you're a good attorney, Bob. A good attorney will find a way."

He grinned. "Touché."

23

The air felt thin and stifling, the night heavy, pressing in on her. The quiet sounds of crickets outside her window that should have been restful seemed to swarm and fill the room with a chorus of monotonous sounds that droned on and on. Unable to sleep, Autumn stared through the dimness at the ceiling. The call had come an hour after she had left Bob. Bob wouldn't say how he had accomplished it, but he had made an appointment for her with Douglas Osborne at nine o'clock the next morning. Be punctual, Bob had said, and dress feminine, very feminine. And good luck.

Her head cluttered with thoughts, she rolled from the bed and went into the kitchen. She mixed a drink and sat staring at the amber liquor, acutely aware of being alone for the first time in her life, totally alone. She had never spent even one night away from Molly; then there was Lonnie. After Lonnie there was Artie—platonic, but he was there. Everett had been so dependent on her that she had felt somewhat alone, until Lloyd. For the last few years, the big Irishman had been only a phone call away.

She finished the drink, reached for the bottle, hesitated, and then shrugged. What the hell? She was alone. If she slipped, no one but the crickets would hear her accent. And she was Irish. The Irish were supposed to be hot-tempered, hard-fighting drinkers. She picked up the bottle, mumbling, "Wouldn't want to disappoint anyone."

Two more drinks and her lids became heavy, her muscles unwound, and her thoughts became a lazy unimportant jumble. She returned to bed, but stared at the telephone. Was the big Irishman still only a phone call away? She pulled the instrument into bed, then hesitated. It was two o'clock in the morning in California. He'd be asleep—or he could be with someone else. It would be rude to call him, unthinkable. Then again, wasn't she one of the impulsive Irish? And a bit tipsy. She dialed his number.

First came a sleepy-sounding Arnold; then Lloyd's deep baritone came on the line. "Were you in bed?" she asked.

"Just."

"Are you alone?"

"I'm alone. Is everything all right?"

"No. I miss you. I want to hold you and make love to you and all that corny stuff."

"I'll send the plane."

"I can't leave. I'm meeting with Douglas in the morning."

"Then I'll come there. Where do you want to meet?"

"Louisville. I'll make hotel reservations."

"Fine. I'll let you know in the morning what time my plane will arrive. Can you meet me, or shall I have a car waiting?"

"I'll meet you." She grinned and thought of her ugly Honda and what his reaction would be. "Is there anything else?"

"Yeah. Bring that lacy black thing."

"You ripped that lacy black thing, but I'll buy another." She dropped back into the pillows and wiggled under the sheets. "Good night, Lloyd."

"Good night, sweetheart."

Autumn replaced the receiver in its cradle and stretched contentedly. The big Irishman was still only a phone call away.

At exactly five minutes to nine, Autumn left her car and entered the tall brick building. She was dressed in a calf-length gray skirt and white blouse. The ruffles at the neck made her look a little prim, but it was feminine. She took the elevator to the top floor and walked down the hall toward her meeting with Douglas Osborne.

Sleep and the morning light had calmed her jitters and she walked with a slow and easy stride. Strange, she thought. She had seen Douglas Osborne only once, briefly, on a street corner, yet the three were linked solidly: she, Lonnie, and Douglas Osborne.

Unlike the first time she had come to his office, the secretary motioned her in without delay. Autumn paused on the threshold, held the ivory knob for a moment, then shoved open the door and walked into the room.

Douglas stood beside a fish tank, his back turned to her. "Take a seat," he said in a bored tone.

The furnishings were antique. Wingback chairs covered in a scratchy-looking fabric sat at proper angles. Some faced a large desk with ornate carvings. Family portraits lined one wall. Autumn chose a chair that faced both him and the sofa, watching as he fed the colorful fish. Her hate was still there, lying subtly below the surface, but seeing him made no real impact on her. She had hated him for so long and so furiously that she felt burned out inside.

"Do you like fish?" he asked.

"Not especially."

"Why?"

"I like a pet I can hold."

"Puppies?"

"Yes, very much."

"Puppies are too damned much like women. All they want is to sit on your lap and be petted." He turned then and looked at Autumn. She knew from her files that he was fifty-nine. His hair was thick and silver now, contrasting with a deep golden tan. Like most large-framed men, he had a resilient body that had withstood the passing of time. He still looked lean and firm. His eyes, large pockets of icy blue, stared at her for what felt like a full five minutes. "You're a mighty fine-looking woman."

"Yes, I know."

"Not at all modest, are you?"

"Why be coy? If a woman is pretty, she knows it."

"You have a point, Mrs. McAvan." He crossed the room and sat on the sofa with an arm resting across the back. "I'm told you want to lease one of my buildings and open a dress shop."

"Yes, the one on Blocker Street."

"Do you plan to sell brassieres?"

She looked at him oddly. "Yes."

"Good. Do you suppose you can find one in the lot that will fit you? This is a small town, Mrs. McAvan, with small-town people. The women here aren't going to take kindly to you parading around with your tits bouncing and your pretty nipples poking at their husbands. If you want to do business in this town, you'll have to dress the part."

Autumn gazed at him directly, relaxing back in the chair. "Do you wear a jockstrap?"

His eyes widened in surprise. "No."

"You don't put a cage around your toy. Why should I put a cage around mine?" She lowered her eyes boldly to his crotch. "You can see the swell of my breasts through my blouse. I can see the swell of your genitals through your trousers. Is one less revealing than the other, less provocative? Do you hide yourself when you have an erection, so the bulge won't show and offend some tender soul?"

Douglas appeared nonplussed for a moment. "Well . . . you might have another point, Mrs. McAvan."

She shifted in the chair, her knee jutting through the slit in her skirt. "Could we move on to business, Mr. Osborne?"

"Depends." He glanced at her knee, his brows drawn together in a frown. "Are you really here for business, or are you trying to vamp me, young lady?"

"Why bother? At your age, it would be a waste of time." *No, no. Wrong, wrong!* The need to cut and jab had overridden her control and she was letting words get away from her. What she had intended to be a simple meeting with him was going haywire. Somehow, Autumn had allowed herself to be drawn into a man/woman confrontation. She gazed at him evenly, waiting for a reaction.

His mouth quivered for a moment; then he reared back and roared with laughter. "Mrs. McAvan, you are the most perfect blend of lady and whore that's ever hit this town."

She shrugged. "We try to please."

He looked at her evenly and smiled for the first time. "Tell me about yourself. I understand you're a widow."

"Yes. My husband died a few months ago."

"You're from San Francisco?"

"Yes," she said again. "Before my husband died, we managed a bar there. The owner didn't think I could manage it alone, so he found someone else. I came into some money when my husband died—insurance. I had planned to open a dress shop, but I hadn't decided where until now. I worked in a department store when I was younger, so I'm not jumping in blind. I know something about clothes, Mr. Osborne, and I know management. I looked around. You don't have a decent dress shop in this town. If you have any doubts, you can ask your sisters-in law."

"Bea wouldn't know a good dress if you shoved it under her nose. Harriet already owns every dress made in Paris, London, and New York, as well as your San Francisco." He opened a gold cigarette box and held it out to her. When she declined, he took a cigarette and lighted it with a table lighter. "Why Edisonville?" he asked. "How did you find your way to our remote little town?"

"Purely by accident. I decided to do some traveling before I opened the shop—see a little of the country. I was nearing the freeway exit and felt tired when I saw a sign advertising the Holiday Inn. I decided to rest here for a day or two. Unfortunately, my car broke down and I was stuck here while it was being repaired." She smiled. "I suppose I should say 'fortunately,' because I found the place I wanted to live. You have a nice quiet town here, Mr. Osborne. The people are friendly and outgoing. I was a stranger here, but they treated me like I was one of them. I'm tired of the noise and crowds of the big city. I like it here. I think I could be happy in Edisonville. In fact, I've already made a friend. Her name is Ella. She runs the diner on Fifth. Do you know her?"

He nodded. "I know everybody in this town, Mrs. McAvan."

"Strange. Ella didn't mention knowing you."

"I don't know her personally, but I do know her name and that she runs the diner. I'm on the board at the bank. I approved a loan for her a few years back when the town was going through a bad time. We were being very selective about the loans we granted, but I felt Ella was a good risk. I understand she's doing very well.''

Autumn shrugged, as if she didn't know. "About the building. Could we discuss the terms of the lease, and repairs that are needed?''

He leaned and butted the cigarette against an ashtray. "I'll have to think about it, little lady. I'm not sure this town needs another dress shop.''

"Oh,'' she said. "And how long do you suppose this thinking will take?''

"It's hard to say. Why don't we go to the club tonight, have some supper, and talk about it?''

"I'm sorry,'' she said. "I have plans for tonight.''

"Break them.''

She shook her head and watched as his eyes hardened, revealing the side Bob had described to her. Obstinacy. Tell him he can't, and he will. She had found the gate, but the means by which it would open made her stomach lunge. "I'll be in touch with you, Mr. Osborne. If you won't lease to me, I'm sure somebody else will.''

"No, Mrs. McAvan. No one will lease you a building. Every new business that opens in this town has to be approved by the city council. I control that council. You'll lease from me, or you won't lease at all.''

Autumn nodded her head in understanding. "In other words, I fuck you, or I'm dead in this town?''

"I wouldn't have put it so bluntly, but yes, if I want.''

Autumn gazed across at him levelly, her voice tight with restraint. "Why don't we clear the air that's been full of chitchatty bullshit from the moment I walked in? *Do* you want, Mr. Osborne?''

"I want.''

Lady and whore, she thought. *I'll* give you lady and whore, bastard! She propped her elbow on the chair arm, her cheek on her hand. "I would have to know the terms, Mr. Osborne. I would think of this as a business deal. As you know, a business is only as strong as the support behind it. What's your offer? Am I to be your mistress, or a one-nighter?''

He drew his hand down and around a jutting chin. "I don't approve of women in business, but I realize you girls have your little whims. I'll indulge you. The building is yours. Take it and do anything you want with it. Just send me the bills."

Autumn smiled derisively. "Suppose you invest all this money and then find you don't like having me around? Wouldn't that be a loss you couldn't deduct from your taxes? And what about me? You wouldn't want an unfuckable woman around, and I'd be branded your whore, a hussy that parades around town with her tits bouncing. I'd be an outcast." She leaned toward him and spoke with a hint of ridicule. "Do you realize you've known me only about twenty minutes? Do you always give so little thought to selecting your mistresses?" She shook her head and clucked. "That's like buying a car without driving it first."

Douglas only looked amused. "I know when a woman excites me."

"Do I excite you, Mr. Osborne?" She glanced down at the revealing swell of his trousers. Then she straightened in the chair, her back stiff as she touched her forehead in salute. "It seems I did you an injustice, and we do want to be just, don't we, Mr. Osborne?" She rose and stood over him. "The whore in me is greedy and would like to accept your offer, but the lady has to refuse. I have never been, nor will I ever be, any man's mistress. I'm for sale, but marriage is my price." She bent and picked up her purse from the coffee table. "I would of course expect a large settlement. At least a hundred thousand when we marry, and another similar amount should you die."

His eyes actually warmed. He rose from the sofa, shaking his head in wonder. "You are incredible."

"Think about it, Mr. Osborne. It's the only way you'll ever fuck me." She walked briskly from the room, but closed the door quietly. "Dirty, ignorant, pee-in-the weeds person."

His secretary quirked an eyebrow. "I beg your pardon?"

"Yes, you do that." Autumn left the office and stalked down the hall. She took the elevator to the ground floor, rushed from the building, and slid behind the wheel of her car. When she turned the starter, the only sound that came from the engine was a weak, mournful groan. The fury she had held in tight control suddenly exploded and she kicked her foot hard against the accelerator. "Start, you blue motherfucker!"

It started.

24

Bobby Joe and Ella sat in the office at the diner with Autumn. She looked from one to the other, concerned that her actions would involve them in something that could possibly ricochet and hurt them both. She had told Bobby everything, but at this point he appeared only as a go-between for her and Douglas. Ella was simply a woman she had met, but what about later? If Douglas learned they were more closely involved, he could ensure that Bobby never practiced law in Edisonville, and he could make things hard for Ella and her family. Somehow, she would have to keep them in the background.

Autumn looked down at the dark liquid in the coffee cup and spoke with awe in her voice. "It was a walking, talking wide-awake nightmare. Crazy. The conversation went from fish, to puppies, to brassieres, to mistress. I don't understand why he agreed to the appointment. He was interested in talking about me, but he wasn't at all interested in discussing the building."

Bob looked at her with a young, sheepish grin. "I was playing the hotshot lawyer, Autumn. I didn't wangle an appointment with Douglas. He saw us together at the club and called me at the office. He wanted to know everything about you, who you were, why you were in town, where you were from, and if you were married. He seemed especially interested in your marital status. He had me arrange the appointment. I'm sorry, Autumn. I should have told you.''

"Yes," she said, "you certainly should have." Autumn understood now. Douglas had seen her and decided to add the new woman in town to his string. What she had thought was a snap decision had been well-thought-out. "I really charmed him," she mumbled. "I said some things. I'm not sure what his reaction will be. If he calls while I'm away, just go on as we planned. You don't know anything, except I want to open a dress shop." She looked at Ella. "I told him we were friends. If he calls, we met here in the diner. You don't know anything else." She paused and frowned. "He told me about the loan you got from the bank a few years ago. He approved it even though the town was in trouble and it was a considerable risk. That doesn't sound like the man I've heard so much about—or like the man I talked to today. He's ice.''

"Sure," Ella said in a sour tone. "He knew the bank would get its money. The bastard wasn't doing me or anybody else a favor in those days. If the diner failed, he knew I could always go back to selling my ass in one of his joints.''

"Now, that sounds like the man we all know and love." Autumn set the coffee cup on Ella's desk and rose from the chair. "I have to go. I'm meeting Lloyd's plane in a few hours, and I have a dab of shopping to do first.''

"Can I come?" Bob asked, grinning.

"No, child, this is a party for grown-ups." She smiled at Ella, grabbed Bob by the collar, and nudged him along with her. They left the diner and were nearing their cars when she paused and looked at him soberly. "Don't ever hold out on me again, Bob. I'll never put you down for failing, or making a mistake, but I'll have your hide if you keep something back from me again.''

He nodded, and his face showed that same boyish look she had seen before. Autumn wilted. Bob was the good part of her past. The part she liked to remember. Impulsively she grasped his shoulder and searched his face for a scar that might have been left from her lunch pail. There were none. His skin was young and flawless.

"Damn," he said when she drew away. "For a minute

there I thought I was going to be kissed by that wild McAvan girl.''

Autumn laughed, stretched to tiptoe, and kissed him on the mouth. There was something reassuring about having Bob there, except for one small doubt that had stayed with her. Autumn had told herself it was nonsense, but she couldn't seem to shake the thought. ''I hope I can trust you, Bob.''

He looked at her oddly. ''Why would you think otherwise?''

''You know everything. You could go to Douglas with what you know. He has more money than I.''

''Would you go to him?'' he asked.

''No.''

''Why not?''

''We're hill people. We stick together.''

''Right,'' he said. ''I'm ambitious, but I wouldn't go against one of my own kind. It just *ain't* done.''

She nodded and touched his cheek lightly. ''We both made mistakes today. I'm sorry, Bob.''

''Yeah . . . well . . . there's only one way you're going to worm your way back into my heart.''

She grinned. ''And just what might that be?''

''Pucker up!''

An opening appeared in the side of the silver Lear jet and Lloyd stepped through. Autumn felt a wash of warmth as he walked toward her. Two weeks? It seemed so long. She wanted to race into his arms and chatter nonsensically, touch, hold and be held by his massive body. She tried to force herself to wait quietly, but as he neared, the urge grew stronger. When he smiled, soft airy laughter rolled from her lips and she leapt into his startled arms, sending his suitcase flying.

Knocked off balance, he stumbled with her, erupting into a burst of surprised laughter. ''My unpredictable darling. Thanks, sweetheart. I needed that.'' He gazed at her with a probing expression. ''How's it going?''

''Fine.''

He turned abruptly and picked up his bag. ''Where is your car?''

His tone had been aloof, and she gazed at him, confused. When he shifted his bag from hand to hand as if impatient, she turned and led him from the private section of the airport to her car. As they approached the Honda, she pulled a ring of keys from her purse and held them out to him. "Do you want to drive?"

He looked from the car to Autumn. "Drive it? I don't think I can even get in it. I thought you were going to buy a new car."

"It *is* new, to me."

"I had something different in mind."

"I know. It's ugly, but it fits Edisonville and it was cheap."

He tossed his suitcase onto the backseat and took the keys. "Okay, Scrooge. You point the way, and I'll drive."

She slid in beside him, smiling as he curled his large frame around the steering wheel. After giving him directions to the hotel, she tried to draw him into small talk, but he was unusually quiet, seeming distracted when he spoke. She glanced at his profile from time to time. It had to be a personal problem that had him so preoccupied. She had been on the board at Murphy's long enough to know the company had never been in a better state. He was nationwide now, and climbing. Ten more years and he'd be right up there with Sears and J. C. Penney's. It could be his daughter, Lindy. Lloyd had some old-fashioned ideas about divorce. If Lindy was having trouble with her marriage, he would be upset by it. He doted on Lindy and his grandson. Whenever they had a problem, he always found a way to solve it. "Is everything all right with Lindy?"

He turned to her as if pulled from some kind of fog. "Yes. Why?"

She shrugged. "Just asking."

He pulled the Honda up in front of the hotel. "I'll get in touch with my people here and have them arrange for different transportation. I'm not going to ride around in this damned kiddie car for three days."

"Yes, grump."

He smiled slightly, uncurled his large frame from the car, and tossed the keys to the waiting valet. "See if you can't lose it." He showed her the little courtesies, but with the same detachment as when they had driven to the hotel. Once reaching their suite, he took the keys and opened the door.

Autumn entered the room, turning on him with her hand against her hips. "Will you please tell me what is going on? I'm not some call girl you've rented for three days, Lloyd. I'm Autumn. Sue Anne Corbett, partner, businesswoman. This kind of business I don't like. If you're here just for a fuck, anyone can help you out. I'll go back to Edisonville and you can call in a hooker. If you've got a problem, then tell me. Maybe I can help."

"The only problem I have is you, babe." He tossed his suitcase to the floor, pulled her into his arms, and drew his hands down over her buttocks, grasping her hips with a jerk that slammed her pelvis hard against his. He kissed her then, deeply, his mouth probing hers. Mumbling inaudibly, he swept her up in his arms and crossed to the bed.

With Lloyd it came so quickly, an overwhelming sensation that gripped her lower stomach and made things happen, priming her body until it was wet and responsive. The argument was forgotten, the lacy black thing forgotten. Stripped of her clothes, she sat down on the bed to wait. When he removed his shorts, she swirled her fingers through the fine hair on his chest, down the taut line of his hips, and pulled him forward, feeling him tremble from the touch of her lips.

He held her head between his hands and gazed at her a moment, then a deep rumbling groan burst from his lips and he picked her up by the armpits. She curled herself around him as he lowered her to bed, and gazed into green eyes dulled with wanting as he penetrated. He was Lloyd, yet he wasn't the Lloyd she knew. He was more intense, attacking her body voraciously. Rough, but not rough. Gentle, but not gentle. She pulled his face down until her lips were against his. "I adore you," she whispered. "You make me love being a woman."

Autumn pulled the black gown over her head, smoothed it down over her hips, and stretched out on the bed beside Lloyd. His hair was damp from the shower and he had a towel wrapped around his waist. He was propped on pillows, smoking a new pipe, or at least it wasn't the one she had hammered on the table edge. She touched the cleft in his chin with her finger. "How do you ever shave in there?"

"Very carefully."

She leaned and touched the hollow with her tongue. "You were so rakish. One would think you hadn't had a woman in weeks."

"Two weeks."

"Really? Why?"

"Too busy."

"Too busy for sex? That doesn't sound like the Lloyd Murphy I know."

"True."

"You came here."

He looked at her with a quiet smile. "I'll always come to my redhead." He knotted fingers in the back of her hair. "What about you, Autumn? Has it been two weeks for you, too?"

"Yes. I haven't wanted anyone else, but I don't expect the same from you."

"You wouldn't be jealous?"

"I didn't say that. You've picked the wrong time to ask such questions. I'm always possessive of you after we've made love."

His mood suddenly shifted. The tension eased from his face and he actually laughed. "How are things in cricket country? Did you meet with Osborne?"

"I met, and it was terrible. He'll either give me the key to the city or have me tarred and feathered. The moment I faced him, all your years of teaching went down the drain. I'm afraid I blew it." She drew her finger along his jawline and thought how alike the two men were. Both were large in build, dynamic, self-possessed, egotistical. There was one big difference, though. Lloyd fought hard for what he wanted, but he'd never resorted to murder. She pulled away from him, the scene in Douglas' office fresh in her mind. The word "marriage" had been thrown out on impulse to tantalize him, but she knew it would be the ultimate victory. The family name he valued so highly, his home, his shrine, desecrated by his own wife. And it would put her in reach of the records in the basement, along with any other secrets the family kept locked as tight as Fort Knox.

She glanced at Lloyd from the corner of her eye. "What would you think if I married Douglas Osborne?"

His head snapped around and he looked at her with an incredulous stare. "You're joking."

She nodded with an impish grin. "I'm joking."

He chewed the stem of his pipe and eyed her skeptically. "You wouldn't, would you?"

"I told you the meeting went rotten. I even joked about him being too old to fuck anymore. It wouldn't surprise me to return and find my bags packed and sitting under the highway sign. Banished. Kicked out of the biggest little town on earth. Home of the Osborne distillery."

Chuckling, Lloyd swung his legs over the edge of the bed and went to his suitcase, returning to Autumn with a small velvet box. He took her hand and slipped an emerald, set in a circle of diamonds, on the finger next to her wedding band. "Happy birthday, sweetheart."

She stared at the ring blankly. "Birthday?"

"Yeah. Birthday."

A lump gathered in her throat at his thoughtfulness. It was her twenty-eighth birthday, but she had been too busy even to remember. "I forgot," she whispered. "I forgot my own birthday." She looked at him with warmth. "It's lovely, Lloyd, and so are you."

He bent and pecked her on the lips. "Put on something lovely and green to match the ring, and I'll take you to dinner."

Their table was in a dim corner of the dining room. The dinner was good, the conversation light and nonsensical. Lloyd looked striking in a tweedy cream-colored suit. She hadn't brought anything green to match the ring, so she wore white instead, which gave her an angelic air, according to Lloyd. The drinks kept coming, and she kept sipping until her speech become slow and drawled. Lloyd teased and mimicked her, but she knew he liked her accent. Delightfully refreshing, he had once said.

They had long since finished dinner when Lloyd brought

up the subject of Bob Proctor, and then became quiet and watchful as she told him about growing up with Bob, and the school fight. "Ironic that we should meet again in Edisonville. He's still wet behind the ears, but shows potential. He's actually very bright, when he isn't trying to impress me. I've been playing with the idea of bringing him to San Francisco later. With your help, I could get him into a good firm there. What do you think?"

"I think you should drop the whole damned thing and return to San Francisco."

His remark was so unexpected and off the track that she sat nonplussed.

"I'm not asking that you forget Douglas, but there are other ways to handle this. We'll hire the best detective agency in San Francisco. They can find out the things you want to know, and in much less time. You've been in Edisonville for two weeks, and you haven't learned anything of importance. At this rate, it could take months."

"I'm not stupid, Lloyd. I hired private detectives about a year ago. I was afraid to have them ask too many questions for fear of alerting Douglas, but I had the brothers watched for two months. Nothing."

"Any man can be good for a couple of months, Autumn. The reason the meeting with Douglas went badly is that you can't relate to him on a professional level. You're too personally and emotionally involved. Let me turn a few good men loose on them."

She shook her head. "I'm in a position now to move in circles a detective can't. I can ask questions and it will seem like gossip. You don't know these people like I do. If you send a stranger here to snoop, their mouths will snap shut like steel traps."

Lloyd frowned in annoyance. He threw his napkin on the table. "I've been waiting years for you to be free, years for you to grow up. You're free now, and almost grown-up, but I'm still waiting. I want you with me now. Not next week, or next month, but now. Either you come back to San Francisco, or you don't come back at all. At least not to me."

Her body recoiled, as if from a stinging blow. She shook her head from side to side. "Unfair. You're being so unfair. You knew this could take months. Why the sudden change?''

He rose from the table and gazed at her with a set, stubborn expression. ''I think we should talk about this in our rooms.''

''No,'' she said strongly. ''I think we should talk about this here and now.''

''You've had things your way long enough, sweetheart. It's time I had things my way now. It will be my way, or not at all.''

Autumn knew by the tone of his voice that no amount of talking would change his mind. Lloyd had been like a lifeline for the last seven years and she could feel a stunning coolness beginning to spread through her. How many more people would she have to lose before it was over? She gazed across the table at him and spoke with sadness in her voice. ''I don't like to be alone. I hate it. And I don't want to lose you, but this is something I have to do.'' When his face remained set, she pushed away from the table. ''Good-bye, Lloyd. I hope you have a safe flight home. My thoughts will be with you.''

25

Autumn hadn't known what to expect after the storm she had raised in Douglas' office, but there were calls from him waiting on her answering machine when she returned to Edisonville. Trying to mend her fences, she returned his call and accepted a dinner date. By the end of their first evening together, she had learned something about the man that he wasn't aware of. Douglas Osborne was very lonely, and bored to the point of frustration. She had walked into his life in a vulnerable moment and added a touch of excitement, a new challenge.

The one dinner led to another, and another. To her surprise, he was easy to talk to, and easy to be with. He had a way of making a woman feel special; he was courteous to the point of being old-fashioned. They talked about the dress shop off and on, but Autumn could see it was difficult for him to discuss business with a woman. It was simply not of his world.

Two weeks after their meeting in his office they were having dinner when he tossed a paper at her. "I had John Allison draw this up a few days ago. Read it over and see if you agree with the terms."

Autumn thought the paper had to do with the dress shop. "A lease?" she asked.

"No. It's the agreement you asked for. We're getting married."

She smiled. "We are?"

"We are."

"And when is this great event going to take place?"

"Tonight. I've made all the arrangements. The *Cart* is ready and waiting to take us to Reno. By tomorrow you'll be Mrs. Douglas Osborne, mistress of Osborne House."

Autumn heard only the words "mistress of Osborne House." She thought of the records in the basement, then smiled and nodded.

Marriage had been a thought she allowed her mind to play with in idle moments. After the breakup with Lloyd, she had felt severed from him and all other ties, desperate to end what had begun with Lonnie's death. Marriage to Douglas had seemed the quickest and easiest way to move her from point nowhere to the middle of the kingdom. Now as she stood gazing at the chalet in the distance, surrounded by wildflowers and the sounds of summer, it seemed incredible that she had actually married Douglas Osborne—the dragon.

Douglas was a complex man: thoughtful, gallant, and generous. Very generous. In the few days since they had married, he had lavished her with furs to keep her warm during the cold Kentucky winters, jewels to make her sparkle, and a Jaguar to replace the Honda. He had slipped his ring on her finger next to the gold wedding band without any objections or questions. One hundred thousand dollars had been deposited in her bank account, along with a separate account he called her pocket money. He was gentle and treated her with the highest respect, but he had an irascible temper that could explode over the smallest incident.

His favorite food was Chinese. Shortly after their marriage, they had flown to Chicago for dinner and she saw his anger released for the first time. Somehow, the waiter confused their dinners and brought almond fried chicken instead of the sesame-seed they had ordered. Within moments, Douglas was raging. He had the waiter, the head-waiter, and the manager at their table and demanded the man be fired. It wasn't until their flight home that she learned he owned the restaurant and hated nuts of any kind. The waiter was fired, not because he had made a mistake, but because Douglas hated almonds.

Autumn glanced at the square diamond he had slipped on her finger, watching as the sun caught against the stone, and thought of Brian, and the night she had spent with him at Rex's. From son to father in ten easy years, she mused. From a two-hundred dollar whore to a hundred-thousand-dollar pet. The two men had at least one thing in common. Both were willing to pay top dollar for what they wanted.

Molly would have to be told, and Autumn turned toward the chalet, knowing she had stalled as long as possible. Turtle Ridge was ninety miles from Edisonville. It took a while for news to find its way to the hidden little town, but sooner or later Molly would learn about her elopement. Autumn felt tension pulling between her shoulder blades and broke into a hard run, something she had added to her morning routine. A few laps around the grounds helped her get through the day. Several laps in the pool left her exhausted and helped her get to sleep at night.

Molly laughed when Autumn bolted into the house. "It's good to see you running around again. You've been so quiet and mopey the last few times you've been here that I've been worried about you." She took Autumn's face and turned it toward the light. "You look a little pale. Are you eating right? That habit you have of skipping meals ain't good for you."

"I'm eating." Autumn sat down on the sofa and patted the cushion next to her. "Sit down, Aunt Molly. I have something to tell you." The years seemed to roll away as she drew Molly into the past with her. The chalet became a small frame house with Lonnie sitting on the porch, listening to her sing and play the guitar, walking with her in the woods, making love to her in the moonlight. Her tone became tense as she recalled for Molly the mine explosion and the day Lonnie's car went over the embankment. Cold and hard when she explained why she had returned to Edisonville and why she had married Douglas Osborne.

Molly shook her head reproachfully, her voice filled with concern for Autumn. "Lord, what if he finds out?"

"He won't. To Douglas I'm just a woman with nothing more important on her mind than spending his money, flashing my jewels, and speeding around in my fast new car."

"And he married you thinking this?"

"Douglas is pushing sixty, Aunt Molly. He isn't looking for love and babies and devotion. I put myself up for sale, and he bought himself a pretty wife to dangle on his arm and take to the four poster." Autumn sprang from the sofa and went to a window that overlooked the river.

During their period of "courting" she had kept Douglas at arm's length, as promised. And once they were married, she coupled with him by reflex. He preferred to sleep alone, so as soon afterward as possible, she went to her quarters and scrubbed in a hot shower or took a long swim.

Autumn turned from the window and looked at Molly. "I don't want you to worry. Everything is going to be fine. I'm sending for Artie. He'll be in town if I need him."

"I can understand how you feel about Lonnie's death, but this is no good. Revenge is bad, Autumn. It corrodes and sours the soul. You'll be the one to pay the most in the end."

"I'm not after revenge, Aunt Molly. All I want is justice. If the law in Edisonville had done its job, I wouldn't be here now. I'd much rather be in San Francisco taking care of my hot-dog stands."

"Lloyd," Molly said. "Does he know you're married?"

"No. I haven't told him." She turned from the window and walked quickly toward the phone. Autumn didn't want to talk about Lloyd, or even to think about Lloyd. He had made his decision and she had accepted it. What she did now, and whom she married, were no longer his concern. They were business associates, nothing more. "I'm going to call Artie, then I have to leave. Douglas is having a dinner party tonight to introduce his new wife to family and friends."

Autumn gazed up at the high old-fashioned ceiling and slid down in the big marble tub. There was a room for everything in Osborne House, and everything had its own room—a morning room, a sunroom, a sewing room, a music room—thirty-nine rooms in all, with a ballroom large enough to land the *Donkey Cart*.

A four-foot chandelier hung from a high gilt celing that rose in a dome above the foyer. The foyer ran the width of the house, with corridors leading to the east and west wings. Autumn's favorite place was the sunroom. It was small, with a chair covered in old rose and gold chintz. The chair faced a row of windows that overlooked a rose garden where a fountain sprayed into a lily pond shaped like a cloverleaf.

She stretched lazily in the foamy bath and was closing her eyes when Daisy rushed in and hurried her from the tub. Daisy was thin, pale-skinned, and wore her salt-and-pepper hair in a kinky permanent wave. She was the only one in the house with guts enough to stand up to Douglas.

Daisy talked a mile a minute while fussing Autumn into a dress with gold beading that twined around her breasts. She loved to chat and Autumn had learned from her that Homer liked the cards too much. And that Bea, Homer's wife, doted on her husband. There wasn't anything Bea wouldn't do for Homer.

Daisy liked to keep a bottle in her room, and when she'd had a few sips she became even more talkative. Autumn could smell the fumes of whiskey with every breath Daisy exhaled. Autumn pushed at her hands. "I can dress myself, Daisy."

"It's always been my job to help the womenfolk in this house get ready for parties." She shoved Autumn down at the dressing table and fought her for the comb. "I'll do it. I'm good with hair."

Autumn looked in the mirror at Daisy's mop of frizz and shuddered. If Daisy had a title, it would have to be that of housekeeper. She had been Edith's maid, and then nanny to Brian, and was still loyal only to him. Autumn had yet to hear her say one good word about Douglas, although he continued to keep her on. Daisy brushed at Autumn's hair, chattering. "It's sure enough good to have a woman in the house to do for again. Mr. Douglas has been awful lonesome since Brian left. 'Course, like I told him, it was all his fault. Brian is strong-willed like his pa. You can't take a boy like that and boss him around like you can the brothers.''

Daisy whipped Autumn's hair this way and then that. ''I don't know why Mr. Douglas didn't remarry sooner. He's the sort that needs a woman of his own. He can be a real mean one, but he's got a soft spot for the womenfolk. 'Course, he expects them to toe the mark. He took Harriet's side and gave George the very devil when he got tangled up with that last gal over near Potsville. He warned George. One more time and he was out.''

Autumn had been only half-listening to Daisy's chatter. Now she sat alert. ''Does Goerge like the women?''

''Yeah, but he's afraid to do much about it now. He's scared to death of Douglas and Harriet. Not that I blame George. That Harriet is a coldhearted bitch. She jumped into bed with Douglas, giving no never-mind to Edith, dying in this very room.''

Autumn turned and faced Daisy. ''Douglas had an affair with his brother's wife?''

''Yeah. Old Harriet thought when she married George that she was getting a rich man, but she got fooled. Harriet thought she was going to trade the poor brother for the rich one, but Douglas is too smart to buy the cow when the milk is free. Edith had the cancer, you know. I have to give Mr. Douglas credit. He did everything he could to make her last days as easy as he could. He loved Edith and he was true to her almost till the end. I guess sleeping in that big bed alone got to be too much for him. He turned to Harriet for a time there. Harriet's got a real nasty tongue, but don't you let it bother you none.''

''It's good Homer doesn't have the same problem, or Douglas would really have his hands full.''

''Huh,'' Daisy snorted. ''Homer ain't no angel. Some years back, he got in deep with the cards and lost a piece of property Mr. Douglas had put in his name for a tax something-or-other.''

''Dodge?'' Autumn asked.

''Yeah, that's it. A tax dodge. Anyway, he got carried away and lost the property. Douglas was fit to be tied. He almost killed Homer. He made Homer pay back every last penny."

"How do you know all this?"

Daisy grinned, moved closer, and breathed sour breath at Autumn. "I listen at keyholes. There ain't much goes on in this house I don't know about."

Autumn made a mental note to be very careful and guard her own keyholes. She glanced in the mirror and pretended to be peering at her reflection. "Tell me about Dale. Does he like the cards too?"

"No, and he don't like the women, either." She gave Autumn a nudge. "If you know what I mean."

"He's gay?" Autumn asked, her eyes wide with surprise.

"I don't know how gay he is, but he's as queer as a three-dollar bill. He takes the women out now and then, but it's only for looks. Orders from Mr. Douglas. He can have his funny sweethearts, but only if he's quiet about it."

Autumn exploded into laughter, turned, and was hugging Daisy when Douglas entered the room. He frowned in annoyance. "Will you get her ready, Daisy? People are beginning to arrive."

"I don't need you hurrying me, big boy."

Douglas looked at Autumn's hair and gave Daisy a push. "I think Autumn had better do her own hair. And stay off the bottle. You smell like a still."

"You oughta know." Before leaving, Daisy bent and whispered, "Don't you breathe a word about what I told you. That old shit would kill me dead if he knew I was snooping around."

Autumn shook her head, took the brush, and began arranging her hair. "This will only take a moment."

He caught her eye in the mirror. "I want you to be a good little girl tonight. This isn't San Francisco, and you're not in a barroom. You're Mrs. Douglas Osborne, mistress of Osborne House. I don't want you to tell somebody to go fuck off simply because you don't like something they said."

"Who, me? Never. Incidentally, I invited Bob Proctor. I wanted somebody here on my side."

"Are you nervous about meeting the family?"

"Why should I be nervous? I doubt you'll kick me out if they don't approve."

"You're damned sure of yourself, woman. You think you've got me laced up all nice and tight, don't you?"

She smiled at him in the mirror. "Haven't I?"

He chuckled and pulled a gray velvet box from his breast pocket. "I'd like you to wear this tonight. It's a family heirloom. I can't give it to you, but you're free to wear it anytime you want. Every Osborne wife has worn this pendant. Someday it will be worn by Brian's wife—if he ever settles down long enough to find one." From the box he removed a ruby pendant the size of a quail's egg and draped it around her neck. The stone lay in the hollow between her breasts, the color of rich red wine against her fair skin.

She touched the gem with her fingertips. "It's lovely," she said sincerely.

His eyes swept over her approvingly. "You're a prideful-looking woman, Autumn, and tall. You carry the jewel well. Edith was small. The ruby looked ridiculous on her." He took Autumn's arm and urged her toward the door. "Come, or we'll be late for our own party."

"Yes," she said, and grinned. "I'm looking forward to meeting your family. I've heard so much about them that I'm burning with curiosity."

"Oh," he said, and arched an eyebrow. "And just what does that mean?"

She smiled. "That they are very interesting people, with many, many facets."

26

Four peas in a pod, Autumn thought after meeting the Osborne brothers. The four men were all tall, with graying blond hair and blue eyes. She soon realized there were vast differences. George never stopped selling himself; an overzealous blowhard, he seemed more the politician than Homer. George had a ruddy complexion, a nervous, snorting kind of laugh, and a thickening waistline. His eyes seemed strongly attracted to the ruby, or to her cleavage.

Homer, on the other hand, was trim, with a slightly crooked mustache that separated him in appearance from his brothers. He had a quick, easy smile, but his eyes never really looked at you, and he moved and spoke with an unnatural calm. He reminded her of a simmering teakettle that could explode any moment in an ear-splitting hiss.

On the surface everybody seemed friendly, but throughout the evening Autumn could sense the family's disapproval, save for chubby, rosy-cheeked Bea. And open hostility from George's wife. Harriet had a slithering way of walking and a habit of twining a strand of dyed hair around her finger like a naughty little girl. Her dark eyes flashed and she spoke rapidly, at times dominating the conversation. Her hands moved as she talked, diamonds flashing.

Autumn could understand why Douglas had been attracted to her. It was evident that she had once been a beauty. Unfortunately, she didn't have the skin or features that withstood time well. The years, or living with an Osborne, had left her a middle-aged, disenchanted woman.

There were thirty-five guests, but Autumn was only interested in the brothers. She stood with Douglas after dinner, nursed a drink, and watched as they moved about the room from group to group. At times Dale had caught her watching him and smiled faintly. He was the youngest of the four brothers, soft-spoken, with a gentle manner. He kept to the edge of the gathering, as if he were there only because it was demanded of him. She sensed a strength of will in Dale that was lacking in George and Homer. If what Daisy had said was true, Dale would need strength to survive in a town full of bigots like Edisonville.

Autumn watched Dale sipping his drink and rested her hand on Douglas' arm. "I think I'll mingle for a while." When he nodded, she turned to leave, but Harriet approached them.

Harriet smiled a smile that never quite touched her eyes. She patted Autumn on the cheek as one would a small child. "She's so young, Douglas. Doesn't it make you feel absolutely ancient to have such a young wife?"

"On the contrary," he said. "I've never felt younger."

"How nice," she said dryly. Harriet slipped her fingers under the ruby and lifted it from Autumn's breasts. "How did you ever pry this from him, my dear? I asked to wear it once and he almost took my head off."

Autumn smiled and patted Harriet on the cheek. "There are ways, my dear." She turned to Douglas. "I definitely think I should mingle now."

He smiled. "Yes, I definitely think you should."

Autumn left Douglas to deal with Harriet and crossed to the quiet corner where Dale sat. The most noticeable thing about Dale was his ears. They were a shade too large for the rest of his head. He smiled vaguely when Autumn sat down in a chair next to him. "Foolish woman," he said.

Autumn tipped her head to one side. "Am I foolish?"

"You came to this town and you married my brother. That is very foolish. You'll find the money isn't worth it."

"Do you think I married Douglas for his money?"

"I don't think you married him for his sweet disposition. That leaves money."

"Do you dislike me for it?"

"No, but there are others who do. George, because he would like to have you for himself, and can't. Homer, because he's afraid you'll take something from him. Harriet, because you're young and she isn't. And because you've replaced her."

"Replaced her, how?"

"After Edith died, she became the queen. She was *the* Mrs. Osborne. Now she's only Mrs. George Osborne. Harriet doesn't like second place. She'll make your life miserable." He leaned toward her, his eyes narrowed. "My advice is to run, run as fast as you can. Get out of town and away from my brother before you're gobbled up by him and Edisonville."

"You sound as if you hate the town and your brother."

"No, I don't hate them, but I do hate their antiquated thinking."

Autumn felt reasonably sure now that what Daisy had told her was true. There was a softness about Dale, but then, she had known other men with feminine features and they were known to be devils in bed. And she had known men in San Francisco who were very masculine in appearance, but homosexuals. There was only one way to be sure, and she watched him closely. "When did you first realize you were gay?"

He looked flustered for a moment and glanced at Douglas. "I'm surprised he told you. Doug tries to pretend I don't exist."

"Douglas didn't tell me," she said. "I guessed. I've known several homosexuals in San Francisco. After a while you learn to spot the little differences. Why don't you leave this town and go someplace where you'll be accepted?"

He smiled mirthlessly. "In case nobody has told you: Dale doesn't know how to do anything. When the mine was open, I had a job and an income. I had an office with my name on the door, and a big mahogany desk. I even had a secretary. When the Black Jewel closed, Doug pensioned me out. I'm forty-four, Autumn. That's too old to start all over."

"Money?" she asked. "Is money what holds you here?"

"Money and fear. I'm like a woman who has been protected all her life by a husband. She would be terrified to go out and make her way alone. She won't, unless she's forced to." He paused and took a sip of his drink. "If my own brother won't give me a job, who will?" He set his glass on the table and rose from the chair. "Think I'll go home and curl up with a John D. MacDonald." He turned and was halfway across the room when he hesitated and looked back at her. "College. I knew my first year of college."

Autumn sat quietly for a while and watched the fancy folks of Edisonville as they milled about the room. She listened halfheartedly to the hum of their chatter, the tinkle of ice against crystal. She thought about Dale and how she could use what he had told her. He might need a push, but there was a way she could help him, and herself at the same time.

She was both surprised and pleased that he had opened up and talked to her so freely, as if a pressure had been relieved in having her know the truth. He was the first in the family to have shown her a friendly gesture, save for Bea. Shortly after they had returned from their fast trip to Reno, Bea had hurried over with her special Apple Betty pie, which Douglas could not refuse.

There was a sweetness about chubby, rose-cheeked Bea. It had taken only a brief conversation with her before Autumn realized Homer was the moon, the sun, and the stars to Bea. The church and the Edisonville children's shelter were her second love. Since their first meeting, Bea had been nagging Autumn to help out with the children.

Bea did have one habit that drove Autumn up the wall. Right in the middle of a conversation she would fall silent and stare off into space, her eyes glazed over. The only way to bring her back was to give her a quick nudge. Daisy called her daffy, but good-hearted.

Autumn mingled for a while and then went to where Douglas stood with John Allison, his attorney. After talking with them for a few minutes, she drifted away to look for Bob. She found him sitting on the stairs in the foyer with Lisa, Dr. Albright's daughter, and Brian's onetime

fiancée. Lisa was divorced now and living in Edisonville.
One word could describe Lisa: voluptuous. Long blond
hair lay on bare shoulders, tanned a deep golden brown.
She had a pout to her mouth, and a lazy, bored way of
speaking.

"Would you mind if I borrowed Bob for a while?"
Autumn asked. "I need to talk to him."

Lisa shrugged, and her large bust quivered. She rose
from the stairs, glancing briefly at Bob. "I'll be at the bar,
or damned close to it."

Bob watched her walk away and grinned. "Mmmmm-
hmmmm. That is one sassy lady. One roll in the sack with
her is the equivalent of a week of fasting. The last time I
spent a night with her, I lost two pounds."

Autumn patted him on the rear. "Better make it one
night only. Your little butt can't afford too much aerobics."

"Whatcha mean? I've got a nice ass."

"Nice, but skinny." She hooked her arm in his and
turned toward the terrace. "It's stuffy in here. Let's go
outside and grab some moonlight." People were scattered
about the terrace, so she led him along the path to the rose
garden. As they walked, Autumn told him what she had
learned from Daisy and Dale. "I want you to wait about a
week, then go to Dale and offer him fifty thousand for his
block of stock in the Black Jewel, and a job with my
company. If he accepts, I'll get in touch with my people
and have it set up."

"A little close, wouldn't you say?"

She nodded. "I'll have him sent to our offices in Seattle. He thinks he can't do anything, but no man sits in an
executive's position for years without learning a good
deal. He's frightened, so we might have to give him a
push."

"What kind of push?"

She shook her head. "Not now."

He frowned annoyed. "Dammit, Autumn. I can't work
blind. I never know what you're going to do until you do
it. As your attorney, I need to know what you're planning."

"I'm a loner, Bob. When I think you need to know
something, I'll tell you." She smiled as they reached the

fountain. "Besides, I don't always know myself, until I do it."

"You're impossible—but I shall obey." He jumped suddenly, grabbed the air, and held his hand out to her. "A gift for my fair maiden."

She laughed at his silliness and clasped her hand over a breast. "What, brave knight, have you for this lowly maiden?"

He bowed. "A handful of moonlight."

"Ahhh, 'tis a gift to cherish when I be old and lonely." She dropped down on the bench near the fountain, felt a fine mist of spray against her back, and shuddered at its coolness. "I think there's a bit of the romantic in you, Bob."

"Yeah," he teased, and lunged at her. "Wanta neck?"

"Autumn!" Douglas stepped from the shadows. He smiled at Bob as he took Autumn by the arm. "You're neglecting your other guests, Autumn." He whisked her away and into the house, where he became very festive. He danced with Autumn, joked about their hasty marriage and his good fortune, popped a cork and toasted her with champagne. However, he looked relieved when the last guest had left.

"What's the verdict?" she asked. "Did I pass the town's scrutiny?"

"That is still to be determined." He led her up the curving flight of stairs, his lips set in a grim line.

She hesitated when they reached her room, and looked at him oddly. "Is something wrong?"

"Don't play innocent, Autumn." Placing his hand on the small of her back, he opened the door and shoved her into the room, drew back his hand, and slapped her across the face with a blow that cracked in the silence of the room.

The strength and force of his hand sent her reeling backward. She grasped wildly at empty air, stumbled, and struck her cheekbone against the scalloped edge of a chair. Pain shot up the side of her head and blurred her vision for a moment. Stunned, she stared as he paced and yelled. His speech was disjointed. "Married only days and you've disgraced me in front of the entire town . . . seen by

Homer . . . playing with Bob's ass . . .ridiculed . . .
warned by George . . . keep an eye on my sexy young
wife . . . Harriet . . . gloating that she saw you romping
in the rose garden with Bob.''

Autumn listened, suddenly swept by a blinding rage.
When he took a step toward her, she ran to the bed, jerked
open the drawer on the nightstand, and pulled out Lonnie's
gun. "You rotten son of a bitch. You hit me again and I'll
shoot your ass off.''

He stopped in mid-stride, his eyes staring at the pistol.
The sight of the metal barrel pointing directly at him
seemed to jolt him back to his senses and he spoke quietly.

"You crazy woman. Do you know what you're doing?
Do you even know how to use that thing?''

"Hell no, but at this distance, I have to hit you somewhere.'' Her voice quivered as she screamed, "Get out,
get out of here—get away from me.'' She tore the ruby
from around her throat and threw it at him. "And take your
fucking heirloom with you.''

He gazed at the gun held awkwardly in her trembling
hand and backed toward the door. "We'll talk tomorrow—
after you've had a chance to cool off.''

The pain in her head had become a roar that blocked out
all rational thought. Autumn wanted only to get away from
Osborne House and Douglas. The ruby was still lying on
the floor and she kicked the stone and sent it rolling. Then
she ran to the dressing room and pulled a suitcase from the
closet. Clothes were thrown in the luggage in an untidy
ball, the gun crammed in her purse. She grabbed the
suitcase and hurried from the room and down the long
flight of stairs. In her haste, the suitcase banged and
clattered against the rails of the banister, an echo that
bounced off the high gilt ceiling and back to the pain that
soared in her head.

The Jag was still parked in front of the house where it
had been since her return from Turtle Ridge. She tossed
the suitcase onto the seat, climbed behind the wheel, and
fumbled the key into the ignition. The big engine sprang to
life and she slammed the car into gear, the tires screaming
as her foot jammed against the accelerator.

The tall trees along the winding lane blurred as the car

sped away from Osborne House and Douglas. The end of the drive loomed in the headlights and her foot hit the clutch, the brake, fishtailing onto Oakwood Drive in a slide. Autumn swore and cut the wheel into the skid. Downshifting, she pressed the accelerator. As the wheels caught, the Jag straightened and the engine roared, thunder against the stillness.

The needle on the speedometer rose higher and higher, but Autumn didn't slow down until the streetlights of town glowed in the distance. Gearing down, she turned onto Mason, and then onto Broadway, and cut sharply into the curb near a phone booth. All the change she had in her purse was two quarters. Swearing, she left the Jag and made the call collect. Shortly the connection was made and Lloyd's deep voice came on the line.

San Francisco seemed years away; Lloyd seemed years away. She had promised herself not to pull him in again, but this was something she couldn't handle alone. All he had to do was snap his fingers and the world unfolded. What was needed, he could have in Edisonville in a matter of hours.

He spoke her name several times before she finally spoke. "I'm here, Lloyd. I'm sorry to call so late, but I need a favor. Two favors."

"You sound upset. Are you all right, Autumn?"

"Yes. About the favors . . ."

"What is it you need?"

"I need a hooker. She has to be young, but not too young. Dark, sultry, unscrupulous, but smart enough to know who is buttering the bread. And I need a cardsharp. I'd like a woman. She doesn't have to be pretty, just have the same qualifications. Loyal only to me. Can you manage it?"

"The hooker is easy. The cardsharp will take a couple of days. What's happening, Autumn?"

"I don't feel like talking now. I'll be at the Holiday Inn. Call me tomorrow."

"Look, honey. You call me in the middle of the night, obviously upset, and ask for a hooker and a cardsharp. Don't you think you owe me an explanation?"

"Please," she whispered. "Just send them."

27

Early dawn was cresting before Autumn slept, and then
fretfully. She woke feeling tired, pulled the blanket over
her head, and tried to escape back into sleep, but thoughts
and images crowded into her mind. Bob, laughing and
playing foolishly in the moonlight. Douglas, shouting like
a man suddenly gone mad. Herself, holding Lonnie's pistol, the gun she had hardly touched in all these years.

Autumn crossed to the bathroom, stepped into the shower,
and let the hot water beat against her back, faced with the
aftermath of the storm at Osborne House. The night seemed
unreal now, but for one brief moment Autumn had known
she could kill Douglas Osborne. The thought was staggering. She had run from the house, not only in rage, but
fear. Rage at Douglas and the family for twisting something innocent into a sticky mess, and fear because of her
own violent emotions. She had always scoffed at the saying
that anyone is capable of murder under the right circum-
stances. Last night had taught her it was true.

She left the shower, toweled dry, and stepped to the
mirror over the vanity. An angry-looking bruise covered a
two-inch circle on her cheekbone. She touched it gingerly
with a fingertip, winced. A soft spot for women, Daisy
had said. Possibly for his late wife, Edith. He had sprung
at her like an enraged lion. Douglas' way of making his
women toe the mark, no doubt.

The bitterness of the night before felt caught in her

mouth. Autumn ran her tongue over her teeth and wished for a toothbrush to wash away the taste of the Osborne clan. After rinsing her mouth with water, she left the bathroom and pulled on a slip from her suitcase, fished a comb from her purse, and was tugging at tangled curls when the phone rang.

Autumn swore under her breath. Lloyd was the only one who knew about her checking in at the Holiday Inn. He would want to ask questions she wasn't ready to answer. Her marriage to Douglas wasn't something she wanted to tell him over the phone. Autumn listened to the shrill ring several times before picking up the receiver. "I'm sorry about calling you last night," she said. "I shouldn't have."

"Have you changed your mind?"

"No. But I could have waited until today to call."

"What happened?" Lloyd asked.

"I found out some important information. George has a fondness for women who aren't his wife. Homer has, or had, a fondness for cards. They've both been warned by Douglas, so I might be wasting my time. I have to try, though."

"You were upset last night. What happened?"

"Nothing," she said quickly. "I was just being female. Artie will be here in a few days. It will be easier then. I won't feel so alone."

There was a long pause at his end and she could see him in her mind's eye, thoughtful, thumbing the cleft in his chin. His voice was even when he came back on the line, but she was sure a frown was on his forehead. "Why aren't you in your apartment?"

"Paint," she said in a rush. "I'm having my apartment painted and the smell was making me sick." She leaned back against the pillows on her bed, quick to change the subject. "Have you given any thought to what we talked about last night?"

"Yeah. The woman I have in mind is Ginger Olson. She's worked for me before. You can trust her, if you keep the money coming. Ginger is twenty-four, tall, long black hair, green kitty-cat eyes, and a body that will give your man wet dreams."

"That good—huh?"

"That good."

"Brains, too, I hope."

"Enough."

"Explain to her that this is more than for a night or a weekend. She could be here for several weeks. George isn't to know she's a call girl. I want him to think she's handing out all that good stuff just for him. When and if she gets him, she's going to have to be smart enough to hang onto him. I want her to drain his bank account dry, take him for anything she can get. I need him crying for money."

"Brutal!"

"Yes, you taught me well, Lloyd. Besides, I'm only providing the cookie jar. He doesn't have to stick his hand in. The same applies for Homer. I'll set the stage, but he doesn't have to sit down at the poker table. Anything there yet?"

"No, but I've got my people working on it. I should have something by tomorrow. I'll get back to you."

"No," she said quickly. "I'm not sure where I'll be for the next few days. I'll call you."

He was silent for a long moment and when he spoke again his voice sounded distracted. "When will you be in San Francisco?"

"I wasn't planning to come until your board meeting in August. Why? Is there a problem?"

"No . . . no problem. I want to talk to you, but it can wait. I'll see you then, sweetheart."

Juggling, she thought. Juggling Douglas, juggling Lloyd. Marriage had moved her objective within reach, but it had created new problems. The house couldn't be used as an address, and she had been afraid to make or receive any out-of-town calls that could be spotted by Douglas. She had given Ella's number to her office in case they had to reach her, and she and Lloyd hadn't been in touch, so the phones hadn't become a problem until now.

She heaved her suitcase onto the bed and pulled out Levi's, pullover, and underwear. She had one leg in a pair of panties when a knock sounded at her door. The taps were soft but steady. When they grew more insistent, she jerked the panties on, crossed the room, and threw open the door. "Good morning, you old bastard. How did you find me?"

Douglas entered the room and closed the door quietly. "It wasn't hard. You have the only red Jag in town. It stood out in the parking lot like a neon sign."

"What do you want?"

"My wife. I came to take you home."

"I can't go back, Douglas. I'd end up killing you and your whole family."

"No, you won't. Because last night isn't going to happen again. I've already talked to my brothers and Harriet. They won't be telling any more tall tales. As my wife, you'll be treated with the same respect that was shown to Edith. From me and my family." He took her chin and frowned as he examined the bruise. "I've never hit a woman before. But then, no woman has ever made me as angry as you did."

Autumn pulled away from him and crossed to the window, gazing down at the hotel pool where children splashed. She didn't hear him walk across the soft carpeting, but she could feel the heat of his body behind her. He wanted her to come back for many reasons, the strongest being his obsessive pride. If she was careful, Autumn knew she could make the incident work for her. "I'm willing to forget last night, but there are other things at Osborne House I don't like."

"What? It's your home, Autumn. I want you happy there."

"I don't like sleeping in your wife's bed."

"Is that all?" He laughed at her and drew a finger along the strap on her slip. "I don't give a damn what you do to that room. Buy anything you want. Make any changes you want."

"I would like a private phone line, too. I'm tired of the servants listening in on my calls."

"Fine—order it."

"And my cream of wheat. I've told the cook several times how I like it, but she insists of doing it her way. It's lumpy."

"Talk to Daisy. She'll straighten out the cook."

"There's more." She turned from the window to face

him. "The servants cater to me, pamper me. They hardly let me feed myself, but they're your servants, not mine. The house is yours, the furnishings are yours, the people are yours. There isn't anything or anyone at Osborne House that is mine. I feel out of place, like a guest."

He shrugged. "What can I do about that?"

"Well . . . I'd like to have a couple of people of my own on the staff. My brother-in-law. He's out of work. You could give him a job around the house."

"Brother-in-law?" He looked surprised. "I didn't know you had a brother-in-law."

"You didn't ask me. His name is Artie McAvan. He was very good to me after my husband died. I'd like to do something for him now. Will you give him a job?"

"Doing what? The house is overstaffed as it is."

Autumn hadn't thought past the moment, and her mind raced through all of Artie's jobs for one that might be useful now. Struck by a sudden thought, she smiled into Douglas' eyes. "Chauffeur," she exclaimed. "Artie would be perfect, Douglas, and he's a top mechanic. You were complaining only a few days ago that the Mercedes was running rough and would have to go into the garage. And when the weather gets bad this winter, I certainly won't want to have to drive in the snow. If you'd rather not have him in the house, he could move into the apartment over the carriage house."

He smiled and nodded. "I think that can be arranged. Is there anything else ruffling your feathers, Mrs. Osborne?"

"Not at the moment."

"Good." He went to the bed and searched first the suitcase, then her purse, until he found the gun. After checking the safety, he tucked the barrel into the waistband of his trousers. "You know," he said, "I think you actually could have killed me for a minute there. I think I've married a bit of a wildcat."

She gazed into eyes that were bright and penetrating. "And that excites you?"

"Everything about you excites me." He took her hand and rubbed it against the swell in his trousers, pulled her into his arms and down onto the bed.

* * *

Autumn stared pensively out the window of the Mercedes. Douglas had kept the gun and insisted she ride with him and send for her car later. He whistled softly, reached out and touched her hand. Douglas' lovemaking didn't seem to fit the man. He was intensely passionate, but generous and tender. And she hated it. Autumn would have preferred him to be abrupt and indifferent. She wanted him all black. It confused her when he stepped out of character.

She caught him stealing a glance at her. He chuckled. "Do you have any more family tucked away that I don't know about?"

Autumn knew it would be wiser to deny Molly, but said, "I have an aunt somewhere. We don't get along." She straightened in the seat as Douglas turned the car into the drive and Osborne House appeared among the towering oaks. "Beautiful," she said sincerely.

"What's beautiful?"

"The house. It has a grandness about it. A sense of roots. Sometimes when I look at the old mansion I feel awed by it."

He glanced at her with a pleased smile. "My grandfather came home from a trip to Louisiana intrigued by some old plantation homes. He had it built shortly afterward. Someday it will belong to Brian."

"Not your brothers?" she asked.

"No. According to the will left by my grandfather, the firstborn son will inherit. The same is true of the ruby. The only way my brothers will get their greedy hands on Osborne House is through my death and then Brian's."

"What about the rest of the estate? From what I heard, you disinherited Brian. I heard, too, that Brian didn't want it. Will you leave everything to your brothers?"

"Hell no. I haven't got a brother smart enough to pour piss from a boot. I didn't disinherit Brian. He's my son, and a good deal like his old man. When the time comes, he'll return and do what's right. I have no doubt about that. Brian is off playing games and running away from himself and from me. He has a keen head for business. He can deny it, but it's there. His brain was meant for finance, not for digging in some tomb, but it's something he'll have to discover for himself." Douglas pulled the

Mercedes up in front of the house and urged her from the car. "Why don't we have some breakfast, and then saddle a couple of horses and go for a ride?"

Autumn looked at him stupidly. She knew only that a horse had four legs, a mane, and a tail. "I don't know anything about horses, Douglas. Even less about riding one. They're pretty to look at, but I prefer something with a steering wheel and a brake."

He grinned and slipped his arms around her waist. "I'll fix that. Before I'm through with you, I'll have you ready to ride the hunt. I'll arrange for you to have lessons. In the meantime, you can ride Penny, Brian's horse. She's fifteen years old and never gets out of a trot unless she's forced. I don't know why I keep her around."

"Maybe for the same reason you keep Brian's room exactly as he left it. And his sports car in the garage."

His face closed in a scowl and he hurried her toward the house. As they passed between the columns, Jasper, a black man with a crop of snowy white hair, came toward them. Douglas began to snap orders. "Bring Mrs. Osborne's things inside, and have her car brought from the Holiday Inn. Have my horse Thunder saddled and saddle Penny for Mrs. Osborne. Tell cook we'll be wanting breakfast now."

Douglas led Autumn into the house, where they were met by Harriet, who almost ran into them as she came out of the study. "I lost my earring last night," she said.

Autumn smiled, but knew Harriet hadn't lost an earring. She had seen Harriet to the door and a diamond had flashed on each ear. Harriet had come to see how much trouble she had caused. "Did you find it?" Autumn asked.

"Yes, it was in the sunroom." Harriet looked closely at Autumn's face, and the hint of a smile tugged at her mouth. "My. What happened to your cheek, dear?"

Autumn smiled sweetly. "Douglas and I were getting it on in the shower. I got so damned excited that I fell and hit my cheek on the water tap."

Harriet's eyes widened in shocked surprise. "Well . . . I never!"

"Really? Douglas, you're going to have to speak to George. He's neglecting Harriet."

"Cats." He took Harriet by the shoulders and directed her toward the door. "I have a few free hours to spend with my wife. I intend them to be peaceful. Scat!" He returned to Autumn, but before they could leave the foyer Daisy appeared at the head of the stairs and called out to Autumn.

Though she was well into her fifties, Daisy bounded down the stairs like a fifteen-year-old. "The maid you hired got here a little while ago. I thought you might want to talk to her, so I put her in your room to wait."

Autumn looked confused. "A maid? I didn't hire a . . ." She paused in thought. "What does this woman look like?"

"Well," Daisy said, "she's white-haired. A good fifty-five, or more. Tall, wears her hair in a braid around her head."

"Oh yes," Autumn said. "Now I remember."

Douglas looked amused. "My wife seems to be building a nest of her own at Osborne House."

"I think I should talk to her now," Autumn said. She ran up the stairs to her room, looked at Molly, and shook her head in wonder. "What are you doing here, Aunt Molly?"

Molly sat beside a window, her body rigid, arms crossed over her bosom. "I'm here, and I ain't leaving."

"That isn't what I asked you. Why did you come here?"

"I knew yesterday there'd be no changing your mind. I'm here to see that nothing happens to you. What you're doing is no good, crazy, and you're gonna end in deep trouble. You'll be needing me." She rose from the chair, looked at Autumn closely, and frowned. "What happened to your cheek?"

Autumn groaned. "A jackass kicked me."

28

❧

The only light in the room was one bulb that hung from the ceiling on a dusty cord. Cobwebs draped and caught like tickling fingers at Autumn's face and hair. Layers of dust puffed as she walked to the stack of documents that had to be six feet high, twenty feet deep, and thirty feet long. The dank-smelling, dimly lit room was located off the wine cellar. The history of the Osborne mines was in this one room, but it was going to take months to find what she needed.

Clouds of dust rose as Autumn pulled a folder from the stack, squinting in the dim light as she read a memorandum from Douglas. According to the memo, people were turning more and more to gas and electricity, and the use of coal was dropping at an alarming rate. Douglas would have been in his twenties when he wrote it. It was about then that he gained control of the Wellington distillery.

Stationing herself at the edge of the stack, she spent the next hour digging through records that were tossed at random, year twenty mixed with year sixty and so on. Annoyed and slightly discouraged, she kicked at the files and then sneezed from the dust that rose in the stale air.

Autumn knew Douglas would become curious if she spent too much time in the cellar, so her trips to the files were short and at odd hours. Douglas would be home shortly, so she left the room, grabbing a bottle of wine in passing as an excuse for having been in the cellar.

She climbed the stairs to a room off the kitchen that was used by the servants as a lounge. Artie was there with a glass of iced tea, which meant Douglas must be home. For some reason, her husband had suddenly wanted to be driven everywhere. Artie had arrived at Orborne House soon after Molly. He had been there well over a month. Douglas treated him with the same indifference as the servants, but acknowledged his relationship to Autumn by paying an exorbitant salary. Artie wasn't the kind to humble himself, so the farce was sometimes harder for him to bear. Unguarded, his gaze on her husband was pure acid. Fortunately, Douglas never looked directly at any of the staff.

Autumn set the wine on the table and tickled Artie under his thick beard. His eyes twinkled at her and she felt the familiar surge of affection. "No man should be as beautiful as you."

"No man is. I'm unique."

"Cocky, too." She sat down in a chair near him and propped her feet on the ottoman. "The files are a rat's nest. I don't know why I don't just give up."

"That's what you said the last time you were down there."

"Yeah, I know. They draw me like a magnet. Like a gambler, I keep telling myself: This time, I'll find something this time." She picked up his glass of iced tea and took a sip. "Where's Douglas?"

"In the study. Harriet was waiting to see him when he got home."

Autumn felt a momentary wave of apprehension. Lloyd had sent Ginger as planned, and Autumn had indirectly arranged the meeting with George. When sent to the Chicago offices on an errand for Douglas, George always stayed at the same hotel. Autumn simply placed Ginger within easy reach. Since then, George had installed the sultry lady, so much like his wife, in an apartment in Evansville, Indiana. In the last month Ginger had collected over sixty thousand dollars in gifts from George, which in addition to Harriet's demands had set his bank account quivering dangerously.

"Do you think Harriet suspects something?" Autumn asked.

"I doubt it. Besides, I don't think George would care. Ginger told me he's mentioned divorce several times. The old guy thinks he's in love with her."

"He can mention it all he wants. Douglas would never allow it, love or no. It would bring shame on the family name." She left the chair and brushed dust from her Levi's. "I have to get cleaned up before dinner. I'll talk to Douglas and find out why she's here." Autumn left Artie and walked down the corridor toward the foyer. She didn't like Ginger, but Artie did. When George wasn't with Ginger, Artie was. It was foolish and very risky, but Artie went where he pleased, and saw whom he pleased.

She turned into the foyer as an angry faced Harriet left the study. Glaring at Autumn, she shook a finger. "One of these days Douglas is going to see you for the cheap little slut you are. Then what will you be?"

Autumn grinned broadly. "A single woman with a hundred thousand dollars more than I had when I married him." She laughed and mounted the stairs to her room. Since Harriet believed her old affair with Douglas was carefully hidden, she thought she had license to judge other people. Harriet was a self-righteous cat, but harmless.

Molly sat near a window, mending what looked like a pair of panties. The house was overrun with servants, so Molly had nothing to do all day; consequently, she mended clothing that should be thrown away. Her aunt was bored and rambled around the old mansion with a lost kind of expression. Several times Autumn had tried to convince her to return to Turtle Ridge, but Molly's stubborn Irish feet were firmly planted in Osborne House. The most difficult thing about having Molly there was remembering not to call her Aunt Molly when people were around. "I'm going to take a bath."

"I'll fix your water," Molly said quickly.

Autumn rolled her eyes and nodded. She peeled out of her clothes, then pulled a drawing from her pocket and propped it on her desk. It was a watercolor of a very cockeyed house drawn by one of the children from the shelter. Bea had, over the weeks, nagged until Autumn agreed to help out there. Autumn enjoyed the children and went to the shelter several times a week. She took the smaller children for walks, played her guitar and sang to them. Sometimes she took a group to the movies, or to Osborne house to play in the pool, or to the stables to pat the horses. Autumn knew she would miss them terribly when the time came to leave Edisonville.

She went into the bathroom and climbed into the tub. Molly had added bubble bath and the tub was hidden in a mountain of suds that made Autumn feel light and giggly as she slid into the soft foam. Molly appeared in the doorway with Autumn's dusty clothes. "I think I'll take your things down to the washroom. Then maybe I'll go and cut some roses for your room. They got some mighty pretty roses here. The reddest I've ever seen."

Closing her eyes, Autumn directed a lazy nod at Molly. "Roses would be nice. Cut some for your room too."

"I can't. The servants aren't allowed to cut the roses for themselves."

"You're not a servant, Aunt Molly." Autumn sat upright in the tub, angry at the pettiness of the Osbornes and the subtle ways they found to separate themselves from what they considered the lower classes. It seemed that roses were only for the rich. "You tell everybody that the mistress of Osborne House has given permission to keep one freshly cut rose at all times, should they want. I'll see that bud vases are sent to each of them."

"It's a little thing, Autumn. Why make such a fuss?"

"It isn't little to me. If there should be a problem, I'll take care of it." Autumn threw herself against the back of the tub and wished for the day when she would be free of the Osbornes. Her plans for George were progressing nicely, but not so with Dale and Homer.

Bob had gone to Dale with the offer to buy his share of the mine, and a job offer the early part of June. Dale hadn't refused, but he had wanted time to think it over. It was the middle of July and he was still thinking. After Lloyd sent the cardsharp, she had set up a floating poker game, and then sent Bob to Homer. Bob bragged about winning enough to open his own office, snickering that a woman was in charge of the game—like taking candy from a baby. Homer had been intrigued; still, he hadn't gone near the hotel where the game was held. He had asked Bob about the game several times since, but he hadn't made a move toward the hotel. Autumn was afraid his fear of Douglas outweighed the pull of the cards.

Autumn scooped a handful of bubbles, blew, and watched as they disintegrated into tiny flakes. Like drifting snow, she thought, and the night with Brian came into her mind's eye. She remembered standing at the window, watching the snowflakes swirl in the wind. Brian had been stretched on the bed; now, ten years later, Autumn had emerged as his stepmother. The thought made her laugh out loud.

"What's so funny?" Douglas asked. He entered from his dressing room and crossed to the tub.

Startled, she sat upright. "Bubbles," she said. "They make me giggly."

He sat down on the edge of the tub, tipped her face, and kissed her lightly on the mouth. "What kind of mischief have you been up to today?"

"The usual. I saw Harriet earlier. What kind of mischief is *she* up to?"

He smiled slightly, dipped his finger into the suds, and smeared them across her cheek. "Inflation has hit George. He told Harriet he couldn't afford to send her to Europe this winter as usual. She came here screaming for me to give him more money."

"I gather you said no. Harriet looked a bit unhappy when I saw her."

He nodded. "Regardless of how much money I give my brothers, they find a way to spend it."

"Dale too?"

"No, Dale prefers to live simply."

Autumn picked up a sponge and drew it across her breasts. "Speaking of Dale. I was having my hair done today when I heard some women talking about him. They were whispering and laughing about his lover." She looked at Douglas with an innocent smile. "I didn't know Dale had a lover. Do you know who she is?"

His face went through a series of angry contortions. "No," he said. "I don't know her." He stood abruptly and left the room at a fast, jerky walk.

Autumn hurried from the tub, grabbed a towel, and followed through their joining bathrooms. She paused in the doorway that was in earshot of the phone in Douglas' room, heard the sounds of dialing, then his voice, low but cold and hard as he ordered Dale to come to Osborne House.

Autumn turned and walked slowly back to her room. She had given Dale the needed push that would send him running to Bob. Dale's shares in the mine would soon be hers, but she felt no triumph.

From where she stood near the terrace doors, Autumn could see and hear the two men in the study. Douglas, his face twisted with revulsion, shouted that Dale was a sickening fag, a degenerate that should be locked away from decent society. Dale pleaded that all he wanted was to be left in peace.

When their voices rose, Autumn braced herself and entered the room. "Douglas," she said, "I can hear you all over the house."

The men stood near the desk within arm's reach of one another. Douglas turned from Dale and looked at Autumn as if he wanted to hit her for intruding. "Get out of here, dammit!" His narrowed glance returned to Dale. "No—stay. I'm sick of protecting this facsimile of a man. The lover the women were referring to is Dale's houseman. This thing I call a brother is nothing but a worthless fag."

"Leave her out of it," Dale said.

"I'll leave her out, and you too." He shook his finger in Dale's face. "You listen, and you listen real good. I want that faggot you're living with out, and I mean out of my town. Furthermore, you are not to see him again. I've heard enough to know you can function as a real man. I don't care who, but I want you safely married, and all talk about you stopped. I'm giving you two months to find a wife. Otherwise, you're out too, and I mean all the way out. There won't be any more allowances, and no job in my town. You can dig ditches for all I care."

The color drained from Dale's face and a deep rumbling growl rolled from his lips. He lunged at Douglas, his arm drawn back, his hand curled into a tight fist. Sidestepping, Douglas shoved Autumn aside, blocking Dale's swing with one hand, backhanding him with the other. Enraged, Douglas curled his fist and swung again. Each blow from Douglas came harder, faster, until Dale was driven to his knees, his arms coiled over his head. Still Douglas pelted him.

Autumn stood transfixed. Blood gushed from Dale's mouth and nose and trailed down his chin in a thick stream. It dripped and stood stark against his white shirt in crimson spots. Then he wailed, a long anguished cry that tore at Autumn.

"Stop it!" she cried. "Stop it." She rushed forward, grabbed Douglas by the arm, and tried to pull him away from Dale. But it was like trying to move a mountain. Frightened for Dale, she shouted at Douglas and pounded on his back. He turned and stared at her with a dazed expression, then slowly lowered his fist.

Douglas frowned and looked at Dale with contempt. "Don't you ever come at me like that again, or so help me I'll kill you." He straightened his tie and stalked from the room. "See that he's cleaned up, Autumn."

29

The days slipped into a scorching hot August. Temperatures were running in the high nineties. The hills were seared to an ugly brown. What little air stirred was hot and muggy. Autumn brushed aside damp strands of hair that clung to her cheeks and parked the Jag in front of the children's shelter.

She left the car, listening to the sounds of children's voices as they played at the rear of the house. Bea had called Autumn about a little girl they had taken in. The father had abandoned them and the mother was having some problems, both financially and emotionally, so Bea had taken the child for a while.

Bea was in the kitchen with her hands buried in flour. She looked up when Autumn entered and said, "I hope you can cheer the little thing up. She won't play with the other children. She just sits in her room and mopes."

Autumn slid onto a kitchen stool and propped her guitar between her legs. "What's her name?"

"Betsy." Bea turned back to her flour. "It breaks my heart to see the little tyke so sad."

Bea's love for children was so obvious and all-consuming that Autumn asked why she didn't have some of her own. Bea turned, wiping her hands on her apron. "Harriet and George didn't have children because Harriet didn't want them. Homer and I wanted them, but I couldn't have them. It doesn't seem fair." She looked around the kitchen.

"Working here at the home has helped, and there was Brian. He used to stop on his way home from school and check my cookie jar." She smiled with a faraway look in her eyes. "He sure grew up to be a fine man—most of the time. He's a bit of a scrapper, though."

Bea talked about Brian as if it were only yesterday that he was a child. "You don't hear from him much, do you?"

Bea nodded. "I've had postcards from all over the world. He never says much, but it's good to know he's alive and well."

"Does he write to his father?"

"No. I'm the only one he writes to." She smiled and shook her head, clucked a little. "Douglas would get so mad at him. He would shout and rave at Brian. The boy would smile and agree, then do as he pleased."

"Do you know where he is?"

"Egypt. I haven't heard from him in months now, but that's not unusual. The last card I got was mailed from Patagonia. He had joined a foundation and was going to Egypt." Bea turned back to the counter and stirred the batter vigorously. "Brian's mother left him a large trust fund, and when his grandparents on Edith's side died, they left him quite a bit of money. He doesn't have to work unless the mood strikes him." Bea paused and gazed out the window. "When I found out I couldn't have children, I hated Edith because she had Brian. Really hated her."

Bea's use of the word "hate" sounded strange and out of place. "I can't imagine you hating anybody."

"Well, I can. There's been times when I hated the ground Douglas walked on. I don't care for myself, but he is so mean to Homer. It's hard to grow up with an older brother that never fails at anything. Every time Homer does something Douglas doesn't like, he threatens to remove him from office. That would kill Homer. Being mayor is the most important thing in his life. It's the only thing he can point to with pride. Now that devil is after him again." She waved the spoon in the air and turned back to the counter. "That Douglas. Sometimes I feel like putting a spider in his Apple Betty pie."

Autumn smiled to herself. "If you feel that strongly, why do you always bake pies for him?"

Bea shrugged her chubby shoulders. "I don't know. He makes a fuss over my pies and it makes me feel good. My Apple Betty pie is the only apple dish he will eat. I guess the one thing I can point to with pride is my cooking. Like Homer, we all need something." She paused and stared down at the bowl of batter, her eyes widening. "My word! Would you look what I've done? I just mixed chopped dates in my brownie batter instead of the nuts."

Autumn grinned and twirled the guitar between her legs. Last week it was raisins in her banana bread. "What did you do with the nuts?"

"I suppose they're in the date bars. Oh, well. The kids won't care. They'll eat anything."

"I'm distracting you," Autumn said. "I'll go and talk to the little girl."

Autumn left Bea and walked down the hall to a room where a little girl sat alone on the edge of a bed. For a moment Autumn felt as if she were seeing herself at that age, alone, lonely.

Betsy's hair wasn't auburn, but a light brown, woven into pigtails as Autumn's had been, and her eyes weren't brown, but a sad blue. The little girl looked at Autumn for a moment, then glanced down and picked at the tail of her dress as Autumn crossed and sat on the bed beside her. "What's your name?" Autumn asked.

"Betsy."

"That's a very pretty name. How old are you?"

Betsy didn't look at her, but she held up five fingers, then popped her thumb in her mouth and mumbled around it, "I want my mommy."

"I know," Autumn said. "You'll be back with her soon. While you're waiting, would you like to be my friend? My name is Autumn, and I don't have anybody to play with."

Betsy looked at her out of the corner of her eye. "You're grown up. You don't play."

"Sure I do. I play the guitar all the time. Would you like me to play for you?"

Betsy shrugged and Autumn pulled the strap over her

head and settled the guitar on her lap. She strummed for a while, glanced at Betsy with a teasing smile, and began to sing. Slowly, bit by bit, Betsy began to smile. After a while she sang along with Autumn. Once the sadness had left her little face, Autumn said good-bye, and promised to return again soon.

Autumn tossed her guitar into the car and drove the six blocks to Ella's diner. It was midafternoon and the place was empty, save for one man at the counter. He looked to be in his seventies, a wrinkled, spidery little man with four long gray hairs standing straight up on the top of his bald head. His eyes were bright, though, and swept over Autumn with a lewd expression.

Autumn grinned in amusement and slid onto a stool as Ella entered from the kitchen. He tossed a dollar on the counter and rose, still with the same lewd expression as he looked at Autumn. "Why would a pretty thing like you marry that old son of a bitch Osborne?" Without another word, he turned and bounced out the door.

Autumn looked at Ella and grinned. "What was that all about?"

"That's Fritz Jergenson. He owns the Edisonville *Times*, and he hates Douglas' guts. There's nothing he would like more than to smear the Osborne name across the front page of the paper."

"Really? Could he be helpful to me?"

Ella shook her head. "He doesn't know anything. If he did, it would already be in his paper. Old Fritz is an honest man, and a real journeyman. He wouldn't publish anything unless it was backed up by absolute proof." Ella turned toward her office. "Let's go back and have some shine."

Autumn followed, but her face was solemn now. Being with Betsy had helped for a while, but the scene between the two men was back, weighing on her mind. She took a drink from Ella and threw herself down in a chair. "Even the air in the old house stings with tension since the fight with Dale. I knew Douglas would be angry, but I didn't expect one remark to wreak such havoc. Dammit, Ella. I didn't want Dale to get hurt this way."

Ella leaned back in her chair, her feet propped on the

desk. "You swore you'd turn this town upside down. Are you going to run now that you've tilted it a little?"

"No, I can't do that." Talking about Dale brought the scene in the study sharply to mind. Autumn rose abruptly, tipped her glass and drained it. "I'm too restless to just sit, Ella. I'll talk to you later—tomorrow."

Autumn rolled a pea around her plate and stabbed at it with a fork. Douglas raised an eyebrow at her from across the dinner table. She gave her napkin a toss. "I'm not hungry." Earlier, she had overheard Homer and Douglas in the study, their voices raised.

She picked the pea from her plate with a finger and shoved it in her mouth. "Are you and Homer having another disagreement?"

"I'm always having a disagreement with one of my brothers. Because Homer is mayor, he thinks he can get around me. His title doesn't mean shit. I run this town. I put him in office, and I can take him out."

"What is he doing?"

"Fucking up." He smiled suddenly, picked the napkin up from his lap, and placed it alongside the plate. "How would you like me to teach you to play chess?"

Autumn looked at him in surprise. A chess set was kept ready in the study, but the only person she had seen him play with was John Allison. "I know the game," she said. "My late husband taught me."

He nodded and rose, took her arm and led her from the table. She glanced at him as they walked through the foyer to the study. "Are you sure you want to play with a woman?"

He only smiled.

She slid into a chair across from him. "Why don't we make this really interesting? A hundred dollars if I can checkmate you in six moves."

"You're on."

"What will you give me if I checkmate you in five moves?"

"What would you like?"

"A shopping spree in San Francisco."

He nodded his agreement and engaged her in small talk.

"How are your riding lessons? Are you ready to move up to a swifter horse?"

"Far from it!" She slid an ivory pawn ahead two spaces. "That gentle mare of Brian's shied and dumped me on my rear."

He chuckled and moved a pawn, was silent for the next two moves, and then brought up the subject of video games. "I won't have them in my town."

"Aren't you being a little stodgy, Douglas. Video games are harmless."

"Not to my way of thinking. I'm not going to have the kids in this town shoving their lunch money down an empty hole. They have better things to do with their time, and better places to spend their money."

She looked at him derisively. "Like the slot machines at the joints, or in the back room humping some whore?"

Douglas leaned back in his chair, frowning. "What do you know about the joints?"

"I know they exist. I know kids go there to drink. I know they play the slots. I know some of the boys ride the whores."

He waited until she had made a move, then slid a chess piece forward. "The men need a place to let off steam, and the kids need to sow a few wild oats. When Brian was fourteen, I took him to one of the joints. I gave him a hundred-dollar bill and turned him loose. He looked like hell when I picked him up the next morning, but he had a grin that spread from ear to ear." Douglas paused and watched as she moved a chess piece; then he slid a bishop across the board. "Anything that can make a boy grin like that can't be all bad . . . Check, and mate."

"Damn! Does this mean I don't get the trip to San Francisco?"

"No," he said, laughing. "Go! Spend—enjoy."

30

Autumn spent the evening before leaving for San Francisco in the study with Douglas. He had been unusually quiet, and she wondered why. He sat at his desk, as if waiting, watching her with a thoughtful expression. She was searching the shelves for a book to read, when George entered the study unannounced.

He stalked across the room in his flamboyant way, dressed in a bright plaid jacket. "I got a message you called. Where are you sending me now?"

"To hell!"

Autumn glanced at Douglas with surprise.

Douglas motioned George toward a chair. "Sit down!"

George dropped immediately into a chair. "Is something wrong?"

"Yeah, a broad named Ginger."

George half-rose in his chair, easing down as if suddenly weakened. "What do you know about Ginger?"

"Everything. Harriet came to me a few weeks ago and told me you couldn't afford to send her to Europe this year. I know how much money you make, and I know how much you have going out." He smiled with rancor. "I did some checking, and what did I find? I found a sexy young gal set up in a fine apartment in Evansville, wearing a few diamonds and driving a new car. She's a good-looking piece, George, but she has to go."

George squirmed in his chair, looked at Autumn and

then to Douglas. "You know what living with Harriet is like. Leave me alone, Doug. I'm not hurting anyone. You have Autumn. Let me have Ginger."

"I can afford Autumn. You can't afford Ginger. She's too rich for your bank account."

"I won't do it," he said, like a nervous boy opposing his father. "I love Ginger. I'm leaving Harriet."

"The hell you are." Douglas leaned forward, his hands folded and resting on the desk. "I don't care if you fuck every whore in the county, but this one has to go. She's using you, George. I had your little woman watched. When you're not around, she has a young stud servicing her. Ginger loves your money, but another man's cock."

Autumn realized Artie had been caught and that she would have some explaining to do. She looked at George, who now sat with his shoulders slumped. He looked at Douglas, raw hate in his eyes. "I could kid myself that you did this for me, but it would be a lie. You did it to hurt." He rose, his face void of emotion as he walked toward the door.

Douglas pushed away from his desk and stood. "I'll give you one week to clean up your mess."

"Maybe I will, maybe I won't."

"It's up to you. Either she goes or you're out. Think about it, George. There aren't many places that will pay a forty-eight-year-old man the kind of money I pay you to run errands."

George stood in the doorway. "Someday, someone is going to put a bullet through that thing you call a heart."

Douglas laughed. "It sure as hell won't be you, brother."

Autumn waited until George had left the room, then crossed to a chair. "Rough on him, weren't you?"

"Sometimes I have to be. My brothers are growing old without ever growing up. They still need a keeper." He left his desk, took a chair, and gazed at her curiously. "What do you know about this, Autumn?"

"Why would I know anything?"

"The young stud is Artie."

Autumn forced her face to show surprise. "Really? I wonder how he met her. You did say she was from Evansville, didn't you?"

"I don't know where she's from, but that's where she's living now. I don't want to go into it tonight, but when you come back from San Francisco we're going to sit down and have a long talk with your brother-in-law. I want to know why and how both men became involved with the same woman."

"Fine," she said, and yawned. "I'm tired. I think I'll go to bed." She felt a wave of panic, but forced herself to leave the room calmly. Once in the foyer, she raced up the stairs to the phone in her room. Artie wasn't in his apartment over the garage, but she reached him at Ginger's.

He thought it was amusing and laughed. "Relax, Autumn. Ginger isn't going to let George get away, and I'll think of something to tell Douglas."

"What? How the hell are you going to explain this?"

"Not to worry. I'll come up with a good one. By the time you get back from San Francisco, I'll have everything under control."

"Why don't I feel reassured?"

"Because you worry too much. Take your trip, have fun, and let me handle things here."

Autumn hesitated, but thought of Lloyd's board meeting and finally agreed. "I'll go, but for Pete's sake, play it cool until I get back."

After the heat of Kentucky, the cool of San Francisco came as a blessing. After the tension in Osborne House, the rush and clamor of her office seemed like mere child's play by comparison. She skirted her desk and held her hand out to Edward Goodman. Ed had been with them five years now, stolen from McDonald's. She had felt comfortable leaving him in charge. "You're doing a marvelous job, Ed. I won't forget."

He rose from a chair, his bald head shining in the afternoon light. Large downward-slanting eyes returned her smile from behind gold-rimmed glasses. "It hasn't been hard. You have good people behind you."

Autumn thought back to Osborne House and frowned, picking up her purse from the desk and walking toward the door, Ed following. "I had an unexpected setback in my plans that could keep me out of town even longer than I had thought.''

Ed looked curious, but he didn't question her. He paused and opened the door to the outer office. Autumn looked at Grace's desk, the covered typewriter, the bud vase with one lone flower. ''There's something very special about a busy office that's been put to rest. It gives me a feeling of accomplishment, even if I've had a few flops during the day.''

He smiled as they left the room. ''Will you be in tomorrow?''

''No. I have a board meeting at Murphy's in the morning. Later, I'm flying out. I had planned to stay longer, but something came up.''

''The setback in your plans?''

''A whopper of a flop.'' She smiled and gave him her hand. ''Thanks, Ed. Thanks for taking care of things.''

Autumn left the car and mounted the stairs to the back room of the Doghouse. Western music blared as she entered. Wally was at the desk, a deep frown of concentration on his face. Autumn realized she had outgrown the Doghouse. It seemed dirty and seedy now, the music too loud, the waitresses too brassy. She slid onto the corner of his desk. ''I think I've become a snob.''

Wally looked at her and grinned. ''What are you trying to tell me?''

''I think I'd like to sell the place and put the money into something with a better return.''

He leaned back in his chair, nodding. ''I've been expecting it. In fact, I've wondered why you waited this long.''

She looked around the room, recalling the years with Everett and Julie: singing in the smoke-filled room, the dollars she had pulled from the peanut-butter jar. In some ways they were good years, fun years. ''Selling the place will be like selling a piece of myself, but it's time. I don't belong here anymore.'' Her glanced circled the room and rested on Wally fondly. ''How would you like to come to work for the Corbett Corporation?''

"I'm sixty-three, Autumn. I'm too old to jump into that kind of rat race."

"What will you do?"

"Retire. I'll go fishing, hunting, travel. If I can get it up, I'll even try to lay my wife now and then."

"Sure . . . sure. Three months and you'll be going crazy. I'll give you a unit to manage. Four stands. You can do it standing on your hands." She winked. "A new job might put new life in your thingamajig."

"Promises. promises."

She grinned. "You don't have to decide today. I don't think the Doghouse will sell overnight." She slid from the desk and turned toward the stairs to the apartment. "I'm going to take some flowers to the cemetery. Then I suppose I'll come back and go to bed early."

His eyes narrowed impishly. "I would have thought you'd be spending the evening with Lloyd."

"No. I'll see Lloyd tomorrow at the meeting." Autumn climbed the stairs to the apartment above, musing how easily Lloyd had detached himself from her. He knew she was in town, but other than one call, they hadn't spoken, and then it had been brief and strictly business.

Her emotions were in such chaos that it was hard to define how she felt about Lloyd. At times she had an overwhelming desire to see him, longed to be held and to smell his distinctive male odor, partly shaving lotion, partly pipe tobacco. Rolled together they were Lloyd Murphy, the big Irishman with sandy hair and vivid green eyes.

The meeting seemed to drag on and on. Autumn had once found it exciting to sit on a board with so many prominent people. Now she only half-listened through a long, dry quarterly report. There were thirteen members on the board and each had his own long, dry comment. As instructed earlier on the phone, she ayed in a new vice-president and nayed out a nominee. The background of the nay sounded more impressive than the aye to Autumn, and she wondered how many men and women on the board were like her—there only as a prop for Lloyd.

Autumn glanced at him and caught him looking at her soberly. She smiled and after a moment's hesitation he smiled in return. Throughout the meeting she had been acutely aware of his presence at the end of the table, so much so that at one point she had become uncomfortable and slipped off her shoes. When he finally adjourned the meeting, she laughed at herself, slipped her feet back into her heels, and picked up her purse to leave.

As she rose, he motioned with his eyes for her to remain, and she eased back into the chair. They sat quietly until the room had cleared. After a long and awkward silence he said, "You're looking good."

"You're looking good too."

"I've missed you."

"I've missed you too."

He smiled and rose from the table. "You're going to force me to make the first move, aren't you?"

She nodded.

"Okay. Are you free for lunch?"

"Yes," she said. "I'm free for lunch."

Autumn looked at the empty soup bowl and thought back to the party when Lloyd had urged her to eat caviar. She had shuddered at the thought. Since then, caviar had become a favorite, and she had just finished a bowl of bird-nest soup. "Amazing how time and circumstances can alter people, and what they believe themselves to be." She popped a piece of cold lobster into her mouth and crossed to the edge of the terrace where she had stood and necked with Lloyd, a mere girl. Nearby was a potted rose tree that scented the air.

She could feel Lloyd's eyes on her and turned toward him. He sat at the table, his tie loosened, his jacket thrown across the back of a chair. "I've made a mess of things," she said.

"Me too. I was wrong in Louisville. I knew how much going back meant to you, but I had to play the macho male." He left the chair and went to where she stood, his large hand embracing her smaller one. "When you told me about Douglas and your plans to go back, I sent men to watch you. Not to check up on you, Autumn, but to watch over you. I was afraid for you." He hesitated and smiled faintly. "That night in Louisville, I'd received a call from one of my men shortly before we sat down. He reported seeing you kissing Bob Proctor in front of Ella's diner. I broke my own rule. I became jealous and tried to force you back to me. I was wrong.''

Autumn nodded, understanding his strange behavior in Louisville now. She thought of Bob and smiled. ''If I were going to take a lover, it would be a man, not a baby like Bobby. To me he's still the little boy I licked in a school fight.'' She glanced down at his hand holding hers, at the diamond Douglas had slipped on her finger, and had a sudden dreadful thought. ''Are your men still in Edisonville?''

''No. I felt you were fairly secure when Artie moved into the apartment over the garage at Osborne House. He was closer to you than my men could ever be.''

''You know?'' she asked.

''Yes, I know.''

''I wanted to tell you, but not over the phone. Then, when you were so distant, I didn't think it mattered.''

''In a way, I feel I pushed you into it. If I hadn't been an ass and left you when I did, you wouldn't have married him. I'm not happy about your so-called marriage, but it doesn't change a damned thing. You were always more mine than Everett's. You're still more mine than Osborne's.'' He kissed her then, lightly, on the edge of the mouth. ''My desk is cleared. The yacht is ready. The crew is waiting, and a black lacy thing, your size, is in the cabin. All you have to do is say yes.'' He smiled when she hesitated. ''Qualms?''

''No. I don't owe Douglas anything, least of all loyalty. But I'm expected back tonight. I'll have to call home.'' She slipped her arm around his waist and they entered the living room together. She stood in the curve of his arm as she dialed. A secretary answered on the second ring and drawled slow and easy that the caller had reached Mr. Osborne's office. ''This is Mrs. Osborne,'' Autumn said. ''I'd like to talk to my husband, please.''

Autumn's face went still, her body rigid in Lloyd's arms. ''When?'' Her voice snapped the word. ''How?'' She looked at Lloyd and her tone lowered to a whisper. ''Yes, I'll be home as soon as possible.'' She eased the receiver down on its cradle and stared at Lloyd with a dazed expression. "He's dead. That son of a bitch is dead."

"Who is dead?"

"It isn't fair," she said. "I've waited years, and he drowns. That fucker drowned in his own damned pool." She spun on her toes, her hands gesturing wildly. "I had them all. All of them. Dale would have accepted Bob's offer eventually. Now he's free. And George. There was a mess with George, but he would have agreed to sell his share in the mine before giving up Ginger. Homer was still a problem, but I would have found a way."

Autumn was shouting and Lloyd took her by the shoulders, shaking lightly. "You're not making any sense, Autumn. Who is dead? Who drowned?"

"Douglas. He drowned in a pool. Damn him. Damn him to hell for dying."

"Then it's over?" Lloyd asked.

She gazed at him and waited for something magical to happen, a freeing inside, a sense of release, something. "Over? I don't know. I feel odd. I have this feeling of something unfinished, ends hanging loose. Like dirty dishes in water, soaking, waiting for someone to come and wash them clean." She turned to Lloyd and shook her head. "It's not over. I have to go back. Dammit, I have to go back."

Autumn paced the room, rubbing her hands together. "The one thing Douglas valued more than life itself was the Osborne name. Maybe I can't smear the man, but I can play hell with his memory. Before I leave Edisonville, the town is going to know that Douglas was responsible for the deaths of fourteen men. They're going to know about Lonnie and how he died. And they're going to know that Douglas and their fine mayor and their fine chief of police are behind the bootleg whiskey and prostitution in their fair town." She paused and looked at Lloyd with a quiet expression. "The first time I left Edisonville, I left in darkness—a thief, a whore, sick inside. The next time I leave, it will be in the sunlight with no shadows following me."

"I understand where you're coming from, honey, but hell, it's not—"

"No," she said quickly. "I'm not tied to a husband now. I'll come whenever you want. It will be different this time, if you'll try too."

He gazed at her as if undecided, but finally nodded. "Want a drink?"

"Please. Whiskey." She sat down on the sofa and tried to relax, but everything was churning inside. Thoughts darted crazily from Douglas to the night with the son and back again to Douglas, round and round and back to Brian. She still felt a lunge of shame when she remembered that night with Brian. He'd called her a whore, thrown her on the bed, and devoured her body as though she were a piece of meat. Trapped beneath him, she had promised herself that someday he would treat her with respect, and not as a whore. Yes, the night with Brian was part of it too, a shadow she would have to face and deal with.

He'd been a boy then, and drunk. What would he be like as a thirty-two-year-old man? She remembered him as tall, with shoulders that strained against a leather jacket, jutting chin, a strong body tanned from vacationing somewhere hot and sunny. The thick mat of hair covering his chest was darker than the mass that tumbled and fell across his forehead. His eyes had been the most disarming: a clear blue that seemed to change colors with his moods, lightening in tone when he teased, until they appeared silver, then darkening to a green-topaz when he was aroused. A handsome, spoiled little rich boy with a fetish for redheads.

Autumn laughed freely as Lloyd came toward her. "I have a feeling things are going to be very different at Osborne House now, maybe even fun."

His eyes narrowed curiously. "What are you planning now?"

"How to stick it to a smart-ass little rich boy."

"What rich boy?"

"The son. Brian will be coming home."

IV

❧

Brian

31

Brian drew fingers down and around his freshly shaven chin. Off with the old, on with the new. The skin around his mouth was tanned a deep bronze, but pale where the shaggy beard had once grown, which gave him the look of a raccoon, or at least a man wearing goggles. A few days in the sun would take care of the mask, and his clean-shaven face would blend with the stiff business suits that were part of his inheritance, an unwanted part. His father had threatened disinheritance, but both men had known it was an empty threat, unfortunately.

Brian heard the sounds of splashing water and glanced at the door between his bathroom and Autumn's. He was curious about the woman, and why his father had married her. She wasn't anything like his mother. Edith had been short and blond, with timid blue eyes. Autumn was tall with auburn hair and deep-set hypnotic eyes. He'd looked, and felt himself being drawn deeper and deeper into velvety pools of soft brown. Perhaps Douglas had looked and been sucked in so deeply he couldn't climb out. Her reasons for marrying were clear, and Brian liked and respected honesty. He couldn't resent the woman; he felt mildly amused that somebody had finally touched a weak spot in a man with a hide like armor.

His strides were even as he left the room, but Brian felt as if his body were moving in slow motion. He wanted to stagger to the four-poster and put his jet lag to bed, but the family was downstairs waiting for the reading of the will. He tried to visualize his father thrashing, gasping, drawing his last breath before the water claimed him, but the picture wouldn't come. His father had been too strong, invincible. Brian could hardly believe the big man was actually dead.

He felt more guilt than grief. He'd tried to get close, but his father had kept him at arm's length. At the same time, Brian had always known that he was loved by his father. But Douglas' need to control had sent his only son running. Brian had felt choked by the town, by his father, and he'd had an unappeasable appetite for adventure. In the beginning he dreamed of making the big find, but the big finds had already been found. Disillusioned, he drifted, brawled, and drifted. Now and then he had felt the need to prove himself a man in his own right. He had joined with one or another foundation, but always a nagging voice pecked away at the base of his brain: "Forget it. Your future is already neatly planned and charted."

It came as no surprise to find the house as he had left it: the white marble floor in the foyer, walls paneled in dark oak, the curving staircase covered in rich wine carpeting. A crystal chandelier hung from the high old-fashioned ceiling. Brian remembered times when it quivered and made a soft tinkling noise, an eerie kind of music that had half-frightened, half-fascinated him as a child. He had thought the house must be haunted, until his mother explained it was only the men setting off blasts in the mines below.

Tension pulled the muscles tight across his shoulders as he entered the study. He glanced at the family scattered about the room and felt the gates of responsibility closing behind him. Brian had run fast and hard, but had always known he would have to come back eventually. His father had instilled in him the importance of the family and the family estates. His summers had been spent working the mines and distillery, following at his father's heels to see how the big man did it. While other boys were having wet dreams, he was having nightmares about mining and distilling with rows of numbers dancing before his eyes. It was all his now, and it would have to be managed somehow.

One by one the uncles rose and shook his hand, patted him on the back, and welcomed him home. Harriet flashed heavy diamond fingers, and Bea, his favorite aunt, gave him a tight hug, a pat, and a kiss on the cheek. Jasper and Daisy sat in the far corner of the room. John Allison smiled and nodded from behind the desk. Brian waited until everybody had returned to their chairs, then went to the liquor cabinet and mixed a Scotch and water to help loosen the tight muscles. He crossed the room and stood in front of the desk. "How did my father die?"

"He drowned," George said. "Didn't Autumn tell you?"

"Yes, but she didn't seem to know how."

"She knows as much as the rest of us."

Homer left his chair and went to stand beside Brian. "It happened when he took his nightly swim, but we don't know the exact circumstances. Autumn was in San Francisco. The servants were here, but asleep. Artie was the one that found Douglas the next morning. The police questioned him, but he didn't see or hear anything."

"Was there an autopsy?" Brian asked.

"Of course," Homer replied. "They had to determine cause of death. Everything pointed to accidental drowning."

"That's what they say," Harriet snapped. "I don't believe it. Douglas was a healthy man and a strong swimmer. If you ask me, there's some monkey business going on, and the monkey is upstairs."

"Meaning?" Brian asked.

"Autumn."

Homer frowned derisively. "What do you think Autumn did, Harriet? Sneak back from San Francisco and hold him down in the water? Somehow I can't imagine a hundred-and-ten-pound woman drowning a two-hundred-pound man. There's nothing out of line about Douglas' death, Brian. There was water from the pool in his lungs. There weren't any marks on the body, or traces of drugs or poisoning." Homer returned to his chair, but looked at Harriet with a scowl. "As usual, Harriet is trying to stir up trouble."

When Harriet made a face at Homer, Brian felt some of the tension begin to ease. "What do you think, Uncle George?"

"I agree with Homer. I don't think Autumn had anything to do with this. Why should she want him dead? He gave her everything she wanted.''

''And then some,'' Harriet snorted.

Brian looked at Dale, his favorite uncle. ''What do you think?''

Dale shrugged. ''A cramp maybe. Doug thought he couldn't go to bed without a snack and a swim first. I suppose his body could have had a reaction this time. I'm surprised it hasn't happened before.''

''I still think it's odd,'' Harriet said. ''For instance, why couldn't Autumn be found when we tried to locate her?''

''Autumn explained that,'' Homer intervened. ''She had reservations at one hotel, but there was a mix-up. They didn't have a suite for her, so she checked into another hotel.''

Harriet glanced at Homer. ''Why are you sticking up for that cheap little bitch?''

''Because you're trying to make something out of nothing.''

Brian looked at each family member, sighed, and turned to John Allison. ''Do you feel all right about Dad's death?''

''Yes,'' John replied. ''His death was sudden, so I looked into it. There's no evidence that Douglas died from any cause other than accidental drowning.''

Brian nodded and leaned against the front of the desk. He took a sip of the drink and his glance again swept the room. ''Tell me about Autumn.''

''A slut,'' Harriet said. ''She appeared from out of nowhere and wrapped Douglas around her little finger.'' She paused as if gathering steam, and her voice became tense and high-pitched. ''There's something odd about the woman. Take that maid of hers. I asked Molly to get me a cup of coffee one day. Autumn heard and came unhinged. She told me in no uncertain terms that Molly was not a servant and if I wanted coffee, I could get it myself.'' Harriet straightened in the chair and drew a breath. ''And there's that brother-in-law of hers. There's something odd there, too. Douglas was a fool to bring him here.''

Daisy displayed her disgust by rolling her eyes and tossing her kinky head of hair. Brian grinned, wondering if there was an unbiased view of Autumn in the room. "I'm not interested in Autumn's morals, or in domestic squabbles between you gals, but I would like to know where she came from and how she managed to marry Dad."

No one spoke, but all eyes turned to John Allison. He shrugged. "I don't know anything. She came here from San Francisco and wanted to open a dress shop. Your father had a piece of property she wanted to lease for the shop. It was a small matter, so I let Bob Proctor handle it. He brought them together. You all know the rest."

Brian set his drink on the desk and went to Bea, leaning forward and resting a hand on each chair arm. She was gazing out the window; nudged to awareness, she smiled and patted him on the cheek. "You're so pretty, Brian. I would have loved to have a son like you."

He bent and kissed her chubby cheek. Brian didn't know how gentle Bea had survived the years. Possibly because she had a way of fading into the background when things got rough. "What do you think of Autumn, Aunt Bea?"

"I like her. She's a little misguided, but that's understandable, coming from a wicked place like San Francisco." She turned from Brian when the terrace doors burst open abruptly. Brian straightened as Autumn breezed into the room.

She paused in the middle of the floor, wearing a black dress with a swooping neckline and a slit that reached to the knee. "Hi, folks. Ya'll waiting on me?"

Harriet's voice could be heard over the murmur of disapproval. "Have you no respect for the dead, no decency? How could you come here wearing a dress like that?" She turned to Brian, but pointed a finger at Autumn. "Look at her."

He smiled, but wondered why the dress. She had to have worn it deliberately, to incite—provoke. Why?

"My, my," Autumn said. "Such a fuss. I'm wearing black, aren't I?"

Harriet's mouth snapped shut, Daisy snickered, George leered, Dale grinned, Homer cleared his throat, and Bea turned back to the window. Autumn looked amused and took a seat on the sofa. Brian crossed to sit beside her, but avoided looking into the velvet pools. He focused on a knee that jutted through the slit. "You're looking good, Mother."

"Thank you, son."

"Nice legs."

"They get me where I have to go." She turned from Brian and glanced at John Allison. "Could we get on with this, please?"

He nodded. "I'll begin by saying that Douglas has left the bulk of his estate to Brian."

Brian groaned inwardly. *Thanks a lot, Dad.*

John's gaze circled the room. "Douglas was very specific about his will and how he wanted it read. These are his words, not mine." John looked directly at Daisy. " 'Daisy, you mouthy bitch, I'm leaving you fifty thousand dollars for the love and care you gave my wife, Edith, and my son, Brian.' "

"Fifty thousand dollars," she shouted. "What in the world am I going to do with fifty thousand dollars?" She looked at Brian and grinned. "You give my money to Mr. Brian. He can take care of it for me."

John smiled and turned back to the will. " 'Jasper, you black bastard, I'm leaving you twenty-five thousand dollars so you can die a high-class coon.' "

Jasper looked at Daisy with a white-toothed smile that spread across his ebony face. "I ain't gonna have no trouble spending my money. I'm gonna buy myself a big fine boat and go fishin'."

"You would," Daisy said. "You best think about your old age. It ain't far off."

John motioned for quiet, then returned to the will. " 'I have always felt my brothers failed to reach manhood because I was there to protect and keep them from harm's way. I intend to right that wrong. To my brothers, Homer, George, and Dale, I leave one dollar each. Brothers, you're on your own. To my sisters-in-law, I leave my sympathy.' "

No one spoke, but the room vibrated with tension and the shuffling of feet. John waited until the room had quieted, and then continued. " 'To my wife Autumn, I leave my deep respect.' " John paused and cleared his throat. " 'So she will never have to marry for money again, I also leave my wife, Autumn, one million dollars.' "

Brian's head jerked around and he stared at Autumn. Her face showed unmistakable surprise. He tipped his glass in a salute. "How does it feel to be a rich widow?"

"Super." She looked at Harriet and smiled sweetly. "One million beautiful dollars. I think I'll take a trip to Europe."

"Bitch!" Harriet leapt to her feet and rushed over to Autumn. "Scheming bitch. You have been an embarrassment to us from the day Douglas married you. He's dead now and there's no one here to protect you. I suggest you take what he left you and get the hell out of Osborne house. Better still, get the hell out of town."

Autumn rose from the sofa, but looked at Brian with a smile that was slightly challenging. "It seems I've just been ordered from your house. I'll start packing. I wouldn't want to stay where I'm not welcome."

Brian watched as Autumn walked toward the door. "No," he said strongly. He set his drink on a table, rose, and glanced at each member of the family. "Autumn was my father's wife, and I respect her as his widow. This is my house now, and she is free to stay for as long as she wants—peacefully." He looked directly at Harriet, held Autumn's arm, and led her from the room. "You took a big chance in there, Autumn."

"What do you mean?"

"This." He hooked a finger in her shoulder strap and gave it a tug. "I don't know why, but you walked in wearing a dress designed for an evening out on the town. Then you incited Aunt Harriet into a jealous rage, which forced me to make a choice. I think you've done enough for today." He turned her toward the stairs with a light shove. "Game's over, Mother."

"Don't call me Mother!" She raced up the stairs. Reaching the landing, she paused, looked down at him, and laughed, a mischievous laugh that seemed to float and wrap around him. "Thank you, Brian. I accept your invitation to stay on in Osborne House."

32

A medley of russet colors, like abstract forms on a canvas, dipped and rippled, and soft laughter crescendoed around Brian. His mind was caught in that brief span between deep sleep and conscious awareness and his body floated, suspended. A distant voice whispered his name. He liked the sound of the voice and the silky way it called to him: "Brian . . . Brian . . . Brian."

He forced heavy lids to open and blinked against the sunlight that spilled into the room. He felt confused about the russet-haired woman who stood beside his bed. Brian looked about, trying to orient himself. The sounds of birds filtered through the open window and sun patterns played against the walls in his father's room. Reality came swift and harsh: his father was dead, and he had come home to try and fill the big man's shoes.

"Good morning," Autumn said. "Or should I say good afternoon?"

He drew his hand over a face that was stiff from sleep, stretched, and flexed his numb muscles. "How long have I been sleeping?"

"Almost twenty-four hours."

"You're kidding?"

"I kid you not." Autumn held up a breakfast tray. "There's a man waiting. He was here earlier, but I sent him away. He returned this afternoon and insisted he had to see you. I thought you might like breakfast while you talked with him."

The scent of bacon and steaming coffee stirred his senses and hunger pains gnawed. Arranging the pillows against the headboard, Brian propped himself in bed. "Who is he?"

"Amos Patterson." She leaned over with the tray, her face a few inches from his. Subtle perfume teased his nostrils and sent erotic images to his brain. Her lips were moist, slightly parted. Impulsively he caught the nape of her neck, pulled her forward, and kissed her on the mouth.

She pulled away, smiling. "Are you always so playful when you wake?"

"Only when I wake to find a sexy redhead bending over my bed."

"My hair isn't red. It's auburn."

Her tone of voice was curt, and he grinned. "Sorry, my mistake." He took the tray from his lap and held it out to her. "The food looks great, honey, but nature is calling. Hell, it's shouting."

She nodded her understanding, and set the tray on the side of the bed. "I'll give you a few minutes."

Brian waited until she had left the room, then dashed naked to the bathroom and stood over the toilet for what seemed like a full five minutes. Then he splashed cold water over his face, which helped to clear the cobwebs. His stomach growling, he returned to the bedroom, climbed into the four-poster, pulled the tray onto his lap, and dug heartily into steak and eggs, country style.

He bit into a biscuit and gazed out the far window pensively. It hadn't taken them long to pounce on him. Amos Patterson managed the feed store and ran the bootleg operations. The places had been around for as long as he could remember. At one time there weren't any controls, so fights broke out constantly over women, cards, and something as asinine as a spilled drink. After a stabbing, his father had stepped in and taken them over. To Brian the joints were a nuisance, and damned risky. He would rather take advantage of local option and bring liquor into the town so there wouldn't be a need for the joints at all.

Brian poured himself another cup of coffee, mopped egg yolk with a biscuit, and was popping a piece in his mouth when Autumn tapped at his door. He mumbled for her to come in. She entered the room, followed by Amos, a stout man with a ruddy, weather-beaten face. Amos walked with a limp and fumbled with a brown felt hat. His face broke into a smile, and he crossed to the bed and shook Brian's hand. "Mighty sorry about your pa. The town's lost a good man."

Brian nodded, but glanced at Autumn as she turned to leave. "Stay, Autumn. I want to talk to you later."

Amos looked with surprise from Autumn to Brian. "I need to talk to you about . . . the . . . places. Your pa didn't mix this sort of thing with the womenfolk."

Brian knew he was going to hear this remark over and over. He cleared his throat and spoke firmly. "I'm not my father. He had his way of doing things and I have mine." He watched as Autumn took a chair near the window, then motioned for the man to be seated. "What is it, Amos?"

Amos pulled the chair up near the bed, still fumbling with the hat. "We got a problem. With your pa gone, I thought it best I come to you."

"What's the problem?"

"A bunch of youngsters from out of town came to Rex's place last night and mixed it up with some of the local boys. It turned into a real free-for-all. By the time Rex got things under control, the place was a shambles. The windows got broken. Ain't nothing left of the tables and chairs but splinters. The jukebox just ain't no more. The walls are so banged up they look like Swiss cheese. There ain't nothing there worth keeping."

"Was anybody hurt?"

Amos shook his head, looking at Brian with an incredulous expression. "Nothing serious. I imagine there's a few black eyes this morning, and a few sore spots, but no real bones were broken. Nobody got cut up."

"What started the fight?"

"A woman, of course—two men wanting the same

whore.'' He glanced quickly at Autumn. ''Beg pardon, Mrs. Osborne, but that's what was told to me.''

''Shocking!''

Brian grinned at Autumn, then rubbed the nape of his neck and turned his attention back to Amos. ''Did the kids all get home all right?''

Amos nodded and rose from the chair. ''What do you want done with the place? Do you want us to try to put it back together, or keep it closed?''

''Leave it closed for now.''

''What about Rex? He'll be out of work.''

''Give me some time to think about it. I'll come up with something for him.''

''All right, Mr. Osborne.''

Brian dropped back against the pillows as Amos limped from the room. He spoke in a grumbling tone: ''Welcome home, Brian.''

''Why don't you call the police?''

''Very funny, Autumn.''

''You do have protection, don't you?''

''Of a sort. The police protect us from themselves, not from outsiders.''

She left the chair and went to the bed. ''What is it you wanted to talk to me about?''

''You.''

''What about me?''

''Everything. How you came to Edisonville, and how you came to marry my father.''

''It's a tired story.''

''Not to me. I haven't heard it yet.'' He set the tray off to one side of the bed and motioned for her to sit beside him. She stood for a moment, considering, then eased down onto the bed and sat with one leg curled beneath her. Autumn painted a fairly clear picture of coming to town and marrying his father. She was soft-spoken, yet he picked up a tone of authority in her voice, as if she were used to giving orders and having them obeyed. For the most part her eyes were direct, but he noticed she kicked off her shoes when talking about her life with his father. Her glance dropped now and then to the Egyptian coin he wore around his neck. It was set in gold and hung from a heavy chain that lay partially buried in blond chest hair.

He vaguely remembered dreaming about Autumn, or at least he thought it had been a dream. She had stood beside his bed in the shadows, pulled the sheet up to his neck, and whispered in a caustic voice, "Why am I always covering you, little rich boy?"

Autumn had been wearing a white robe. She wore a tan sleeveless dress now, a simple cotton buttoned to the neck, but she wore it with flair. She had a reserved indifference that acted as an aphrodisiac. He felt a rush of heat to his loins, but a tiny voice whispered: "No, no, she's my dad's woman." He drew a fingertip along her cheek. "You're very pretty, Autumn. I imagine many men have loved you."

Autumn laughed quietly. "Hundreds!" She eased from the bed and slipped her feet into sandals. "I told Bea I would help her at the shelter this afternoon. If you plan to be out, I'll arranged to have your father's things taken out of this room before I leave."

He nodded. "I want to have a look at the town. Later, I'll probably go to the club and see if anyone I used to know is still around."

"Lisa is here."

A picture of Lisa in the hayloft flashed into his mind, and he grinned. He'd only been a kid, but after a night at one of the joints he had talked Lisa into the hay to teach her what he'd learned. Daisy had caught them, and a long speech on the pitfalls of sex had followed. "Is she still married?"

"No. She's free and very available."

"Do you know her?"

"Only slightly. A friend of mine takes her out from time to time. His name is Bob Proctor. He's my attorney."

"You don't use John Allison?"

"No." She turned abruptly and walked to the door, but paused suddenly and looked back at him. "I wanted to ask you about the records in the basement."

"What about them?"

"I found them while exploring the house. They're fascinating. The entire history of the Osborne family is in that room. I even found a memorandum written by your grandfather. I'd like to hire a couple of people to help me put them in order. Someday, when you have children, you can take them to a file and pull out papers dating back to the 1800's—show them notes written by their great-great-grandfather."

"That's very nice of you, Autumn, but it sounds like a lot of work. Are you sure?"

"Absolutely. The records from around the time of the explosion should really tell a story."

"Hardly. There was a fire shortly after the explosion. All the records for the last five years were destroyed."

A shadow seemed to pass over her face. "What a shame. That's like reading a book and then finding the last few pages missing."

33

The first few days were hell. Brian was told over and over, "This is the way your father did it." Sometimes the line was varied: "This is the way Douglas did it." Most of the people had been with them for years and had known Brian as a boy. They joked, patted him on the back, and treated him as if he were still ten. Before someone made the mistake of offering him a lollipop, he called a staff meeting. Sprawled on his father's chair at the head of a long table, he looked at each of the twelve officers and wondered if the number had any significance: *Jesus and his twelve disciples*.

Hank Miller, who had been with the company for twenty years, sat on Brian's left. "How's the wife and kids, Hank?"

"The wife is fine. The kids are all grown now. My boy works in the distillery as a manager. Lee Ann is married and has two kids of her own. She married a boy over in Hopkins County. He works the mines as an engineer."

Brian nodded and worked his way around the table until he had spoken to each man. His glance moved over the circle of men. Most were graying, and some were balding, but they all wore the same stiff business suits. "This won't take long," he said. "I don't have much to say." He dropped his hands between his spread legs and spoke in a lazy, relaxed tone. "I think I know what every man here has on his mind." He grinned. "Yes, I'm young. And no,

I don't know as much as my father. And yes, I'll make mistakes. That's not your concern. If I make a mistake, I'll take care of it." He paused and looked at four of the most troublesome men. "I'll be working with John Allison. He's been managing Dad's affairs for years and knows this company inside and out. I respect his judgment and I'll follow any advice he gives me. I'd like a full job report from each of you. I want to know what each job entails, and how I can best work with you." Brian glanced around the table. "Are there any questions?"

Hank Miller cleared his throat. "We have hard set policies, Brian. Changes could interrupt the flow."

"Whose policies?"

"Your father's."

Brian gave his chair a spin and rose to his feet. "Dad is dead. I can't run this company from his head. There can only be one chief. Like it or not, you got me." He turned toward the door. "I'll be in my office if anybody wants to talk to me."

He left the staff room and took the elevator to the office where his father, his grandfather, and his great-grandfather had ruled for three generations. Generation number four dropped unceremoniously into the chair and stared at the papers on his desk. Not only did he have to win the people's respect, but his father's interests had spread across the United States as well as several other countries. A conglomerate mess that scared the hell out of him.

He rocked in the chair and propped his feet on the desk as his secretary entered the room. Beth had been with his father and still guarded the door as furiously as she had before. She looked at his feet on the hallowed desk and blinked disapproval. "Your Uncle Dale is here to see you."

"Good," Brian said, and stretched. "Why don't you send him in." He folded his arms behind his head and watched as her stiff back disappeared through the doorway. Brian had always known his uncles were weak, but he also understood them. George was like a sneaky kid. He lied, boasted, was an eager beaver without the ability to live up to his promises. Dale had been Douglas' cross to bear. A soft man, he had survived by staying as far from his older brother as possible. Homer had tried at least. Even as a boy, Brian remembered how important Douglas' approval was to him. Sadly, when Homer made a decision it was usually the wrong one, or not the one Douglas wanted to hear.

Brian put his feet down as Dale entered the office. His uncle smiled cheerfully and took a chair. "How are things here in heaven?"

"I don't think I'd call this place heaven."

"That's how Douglas thought of it. This is where god made all his decisions and handed down his punishments. Here, and in his damned study."

"You sound bitter."

"Yeah, I suppose I am."

"Is there something I can do about it?"

Dale shook his head. "I'm fine. Better than fine. I've made some decisions and I wanted you to know. I was approached by Bob Proctor sometime ago about selling my share in the mine. I hesitated for a while. I suppose I was afraid of Douglas. Anyhow, I signed the papers this morning."

Brian looked at him stupidly. "The mine? Who would want it?"

"An outfit from California."

"What are they planning to do with it?"

"From what I was told, they plan to work it."

"There's nothing there worth mining."

"I know. It sounds crazy to me, too."

"Who made the offer?"

"The Corbett Corporation. Attorneys from San Francisco approached Bob Proctor and asked him to handle it from this end. That's all I know. I was offered a job with the company, too. I accepted. I'm putting my house on the market and leaving for Seattle next week."

Things were happening too quickly and Brian was confused. The Osborne men had always worked together as a family. "Why?" Brian asked. "If you want to work, I'll give you a job. I know from John about the allowance Dad paid you. It was cut off with his death, but I had planned to continue it on my own. I assumed you were happy with the arrangement."

"No, I was never happy. I'm a man, Brian, with pride. I want to live my life like any man, not a kept woman. The allowance was Douglas' way of keeping me hidden. He didn't want people to know his brother was queer."

"Hey—I don't give a damn about your sexual preference. If you want to work, I'll find a spot for you."

Dale shook his head. "I don't know if you can understand, but I suddenly feel like I've just been released from a life sentence in prison. Away from the town and the Osborne name, I can be myself. Even if you sent me elsewhere with the company, I would still be connected with the family. Gossip would leak back. I don't want to bring shame on the family name. In Seattle, I'll just be Dale Osborne, that nice—but gay—guy."

"I understand," Brian said. "My name is Osborne too." He shuffled the stack of papers on his desk. "Are you aware how large Dad's estate is?"

"I have a fair idea."

"It scares the hell out of me."

"Don't be intimidated, Brian. One man can't know everything. When you come up against something that's mind-boggling, go out and hire the best brains to unscramble the puzzle. That's the advantage of being big. You can hire the best. Douglas transported John Allison from a large firm in New York." Dale paused and looked at him with a quiet smile. "I have to be going. I've got a lot to do before next week."

Brian rose and held out his hand. "I'll miss you, Uncle Dale. I've always enjoyed talking to you. Thanks for always being here." Brian gazed at his uncle, remembering how he had gone to Dale after the fight with his father that separated them for years. Dale had told him to run, run, and never look back. "I have one more question. What do you think of Autumn?"

Dale chuckled. "Women aren't my specialty."

"What do you think of her as a person?"

Dale was quiet for a moment. "I don't know. She's a complex woman. I've always had the feeling there was more to Autumn than she lets anyone see. As a woman, she's lovely. As a friend, I'd trust her in a pinch. Does that tell you anything?"

Brian nodded. "Thanks, Uncle Dale." He waited until Dale had left the room, then pressed the intercom. "Beth, would you get Mrs. Osborne on the phone—Autumn," he added as an afterthought. Then he waited, drumming a pencil on the desk.

After what seemed an unusually long time, Beth's voice came through the intercom. "Mrs. Osborne is on line four."

Brian pressed the button and spoke impatiently into the receiver. "What's the matter, honey? Did I pull you from your bubble bath, or were you polishing your nails?"

"Masturbating."

Brian sat nonplussed for a moment. He never knew what she was going to say or do next, but that was what made her so appealing. He started to speak, but she cut in again. "Some men I know think all women are muddle-headed morons with nothing better to do but sit on their fannies and pamper themselves. We do have brains, Brian, and most of us use them when we're allowed to."

"Yes, ma'am."

"Don't you patronize me."

"No, ma'am."

"Brian!"

He laughed at the exasperation in her voice and relaxed back in the chair. "Would you by chance know anything about the Corbett Corporation? It's an outfit out of San Francisco."

"Yes," she said. "It's a string of hot-dog stands along the west coast. Why?"

"For some crazy reason, they're buying stock in the Black Jewel. Uncle Dale sold his shares this morning."

"Why is that crazy?"

"The mine is worthless."

"They're probably planning to use it as a tax write-off. They'll throw a bunch of money in, then declare a loss."

"Maybe. They offered Uncle Dale a job with the company, too."

"That's great. It's still a fairly small company, but growing rapidly. I've read that they're planning to expand to the east coast. It's a good time for him to get in."

"Why hire Uncle Dale?"

"Why not? Is he stupid or something?"

"No, he's a highly intelligent man."

"Okay. There's your reason."

"I don't know," he said. "Something doesn't quite fit. I have a funny feeling about it."

"What doesn't fit is your uncle leaving town. And the mine has been in the family for such a long time. It's hard to let go of people and possessions. We tend to look for hidden reasons that just aren't there."

"Yeah, you're probably right. Uncle Dale is leaving in a week. Why don't you get some people together and have a dinner party for him?"

"Okey-dokey."

"Very good, Autumn. You're sliding into the local jargon quite nicely."

"Why, honey chile, ya'll ain't heard nothing yet."

Brian laughed. He liked Autumn; she had a lifting quality. There were moments when she emanated warmth, other times he had caught her looking at him with a narrowed glance that was pure granite.

He rocked in his chair and thumbed through the stack of appointments. "Time is rushing in on me, honey. I'll let you get back to what you were doing."

"Ella is here. She's opening a new restaurant and I'm helping her with the planning."

"A little sudden, isn't it?"

"Not really. We came up with the idea before your father died. We're trying to pull things together so we can get moving on it."

"Can I be of any help?"

"Thanks, but I can manage."

"Are you sure? I wouldn't want you to put too much strain on that pretty little brain of yours."

"Piss off, Brian."

Grinning, he jerked the receiver away from his head and returned it to its cradle. He turned in the chair toward the line of portraits and gazed at his father's face. A strong man, Douglas Osborne, both in mind and in body. Brian remembered that his only flaw had been an allergy to nuts, which he felt was a weakness and kept well hidden. His father's death had a funny feel about it, too. Or was it as

Autumn had said? It's hard to let go of people. You look for hidden reasons that just aren't there.

Brian's face softened as he gazed at features so like his own. "It wasn't easy, Dad, but I loved you, you old fucker. I hope to hell you were happy with that gorgeous creature you married."

34

Lisa placed a cup of coffee on the table in front of Brian and slid onto a chair. She was draped in a mist of black chiffon, and the front of her nightgown gaped open as an overabundance of dips and dimples spilled over the bodice. A lot of memories were wrapped up in Lisa: playing in the treehouse, riding to the hunt, slipping off to the woods to neck, the hayloft, the senior prom. But they were both over thirty now and no longer kids.

Lisa had been married twice and had a child from each marriage—a boy and a girl who were already calling him uncle. From the looks of her house, both settlements had been good. Her first husband was from Louisville, her second was Norman Heckler. Norman and his father owned the mill, or at least forty-five percent. Brian owned the other fifty-five percent. He was discovering that his father had reaped the harvest when the mine closed and the town went into a slump. If a man needed a boost, his father had generously provided—for a small consideration.

Brian felt his stomach growl and nodded toward the coffee. "Is this all I get, or can't you cook?"

"I can cook, but that's all you get. I want you out of here before the children get up. You can't spend the night here again, either. You know this town. Norman will be screaming that I'm an unfit mother."

Brian smiled to himself. "How many uncles have the kids had?"

"A few."

"Am I cutting in on someone?"

"No. Am I?" She smiled across at him. "Are you in love? Have you been in love?"

"No to both."

"Why not?"

"I don't know. I didn't run from it. It just didn't happen."

"Oh boy, when you late bloomers finally fall, it's usually hard and all the way." She touched a small scar at the rim of his mouth. "How did you get that?"

"Brawl in Tangier."

"The one on your leg?"

"Brazil."

"Your shoulder?"

"Haiti."

"Christ, Brian. I thought you were an archaeologist studying ruins, not creating them."

"It happened a long time ago. I finally realized I was getting the worst of it and learned to keep my mouth shut."

She took a sip of coffee and smiled playfully at him over the rim. "What do you think of your new mother?"

"Interesting lady."

" 'Lady' isn't the term used for Autumn in this town."

"Why?"

"Jealousy, I guess. It doesn't help that she wasn't born here. Autumn is standoffish, too. She won't let anyone get close enough to be her friend. Of course the gossips wouldn't have dared say anything about her in earshot of Douglas. Now it will be different." Her eyes smiled at him and she set the cup back in its saucer. "There was some talk after a party. Word went around that Autumn was seen playing with Bob Proctor's ass. They were later caught in the garden by your father. He dragged her into the house. It provided some juicy gossip for a few days."

"Bob Proctor," Brian said, and thought back to his conversation with Autumn. "He's her attorney."

"Yes. They're close, but I don't think there's anything there but friendship. I used to tease Bob about her. He shut me up by saying no man with less than ten million dollars would ever get into Autumn's panties."

An image of Autumn and their first meeting came into his mind's eye. "Why did you marry my father?" he had asked. "For his money," she had replied. He had laughed then, and he laughed now. "It must have caused one hell of a stir in this town when Dad married her."

"A shock. So was his death." She leaned forward and rested her hand over his. "I'm sorry, Brian."

At the mention of his father's death a tightness spread across his shoulders, and the same uneasiness he had felt before gnawed at his mind. "Did your father ever mention that Dad had a health problem? Maybe something that could have caused a strong man to take a swim and drown?"

"No, but as a doctor he wouldn't. Mom and Dad just returned yesterday from a month in the Caribbean. They were stunned when they heard. You can talk to Dad if you want. Maybe there was something."

Brian nodded. "I tried shortly after I got home, but his office said he was out of town. I'm going to make a point of seeing him today." Brian paused. "Things are changing too damned fast. Dad's dead. Uncle Dale is leaving. Some outfit in California is buying up the mine. I think Bob Proctor can clear up at least one question."

"Such as?"

"Why anyone would buy up a worthless mine." He picked up his empty cup and waved it under her nose. "If you're not going to feed me, I'm going home to my beautiful new mother."

"She is pretty, isn't she?"

"Mighty." He rose and circled the table, bent and kissed her on the forehead. "If I can get away from the office before midnight, I'll take you to the club for dinner."

"Not tonight. I have a date with Bob."

"Oh yes, Bob. He does get around, doesn't he?" Brian glanced at her mounds of dips and dimples and drew a finger along the edge of her gown. "Save a little something for me."

"All you have to do is say the word and I'll save it all for you."

"Now, Lisa. Let's keep everything free and easy."

"Still afraid of being tied down, aren't you?"

He turned and walked quickly to the door, escaping before Lisa could bring up the past and why he had abandoned her for a bunch of dirty old ruins. Lisa would never understand. He left the house and slid behind the wheel of his twelve-year-old sports car, gazing at Lisa's three-hundred-thousand-dollar settlement as he started the engine. Was this to be his future? Coffee-klatching and gossiping about who patted whom on the ass at whose party?

Brian shuddered at the thought and hit the accelerator, speeding away from Lisa, the luxurious cottage, and all it implied. He sped through the empty streets, across Main to the outskirts of town, and up the winding hill to Osborne house. Gearing down, he turned into the drive. The engine rumbled quietly as he pulled up in front of the old mansion.

He left the car and entered the foyer, expecting everybody still to be asleep, but soft teasing laughter came from the direction of the stairs. He looked up at Autumn, who stood on the landing. "Up early, Brian, or out late?"

Suddenly aware of his appearance, he glanced down at his wrinkled clothes and touched the stubble on his cheeks. "Both." He mounted the stairs as she came toward him, her hips moving in an arrogant sway. She had a lofty touch-me-not air that irked him at times. When she swept past him, he reached and patted her on the rear.

She didn't stop or even pause. "Be nice, Brian, or Mother will spank your ass."

"Why are you always trying to be so tough?"

She stopped then and looked back at him. "I am tough, so don't fuck with me."

"You could try cleaning up your mouth, too."

"Yes, but then I'd spoil my image. It's what the family expects. I wouldn't want them to be disappointed."

"And that bothers you?"

"No," she said, and looked at him squarely. "A very wise and dear person once said to me, 'Be what you are, Autumn, not what folks want you to be.'" She waved her hands down in gesture over her body. "What you see is what you get."

"Yeah, provided you have ten million dollars."

She smiled and her glance moved over him. "Did you and Lisa have fun making mud pies?"

At one time in his life, Brian had made mud pies with Lisa, and now he felt foolish. "You are a very frustrating woman."

"Yes, I know." She turned and walked down the stairs, and he turned and walked up the stairs to his room, where he showered and dressed for another fourteen-hour day.

35

❧

Dr. Albright had a rolling way of moving his pudgy frame from one point to another, and a habit of pushing his half-glasses up and over the bridge of his nose. Gray hair ringed the back of his head, and the top was bald and shiny. He pumped Brian's hand and led him to a chair in front of his desk. Dr. Albright had brought Brian into the world, then gagged him with tongue depressors, mended a series of broken bones, and grounded him to the bed when bouts of flu, mumps, chicken pox, and other assorted childhood ailments, as well as stabbing him in the derriere with a thousand sharp needles.

Brian grinned fondly at the older man. "Are you still tormenting kids with your wicked little spears?"

"Every chance I get." He chuckled good-naturedly and used his hands to cross one chubby leg over the other. "I've thought about you a great deal these last few days. You and Doug. I wish I had been here, not that it would have changed a thing." He gave his glasses a nudge and settled back in the chair. "Lisa called me this morning. She tells me you're having trouble accepting your father's death."

"No," Brian replied. "I can accept his death. I'm just having trouble accepting how he died." Brian felt edgy, confined by the stiff business suit. He wiggled his shoulders uncomfortably and loosened his tie. "Did Dad have any kind of health problem? Maybe something he was keeping from the family?"

Dr. Albright shook his head. "Your father came to me for a checkup shortly before he married Autumn. He was in good health—fine shape for a man his age. More like a man in his late forties."

"Why, then?"

"I can't answer that, Brian. I know it seems unreal and unfair, but things happen. We can't choose the way we die, or when."

Brian rose and paced the room restlessly. "A strong man like Dad doesn't go for a swim and drown. Not in his own backyard."

"Yes, they do. Sadly, I see the young, as well as the old, die for no earthly good reason. Doug could have gotten a cramp and panicked."

"Dad wouldn't panic."

Dr. Albright smiled. "Doug was a powerful man, but he wasn't immune to fear or death. When our life is threatened, any one of us can panic."

"I hear what you're saying and I understand. It just doesn't apply to Dad. He was a mountain, immovable, volcanic. When they go, they go in a blaze of glory. They don't simply ease away in the quiet of the night."

"What, then? Foul play?"

The thought was humorous. People in Edisonville didn't even bother to lock their doors. "Well . . . no." Brian grinned.

"All right. We've eliminated a health problem and foul play. That leaves an accident."

Brian shoved his hands in his pockets and jingled some change. "I keep telling myself I'm thinking like an old woman. I push the thought aside, but it sits back there and rubs on my mind." He ran a finger along his neck, grimaced, and gave a pull at his shirt collar. "Everybody is satisfied, even the coroner. Why can't I just let it rest?"

Dr. Albright looked at him with understanding, removed his glasses, and slid them into the pocket of his white jacket. "Give it some time, Brian. A year from now, and everything will look a lot different."

"Christ, I hope so. Dad's left me with one long headache. Home a week, and already I'm buried in paper to my eyeballs. Which reminds me. I have a briefcase full of work to go over tonight.'' He crossed and held out his hand. ''Thanks, Doc.''

Dr. Albright left the chair and walked with him to the door. He rested a hand on Brian's shoulder. ''Why don't you ask for a copy of the autopsy report? Maybe if you read it yourself, it will bring things into perspective for you.''

''John Allison has seen a copy. If anything was out of line, he would have spotted it.''

Dr. Albright smiled faintly. ''Do I sense some reluctance here? Maybe you don't want to read about Doug's death in black and white.''

Brian smiled sheepishly. ''You're right. I haven't wanted to see it in cold hard print.''

''Do you want me to have a look at it?''

He grinned. ''Yeah, but that wouldn't help me much, would it?''

''No. You're the one with the uncertainties.''

Brian nodded and turned toward the door. ''Tomorrow. I'll have a look at it tomorrow.''

That night Brian was pulled from a deep sleep by a prickling sensation at the nape of his neck—the same warning signal he had felt in waterfront dives when some angry drunk came at him from behind. He sat upright in bed, his dulled senses alerted to the sounds of panic in the house. The hum of voices tinged with urgency cut the stillness, and the rush of scurrying feet filled the old mansion.

He didn't stop to think, but scrambled from the bed, grabbed a robe, and left the room at a run. Autumn was in the corridor with Daisy. Jasper, wearing an old gray wrap, stood in the foyer with two police officers. Molly appeared from the rear of the house and looked up at Autumn. Their eyes met and silent messages seemed to pass between them. He heard Autumn choke back a scream. ''Dear God! Please, not again.'' She broke into a run, Brian following, down the curving stairs and across to where the officers waited. ''Daisy told me there had been an accident," she cried, her eyes wide, searching the officers' faces. "Is he dead? Is Artie dead?"

"No," the officer said quickly. "He's alive."

Brian had been home only a week, so other than Chief Hadley, he didn't know anybody on the force. He turned to the older of the two officers. "What happened?"

"We don't know much, Mr. Osborne. The car was traveling south on Snake Road when it apparently left the pavement and rammed an embankment. There was a woman with him. She died on the way to the hospital. A Ginger Olson." The officer turned to Autumn. "Your brother-in-law is hurt pretty bad."

"Yeah," the younger policeman agreed. "If he lives through the night, it will surprise me. I never saw anything like it. There's nothing left of his car but a handful of metal. Blood, running like a river. My stomach—"

"That's enough, dammit." Brian put a comforting arm around Autumn, furious with the small-town policeman. "All we need are the facts, not your ramblings."

Autumn pulled away from Brian, her speech disjointed, her eyes stunned. "I . . . I should be there. He'll need me. Artie will need me now." She looked down at her robe and fumbled with the sash. "I have to go to him."

Brian nodded. "I'll drive you."

"No!" She turned on him with such violence in her voice that he stepped away for a moment, startled. She stood with her hands in fists at her sides, her eyes filled with hostility. "Artie is nothing to you. I'm nothing to you. You don't belong there."

Brian felt her animosity and cringed, but he understood. She was alone, a stranger in a class-divided town, and his family was certainly no exception. His eyes softened and he reached out for her. "Let me help you, Autumn."

She jumped backward, waving her hands in a pushing motion. "Don't touch me. Don't you dare touch me—you son of a bitch."

Molly rushed forward and grabbed her by the shoulders. "Autumn. Miss Autumn. Be still. You don't know what you're saying."

"I know. I know." She pushed away from Molly and turned on Brian again. "I despise you. All of you. You're a pack of sanctimonious assholes. I don't need you. I don't need any of you. I can take care of Artie.''

Though angry, Autumn looked so defenseless and vulnerable, the fear so raw in her eyes, that Brian instinctively reached out for her again. She came at him then with a force that almost knocked him off his feet, clawing and pounding her fists against his chest. He realized the damned fool cop had thrown her into a state of hysteria and caught her wrists, first one and then the other. He pulled her tight against him and held her hands clasped behind her back.

Ignoring her struggles and garbled words, he frowned and glanced at the row of servants that stood gaping. ''Jasper, show the officers to the door. Daisy, get everybody back to their rooms. Molly, you stay here with Autumn.'' The calm of his voice and the rational manner in which he spoke seemed to bring sanity back to the room. Autumn collapsed against him, breathless but quiet. He loosened her wrist but held her in his arms and spoke gently. ''You were my father's wife, Autumn. And an Osborne. Artie is your brother-in-law. I want to help you if I can.''

Her entire body seemed to sigh and she grasped at him so tightly that he could feel her nails cutting into his back. ''Scared,'' she murmured. ''So damned scared.''

''I know.'' He stroked her hair and tried to reassure her, but the words sounded hollow even to him. He stood quietly, just holding her.

As if realizing suddenly that she was being held by strange arms, Autumn straightened and moved away. ''I'm sorry,'' she said. ''I don't know what happened. I lost control.''

Brian expected to see tears, but her eyes were dry. She had pressed her face so hard against the opening of his robe that the coin had left an imprint on her cheek. The mark bothered him. He rubbed his thumb against the blotch. ''I'll take you to Artie whenever you're ready.'' He left Molly with Autumn, then crossed to the study and called Chief Hadley. The conversation was short. ''One of your men just came to my house and scared the hell out of Autumn. If this ever happens again, I will personally hammer the man's head with his own billy club. Good night, Chief.''

The moment Brian stopped the Mercedes, Autumn leapt from the car and ran toward the emergency room. By the time Brian reached the building, Autumn was screaming at nurses. She grabbed at his arm. "They won't tell me anything."

The nurse looked at Brian. "We don't know anything yet. It's too soon."

"Can I at least see him?"

The nurse shook her head. "No one is allowed in the emergency ward."

"Is he going to die?"

The nurse spoke with patience. "The doctors are with him. He's being taken care of."

"You didn't answer my question. Is he going to die?"

The nurse looked helplessly from Autumn to Brian. He took Autumn by the arm and pulled her to a chair, forcing her to sit. "All we can do now is wait."

It was over a week before they knew if Artie would live, and even then there was some doubt as to whether he would ever walk again. He had massive internal injuries, a ruptured spleen, intestinal damage, and a lower-back fracture with injury to the spinal nerves causing paresis of the left leg. He had been in and out of surgery three times, and was going in for a fourth.

Brian hadn't known the woman and he knew Artie only slightly, so he was relatively untouched by the accident; however, there was Autumn. He had tried to be supportive, but she turned away from him along with everyone else at Osborne House. The only people she wanted around her was Molly, Bob, and Ella.

At first Brian had thought of Autumn as his father's playmate. During the days following the accident he learned to look at her with new respect. Within twelve hours she had some of the best surgeons in the country either there in town or consulting. Amid the chaos, she contacted Ginger's parents and made all the arrangements to have the body returned to her family. She stayed at the hospital near

Artie until forced to go home by the doctors, and then she paced, sleeping only briefly. Day by day, Brian watched the shadows under her eyes deepen, but if she cried, she cried in her room alone.

Brian left his car and went into the house. Jasper met him in the foyer and took his briefcase. "Supper will be on the table directly, Mr. Brian."

"I'll have it at my desk. Is Autumn here?"

"No, Mr. Brian. She's still at the hospital."

"Have you heard how Artie is?"

"No, but I imagine Molly will know."

"Yeah," Brian said with a half-sigh. He tugged off his jacket as he climbed the stairs. It was late September, but warm and humid. He turned toward his room with thoughts of a cool shower, but Molly came through Autumn's doorway, her eyes so intent that he immediately thought of Artie. "What is it, Molly?"

"I was wondering if I might talk to you for a spell?"

"Is it Artie?"

"Him . . . and Autumn. Artie is doing fine. The doctors think they've got everything fixed now. They don't expect him to do any more bleeding. 'Course it'll be a while before they can say for sure. It's Autumn I'm more worried about now."

He nodded and led Molly to his room, tossed his jacket and tie on the bed, and motioned her toward a group of wingback chairs. It was hard for him to think of Molly as a servant. She had a gracious, independent air and a directness that invoked respect. A little like Autumn, he realized. They were unusually close for maid and mistress, but he had seen it before. Daisy and his mother had been like sisters. "What is it you're worried about?"

Molly hesitated a moment. "Well, Autumn has been under a strain for a long time now. This thing with Artie ain't helping none, either. I've tried to talk to her, but once she's got her mind made up, there's no stopping her. She ain't sleeping, and she ain't eating." Molly's brows furrowed in a deep frown of concern. "She ain't slept more than a few hours all this week. If somebody don't take her in hand, she's gonna make herself sick. I know ya'll get on each other's nerves and spat a lot, but I've watched you, Mr. Brian, and I know you're fond of Autumn. I thought maybe you could go and make her come home.''

Brian smiled a little. ''I don't think any man can make Autumn do something she doesn't want to do, Molly.''

''Why? You're bigger than she is, ain't you?''

This brought a chuckle from Brian. ''Are you suggesting I go and drag her home?''

''If you have to. I watched you the night Autumn went to pieces over Artie's accident. You handled her real good, better than anybody else I know. She needs your kind of calm and order now. Maybe she don't know it, but she does.''

Brian had wondered about the strong bond between Artie and Autumn, but they were so open with their affection that he had accepted it for what it was—a brother-and-sister attachment. ''It's rare for in-laws to be so close.''

''Autumn don't have much family of her own, so she's mighty partial to the dab she's got.'' Molly fell silent and gazed at him as if considering. ''Artie and his brother were twins. I imagine Autumn sees her dead husband in him. He died in a car wreck. I reckon she's kind of living it all over again. That was a bad time for her. After her man died, she lost her unborn baby too.''

''I didn't know she had lost a child.''

Molly nodded. ''There's been some kind of war brewing inside her since. That war is gonna come to an end. When it does, I don't know what will happen to Autumn, and it scares me.''

''War?'' Brian asked curiously. ''What kind of war? When was this?''

Molly rose abruptly. ''I guess maybe I'm saying too much. That's part of Autumn's past and not for me to be rambling on about.''

Brian knew from the closed look on her face that further questioning would be pointless. He rose along with Molly. ''I'll grab a quick shower, and then I'll go and bring her home.''

Molly nodded. ''Thanks, Mr. Brian.'' She paused at the

door. "If Miss Autumn kicks up a fuss, you just kick up a bigger one, but keep a close eye on her. She's as sly as a fox."

To avoid as much argument as possible, Brian first talked with Artie's doctors and learned he was out of recovery, back in his room, and expected to sleep through the night. He then hunted down Dr. Albright for sleeping pills. Armed with a packet of Dalmane, he went in search of Autumn. After covering the most likely places without finding her, he spotted her crop of auburn hair in a corner of the cafeteria. She sat with coffee and a plate in front of her, but she wasn't eating. Her elbows propped on the table, she stared down at the plate and poked at her food with a fork. As he approached her from behind she mumbled, "Hello, Brian."

"How did you know it was me?"

"The after-shave. I have a sensitive nose."

He took a chair and motioned toward the plate. "Why aren't you eating?"

"It's lousy. If Artie has to live on this stuff, he'll never make it."

"The food at Osborne House isn't lousy. Why don't you come home and have some dinner and get some sleep?"

She dropped the fork onto the plate and shook her head. "I'm the only person Artie has. I want to be here when he wakes up."

"I've checked. Artie will sleep through the night. Even if he did wake up, he'd still be so dopey he wouldn't know if you were here or not."

"I know, but I'll feel better if I stay."

"You'll feel better if you come home and get a good night's sleep." He rose, took her by the hand, and pulled her along with him.

She glanced at his hand on hers, looked at him quizzically. "What the hell do you think you're doing?"

"I'm taking you home."

"No you're not."

"I could carry you."

"You wouldn't."

"I would."

She stared into his eyes for a long moment, shrugged, and followed him to the car. During the drive home, he tried to start a conversation, but she stared at the side window and refused to answer. When he turned into the drive at Osborne House, she asked abruptly, "Have you ever been afraid, Brian, really afraid?"

"Yeah. Most of my life."

"I can't imagine you ever being afraid of anything."

"Not physically, but from the time I was old enough to know what was expected of me, I was afraid I couldn't measure up. As a kid I had to crane my neck to look up at Dad. Even after I had grown to be six-feet-two and could look him square in the eye, I still had that same feeling of craning my neck. It gets damned painful." He pulled the car up in front of the house and turned in the seat to face her. "Maybe if I had come home as a man, it would have been different. As it is, I'll never know."

"And you feel guilty?"

"Yeah, I feel guilty. I should have come home sooner, at least for a visit. I kept telling myself: Next time. The next time I'm in the States, I'll go home. I wanted to come back and make peace with Dad, but I was afraid I'd be trapped here, unable to walk away a second time." He paused and smiled faintly. "There's that word again."

She smiled too. "For what it's worth, your father was proud of you for standing up to him. He loved you very much, Brian."

"He had a hell of a way of showing it."

She swung the car door open and slid from the seat. "Your father had a hell of a way of doing most things."

He left the car and followed her into the house, took the pills from a breast pocket, and held them out to her. "Sleeping pills. Take two and go to bed. I'll have Molly bring you up a tray."

"I don't want dinner, or pills."

"Take them," he urged. "They'll help you sleep more deeply."

She gazed at the pills, then at Brian, snatched the packet, and turned toward the stairs. Brian watched her until she reached the landing. When she glanced back and smiled, he had a quick thought. It had all been too easy. Once she entered her quarters, he mounted the stairs and sat on a velvet settee across from her room.

Near him was an oval table with a vase of red roses. He couldn't remember when there hadn't been flowers of some kind sitting on that table. Once when he was six or seven he had grabbed a rose in passing and taken it to his mother. She had looked so pleased that he'd grabbed a flower from the vase every time he went in to see her. The vase was usually looking a little bare by the time the servants brought new flowers.

On impulse, he snapped off a bud and twirled the two-inch stem between his fingers. Autumn *was* sly. It was perhaps ten minutes before the door cracked slightly and auburn curls appeared. She looked up the corridor to the left, and then at Brian. He grinned and winked. "Going somewhere, Autumn, like maybe the hospital?"

She threw the door open wide. "Damn you, Brian."

He left the settee and shoved the rose into her hand. "Have a flower, pretty lady."

She gazed at the rose, the fatigue in her eyes was replaced by a look of pleased surprise. She touched the soft petals against her lips and glanced at him with a teasing smile. "Not much on stems, are you?"

He shrugged. "Where are the pills?"

"The nightstand, but I'm not taking them."

He nodded and went to her bed, pulled back the sheets, shook two pills from the packet, and walked to the bathroom, from which he returned with a glass of water. "Take these."

"I don't take pills, Brian. They make me groggy in the mornings."

"I could sit on you, hold your nose, and shove the damned things down your throat. In case you haven't noticed, I'm bigger than you are."

Autumn grabbed the pills. "I'll get you for this." She chased the pills down with water, then stuck the rose in the glass. "Good night, Brian."

"No way. You're just crazy enough to take off with two pills under your belt. I'm not leaving until you're grounded for the night."

She didn't object when he pushed her down on the bed and removed her shoes and slacks, but when he reached for the buttons on her blouse, she slapped at his hand. "I don't wear a bra."

He looked at her nipples pressing against the soft material and grinned. "Gee, I never would have guessed." Brian turned his back while she finished undressing. Once she was under the sheets, he sat down on the bed. The pleasure brought from the rose had been momentary. The fear, the exhaustion, were back in her eyes. "Scared?" he asked.

"Terrified. And I can't seem to shake it. I've learned how quickly death can strike. I have this crazy thought that if I'm there, I can keep it away."

"Artie is out of danger now, isn't he?"

"For the most part, but there are still many things that can go wrong. There could be more bleeding, infection."

"What about the back injury?"

"They're more hopeful now than they were. There's been some movement in his leg." She clasped the sheet against her breasts and sat upright in bed. "If he does recover, it will be a long hard pull. I'll want to have him close at hand with constant care. I don't think the apartment over the garage will work out very well. If bringing him to Osborne House is a problem, I'll rent a place in town."

"Don't talk shit." He pushed her back against the pillows, but she seemed to want to talk, so he listened. Shortly, though, her words became slow and lazy and her eyes half-closed.

Between yawns, she brushed a finger across his cheeks. "It's gone."

"What's gone?"

"The funny-looking mask you had after shaving that beard you came home with." She yawned. "Did you know your eyes change colors? Beautiful colors."

"Yeah. When I drink too much, they turn a nice rosy red."

She smiled, yawned again, and then she was gone. He sat for a while and watched her sleep. She murmured now and then and breathed deep relaxing sighs. He didn't know why, but strong images of the sleeping woman came to mind: the way the wind caught and tossed her auburn hair, the smile that came suddenly, beginning at her lips and spreading to her eyes. And the long slender legs he had shaken free of slacks, the shadowy line of hair that began at her navel and disappeared behind a bright red bikini.

He felt a rush of feeling for the sleeping woman and drew a finger along the soft skin of her shoulder, her lips, with a velvet touch. If she hadn't been . . . If if if. Brian rose, jerked the sheet up over her shoulders, and snapped off the light. "Good night, toughie."

36

❧

Snow came early that year, in late November. Thanks-giving had come and gone and the stores were gearing up for Christmas. Carols hummed on the air and nudged the townspeople into a spree of early buying. Bundled in a heavy topcoat, Brian left Bob's office and walked through several inches of snow to his new white Ferrari. The old sports car had coughed, spit, and refused to move out of the garage one morning, so Brian had granted it retire-ment, realizing he had formed a strong attachment to the inanimate piece of metal. He had had the car since his twenty-first birthday, a gift from his father.

Brian had finally received a copy of the autopsy report, and had forced himself at last to read about the circum-stances surrounding his father's death. The report went into graphic detail about the size, shape, and condition of his father's organs. After a couple of pages the image of his father stretched on a slab had formed in Brian's mind. He had wanted to toss the report into the trash, but he had made himself at least skim the entire contents. All was in order, so he had shoved the papers in his desk and slammed the drawer closed.

He slid behind the wheel onto leather as soft as warm butter, cranked the engine, and pulled into the flow of traffic. Seeing Bob had been a waste of time. He hadn't learned anything more, save that the Corbett Corporation was owned by a Mrs. Everett Corbett, which he could have learned from other sources. He still wanted to know what her purpose was in buying a worthless mine, and he intended to go to San Francisco and meet the lady, but at the moment other things were more pressing.

What his father had handled easily seemed to take up all of Brian's time. Encased in the office, he had piled up hours while John familiarized him with every aspect of his father's estate. For months now he had worked over sixteen hours a day without a break, jetting from city to city, meeting with staff members, managers, and the political friends his father had scattered around the States. He had begun to think of sleep as a luxury. Having Autumn in the room next to his didn't help any, either. Sometimes she played the guitar and sang at night. Her voice was surprisingly good and occasionally the songs lulled him to sleep. Other times, she chose songs that tantalized him. He lay on the four-poster, alone, listening to the silky sounds of her voice whispering "I Feel Like Making Love" or "You Need a Woman Tonight."

The singing had come slowly. For weeks he heard only the opening of drawers and the sounds of running water from her rooms. He had seen a spark when she learned Artie would walk again; however, it wasn't until she could bring Artie home that the old Autumn really began to surface. Until then Brian hadn't realized how much he had missed her sarcastic wit and unpredictable smile.

Brian pulled up in front of the house and left the Ferrari with the new chauffeur. Autumn had hired him because his name was James. Never mind whether or not he knew jack-shit about cars. She had laughed that every fancy family should have a chauffeur named James. Brian knocked snowflakes from his hair and entered the house, where he was met by Jasper, wearing a new uniform.

Jasper smiled and took his coat and briefcase. "Miss Autumn's waiting supper for you in the family dining room."

Brian cocked a surprised eyebrow. Autumn had installed Artie, along with a male nurse, in the west wing of the house. She had bought a wheelchair, a walker, and hired a psyiotherapist who came in every day. In the week Artie had been home, Autumn had taken all her meals with her brother-in-law. "I'm afraid I'll have to decline. I have a lot of work to do tonight. I'll have dinner in the study."

"Miss Autumn said no. She said you was to have supper with her."

"Oh, she did, did she?"

"Yes, she did." Autumn entered the foyer and swept toward Brian, wearing a long green dress that was belted at the waist. "You have been eating far too many dinners at your desk, and I have been cooped up with Artie far too long. It's time you took a break, and it's time I got back to my own life." She slipped her arm under his and gave him a nudge. "This way, Mr. Osborne."

"I need to wash up."

"Why? Have you and Lisa been making mud pies again?" He laughed, the first good laugh he had had in weeks. "Welcome home, Mrs. Osborne."

Dinner was a feast of roast goose with apple-and-prune stuffing, braised celery, roast potatoes, baked acorn squash, hot rolls and butter, followed by plum pudding with brandy sauce. Pleasantly sated, he settled back in the chair with an after-dinner drink. "I haven't heard you mention how Ella is doing with her new restaurant."

"Fantastic. The place is packed every night. The town needed a good middle-class restaurant. We're seriously thinking about a second place, but that won't be for a year or so."

"We?" he questioned.

"Oh," she said. "Didn't I tell you? I put up the money."

"No, you failed to mention you were her benefactor."

She shrugged. "I had a million dollars doing nothing, so I put it to work. I own half the place."

"What did Ella put up?"

"Herself."

"Wasn't that a little risky? After all, you've only known Ella a few months."

"Ella is special. Besides, I like to see the bad little girls get a break now and then. She was once a hooker in one of your joints."

He took a sip of his drink and looked at her narrowly.

"What if you lose all your money? What will you do then?"

She shrugged. "Marry another rich man."

Brian tossed his napkin on the table and shook his head in wonder. "You never cease to amaze me, Autumn. You're a young, beautiful woman. Don't you want love, children?"

"I've had love, and no, I don't want children. I hate the screaming little monsters." She left the chair abruptly, circled the table, and pulled at his arm. "Let's bundle up and go play in the snow."

"Snow?" he said dully.

"Yes, that fluffy white stuff. How long has it been since you built a snowman?"

Brian couldn't remember, but he liked the thought. He rose from the table and followed her. "Dinner. Snow. Why am I always giving in to you?"

"Because you're a softie and can't say no to a lady."

"Sure I can. Ask to drive my new Ferrari."

"Okay. May I drive your new Ferrari?"

"Hell no. I've seen how you drive—foot on the floor and haul ass." They left the dining room and were walking toward the foyer when voices broke out in the west wing. Brian looked at her quizzically. "Who's with Artie?"

"Just his nurse." She frowned and turned toward the foyer. "Artie isn't handling being an invalid very well. He's probably giving the nurse a hard time. I'll go see if I can calm him down." When the voices burst into a chorus of angry shouting, she set out at a run. Brian followed.

As they entered the foyer Daisy came toward them, her eyes wide and startled. Brian caught her by the shoulders. "You stay here and keep everybody out of the west wing until I find out what's going on." He hurried down the corridor with Autumn. When they neared Artie's quarters, Brian knew there had to be someone other than the nurse with Artie. Several voices shouted curses, and he heard the sounds of scuffling feet. Autumn was in front of him and he motioned her aside and pushed into the room.

Artie hung half out of the wheelchair with a tray of food spilled at his feet. The nurse, a stout, burly man, was wrestling with George, who waved a gun and shouted, "Artie killed Ginger."

The nurse grabbed George's arm and the gun discharged into a cracking sound that grated against every vertebra in Brian's spine. The bullet slammed into the ceiling, spraying them with dust and bits of flying plaster. "Holy shit!" Brian dived for his uncle. Even with the heavily muscled nurse and his own one hundred and eighty pounds, it took the two of them to fight George to the floor. Caught in a mad scramble of arms and legs, the three powerful men rolled on the floor like a pack of rabid dogs. The acid smell of sweat bit against Brian's nostrils and pain shot up his leg when one of the men kicked him.

Brian threw his full weight on George, pinning his uncle to the floor. He grabbed his wrist and held it outstretched toward an empty wall. While Brian held his uncle's arm, the nurse pried the gun from his fingers. Straddling George, Brian shouted his name repeatedly and struck him with an openhanded slap until awareness flickered in his uncle's eyes.

George stared as if awakening from a deep sleep. His body went limp and a low, sorrowful moan whispered past his lips. "He killed Ginger."

Brian moved off George, but kept a firm hand on his chest. The nurse had Artie back in the wheelchair and Autumn was spreading a lap rug over his legs. Artie had lost so much weight that his body looked frail, but his eyes glared with an impotent rage, the veins in his neck standing rigid. "Get that crazy bastard out of here," he shouted.

Separating the two men seemed the most sensible thing to do, so Brian rose to his feet with a hand on his uncle's shoulder. George followed obediently, his head bowed, shoulders slumped, eyes turned away as if ashamed. Brian urged him from the room and down the corridor to the study. He motioned George to a chair, went to the liquor cabinet, and mixed two drinks, stiff ones.

Brian handed his uncle a glass, feeling pity for the man, anger, and confusion. George took the glass, but glanced away quickly. "I suppose you're wondering?"

"A little." Brian sat down across from him and sipped the drink silently, allowing his uncle a few minutes to relax. George had taught him how to ride a horse, drive a car, to laugh, how to be a child in a house filled with sobriety. Now Brian felt the older of the two. "Do you want to tell me what this is all about?"

George took a long swallow of the whiskey and nodded. Once he started to talk, it came pouring out, the words rushing one after the other. He told about meeting Ginger, the money he had lavished on her, Douglas finding out, the threat, the fight between them, the other man.

Little by little, Brian was beginning to understand. To his knowledge, his brash but good-hearted uncle had never even fired a gun before, but George had brooded over Ginger's death until it had grown into a blind, monstrous rage. Then he had come after Artie. Brian sat suddenly forward. "Did you have anything to do with the accident, Uncle George? Did you tamper with the car?"

"No!" His eyes widened. "I would never have done anything to hurt Ginger. I loved her. She was so beautiful—so good."

"Bullshit."

Brian turned as Autumn entered the room. She had spoken softly, but he knew her body language. She was ready to tear into George with a fury. He left his chair and grabbed her by the arm as she strode into the room. "Not now, Autumn."

"There are things he needs to know."

"Later." He pivoted quickly and led her from the room and to the foyer. "The man's upset, Autumn. Now isn't the time."

"I want to talk to him."

"No." He frowned in annoyance. "Using your cutes to coax me into dinner and games in the snow is fine, but I would appreciate it if you left the family matters to me." He turned her toward the stairs. "Wait for me in your room. I'll talk to you later."

"Fine. You take care of your family, and I'll take care of mine. Just make sure that damned fool doesn't come after Artie again. The next time, he could be alone. Then where will your precious uncle be? In jail!"

Brian returned to the study, flexing his muscles against the tightness that pulled at his neck and shoulders. George was leaving the liquor cabinet with another drink. He looked at Brian and shook his head. "I didn't tamper with the car. I didn't even know who the man was until after the accident. I couldn't believe there *was* another man." He sat down across from Brian, still shaking his head. "Douglas told me Ginger was seeing someone else. After he died, I went back to Ginger. She told me Douglas had lied, and I believed her."

Brian listened while his uncle rambled on about Ginger for over an hour. George had become more relaxed, as if getting it out in the open had relieved all the pressure. Still, Brian wanted to be sure. "Do you have another gun at home, Uncle George?"

"No." He smiled faintly. "You don't have to worry, Brian. I don't have enough balls to try this again."

Brian nodded. "Why don't you take Aunt Harriet and go away for a while? Take a month . . . take two . . . take three."

"Yeah, maybe I will. Harriet's been nagging me to get away for the winter."

"Does she know about Ginger?"

As if suddenly very weary, George shook his head and lifted himself from the chair. "Harriet doesn't stop thinking about herself and where her next new dress is coming from long enough to see what's going on around her."

Brian heard the apathy in his voice and felt compassion. He walked with George to the foyer, his arm resting across the other man's shoulders. "Then you will be leaving?"

"Yeah. Tell Autumn not to worry. I'll be leaving."

Brian said good night to George, then turned toward the stairs and Autumn. Now that the skirmish was over, he thought it strange that her safety had been uppermmost on his mind. A man's instinctive urge to protect the female sex, he supposed. Yet Autumn had remained unruffled, very cool and controlled. Not Brian. When the gun had cracked, a streak of yellow fear raced up and down his spine, puckering his asshole like a rosebud. He'd been in a few brawls, but he'd never had any desire to play the hero.

When he rapped lightly on her door, Autumn called out for him to come in. Two chairs sat facing the fireplace, but Autumn was sitting on the floor with her cheek resting on her knees. The room was dark, save for the light from the flames. Shadows played against her face. At first her eyes were cold, but then she smiled suddenly. Tempestuous, Brian thought. Stormy one minute, beautifully calm the next. Autumn heated easily, but cooled just as quickly.

She looked at him, her eyes reflecting the firelight, and his heart actually thumped. He took a step toward her, wanting to . . . What he wanted was for her not to have been married to his father. He turned abruptly and strode from the room. ''We'll talk tomorrow. When it's daylight.''

37

When daylight came, Autumn was gone. According to James, she had awakened him in the middle of the night and asked for the keys to the Rolls. After bundling Molly, Artie, and his nurse in the car, she had climbed behind the wheel and steered the long black limousine through the snow and away from Osborne House.

During Autumn's absence an echoing silence seemed to descend and hover over the old house. And the sky, a remorseful gray, dumped layer upon layer of newly debilitating snow. Two- and three-foot icicles grew and hung from the eaves like long, threatening spears. Weighted down, the naked tree limbs dipped and swayed in the freezing winds.

Road crews had kept the highways passable, and the airports were still operating, but the *Donkey Cart* was grounded. Caught in the small capsulized town, Brian again felt the sobriety he had known as a child. The stillness at Osborne House grated on his nerves and he found himself staying later at the office, or sometimes he called Lisa. She was comfortable and easy to be with, except for her reservations about his staying at her house. Lisa worried about her children, and thought it more exciting to go out of town to a hotel or sneak up the back stairs to his quarters. She often joked that it reminded her of the hayloft.

*   *   *

By the middle of December the white blanket of beauty had grown tiresome. Brian had left his office early for home and was climbing from his car, when Autumn announced her return by slamming him in the back of the head with a snowball. His first reaction was annoyance, but then he saw her. She stood at the base of the house, booted, gloved, capped in mink, and bundled in a sable jacket, the beginning of a snowman at her side. He felt a wave of sudden laughter and tossed his briefcase, grabbed a handful of snow, and slammed it back at her.

After a fast and furious snowball fight, they rolled mounds and finished the snowman, or woman. Autumn wanted it to be female, so the cook's apron covered her middle, a colorful shawl her large bust, a dab of hay for hair and a red scarf tied around her head. They added a face and then stepped back to admire their handiwork. Autumn looked from the snowperson to Brian. "I think we just created a honky Aunt Jemima."

Brian wasn't looking at Aunt Jemima, he was looking at Autumn. She was so cold her teeth chattered and her lips were turning blue. He took her by the hand, paused for his briefcase, and then led her into the house, where they warmed up over hot buttered rums in the afternoon room.

He wondered if Autumn's return with her family had anything to do with the fact that George and Harriet had left for Palm Springs the day before. She didn't give any explanation of why they had left or where they had been, but she did explain about Ginger and how the accident had happened.

"Artie is a rogue," she said. "And he knows it. He usually picks the Gingers of the world so he can come and go without hurting anyone. When he became bored with Ginger, she wasn't ready to let him go. There was a fight and she grabbed the wheel. At the speed they were traveling, he lost control and the car rammed an embankment." Autumn picked up the mug and cupped it between her hands to warm them. "I've been told that there are whores, and then there are whores. Ginger was a real whore, with a whore's heart. She didn't care about anyone—not Artie, not George."

"How did the two men become involved with the same woman?"

"It happens. For instance, there's you, Lisa, and Bob." Autumn looked around the room. "Why aren't there any Christmas decorations?"

Brian smiled at her subtle change of topic. "The house seemed to come to a standstill after its mistress went away."

She nodded and looked down at the mug. "This has always been a bad time of the year for me. I wanted to get away for a while. After I put Artie in a place where I wouldn't have to worry about him, I went to San Francisco. But now I'm back for a while." She rose with the mug and motioned for him to follow. "Since the first day I walked into the foyer, I've thought how much fun it would be to dress this grand old house up for Christmas."

"You like the place?"

"I love it," she said with surprise in her voice. "It has so much *history*." She pointed as they entered the foyer. "I think we should have a big tree here for everybody as a kind of welcome, but a smaller, more personal one in the living room for the family. Some holly and ribbons will brighten things too. Dale will probably be coming home. I'll have a room made ready for him." She paused as if gathering her thoughts and spoke directly and in an authoritative tone. "I think we should have a small gathering for the help early Christmas Eve, then you'll be free to spend the rest of the evening wherever you want. We'll have a big Christmas dinner for the family and friends, of course, and a large New Year's Eve party. A hundred or so. With the snow, some of the out-of-towners might want to stay over. I'll have rooms made ready, and I'll call the caterers. I would like to have the children from the shelter over for games and presents. The ballroom will be the safest place. I'll have it prepared." She patted him on the chest and shoulders. "You can be the Santa Claus. You're certainly big enough. All we'll have to add is the beard and the belly." She paused. "Well, what do you think?"

"I think I'll let you direct my next board meeting."

Autumn looked blank for a moment, but then she grinned. "I'm sorry, but we don't have much time before Christmas. When I feel rushed, my brain clicks a hundred miles an hour. Do this, do that. Bang-bang-bang. Get it over. Get it done.'' She lifted the mug and took a long swallow of the warm rum. ''What would you like to do for Christmas?''

Brian smiled and rumpled her damp, tousled hair. She really had the old house humming again. ''You make the plans. Just tell me when I'm supposed to be here.''

''As Santa Claus?''

''Sure. I'll practice my ho-ho-ho's.''

The house buzzed with activity for the next two weeks, then fell silent again when Autumn, Molly, and Artie disappeared a second time. Autumn was there for the children's party, and she was cheerful and in high spirits during the party for the help. Later, Brian noticed she had become quiet and preoccupied. When he woke Christmas morning, she was gone, as if her duty as mistress of Osborne House had been fulfilled. She returned to hostess the New Year's Eve party, but she disappeared again a week later. This time, she took only Molly.

After she had been gone a month without any word, he became concerned and went to Artie. When Artie shrugged him off, he went to Bob Proctor. Bob was even more evasive, so he went to Ella. Ella was a little more open. She slid a cup of coffee in front of him and sat down at the same table. ''I wouldn't worry, Mr. Osborne.''

''Brian.''

She smiled. ''Don't worry, Brian. Autumn isn't a featherweight. She can take care of herself.''

''Do you know where she is?''

''Yes. We're partners, so she's been keeping in touch.''

''Why couldn't she call me or someone at Osborne House?''

''Autumn is a free spirit. She doesn't check in with anybody. With me it's business.''

Brian glanced at the crowded room, listening to silverware clatter against china, the hum of voices. The restaurant seated over three hundred and it looked as if every chair was filled. The room was dimly lighted, with carpeting and well-padded chairs. A nice middle-class restaurant specializing in barbecued meats. Their mutton was said to be the best. "A very good business, it looks like."

Ella nodded and took a sip of coffee. "We've shown a profit from the beginning. It's unusual and more than we hoped for. If everything goes well, we plan to open a second place over near Hopkinsville. Maybe a third a little closer to Louisville."

Brian quirked an eyebrow. "How many are you planning?

"Autumn doesn't think in terms of one, or even two, but many. I'm going to follow her lead, wouldn't you?"

"Yeah, I probably would." He rose from the table, a teasing smile in his eyes. "I don't suppose you want to tell me where Autumn is?"

"I can't, but don't worry. She'll be back when she's ready."

Brian turned and left the restaurant, accepting that Autumn was Autumn. She returned two days later, but she didn't offer any explanation, and he didn't ask any questions.

Late February brought a warming trend and the hint of an early spring. The icicles dropped and shattered against the ground. The roads cleared. Things had leveled out at the office, and Brian was beginning to dig out from under the layers of paper. Now that he could make decisions without his father looking over his shoulder and judging him, much of the resentment he had felt was gone. Brian admitted there was a certain kind of excitement in juggling millions of dollars.

He had fallen into a routine of breakfast with Autumn, the office, dinner out, or with Autumn. Evenings out, or home with Autumn. Some nights she curled in the chair and read while he worked at his desk. The silences between them were long, but comfortable. When he had to go out of town on business, she often went with him and shopped. If they had to stay overnight, they had dinner together, then went to their own rooms.

In a sense, Brian had put Autumn in a velvet box, taught himself not to think of her as a woman, but as his father's widow—hands off—for the most part. He had slipped only once.

They had had two horses saddled and had ridden to Clearview Lake. Autumn had moved up from Penny to a four-year-old gelding. He was on his father's horse, Thunder. The snow had melted, but the lake was still frozen solid. Excited squeals from kids ice-skating at the other end of the lake drifted back to them on the chilly wind.

Autumn slid from the saddle and tossed the reins over a limb, then sat down with her back braced against a tree trunk. "Douglas brought me here shortly after we were married. There's a cozy corner I singled out for skinny dipping." She looked at Brian as he sat down beside her "You're still wondering why your father married me, aren't you?"

"No. It's obvious."

She frowned, picked up a twig, and snapped it between her fingers. "It wasn't all sex. Douglas felt himself getting older, and he needed something. You were gone, and his business wasn't the challenge it once was. I came into his life in a vulnerable moment." She paused, as if in thought. "When we were first married, he preferred to sleep alone. Then he wanted me to stay after sex. Later, he wanted me there every night. He was lonely."

Brian didn't want to hear about his father or what had gone on in the four-poster. He felt restless, and rose to his feet. "Let's go skating."

"I think we're short two pairs of skates."

"No, I'll show you." He led her to the lake's edge and maneuvered his large frame onto the ice. He broke into a run, stopped quickly with his feet planted flat, and his body went sailing across the frozen surface. He turned to Autumn with an ungraceful bow. "See? Nothing to it."

Autumn followed, and walked on the ice until she had gained her footing. She looked at Brian and broke into a run as he had shown her. Planting her feet, she went flying toward him. He realized she couldn't stop and grabbed her in his arms. In the process, he lost his balance and they both fell with a hard thud, a tangle of arms and legs. Laughing, he pulled her on top of him and off the ice.

She was wearing a silly-looking stocking cap and it sat cocked to one side. He framed her face with his hands and pulled the cap down over her ears. Her cheeks were red from the cold, her lips parted in laughter. For a moment she was just a woman named Autumn and he was just a man named Brian, an archaeologist and doctor of Egyptology. He pulled her into his arms, her mouth down to his. She tasted like fresh air and sunshine and all the sweet things rolled into woman. He pulled away slightly, drew his lips over the soft skin of her cheeks, her eyes, and back to her mouth. His hands moved slowly over her waist and buttocks, then up and under her heavy jacket. He wanted her, to feel the touch of flesh against flesh, and his mind flashed to the four-poster, but then to his father.

Brian pushed her away and laughed. "I know I'm irresistible, Autumn, but would you please stop throwing yourself at me."

She sat upright, her elbow propped on her knee. "You really think you're the cat's meow, don't you?"

"Meoooow. Let's go home. It's cold."

He had made a joke of the kiss, but he had kept her at arm's length from that time on.

It seemed to Brian that April, and the appearance of tulips, was some kind of a signal for Autumn. She ordered the windows thrown open, the house cleaned from the basement to attic, and the pool to be filled. Then she disappeared again for a week.

Brian was in his room with Lisa the night Autumn returned. Dressed in a robe, he half-listened to Lisa talk to him from the bed. He leaned against the window jamb, and watched Autumn's supple body, a misty shadow in the moonlight, as it moved through the water. Lap after lap she swam, furiously, as if fighting a strong current. Back and forth, back and forth, until her strokes had become slow and labored.

"Are you listening to me?" Lisa asked.

"No—yes—what did you say?" He turned and looked at Lisa on the bed, realizing how much Autumn had been in his thoughts lately.

"I asked what you were staring at."

"A mermaid."

Lisa scrambled from the bed and crossed to the window as Autumn climbed from the pool and wrapped a towel around her bare breasts. "Oh—Autumn. I envy her. Everything fits."

"There's nothing wrong with your body, Lisa."

"My tits are too big."

Brian scowled. "Why are women always unhappy with their bodies? Autumn complains because she has seven lousy freckles on her nose."

"Seven? What did you do, Brian, count them?"

He had counted Autumn's freckles, and felt foolish. He shoved the drink he had been sipping into her hand. "Hold this. I want to talk to Autumn for a minute." He left the room and went to stand at the head of the landing. She approached him slowly, her head bent as she climbed the stairs. He waited until she was within a few feet of him, then asked, "Where have you been?"

She looked at him, startled for a moment. "Swimming."

"Don't be flip, Autumn. Where have you been for the last week?"

"Why the sudden interest, Brian? You never asked before."

"I'm asking now."

She stepped around him, but paused at her door. "My birthday was a few days ago. A friend wanted to do something special for me. He sent his plane and I went to San Francisco. I spent the week on his yacht."

Brian had wondered about men in her life, but he hadn't thought of her with a specific man. He didn't like the thought. She was an Osborne, his father's widow. It was his responsibility to look after her. "Who is this man?"

"Who he is doesn't matter. Your father is dead, Brian. I'm free to see anyone I want."

He couldn't find words to argue with her, and stood quietly staring. Her hair had grown and lay around her face and shoulders in wet ringlets. The towel had slipped until it barely covered her nipples. He hooked a finger between her breasts and jerked the towel up to her chin. "You better take a hot bath or you'll catch a cold."

"A cold? It's almost seventy degrees outside, Brian."

Swept suddenly with frustration, he snapped, "Go to bed, Autumn."

"Go to hell, Brian." She slammed the door between them.

He stood for a moment, confused. He hadn't intended to fight with Autumn, and he hadn't known it was her birthday. She had made a point to learn the date of his and then thrown a party.

He returned to his room, picked up the glass from the nightstand, and took a long, deep swallow. Lisa was stretched on the bed, her blond hair framed over the pillow. Full breasts flattened and spread the width of her chest. Blond pubic hair shimmered in the mellow light. She gazed at him, her eyes narrowed. "Are you sleeping with her?"

"No."

"Do you want to?"

He slammed the glass down on the nightstand. "She's my father's widow."

"So?"

"So, shut up."

She stretched long curvaceous legs, reached and fumbled under his robe. "You're hard!"

He bared his teeth and curled his fingers into claws, his voice low and growly. "All the better to fuck you with, my dear." He threw off his robe and climbed between her legs without preliminaries.

Lisa gasped when he lifted her hips and drove his erection into her. "Brian!"

"I'm not in the mood to coo and woo you, Lisa. This is the way I want it, all right?"

"No, it's not all right. We're not kids in the hayloft, and I'm not some sultry floozy you picked up in Singapore."

Brian sighed and offered the little amenities until she was panting and moving her body in response to his. Then he took her with a cold indifference, flipped to his back, and thought of her in retrospect. Lisa's parents and his had been friends since before either of them was born. From the time Brian was old enough to know a boy from a girl, his father had planned marriage between the two. By age thirteen Brian had decided he wouldn't marry Lisa, or anybody else, unless he wanted to.

Life with Lisa would be an easy rut to fall into. She was

a good mother, an easygoing, lusty woman. She would make a good wife. The only problem was, he didn't love Lisa and never would. Brian pulled her onto his shoulder and nuzzled his face in her flock of soft hair. "Sorry, kitten."

She pushed away and sat upright. "I love it when you're wild and raunchy, but I don't like to be screwed when you're hot for someone else."

"What the hell are you talking about?"

"Autumn," she shouted at him. "When you left me, you didn't have an erection, but you did when you came back after talking to her."

"It had nothing to do with Autumn."

"Yes it did. You spent years finding yourself, and you still don't know shit. You want to fuck Autumn and it's eating at you and gnawing at you and turning you into a real pisshead." She threw her legs over the edge of the bed. "Don't call me again unless it's me you want."

38

A cardinal sat perched on a limb of the oak and called cheerfully to its mate. Brian scowled at the noisy bird, yawned, and poked a fork at a Denver omelet. He had spent the night reassuring Lisa. Jealousy had turned a perfectly easygoing woman into a shrew. When they weren't fucking, she was bitching. Over and over she reminded him that he had stolen her virginity in the hayloft and then gone off and left her alone. And how she had waited years for him to come home. Waited, in between two husbands, Brian thought. It was four o'clock before he could finally take her home, and then he had literally dressed her, carried her from the house, and dumped her into his car.

Brian glanced at the bowl of cream of wheat on the table across from him. Autumn had set her breakfast on the terrace, but she wasn't around to eat it. A stack of financial reports was on the table too. He had tried to look them over, but it was too quiet. He couldn't concentrate.

Brian took a bite of the omelet, realizing what a creature of habit he had become. The morning didn't seem right without Autumn across from him chattering. No, she didn't chatter. In fact, she had a fascinating way of directing the conversation away from herself and leading him into doing all the talking. If he added up everything he knew about her, it would amount to practically nothing.

He dropped the fork back on his plate when Daisy

crossed to the table. She motioned toward the omelet. "What's wrong with your breakfast?"

"Nothing."

"Then why ain't you eating?"

"I'm not hungry. Where's Autumn?"

"Jogging. You best not prank with her this morning. She's in a bad mood."

"I don't prank with Autumn."

"Yes you do. You're always picking at her." Daisy turned from him as Autumn approached from the direction of the rose garden. "You mind what I say, now."

"Yes, ma'am."

Autumn dropped into the chair across from him, still breathing heavily. Her hair shone bronze and gold against the morning sun. Sweat beads curled on her upper lip. "Good morning," she said.

He watched her pour milk over the bowl of cereal and then dip a spoon into the mush. "How can you eat this shit?"

"Maybe because I was raised on it. Unlike you, there were times when we didn't have anything else."

Brian didn't know why, but she irritated him. She was wearing track shorts and a jersey shirt, her nipples straining against the thin fabric. "Don't you ever wear any clothes?"

"What's wrong with the way I dress?"

"Too skimpy."

"This town is getting to you, Brian. You're becoming as stodgy as your father."

"That may be," he said, and motioned toward her bosom. "But things that are accepted in San Francisco are frowned upon in Edisonville."

"I have never worn a bra in my life, and I don't intend to start now."

"You're an Osborne. Everything you do and everything you wear are noticed. It's too bad, but that's the way it is. You're just going to have to learn to live with it."

"What about you? You're an Osborne too. Not only are you balling every woman in Kentucky, but you bring them home with you." She fluttered her eyelashes, her voice soft and breathless: "Ooooh, Brrrrian, Brrrrrian. Huff huff, pant pant, and help help, cried the bed springs."

"What were you doing, Autumn, listening at the keyhole?"

"I don't have to. Lisa's voice came through loud and clear."

He stabbed at the omelet with his fork. "What I do is an entirely different matter. You should know that."

"Why?"

"I'm a man."

Autumn stiffened in the chair and her cheeks flushed an angry red. "I won't," she said. "I won't, I won't. Like shit, I won't." She threw the spoon, picked up the bowl of cream of wheat, and dumped it over his head. "Arrogant ass." She ran.

Brian sat ramrod straight as sticky lumps of cream of wheat dropped to his jacket and slimy trails of milk oozed over his face. He looked down and knocked a lump from his lapel, leapt from the chair, and chased after her at a run. As he entered the house, Daisy caught him by the arm and dabbed at his hair with a towel. "I told you not to prank with her today."

He swore hotly and pushed away from Daisy, and stalked through the house, his long legs taking the stairs three steps at a time. Brian glanced at Autumn's door in passing. He wanting to stop and grab her around the throat and shake her hard, but his collar was sticking to his neck and itching like hell. He moved down the hall at a fast pace, entered his quarters, and crossed to the bathroom. Then he caught his reflection in the mirror and burst into wholehearted laughter. His blond hair was plastered against his head, and his eyelashes were coated with grains of wheat. The rest of Autumn's breakfast decorated his jacket.

For the second time that morning, he undressed and stepped into the shower, where he spent twenty minutes washing the grainy wheat from his hair. After toweling dry, he dressed in fresh clothes, slung his jacket over his shoulder, and headed for the door.

His briefcase was still on the terrace, so he took the back stairs, gathered the reports, and went around the rear of the house to the garage. He hadn't expected to see

Autumn, but she was sitting on the fender of his car talking to Artie. She was frowning and gesticulating with her hands. "I'll have everything I need shortly."

Brian felt he was intruding and cleared his throat to alert them.

Autumn turned quickly, looked at Brian and then at Artie with a strange kind of smile. "There's one little thing I have to do. I can take care of that anytime I want."

Artie nodded to Brian, then turned and entered the garage with a slight limp.

Autumn looked at Brian's wet hair and grinned. "I've heard wheat is a great conditioner."

He tossed his jacket and briefcase through the open window on his car, frowning a little. "Next time, you can try it." He picked her up from the fender by the armpits and held her high over his head. "You have a new freckle."

"Where?" She touched her nose.

Brian lowered her to the ground, shaking his head in wonder at the vanity of women. He reached for the handle on his car, then paused. "I forgot." He took her by the hand and pulled her toward the rear of the house. "I have a surprise for you."

She looked at him curiously. "What kind of surprise?"

"You'll see." He gave her wrist a tug. "You'll love it." He led her along the side of the house, through the rose garden, around the marble fountain, past the oak, to the terrace.

She looked at him in bewilderment. "I don't see anything."

"You will." He bent and scooped her up in his arms and walked toward the pool.

Autumn glanced at the water and then at Brian. "No! You wouldn't!"

"Yes! I would." He stepped to the pool and tossed. "I hate cream of wheat."

"Ooooh, noooo!"

Brian waited until she had surfaced, treading water and glaring at him. He grinned victoriously. "See you."

Before going to the office, Brian parked his car and walked down Main Street. He wanted to buy a birthday gift for Autumn, but he didn't know what. Diamonds? He didn't think so. His father had lavished her with icy stones she seldom wore. Brian wanted to get her something different, something she could touch and have with her every day, not cold, hard jewels that had to be locked away in a safe until they were wanted. Unfortunately, buying gifts for women had never been his forte.

Brian passed an antique shop, and he paused for a moment. Surely among all the art objects he could find something that suited Autumn. He had almost entered the shop when a window display next door caught his attention and he smiled in wonder. The size was right, and the color matched her hair perfectly. It *was* Autumn.

He had it boxed and beribboned.

Carrying his package, Brian mounted the stairs to Autumn's room. After the second knock, she appeared in the doorway, scowling. She had changed clothes, but her wet hair curled in ringlets about her face, Brian smiled. "I have a surprise for you."

"Thanks, but I had one of your surprises this morning."

"No," he said, motioning toward the carton. "This is a real surprise."

Autumn looked skeptical, but stepped forward and glanced into the open box. Her eyes widened when a fat, fuzzy Irish setter puppy with a lopsided bow yawned lazily and peeped up at her. "Oooh," she cooed. "A puppy. I've always wanted a dog. What is it, boy or girl?"

"Female."

She looked at Brian, her eyes alive with pleased surprise. "Good. We'll get a male and she can have babies." The moment Autumn picked up the pup, it started to squirm excitedly, wiggling and licking her face with a little pink tongue. It burrowed against her throat, its color so like her own that it was hard to separate dog from long russet hair. Autumn smiled at Brian. "I love her already."

"Happy late birthday, Autumn."

"It's perfect." Then she stepped out of the velvet box and into his arms so easily, her lips soft against his. "Thank you, Brian. It's the nicest gift anyone has ever given me."

*   *   *

When Brian got to his office, George was waiting to see him. The uncle who had gone to Palm Springs had returned an entirely different man. Brian sensed a change in George he liked, a strength of will his uncle hadn't had before.

George sat calmly in the chair in front of Brian's desk. "It's no secret," he said, "that Harriet and I haven't gotten on very well for the last few years. If not for Douglas and his threats, I wouldn't have stayed with her as long as I have. There's never been a divorce in the family before, but things can't go on as they are."

"I don't understand," Brian said. "Are you here to ask my permission to divorce Harriet?"

"No, I'm through asking permission. I just wanted to let you know what I'm planning."

"Does Aunt Harriet know?"

George nodded. "She agreed, but she wants everything. The house and furnishings, jewels, furs, her car, and money. Lots of money. I didn't have the kind of cash she wanted, so I sold my shares in the mine. I signed the papers this morning."

Brian ran fingers through his hair, blond strands tumbling onto his forehead. He had tried several times to get an appointment with Mrs. Corbett, but she was always out of town. He'd even gone to San Francisco once. After being shuffled from office to office he had talked with a man she had left in charge, who knew nothing about the company buying a coal mine. The man had smiled and looked at Brian as if he were some kind of nut from the street. "Our interest is food, Mr. Osborne, not coal mining," he had said.

Brian leaned forward at his desk and gazed across at his uncle. "When was the offer first made?"

"Months ago."

"Why have you waited until now to sell?"

George smiled. "The mine was like an insurance policy. I knew if I sold, Harriet would end up with the money. If I divorced her and then sold the mine, I'd have the money for Ginger and myself." He shrugged. "I don't care anymore. I just want out. If the money from the mine will buy me freedom from that bitch, it's well worth it."

"What about Homer?" Brian asked. "Is he going to sell too?"

"Homer?" George said, and grinned. "Homer would be afraid Douglas would rise from the grave and come after him. No, I doubt Homer will sell. He's happy with things as they are. He's an Osborne, and mayor of Edisonville, and a shareholder in the largest mine in the country. It doesn't matter to him that the Black Jewel is closed."

"What are they going to do with half a mine?"

"Who know? Who cares?" George rose and glanced at the portrait of Douglas. "He was wrong about me. If he'd given me a chance, I might have done better with the company. I think it gave him a feeling of power to have me for his gofer." He looked at Brian. "I really would like to have more responsibility."

"All right. How would you feel about taking over the garment factory? Martin is retiring in a couple of months. Why don't you work with him until you get the feel of things."

"Aren't you afraid I'll blow it?"

"No. I can always fire you."

George grinned and held out his hand. "Thanks, kid. You've got enough of Doug in you to be a winner, but not enough to have a knife shoved in your back."

Brian leaned back in his desk chair as George left the room, pivoted and gazed at the portrait of his father. A knife in the back? His uncle's words rattled around in his head. Foul play in Edisonville had seemed preposterous, but after months of sitting at his father's desk, it didn't seem so unreasonable now. Brian had learned that in building his kingdom, Douglas Osborne had created some strong enemies. There was a long line of men who wanted him dead. Month after month Brian had seen it. The deeper he delved, the more dirt he had uncovered. But here? In his own pool?

He gazed at the desk drawer, slowly pulled it open, and took out the autopsy report. The months had helped, and now he could read it with more objectivity. This time he read it slowly, carefully. After struggling through three pages of medical jargon, his eyes paused on two words.

Nut protein. Brian reread the paragraph a second time, then a third. He frowned in confusion, then left his desk and crossed to Beth's office. "I've got a few loose ends to tie up. Try to get me an appointment with Mrs. Corbett in San Francisco. Keep trying until you catch her in town. And call John Allison. I want him to find out everything he can about the woman."

"Yes, Mr. Osborne."

He turned toward the door, folding the report and tucking it in his pocket. "I'll be out for a while. I have to talk to Dr. Albright."

39

Brian turned the Ferrari into the driveway at Osborne House. It had been two days since he had taken the autopsy report to Dr. Albright, but their conversation kept flicking in and out of his mind. Anaphylactic shock, Dr. Albright had said, resulting in respiratory stridor set off by an allergic reaction. It was easy for Brian to understand now how his father could have panicked, how a strong, healthy man could have drowned in his own pool. His father would have felt his throat tightening and fought to draw a breath. Frightened, he would have thrashed out wildly, gasped for air, and sucked water into his nose and mouth and lungs. His father's death had been a waste, but an accident Brian could understand and accept. His father had eaten nuts accidentally. It had happened to him before, so he had learned to carry the pills Dr. Albright had prescribed; however, he wouldn't have had them in the pool.

Brian turned the car over to James and walked toward the house. As he approached, Jasper came toward him with a pup at each heel. The day after he had given Autumn the puppy, she had gone out and bought a mate, naming them Sir Gerald and Lady Grace. Jerry and Gracie for short. In their excitement at seeing Brian, the pups left wet trails behind them. Chuckling, he bent to a squat and gathered the wiggling masses on his lap. Brian wasn't sure who enjoyed the pups more, he or Autumn.

Jasper scowled goodnaturedly at the puppies. "Them

little rascals has got me running round like a chicken with its head cut off," he said. When they ain't eating, they're shitting, and when they ain't shitting, they're chewing somethin' they ain't supposed to."

Brian eased the pups from his lap, then turned toward the house. As he entered the foyer, Autumn approached from the rear. She looked at Brian with a long, searching stare, almost analytically. He waited for her to speak, but she only smiled, then hurried up the stairs.

Brian gazed after her, puzzled, then shrugged off Autumn's glance as a mood. He went into his study, tossed his jacket on the chair, rolled his sleeves, and loosened his collar. He pulled a sheaf of reports an inch thick from his briefcase and spread them out on the desk. He worked until dinner, then had his meal brought to the study.

After eating he leaned back, spent the next hour thinking. He didn't want to point a finger at anyone, but he was curious as to how his father had gotten the nuts. Foul play was out. No one knew about the allergy but the family and Dr. Albright. To protect his all-consuming pride in his strength and virility, his father had pretended to detest nuts or anything vaguely resembling the taste, threatening the cooks with dismissal if they ever used nuts in food they prepared for him. The attacks usually came twenty or thirty minutes after he had been exposed. That would have given him plenty of time to change after eating and go for a swim. With Dr. Albright out of town, and the coroner unaware of the allergy, it would be an easy thing to overlook. Especially since the body had been in the water for almost nine hours.

Had his uncles wanted to get rid of their older brother, it would have been the perfect way, except they didn't have the imagination, even if they had had the balls. On impulse Brian called for Daisy. She entered the room and looked at his tray. "You can't still be hungry?"

"No, but I have a question. Do you remember if the cook had anybody helping her at the time of Dad's death? Were there any parties that night, or catering?"

"No," she said. "It was a quiet night. I went to the movies, but I imagine he did the same thing he did every night. He worked here in the study and then had his snack and took a swim before going to bed. Why?"

"Just curious. I thought maybe the cook could have had a stranger in helping her, someone who didn't know the family's eating habits."

Daisy frowned thoughtfully. "Now that you mention it, it seems to me it was about that time the cook was feeling poorly and called her sister in to do the cooking. She was only here for a day or two, so I forgot. I can ask the cook."

"No, it isn't important anymore." Brian was satisfied now that the woman, unaware of his father's allergy, had grated nuts into a dish.

Daisy looked at him with a puzzled frown. "Have you and Miss Autumn been spatting again?"

"No, why?"

"She's been acting odd lately, and she was tearing her room apart and boxing up stuff this morning. I reckon she's going to give some of her things to Goodwill again. I'll bet she'll be going off on another shopping trip before long." Daisy picked up the tray and turned toward the door.

Brian spun in his chair and was reaching for the phone to call John when Autumn entered the room, wearing a long black dress that did little to hide all the svelte body underneath. The bodice was sheer and glittery, damned sheer. The only thing covering her breasts was two sequined roses. Just a whisper of shapely leg and thigh teased through the slit in the side as she moved toward him. He drew a deep breath and dropped the receiver back onto its cradle. "Holy shit! Where did you get that dress?"

"San Francisco." She smiled and turned slowly for him, her arms outstretched. The back swooped to her waist in a V. Long auburn hair fell in soft waves around her shoulders. The only jewelry she wore was a diamond bracelet, a ring, and the plain gold band. "Like it?" she asked.

"Nice," he mumbled. He felt a tightness in his lower stomach that was becoming more and more familiar when Autumn was around. He had tried to put her back in the velvet box, but she kept climbing out. When he reminded himself who she was, the words wouldn't penetrate. He cleared his throat. "Who and what are you dressed for?"

"I'm going to the club." She picked up some papers and threw them in the air. "Why don't you come with me?

It will do you good to get away from all this boring stuff
for an evening.''

He looked down at his desk and shook his head. "I
can't. I'm up to my ears in reports.''

She smiled and her eyes lit with teasing. "All work and
no play will make Brian a dull little rich boy.''

Brian shuffled papers, understanding in part why his
father had never had time for him. In the last two weeks,
he had spent only six days in town. It was a treadmill,
yet it was addictive. The deeper he delved, the more
enthralling it all became. He sat for a moment and stared at
the papers, then tossed a few. "Remind me now and then
to dig out from under.''

"Does that mean you'll come?''

"I'll come. You go on. I'll be there as soon as I shower
and change. We'll boogie.''

"You—boogie?''

"No, but if they play a slow one, I'll walk you around
the dance floor.'' Brian waited until Autumn had left the
study, then called John and explained what he had learned.
John agreed that it was unfortunate, but an accident, and
should remain between the three men: himself, Brian, and
Dr. Albright. There was no point in dredging it all up
again, possibly leaving some woman to feel she was responsible for a man's life. Brian expressed his complete
agreement and was about to hang up when John brought
up the subject of the Corbett Corporation.

"I haven't been able to learn very much,'' he said.
"But I have found out a few things. The woman's name is
Sue Anne. She was a Norton before she married Everett
Corbett. He died about a year ago. He left her a bar, but
she sold it back in January.'' John paused for a moment.
"She's connected to the Murphy Company. They own
forty-five percent of her chain.''

"Murphy?'' Brian asked. "Is that the department store
Murphy?''

"That's the one.''

Brian puckered his lips in a whistle. "The lady has
money behind her, big money.''

"I've heard she's also Lloyd Murphy's mistress. Un-
confirmed, of course.''

"What the hell would she care about this hick town? What's her interest?"

"I'm working on it. The lady is hard to get a fix on. She's in and out of San Francisco and has been since her husband died."

"At least we have another name. I can always go to Murphy."

"You can, or I will."

"I'll go. Attorneys are too intimidating."

"Do you want more background on Mrs. Corbett?"

"No. I don't care who she's fucking. Just find out what she wants in Edisonville."

40

The club was crowded. Couples filled most of the tables, while others circled with arms entwined, about the dance floor. The bands they had been booking into the club had improved amazingly, and the atmosphere had changed since Brian had come home. The place was more relaxed, less stiff and formal, and he wondered if the improvements had been brought about by Autumn. She was everywhere in Osborne House and the town. Wherever she went, changes soon took place.

He weaved around the tables to where she sat with Bob Proctor, surprised at the disappointment he felt. Brian liked the man; still, he wasn't in the mood for social chatter. He had expected to be alone with Autumn, or as alone as it was possible to be in the crowded room. He signaled the waiter, then watched the two as they chatted good naturedly. They shared an affinity that was rare between attorney and client; they seemed more like old friends of many years.

Brian felt a twinge of envy, or resentment, or . . . jealousy? It was a startling revelation. His encounters with women had been mostly hit and run: a new country, new faces. He hadn't stayed with one woman long enough to form any strong emotional ties. For the first time in his life he was possessively jealous, and he wasn't sure how to handle it.

When the drinks arrived, Brian reached quickly for his

glass. He took a sip, engaging Bob in conversation. They had only the one thing in common, so he broached the subject of the Corbett Corporation buying the mine. Bob made a show, Brian thought, of looking at his watch, then quickly made excuses and left.

Talking to Autumn had always been easy, but suddenly Brian was so conscious of her that conversation become difficult, leaving long gaps of silence between them, and too, the sequined roses were playing hell with his concentration. He was almost glad when she excused herself and left the table to powder her nose. His glass was empty, so he ordered refills for both, even though he knew she refused without exception to have more than two drinks. Brian had yet to see her even mildly affected.

She was returning to the table when a member of the band approached her to sing. She glanced at the stage and then at Brian. "Would you mind?"

Autumn looked so wistful that he waved her off. She mounted the stage and spoke with the men in the band for a moment, then turned and faced the crowd. "I can't give you Anne Murray, but I can give you one of her hit songs." Holding the mike, her body swaying in time with the music, she broke into the song "Snowbirds."

Some kind of mask seemed to fall away as she sang. Her face became soft, glowing, lost in the sounds around her. Relaxed and breezy, Autumn's voice reflected all the things she was: tart, sarcastic, impetuous, and warm—carrying the listener along with her. Against the lights her dress shimmered and cast colored lights, her hair a gold-and-copper mist.

Brian was surprised by her professionalism. After the first song they asked for more, and more. She knew how to capture and hold an audience, using words and body language to seduce every man in the room, or so it seemed to Brian. After she sang several of the most recent hits by other artists, she switched back to Anne Murray. Then Autumn turned and, half-laughing, looked directly at Brian.

He smiled and lifted his glass to her, admitting finally that Lisa was right. He wanted Autumn more than he'd ever wanted any woman. Living in the same house, they had been thrown together constantly. By the law of averages, they should have made love months ago. If not for his father, and her many disappearances . . . The man with the yacht came to mind. Her lover? Was marriage likely? Not once had Brian thought of Osborne House without Autumn. An odd feeling gripped his middle and he stared at her solemnly.

She finished the song with a bubbly kind of laugh. "Ohh, yeah! I love it, I love it, folks, but the lights are getting hotter and hotter." She returned the mike and walked from the stage and toward Brian with her arms outstretched. "You promised to walk me around the dance floor, or would you rather sit and stare as if you had never seen me before?"

"Is that what I was doing?"

"All evening. You seem a little preoccupied."

"A little." He led her to the dance floor, slipped his arm around her waist, and fell smoothly into step with the music, his senses sharpened by the warmth and feel of her in his arms. Humming, she seemed unaware of the effect she had upon him. If he could do what he wanted, if she were anyone else, he would scoop her up in his arms and race home to the four-poster.

She eased away from him slightly. "Liar. You dance well."

He motioned toward the stage. "You do that well, too."

"I once sang in a bar. I was young and hungry to get ahead. The only money I could make was what I could tease from the men, so I learned to tease."

"With expertise," he mumbled.

"What?"

Brian smiled. "It's getting late. I think I'll call it a night."

"What's the matter, Brian? Are you afraid you'll turn into a pumpkin if you stay past twelve?"

"Might. Are you coming?"

She nodded and he led her from the club. As they approached their cars, Autumn paused. "Want to race?"

"Me against you? A Jag against a Ferrari? You don't stand a chance."

"Ha! Try me."

It had been years since Brian had raced down Main Street. He liked the thought. "Sure. I'll even spot you three blocks."

Brian knew all the shortcuts, so he was home long before Autumn. He was beginning to be concerned when headlights finally flashed and her Jag roared up the driveway. After a quick stop, she slammed from the car. Muttering under her breath, she pushed past him, entered the house, and raced up the stairs. "Poor sport!" he called.

Autumn turned and glared. "I got stopped by the cops."

"Get a ticket?"

"No, just a tougue-lashing about speeding. I didn't have my license with me, so we had to talk about that for a while, too."

"If you didn't get ticketed, then why are you upset?"

"Because it was a stupid thing for me to do." She slammed into her room.

Puzzled for a moment that Autumn would be upset over something so trivial, Brian mounted the stairs to his quarters, undressed, and climbed into bed. But sleep wouldn't come. He rolled and tossed, pushing thoughts of Autumn around in his head. His father's widow, he kept reminding himself. Throwing back the sheet, he swore and sprang from the bed. He grabbed a robe and was turning to leave his room for the study and work when he caught a glimpse from the window of a form half-hidden in the shadows.

Brian thought of his father, but only briefly before taking the back stairs. Autumn was huddled on the grass with a bulky towel around her. Wet hair curled against her back. She sat with legs bent, her chin resting on her knees, gazing pensively into the night. "What has you so thoughtful?"

"Just pondering."

"Pondering what?"

"Life. The past, the present, and the future. Would you sell yourself, Brian?"

"That's an odd question."

She rose and stood facing him. "Would you?"

"No."

"Oooooh, so high and mighty." A slow, strange kind of

smile glazed her eyes. Her lips parted slightly, a pink tongue appeared and traced the outline of her mouth. She dropped the towel and stood naked before him, drew her fingers along the edge of his lapel, and eased the robe from his shoulders. The moonlight fell across his chest and brought the coin to life with glimmering specks of gold that flickered in the night. She swept her hands over the broad span of his shoulders and down the length of his arms. "Come swim with me, Brian."

His pulse quickened, throbbing in his temples like jungle drums. He drew a quick, shaky breath. He had seen her nude before, but never so close. Her skin captured the moonlight and seemed to glow, the pubic hair a raging flame. He watched the rise and fall of her breasts, the delicate shadows they cast against her midriff. With a lingering touch he drew his hand over her shoulder, caressed a pink nipple, and stroked fingers that felt trembly over her belly and the gentle swell of her hips, his voice raspy with wanting. "Autumn is driving me crazy."

"I know." She laughed quietly and swayed toward him. Brian thought briefly of the four-poster, but it was too far away. He picked her up in his arms and crossed to the oak where the limbs dipped low and the grass grew thick and velvety. A light breeze stirred through the trees and leaves whispered and made little sighing sounds. He lowered her to the grass, touched her lips with a fingertip, traced the dancing shadows that played against her bare skin. She reached out for him, her face tipped upward. Her lips were cool and moist, hesitant at first, but then warmed and moved in response to his.

He wanted to please Autumn, but he sensed something unrelenting, as if she were deliberately holding a little of herself back from him. He coaxed patiently. His hands strong and sure, he caressed the hollows and swells of her breasts. His lips tasted her body, satin smooth, sweet as rich cream. Autumn felt frail in his arms, but her touch wasn't soft or timid. She stroked his erect penis, and the tips of her fingers made him shudder like a leaf quivering in the wind. She played games with his body, touched him with lips that felt hot, backed away as if to leave, laughed quietly and reached out for him again. Over and over she played the teasing game until he felt ready to explode.

Unable to wait any longer, he rose and sank into the warmth of her, his body embedded deeply in hers. He had in his arms what he had wanted for months but had refused to accept even in the confines of his own bed. Now he touched her with new awareness, new tenderness, kissed her as if for the first time, felt the rapid beating of her heart against his racing one.

She drew quick, uneven breaths against his cheek, and when he stirred, she moved her body in sweet cadence with his. She murmured to him, her lips and fingers tormenting him until his senses were soaring. He could feel it building up, ready to burst forth when she moaned softly and gazed at him with wonder.

"Son of a bitch," she whispered. "Bastard." But the words were soft, like love words, and she pulled his face down to hers with hunger.

Brian wanted to laugh, to shout, to leap tall buildings in a single bound. The night, Autumn, the rapture—it was wild and wonderful. Rockets to the moon, shooting stars, even the damned bells were ringing.

41

❧

The sun was streaming through the window and creeping toward the four-poster when Brian awoke. Remembering, he reached out for Autumn. Her hair was a disarray of russet curls, but she'd never looked more beautiful to him. Her cheeks were flushed and a pink nipple peeped at him from the edge of the sheet. She was propped on her elbow, watching him with a quiet expression. "What are you doing?" he asked.

"Looking at you."

He grinned and tousled her tousled hair. "You're a mess, woman. Go comb your hair and make yourself beautiful for me."

"Stick it up your ass, Brian." She laughed playfully and tackled him. Tangled in sheets, they rolled on the bed. She bit him on the neck and shoulders until he yelled and hooked a leg around her. "Not fair, not fair," she cried. Autumn nibbled his ear, his mouth, then buried her face in wheat-colored chest hair.

He held her head against him for a moment, then tipped her face until she was looking at him. "Last night. You were everything a woman should be."

She puckered her lips into a rosebud and kissed him on the nose. "Last night was hard for you, wasn't it?"

"Hard, how?"

"Your father. His room. His bed."

368

"Last night was last night. Today is today." He rolled her over, brushed his lips against her breasts and over her belly to the bush of auburn hair. "I love your fuzzy red puss. It's like a hot volcano. A tiny mound that spits fire."

In reply, her stomach rumbled with such a loud growl of hunger that he jumped back startled. "Christ, I think it just erupted."

Her body shook with laughter. "I haven't eaten since lunch yesterday."

"I better feed you before you vanish. Why don't we call down and have breakfast sent up?"

"Are you crazy? This isn't a hotel, it's Osborne House. I can't be found here with you." She sat upright, threw her legs over the edge of the bed, and groaned. "What I need is to soak in a hot tub, not food." She glanced back at him and swept a blond strand from his forehead. "It's been a long time since I made love with a man so young. I'd forgotten how they can screw all night. Your thing is too big, and you're too rambunctious. I have a few sore spots, namely my puss." She left the bed and walked with a pretend spraddle-legged walk.

Phony, he thought. He watched as her bare bottom disappeared through the doorway between their quarters. Regardless of what she said, Autumn was restrained by propriety. Like her gutter talk, her attempt to be brazen and audacious was a farce.

He left the bed, entered the bathroom, and heard splashing water, doors opening and closing in the room next to his. He stepped into the shower and smiled a little. His *thing* wasn't any bigger than the next man's. Autumn hadn't been bouncing in too many beds or she wouldn't have a sore crotch.

He planned to fly to Chicago for a couple of days, but if he left straight from the bed, it would seem he was treating the night with Autumn like a one-night stand. And it had meant much more. He finished showering and shaved so hurriedly that he nicked his chin. Wiping at bits of lather, he opened the door to her room. She stood beside the vanity, pulling on lacy panties. Her hair was pinned up, but loose strands dangled around her face and neck. He hooked the towel around her waist and pulled her against him. "I'm going to Chicago and I'd like you to come with me."

"I can't."

"Why not?"

She ducked from under the towel and stepped away from him. "This isn't the time, Brian. Molly could come in and find us. I'm half-naked, and you've got half a hard-on." She glanced at his penis, then pointed and laughed. "Jesus! The damned thing is crooked."

Brian followed her glance down to his rising penis. It tilted slightly to the left. "So what? It works." He reached for her again, then paused and gazed into the next room. Spread over the bed were open suitcases with clothes scattered about. "Where the hell are you going now?"

"I'm moving out."

"Moving? Why?"

Autumn left the bathroom, went to the bed, and picked up a blouse, glancing at him as he followed. "I can't stay here after last night, Brian. You should know that."

He snatched the blouse from her hand and threw it on the bed. "No, I don't know."

"All right. I'll explain it to you." She gazed at him soberly, her hands resting on her hips. "You know and I know that we can't live in the same house without last night happening again and again. I have no intention of becoming a live-in convenience for you. I don't shack up, Brian. Not with anyone."

"Is that what you think I want, a convenience?"

She nodded and picked up the blouse again. "Your being here only proves my point. Yesterday you wouldn't have entered my room without knocking. Yesterday I was your father's widow, but today I'm your woman, your possession. I'll be leaving town for good in a few weeks. In the meantime, I'll stay at the Holiday Inn until I've completed everything I have to do here."

Osborne House without Autumn? Edisonville without her? It was all happening too fast and he felt an unreasonable moment of panic. He grabbed the blouse from her again, as if it would hold her there. "What do you want from me, Autumn? Marriage? Is that what you want?"

She laughed quietly, picked up a pair of slacks, folded

and placed them in the suitcase. "Sure, Brian. I'll make you the same deal I made your father."

Her words seemed to bounce against the walls and slap back at him. He twisted her blouse into a ball and heaved it at her feet. "Look somewhere else for your next rich husband. I'm not buying."

She smiled. "If the price is too high, I might consider a discount."

"Go to hell, Autumn." He returned to his room, jerked his legs into shorts, his arms into shirt sleeves, swearing when he stumbled while pulling on trousers. The tie wouldn't tie, and he didn't notice until later that his socks were a mismatch of blue and black.

He tore the tie from around his neck, grabbed a jacket, and headed for his car. James had parked the Ferrari in front of the house, and forcing a calm he didn't feel, Brian started the engine and pulled away slowly, but picked up speed once he entered Oakwood Drive.

So what if she left town? Autumn was nothing to him. They had had a great night, but he'd had other great nights. Autumn was no different from any other woman. The night was no different. The world was full of women, beautiful women with much nicer temperaments. Sarcastic, unpredictable. What did he need with a woman like her? She'd drive him crazy after a while. They had never been able to get through more than a few days without finding something to disagree about. No different, he told himself. She's no different from the rest.

Brian was halfway to town when he slammed on the brakes so quickly the tail of the Ferrari whipped back and forth. He sat for a moment listening to his own thoughts and wondering who the hell he was trying to kid. He wasn't going to let Autumn leave.

The night *was* different. Autumn *was* different. He needed her. More, he loved Autumn. He wanted to wake every morning and find her tousled head on the pillow next to his, sit across from her and watch as she ate lumpy cream of wheat, fight with her over silly everyday differences. Loving, caring, needing, had made the night different from all the rest. It had taken him thirty-three years to find

Autumn. If he let her go now, he'd spend the rest of his life looking for something of her in every woman he met.

He cut the wheel sharply and made a U-turn in the middle of the road and headed the car back to Osborne House. He knew he was afraid of Autumn, and his lack of control over her. A piece of paper wouldn't anchor her, but he *knew* what would. He didn't think any man would ever learn all the secrets hidden behind her brown eyes, but he'd found her Achilles' heel. Children. He had watched her with the children from the shelter. She was especially fond of a little girl named Betsy. Several times Autumn had brought her to the house to play in the pool. When the little girl's mother came for her, Autumn had moped for days.

He brought the car to a stop in front of the house and slid from behind the wheel. One year. If he could have her as his wife for one year, he'd anchor her ass to Osborne House so tightly she'd never leave. He crossed the foyer and mounted the stairs to her room and entered without knocking. She was dressed now in a pantsuit.

Autumn leaned over and snapped the locks on her suitcase. "Did you forget something, Brian?"

"Yeah. You want marriage, I'll give you marriage. What were the terms of the agreement with my father?"

"A hundred thousand after marriage, another hundred thousand if he died. The million was his idea."

"Sounds good to me."

Autumn turned from the bed so quickly she knocked her purse to the floor. "You're serious?"

"I'm serious."

"Why?" she asked, and gazed at him studiously. "Never mind. I think I know. Young or old, rich men do buy what they want, don't they?" She turned away from him, but not before he saw shadows of both pain and anger on her face. "Perfect," she whispered. "The perfect ending to a very imperfect story." She turned to him and smiled. "Sure, Brian. I'll marry you."

"There are a few things I want in the agreement, too."

"Such as?"

"A child. You have to agree to give me a baby within a year. Should you want a divorce without good cause, the child will remain with me. Should I want the divorce without good cause, the child will go with you. Other details concerning its welfare can be worked out later."

"A child?" She said the word as if the meaning escaped her.

"Yeah. They wet their pants and cry a lot."

"No." She eased down on the bed, shaking her head and tossing auburn strands against her cheeks. "I can't agree to a child, Brian. I couldn't do that to . . ." She hesitated then smiled suddenly. "Sure, Brian. I'll give you a baby."

He smiled too. While looking for toothpaste in her bathroom one morning, he had seen her birth-control pills and knew her thoughts. "Then it's a deal?"

"It's a deal. When do you want this great event to take place?"

"As soon as John can draw up the agreements." He pulled her into his arms. "I think this kind of thing is usually polished off with a long, lingering kiss." She felt soft and warm in his arms and smelled of summer flowers. He pulled her closer and buried his face in her hair. "Now that it's settled, why don't we go back to bed and make a baby?"

"No!"

"Hard-ass." He left her and returned to his room, thinking back over the night. She had come to his study wearing a dress meant for seduction, and then teased him into going to the club. And later. She had been in the right place at the right time. Autumn had, very nicely, seduced him. He hadn't seduced her. Brian smiled faintly and admitted that he had been set up. Smoothly and sweetly, but set up.

He changed his socks, straightened his shirt, and was going to the mirror to try the tie again when he noticed an envelope with his name written in her hand. He expected to find a note, but instead he pulled out two one-hundred-dollar bills. Confused, he returned to Autumn with the money. "What is this for?"

"Last night." She winked suggestively. "It was *wow!*"

He looked at the money and grinned. "Is this your way of telling me I've been bought?"

"Everyone is for sale at some point in their life. All you have to do is offer them the right price. If they want what you have bad enough, they'll sell."

"If you think I sold my integrity because I made love to my father's widow, you're wrong. I've wanted you since the day we first met, but I didn't want to step on a dead man's toes." He paused and grinned. "Hell, Dad would have kicked my ass for allowing you to sleep in the room next to mine without a tumble. The only sin I've committed is not having you months ago."

She crossed to him and curled her arms around his neck. "It really should have been more than two hundred, Brian. You're terrific under an oak." She drew her lips over his chin, traced his lips with her tongue. "I wouldn't want to make a baby out of wedlock, but we could practice . . . unless you absolutely have to go to Chicago?"

Brian didn't hesitate. He slid his arm around her waist and turned toward the door. As they neared the bed, he paused and looked at her oddly. "Why do I feel like the proverbial snook being led around by his cock?"

Her eyes teased. "I don't know, Brian. Why do you?"

He picked her up in his arms and tossed her to the middle of the bed. "You're at the head of the race right now, but I'll win in the end."

She bounced among the rumpled sheets. "Win what?"

"You have your secrets, and I have mine. Now I'm going to the office and then to Chicago. If you want to come along, I'd be delighted. Otherwise, you can stay here and do whatever it is women do when they're about to be married."

42

Brian and Autumn were married in the rose garden with friends and family looking on. All of Edisonville was there, smiling, sipping champagne, and whispering behind their hands. "Imagine, marrying your father's widow. Shame, shame. Hell and damnation."

Autumn looked ready to scramble over the hedge and run as Brian slipped his mother's wedding ring on her finger alongside the gold band. The ring, a heavy rope of white diamonds, was an heirloom and signified permanency. Autumn might not intend to be around for the full run; however, Brian had other plans.

The following day they flew to New York and fell into a round of parties. During the day they ran through the streets like tourists. Evenings, it was dinner and the theater, or nightclubs with friends, either from college or the archaeology foundation Brian had been connected with, business associates, or old friends of the family. Some had a free style of living, others were stuffy and judgmental. He had wondered with amusement how Autumn would handle herself, but Fifth Avenue or Greenwich Village, sipping sherry or passing a joint, she had the rare ability to shift gears and blend in.

After two harried weeks Brian took Autumn and left for the Bahamas so he could have her to himself. They toured the islands by jeep, sailed, swam the cerulean waters, and played on the white sands until his skin was burned a deep brown and Autumn's fair skin glowed a shade away from beet red and the seven freckles had grown to ten.

Brian had planned to be gone only a month, but one lazy week stretched into another and another. And each week he had fallen more and more in love with his wife, deeper than he had thought it possible to love anyone. Until Autumn, he hadn't realized how alone he had been. She rounded out his life and made him feel whole. She was different away from Osborne House, gayer, more free with herself, laughing at the smallest things. In the weeks they were gone, there wasn't one dark day. Not once had the coldness touched her eyes.

He caught himself watching, waiting for some sign that he was stripping away the barrier. She responded to his lovemaking and whispered endearments, but the right words, the words he wanted to hear, just didn't come. So he told himself to be patient, give it time, give her time. Once, she had come so close.

The day before they were to leave the islands, they were lying on the beach after swimming. Autumn, propped on her elbows, smoothed the sand and drew a heart with their initials. Brian added an arrow. "When we get home I'll carve it in the oak," he said. "I'll even add the date when A.O. seduced B.O. in the very spot."

"I didn't seduce you. I only asked you to swim with me."

"Yeah, and then stood with your beautiful tits peeping at me in the moonlight and your fuzzy bush a blaze of fire, taunting me, driving me wild, witless with passion."

"I said swimming. I can't help that you were born with a big thing that itches every time it comes in contact with a little bare skin." She rolled to her back and smiled up at him. "I don't want to go home."

"Neither do I, honey."

"We have to go home?"

"We have to go home," he echoed.

She drew a finger along the line of his jaw, tenderly across his lips. "These weeks have been like a fairy tale. Once upon a time there was a princess named Autumn, and a prince named Brian. They made love under an oak and then they got married and then they lived happily ever after." She gazed at him with a lingering look, cupped his face and pulled him down to her, touched the tiny curving scar at the corner of his mouth with her lips. It was a tender moment and he waited, for the words. But Autumn pushed away abruptly and ran for the water, calling, "Last one in's a rotten egg."

Brian rose from his chair and held out his hand in greeting as John Allison came toward him. John smiled and gave him a hearty handshake. "You look great, Brian. The Bahamas or marriage certainly agrees with you. How long has it been now?"

"Two months and two days. If you want to wait a minute, I'll count the hours."

John set his briefcase on Brian's desk and took a chair. "How is Autumn?"

"Terrific." Brian thought of Autumn, smiled to himself, and sat down behind the cavernous desk. "Let's get to work." He tried to concentrate, but the afternoon limped past at a snail's pace and his thoughts kept drifting. "I'm sorry, John. What was that again?"

"This thing with the Corbett woman."

Brian looked blank for a moment. "Oh, yeah. What about her?"

"I can't find any tie between her and the town. She started her company with backing from Lloyd Murphy. She began with four stands. The business caught on and spread like wildfire. She's always lived simply. Nothing garish. She poured everything back into the business. Three months ago they branched out to the east coast."

"This Murphy doesn't keep her in style?"

John shook his head. "She lived over the bar she owned until it was sold. Then she moved to a nice but not pretentious apartment in a good but not great part of town. Until a year ago she was totally devoted to the business. I don't know what happened then, but after her husband died, she turned the business over to managers. She's rarely in town now. She returns for a few days and then disappears again. I haven't found out where. If you want more, I'll have to go further back."

The mine and the Corbett woman seemed years past,

unimportant now, and Brian stretched back in his chair, yawning. "I don't know if it's worth bothering with. She sounds like a lady fighting boredom. Her business is off and running and she's looking for new worlds to conquer." He grinned. "Maybe she has some cockeyed delusions about becoming a big coal baroness. Some women will do strange things when they're bored. I don't give a damn about the mine. I was mainly curious about who my partner was and why she would buy up a worthless mine."

John smiled a little, a bit teasing. "While you were gone, the bored little lady picked up controlling interest in the Edisonville *Times*."

Brian snapped forward in the chair. "She what?"

"She bought controlling interest in the paper here."

Brian hit the intercom. "Beth, get me an appointment with Lloyd Murphy in San Francisco. I want to see him as soon as possible."

"Yes, Mr. Osborne."

Attentive now, Brian listened as John explained about the sale, the announcement in the paper, and what he had learned. For some reason, the lady had managed to search out and join forces with the family's longtime enemy, Fritz Jergenson. Brian reached for the intercom again. "Did you get the appointment, Beth?"

"Yes, Mr. Osborne, but the best I could do was two weeks."

"Two weeks? Who the hell does he think he is, the fucking president?" Brian heard her gasp, could see her prim face pucker with disapproval, and grinned. "That's fine, Beth." He turned back to John. "When did all this happen?"

"The sale took place some weeks ago, but they didn't make the announcement until recently."

"How was it handled?"

"Her attorneys in San Francisco, and Bob Proctor."

"In other words," Brian said derisively, "the mysterious lady is handling this the same way she bought the mine shares. A name only."

John nodded, rose, and snapped his briefcase closed. "From what I've been able to learn, old Fritz will remain with the paper, but it will have a new editor. She's bringing in people from San Francisco to give it a facelift.''

Brian left his chair and walked along with John to the door. "The lady is obviously more than just bored. She's after something. I want you to dig deep. Find out who the hell she is and where she came from. In the meantime, I'll find out what I can from Murphy."

As they entered the outer office, Beth looked up and smiled brightly. "I don't understand, but Mr. Murphy's secretary just called. Mr. Murphy will be happy to see you anytime it's convenient.''

"Let's see how happy he is to see me tomorrow morning. Make the appointment and get in touch with my pilot. Tell him to have the Lear ready. And make hotel reservations for me in San Francisco."

"Would you like me to go with you?" John asked.

"No. Attorneys have a way of putting people on guard. I'd like this to be an easy, informal talk." As he spoke with John, Beth made a nine-o'clock appointment with Lloyd Murphy. Leaving the building, Brian walked John to the parking lot. They spoke briefly, then Brian drove to Osborne House to pack a bag. Racing up the stairs, he almost collided with Daisy. "I'll be flying out in an hour. Pack a bag for me, and . . ." He paused and looked around. "Where's Autumn?"

Daisy looked toward Autumn's bedroom and frowned. "She's resting. Miss Autumn's feeling poorly today."

"Poorly, how?"

Daisy shrugged. "I don't know. She was up and around a while ago. Then Molly said she had gone to bed because she wasn't feeling good. Probably picked up something in them islands where ya'll stayed.''

Autumn never went to bed during the day, even for a short nap, and Brian went in to see her concerned. The room was dim, the drapes drawn, and Autumn was buried under blankets. He crossed to the bed, eased aside the edge of the sheet, expecting her to be asleep. When she looked up at him and moaned, he smiled slightly and sat down beside her. "What's wrong, honey?"

She sat upright, naked, and shoved wet hair from her face. "I don't know. I took a shower, hoping it would help, but it hasn't. I feel funny. Kind of pooped. Kind of grumpy.''

He looked at her narrowly. "How long has it been since you've seen a doctor?"

"Six months or so. When I had my last Pap."

"Do you hurt anywhere?"

"No."

"Are you sick to your stomach?"

"No."

He grinned. "What are you, then?"

"Grumpy."

He gazed at her uncertainly. If she was sick, he didn't want to leave her—become like his father: business before life. Where was the dividing line? He wanted to keep the appointment with Murphy, too. "I need to fly out of town tonight. I'll be back early tomorrow afternoon. Will you be all right?"

"I'm just a little tired, Brian. Go—do your thing. I'll be fine."

"Are you sure?"

"I'm sure."

He hesitated. "Why don't I call Dr. Albright and have him take a look at you?"

She smiled and threw herself into his arms, teasing until he felt foolish. Laughing at himself, he left Autumn to pick up his bag. In passing, he snapped off a rose from the vase in the corridor and returned to her room. "A rose for my pretty wife."

Autumn sat up in bed. She held the rose by its two-inch stem and looked at him with a quiet smile. "It's beautiful. I love your little impromptu gestures." She lowered her eyes and gazed at the rose. "Regardless of what might happen, don't forget the islands. Remember, the princess didn't want to come home." She turned away from him and buried her head under the blanket.

Brian settled back on the soft-cushioned seats of the *Donkey Cart*, the Lear jet that was a luxurious whim of his father's. He felt the engines whine as they taxied down the runway, a gathering surge of power, and then the jet lifted smoothly into the air. He unbuckled his seat belt, his thoughts drifting to the afternoon with John. Old Fritz was harmless for the most part, but only because he'd never been able to get anything on the family that would hold up in print. There was nothing Fritz would like more than to bring down the Osborne family. He had certainly tried hard enough over the years. The slightest incident and he had used his paper to take a jab at Douglas or Homer, needling and editorializing about the monarch who used his money and power to rule the town and its people. A step away from a dictatorship, he had shouted numerous times. Douglas' death hadn't changed Fritz's mind. He still saw the town as being controlled by one man, Brian.

Douglas had tried to get the paper away from him, but old Fritz had kept every crack closed. Why he had sold now, Brian could only speculate. He had heard rumors that old Fritz's heart wasn't as good as it once was. Possibly he had jumped at the chance to sell to an out-of-town source, but only if he knew that source was opposed to the Osbornes. There was something stewing in town, Brian knew it. He could feel it. The Corbett lady and old Fritz were up to something.

Brian finished his drink, then turned his thoughts to something soft and yielding, not cold and oppressive. Autumn's skin had felt dewy from the shower, and she'd smelled of bubbles and soaps and colognes—sugar and spice and everything nice. This would be the first time he had slept without Autumn curled next to him in weeks and it felt strange.

As the plane soared, taking him closer and closer to San Francisco, he had the uneasy feeling that he had forgotten something, or left a little something of himself behind among the satin sheets.

43

Lloyd Murphy was in his early fifties, with sandy hair graying at the temples and keen green eyes. He was heavier across the chest than Brian, and a couple of inches shorter. He carried his large frame with relaxed self-assurance. His years of wheeling and dealing had honed him into a polished businessman who remembered to smile at the right time, check discreetly that his tie was always straight, and graciously extend the little courtesies. Charming, but Brian didn't kid himself. Lloyd Murphy looked like the proverbial country squire, but he was the kind of man that could be down and dirty.

Lines crinkled at his eyes when he smiled and held a drink out to Brian. "You make a fine bourbon, Mr. Osborne."

"Thank you. We try hard."

Still smiling, Lloyd sat down in a chair across from Brian. "I have to admit, I've been curious about you. You're much younger than I expected."

Brian had heard that same remark so many times that he had learned to shrug it off. "I don't think Dad had planned to die and leave me the bundle while I was still wet behind the ears. Unfortunately, he was unable to wait."

"Yes," Lloyd said in a consoling voice. "A tragedy."

Brian arched a surprised eyebrow. "Did you know my father?"

"No, not personally, but his name was well known in

the business world." Lloyd smiled again. "From what I've been hearing, you're making quite a name for yourself, too. Which brings me to ask why you're here."

"The Black Jewel," Brian said bluntly. "And why Mrs. Corbett is buying it, or trying to. Since I haven't been able to reach her, I came to you. I understand you're part-owner in her company. Consequently that makes you part-owner in our coal mine. I hope you can clear up a few questions."

"Certainly."

For the next fifteen minutes Brian listened while Lloyd led him around and around with double-talk. Not only was Lloyd Murphy a wheeler and dealer, but he was full of bullshit up to his green eyeballs. Brian smiled to himself at the innocence of the man. Lloyd Murphy was a city slicker selling fashion. He knew nothing about the harsh realities of coal mining. "I'm all for progress," Brian said. "But only if it's in the best interest of the town. Somehow, I wonder if this is the case with Mrs. Corbett. I don't trust people, man or woman, who hide behind attorneys."

"Mrs. Corbett has her own way of doing things."

"She's made several damned stupid mistakes."

"How is that?"

"To begin, she bought the shares without asking for a geology report. Instead of waiting until she could buy the stock as a package, she's been picking up scattered shares. You and the lady own half, but my uncle and I own the other half and we have no intention of pouring money into an empty hole, nor do we plan to sell. Which brings us to a stalemate."

"I believe Mrs. Corbett was led to understand the mine had closed prematurely. From what she tells me, there are two years of work left in the Black Jewel."

"Yes," Brian said. "Possibly three, if you worked small crews. However, the cost to mine the coal by far outreaches any profit that could be made. If the lady had bothered to look at a geology report, she would have known this. As it is, she's poured over a hundred thousand dollars into a worthless mine. It would cost millions alone to replace the equipment that would be needed if the mind reopened. The vein had narrowed over the years, and we

ran into the kind of overburden that required extensive
supporting to make the ceiling safe. Believe me, Mr.
Murphy, if there was money to be made in the Black
Jewel, Dad would never have closed it.''

Lloyd took a sip from his glass, swirled the ice. "I think
we should clear up one point. I own forty-five percent of
the Corbett Company, but I don't own any part of your
mine. Mrs. Corbett bought the mine through the corporation, but she used her own money.'' He waved his hand in
a slight gesture. "If I wanted to get into a court battle,
which I don't, I could possibly force her shares split in my
behalf. In all fairness, it was her money, and her venture. I
have no interest in your mine or your town.''

"What about the Edisonville *Times* she picked up recently? Was that bought with her money too?''

Murphy's eyes widened in unmistakable surprise. "I'm
afraid you have me at a disadvantage, Mr. Osborne. I
don't know anything about this.'' He paused for a moment
and took another sip of his drink. "Mrs. Corbett is a very
independent and determined lady. She doesn't ask my
permission to buy or sell. Mrs. Corbett has been out of the
country for the past couple of months on a much-needed
vacation. We've only spoken by phone, and then briefly.
She hasn't told me about the paper, or what she has in
mind.''

Brian smiled to himself. The man didn't seem to have
very much control over his woman. Brian felt he had
gotten everything he could from Murphy and began easing
the conversation to an end, complimentary chitchat about
the city and its famous bridges and seaports.

Lloyd seemed to appreciate the change in topic and offered him another drink, which Brian declined. Settling
back in the chair, Lloyd smiled. "Have you spent much
time in San Francisco?''

"No, but my wife, Autumn, once lived here. She returns often to shop and visit with friends.''

Lloyd jerked forward in the chair and stared as if Brian
had committed some kind of social blunder. "Your what?''

"My wife, Autumn. She once lived here.''

Slowly Lloyd eased back in the chair. "I didn't know
you were married. When did this take place?''

"Two months ago. We just returned recently from the Bahamas."

Lloyd nodded and looked at Brian with a stiff smile. "I hope you'll excuse me, Mr. Osborne, but I just remembered a very important phone call." He left the chair and held out his hand to Brian. "Marriage at its best can be a tedious thing. You've entered into a hazardous venture. I hope you're more successful than some I know." He smiled thinly. "Give your wife my regards."

Settling back, Brian tilted his chair as he nodded at the men he'd summoned to Osborne House. Recalling his conversation with Murphy, he decided it had ended on a strange note. The man's face had actually blanched when marriage was mentioned, and his parting remarks had been laced with sarcasm, his smile a sour-faced grimace. The trip had been a waste. The only thing he had learned from the man was that he had a mistress he couldn't control and that he found marriage distasteful. Whereas Brian advocated marriage strongly, but only if that marriage was to a redhead named Autumn.

She still wasn't her old self and it concerned Brian. She had been quiet, tired, snappish, her face drawn, her eyes dull and evasive. He had urged her to see Dr. Albright, but she had insisted she was fine. When he saw her at breakfast later, Brian decided, he would demand she see a doctor. Otherwise, he would bring a doctor to her.

Now he turned in the chair and gazed across at the three men he had called to his office, Homer, John, and Chief Hadley. "I think you all know that Fritz sold controlling interest in the paper to a woman from San Francisco. We haven't learned anything about her, but I have a gut feeling she's after something. I think old Fritz is going to come after us, and I have no intention of being caught with my pants down. Since our only weak spot is the joints, I'm ordering them closed. This week."

Chief Hadley, a thin man with bushy eyebrows, shook his head and frowned. "I don't think we need to go to such extremes."

Brian smiled a little. "The twenty percent we kick back

ιo you wouldn't have anything to do with your decision, would it, Chief?''

Hadley arched his thick brows and shifted in the chair. ''That was uncalled for, Brian.''

''I agree with my nephew,'' Homer said. ''Fritz has known for years that we're all tied in with the . . . shall I say, seedier side of town. Fortunately, he's never been able to prove it. I think we should close until we know more about this woman and why she's moving into town. When things calm down, we can open again.''

''No,'' Brian said strongly. ''I have no intentions of re-opening. I've always thought Dad was a fool for support-ing those places. Sometimes I think he did it to tempt fate or old Fritz. I had planned to close eventually, but not until next election. As things stand, I don't think we should wait.'' He paused and looked from Homer to Chief Hadley. ''When the time comes, I want you to get behind me and push the people to let liquor into the county.''

Homer shook his head, along with Hadley. ''The people will never agree,'' Homer said. ''They want their town dry.''

Brian looked at the two men derisively. ''They'll vote the way we want if you don't get on your grandstand and fill them full of bullshit, Uncle Homer.'' Brian straightened his back pompously, mimicking Homer. ''DO YOU WANT YOUR INNOCENT YOUNG GIRLS BOTHERED BY DRUNKS STAGGERING FROM TAVERNS WHEN THE LITTLE DARLINGS LEAVE THE SAFETY OF THE THEATERS?'' Brian grinned. ''What the people don't know is their innocent daughters are not at the movies, but at the joints feeding quarters into a slot machine, and their sons are humping away their allowance in the back room with some whore.'' Brian threw his head back and laughed whole-heartedly. ''Don't try to snow me, Uncle Homer. I grew up here, remember. You don't want taverns because you won't be pulling in twenty percent of the take from them.''

Homer bristled mildly and stroked a finger over his crooked mustache. Chief Hadley still wasn't convinced. ''I think you're running scared, Brian. We don't know that this woman has anything. If you close, the places will open up again, and without us to keep things from getting out of hand.''

"Hell yes, I'm running scared. And no, we don't know that Mrs. Corbett has anything, but I have to ask myself why she would come to a one-horse town and buy a worthless mine owned by the Osbornes. Why hire my uncle and send him to Seattle? Why buy a newspaper that isn't going to show her a hell of a lot of profit? And from a man that's known to hate the Osbornes. A man that wants nothing more than to see the not-so-lily-white name of Osborne smeared across his paper. And as far as the joints opening by someone else: fine, let Fritz go after him. My ass will be clean and so will yours."

John had sat quietly. He spoke now, directing his words at Homer and Hadley. "Brian is right. If Fritz and this woman should come up with something and it gets into print, it could lead to a full-scale investigation. You'll have state and federal agents swarming over the town like honey-sucking bees. I advised Douglas to get out years ago, but he refused. He didn't want anything changed. Brian is trying to do what should have been done years ago."

"Yeah," Homer said. "I have to agree, up to a point. Doug refused to let the town change. I've had several men approach me about bringing in new businesses. This one fellow wanted to open a kind of arcade with pizza and dancing puppets and video games. It seemed innocent enough and I tried to push it through, but Douglas found out. He was furious with me. He told me he wouldn't back me in the next election. He was looking around for a man to run against me." Homer paused and looked at Brian. "What about it, Brian? Are you going to stand behind me?"

"I'll stand behind you, if you'll stand behind me now. This is a good town and I want to see it grow, not stagnate. We can't get people to come here if they have to belong to the country club, the Elks, or go to a dirty bootleg dive every time they feel like having a social drink. I want to see new businesses coming in, new industry. I'd like to see a college here, even if it's only a community college, and a youth center for the kids, my kids. Christ, in the years I was gone, the town just sat here and hibernated, the door locked as tight as a wart on a whore's ass. The only thing new is the Holiday Inn and Autumn and Ella's new restaurant, which is doing great.''

Brian looked at Homer and Chief Hadley. ''When a town grows, the officials' salaries also grow. You're both good men, and you're liked by the people. If you want to go along with me, I'll stand behind you. Otherwise, I'll look around for new men to fill your spots. I can do it, too. I'm Brian Osborne, son of Douglas, fair-haired boy. I'm the cat's meow, and I know it, and I'll use it.'' He pushed away from his desk and stood, his eyes imploring Homer to agree. Brian had come down hard on his uncle, harder than he could have on Dale and George. He didn't know why, but he had never gotten close to Homer. Blood was between them, but Homer was reserved and held himself back from people. He had struggled or years to be like his older brother, to rise along with Douglas, but he lacked the special something it took to shine. ''What's it going to be? Are you in, or are you out?''

Homer nodded and looked at Hadley. ''Would you believe this mouthy nephew of mine used to come and beg brownies from his Aunt Bea? Now he doesn't ask, he tells.'' Homer rose from the chair. ''I guess I'm in, since I don't have anywhere else to go. I've made some bad investments and I'll miss the twenty percent, but I'm still in better shape than I would have been if Douglas were sitting behind that desk.''

Hadley rose along with Homer, his heavy brows arched as he looked at Brian. ''I remember a few things too. I remember turning my back when you raced your damned sports car down Main Street. I remember carting your ass home when I should have arrested you for being drunk and disorderly. I remember stepping in and breaking up a brawl when you were getting your ass beat by a bunch of paratroopers from Fort Campbell. Yeah, I remember a lot of things.'' He turned on his heel and stalked from the room, followed by Homer.

Brian watched them leave and frowned, confused. ''Why can't the damned fools realize I'm looking after their butts as well as my own?''

''They'll come around,'' John said. ''Right now all they're thinking about is the twenty percent.''

"Yeah, twenty percent of nothing if Fritz and Lady Corbett have their way. I don't want to have to play the heavy with Amos Patterson, too. Get with him and explain what's happening. Tell him to close up. I don't want one slot machine, deck of cards, or whore left in the county that can be traced to me, or Uncle Homer, or Hadley." His eyes narrowed and he looked at John closely. "Is there anything I should know, anything in Dad's past business dealings that Fritz could use against me now?"

"No, nothing," John said. "Douglas was a dirty and often immoral fighter, but he had the good sense to stay within the law when it came to other dealings."

"What about the woman? Have you learned anything more on her?"

John smiled faintly and shook his head. "My source in San Francisco did talk to someone who remembered her from when she sang in the bar. He couldn't remember much, just that she was a terrific-looking redhead with an accent, a Southern accent."

Brian instantly thought of Autumn. "Damn. I forgot. There's a terrific-looking redhead waiting breakfast on the terrace, but she doesn't have an accent."

John smiled and walked toward the door. "I'll show myself out." He paused and glanced back at Brian. "Cat's meow?"

Brian grinned and shrugged. "A little something I picked up from my wife. I thought it added a nice touch." He left John and crossed to the double doors leading to the terrace. Autumn was at the table with coffee cupped between her hands. Her lips were on the rim, but she wasn't drinking. He leaned over and brushed his lips against her cheek. "Sorry I'm late." When she mumbled absently, he tipped her face toward his and gazed long and hard. She had tried, but makeup couldn't hide the pallor of her skin. Autumn was ill, fighting it, but ill. He took her hand and slid into a chair across from her. "I want you to see Dr. Albright. Today. No excuses."

"I'm all right, Brian. I've just picked up some kind of bug. I'll be fine in a couple of days."

"That's what you said a week ago." His breakfast was

under a warming tray. She was, or had been, nibbling on a dry piece of toast. "Aren't you hungry?"

"No. My stomach feels shitty."

Brian looked at the toast and then at Autumn. "Maybe you're pregnant."

"No," she said, and shook her head. "I can't be."

"How can you be sure? We've been married over two months, and in those months you haven't had a period."

She shrugged. "My body is just a little off—out of whack. Believe me, I'm not pregnant."

"I think you should see Dr. Albright and make sure."

She frowned, and her voice rose snappishly. "I'm not pregnant, Brian. Please, just drop it."

"I can't. There's a very good chance you're pregnant. The pills you're taking are nothing but sugar. I switched them."

She gazed at him, her eyes confused, as if trying to make sense of what he had said. "You what?"

"I switched them. I knew you were taking the pill on the sly, so I found them and switched them for some sugar pills I had made up. We had an agreement, Autumn. You weren't holding up your end. A baby within a year, remember?"

Her body slumped in the chair, her voice a low moan. "My God. You stupid man. You don't know what you've done." She pushed away from him and raced for the house. Brian followed, calling as he ran. He had expected anger from Autumn, a temper tantrum maybe, but her voice had been strangely quiet, tormented. Molly was on the stairs and she looked at him quizzically, but he rushed past her without speaking.

When he entered the room, Autumn was standing at her desk with a calendar. "Bastard," she shouted, and threw the calendar across the room at him. "I'll abort. I'm not having this child. I can't. I won't bring an innocent child into this mess. I won't."

"What mess?" he asked with a perplexed frown. "What are you talking about?"

Her hands waved frantically and her voice rose with hysteria. "You don't understand. I can't have this baby. I won't." She brushed hair from her face, wringing her hands and pacing. "I can't take this, Brian. I can't take any more. I feel like I'm being pulled in every direction, torn in half." She looked at him and her eyes pleaded for understanding. "We can't have this baby. A child needs love. Two parents. We can't give it that."

He took a step toward her, his hands outstretched. "You're confusing me, honey. Our child will have love, all the love in the world. And two parents. Brian and Autumn."

"No!" She pushed away from him, her voice cracking with emotion. "A child needs to be surrounded by love. Two parents loving it and each other. You don't love me, Brian. You only married me because I had belonged to your father and you wanted what he had had. I've watched you. Oh, I've watched you, Brian. You've been fighting since you came home to best your father at everything. Marry Autumn. Get her pregnant. Do the big man one better."

Confused and angry, he shouted at her. "Love you? Goddammit, woman, are you blind? I've been tearing my guts, waiting for some sign that you cared even a tenth as much as I do." He caught her wrist and jerked her into his arms, but felt the anger slipping away. He spoke quietly. "I married you for one reason, and one reason only. I love you, Autumn. More and more every day, if that's possible. If I lost you, I'd lose the only thing I really care for. Maybe it was wrong, but the pills were to keep you with me."

"Dear God," she moaned. "You weren't supposed to love me." She pulled away from him and Brian watched as his wife crumbled. It wasn't the kind of hysteria he had seen when Artie was hurt, but a kind of disintegration that reached out and tore at him. Her eyes dulled and she gazed blankly. She climbed onto the bed and curled into a fetal position, her hands clasped tightly against her stomach. "Caught in the middle," she whispered. "Poor little baby . . . caught in the middle." Over and over and over, she whispered the same words.

Brian pulled her into his arms, longing to help her, tormented because he couldn't. She was off somewhere in her own private hell, moaning incoherent ramblings now.

Alarmed, he called for Molly, and then Dr. Albright. He, along with Molly, stayed with Autumn and held her, rocking and whispering until Dr. Albright was shown into the room by Daisy.

Dr. Albright took one look at Autumn and then ordered everyone out of the room. Pushed into the hallway, Brian sat on the velvet settee beside Molly, waiting. "Do you know if this has happened to Autumn before?"

"I don't reckon I can say."

"Can't, or won't?"

Molly reached and patted his hand. "Autumn feels things a lot deeper than most. She loves hard, and she hates hard. I reckon folks like that have to explode a little now and then, else they'd break so bad there'd be no putting them back together again." She squeezed his hand and looked at him in a way that was reassuring. "I think the war in Autumn is over now. Just you be patient. She'll need you now more than ever."

Daisy, her arms folded over her bosom, gazed at him. "What happened to Miss Autumn, anyhow? I ain't never seen her like this before."

Brian didn't reply. He rose and paced back and forth in front of the door, filled with recriminations. Autumn had always been so strong, like the steady oak. She would bend a little if the wind blew hard, but never break. He wouldn't have believed she could be flattened so easily. Or was it easily? There were still so many things he didn't know about his wife.

Dr. Albright was with Autumn for almost an hour. When he left her room, Brian leapt at him. "What happened? What's wrong with her?"

Dr. Albright turned to Molly. "She's going to be wanting to sleep. Why don't you and Daisy help her undress and get her to bed." He turned then to Brian. "She'll be all right. I gave her a sedative and we talked. She told me about the child she had lost when she was eighteen. Learning she was pregnant so abruptly jolted her. I think she confused the two babies in her mind. I suspect, too, that there are other things bothering her. I suggest you have a long talk with your wife and get things straightened out.

She's fine now, but I'll want to see her in my office the first thing in the morning.''

Brian nodded. "May I see her now?"

"Yes, but don't excite her. I want her to have complete rest and quiet for the next few days. And no sex right now. She's had one miscarriage. I don't want to take a chance on another one.''

Brian nodded as he left Dr. Albright. He stood just inside the door until Molly and Daisy had put her to bed. He motioned them out, then crossed and sat on the bed next to her. She looked wan and beautiful, wearing an apricot-colored gown. She glanced at her middle and tears welled in her eyes, slipping slowly down her cheeks. "I couldn't abort the baby, Brian. I wouldn't. I couldn't.''

"I know." He reached and wiped at the tears. "Don't cry. Everything is going to be all right. We're going to be all right.''

"I'm not crying. I never cry. I can't cry.''

He smiled faintly and drew a finger over her cheek. "What is this, if it isn't tears?''

She gazed at the dampness on his fingers, rubbed her cheek, and stared at her own hand. Wailing like a child, she threw herself into his arms. Her body quivered, racked with sobs—sobs that healed. "Hold me," she murmured. "Hold me. Tell me again that everything is going to be all right.''

And he held her, and he rocked her like a baby. And he whispered until she had grown quiet, asleep in his arms. And still he held her.

V

Autumn

44

Autumn lay on the terrace, basking in the sun and watching in fascination as a tiny black spider wove a web between two legs of a wrought-iron chair. She hated the ugly, repulsive little critter, but she had to admire its tenacity. Set against a world so many times its size, the spider had carefully and a bit arrogantly planned and then gone about the tedious chore of building its new home: a delicate intricacy of pattern that was both simple and complex.

She and Autumn decided the spider had to be a she to want a home so badly. It ran on its many spindly legs, back and forth, back and forth between the center of the web and the outer edges, spinning a strong network of silver threads. Once she had built the frame, the spider then circled the web, round and round, leaving a silk line that interconnected to build squares that looked about a half-inch in size. Autumn thought the spider was finished when she had worked her way to the center, but her house wasn't quite secure, so she began again, circling the web and spinning reinforcing threads between the squares. Once she had reached the outer edge, the spider scrambled to the center and sat as if exhausted or slyly waiting for some unsuspecting fly to become trapped in her web. She looked smug, until Gracie came lumbering across the terrace and collapsed the web with one whisk of her wagging tail.

Autumn was surprised at the pity she felt for the ugly

little spider, who had dared to build her home in the
middle of their busy terrace. She leaned back in the lounge
chair and watched as the spider, caught in her own web,
fought to free herself and then scurry across the flagstones
to the safety of a thick growth of petunias. "Dumb spider.
I wager you'll lay your plans a bit more carefully next
time."

Autumn pulled Gracie onto the lounge with her and
cuddled the pup lovingly in her arms. If she could have a
next time, which she couldn't, Autumn would lay her
plans a bit more carefully too. Women seldom conceived
the first time they made love, and women seldom conceived directly after taking the pill for years, or so she had
read. Seldom hadn't worked for Autumn. If there had been
a rabbit, it would have died.

Stretching in the sun, she smiled with irony. She liked a
man who fought for what he wanted, and she did admire
Brian's ingenuity, but the dear fellow had thrown one
giant screw in the works. There was no way out, no corner
she could cut, no quick change in plans, no alternate road.
Humorous, but sad. The baby in her belly was growing
each day, and would, in about seven months, pop its little
head into the world and wonder what the hell was going
on, ask to understand why its deceased stepfather was also
its grandfather—a man who had killed its mother's first
husband. And yes, "killed" was the correct word. She
had had to take many alternate roads, but she had all the
evidence she needed. But could she use it now? Wouldn't
she be going against the welfare of her own child? Like the
spider, Autumn was caught in her own web.

The heat of the July sun burned against her bare skin
and she slid Gracie from the lounge. "Go find your mate
and play with him." She gave Gracie a shove toward the
house and rose to her feet, tugging the heavy lounge chair
toward the shade of the oak.

True to his word, Brian had carved their initials in the
trunk, along with the date. Bold and daring for their de-
scendants to read. The family joke. "We had this ancestor
named Autumn. But her name wasn't really Autumn, it
was Sue Anne. She married old Doug, who had killed her
first husband. After Doug drowned in the swimming pool,

she married his son Brian. They had a child that . . ."
What would follow?

Autumn wiped perspiration from her forehead and between her breasts, straightened the bottom of her twisted bikini, then gave the lounge another hard tug. She had thought she was alone, but Brian's voice called out from the terrace doors. "If you want it moved," he said, coming toward her, "there are men around to do it for you. You can't play toughie for the next few months, or have you already forgotten?"

"I haven't forgotten, and that's an old wives' tale. Dr. Albright said I'm healthy as a horse with a body made to have babies. Something to do with the hips, I think."

"I agree. You have great hips." Brian moved the lounge to the shade, grabbed Autumn, and fell to the chair with her in his arms. She nestled her breasts around his rib cage, opened his shirt, and ran her hand across the span of his chest, toying idly with the coin. His jacket was unbuttoned and ink-stained, his tie crooked, his handkerchief balled in his breast pocket. Sun-bleached hair dipped in an unruly mass on his forehead. Compared with Lloyd, he looked like a grubby kid, but so completely and comfortably male.

Her husband was very skilled under an oak, but a baby at love. This beautiful thing emanated from him, in his smile, his eyes, the way he touched her, shouting what she had refused to see, had not wanted. Or had she? In retrospect, Autumn wondered if unconsciously she had plotted to make Brian fall in love with her, just so she could really stick it to him in the end. She had always thought of love as a precious thing, something to be cherished and protected, not used. Unlike Lloyd, Brian was tender. Could she unleash her pernicious plans on him as well as their child? So many many questions, and so many, many decisions to be made. Regardless of what she decided, Brian would be hurt in the end.

She tightened her arms around his waist protectively. "What are you doing home in the middle of the day?"

"Checking on you. Dr. Albright said rest and quiet. I don't trust you to follow his orders like you should."

"I'm so rested I feel exhausted. I saw him again this

morning. He took me off the critical list." She turned in his arms until she was looking at him. "I need to go to San Francisco. There are some people I want to see, and things I have to do. I talked with the doctor, and he said it would be fine."

"Sounds great. You've met all my friends. I think it's time I met yours. Things are fairly quiet at the office. I think I can escape for a few days."

"No," she said quickly. "This isn't a social trip. You can meet my friends another time. I'll be too busy with other things."

"What other things?"

She shrugged. "I have a few business affairs I want to clear up, and I have to shop for new clothes. I'll be needing some fat things, remember."

He chuckled and ran his hand over her flat stomach. "Yeah, you are getting a little pudgy." He stroked her middle. "What are we going to name him?"

"Him? It could be a girl, Brian."

"No, it will be a boy."

"What makes you so sure?"

"Boys run in our family."

"So. Girls run in my family."

He glanced down at her and grinned. "One girl doesn't count, Autumn."

She smiled too. "If it's a boy, we'll name him Brian. If it's a girl, we'll name her Brianna."

"No we won't. I want my son to have his own name." He pulled away slightly, reached inside his jacket, and removed a paper from his breast pocket. "I won't say I'm sorry about the pills. If I did, it would be like saying I'm sorry about the baby, and I'm not." He motioned toward the paper. "This is my copy of the marriage agreement. No woman should have this kind of thing hanging over her head. If the time comes when you feel you have to leave, we'll work out what's best for the child." He tore the paper in half and tucked it in the front of her bikini. "You go and buy your fat things, but if you're not back in a week, I'll come and drag you home. This place is too damned lonely without you." His eyes, so clear and blue, gazed into hers and he drew a finger along the edge of her bikini. "What else did the doctor say . . . about other things?"

"He said I could do anything I did before I got pregnant."

"Anything?"

"Anything."

"Good," he grinned. "How would you feel about a close encounter of the best kind?"

"Your bed or mine?"

He glanced toward the back stairs. "The four-poster. It's closer."

Autumn paused beside an occasional table and picked up the music box Brian had given her for Christmas. Inlaid ivory with jade leaves formed a flower on the gold cover, and when she lifted the lid, soft tinkly music filled the room. Carefully she picked up the two roses with their short stems that she had pressed and then stored in the box. Since Lonnie, no one else had given her flowers—just jewels, and furs, and cars, and money. She had tried to throw the roses away, but each one had been given to her in a moment when she had needed a personal gesture so much. Once after Artie's accident when she had been so frightened. Again after their return from the Bahamas when she'd had to face the harsh reality of what she had done in marrying Brian—what she still had to do.

She returned the roses to the box, pulled the torn agreement from the pocket of her robe, and placed it alongside the flowers. She hadn't been concerned about the agreement; the child bound her tighter to the Osbornes than any piece of paper ever could. She left the table abruptly, crossed the room, and unlocked a desk drawer. The moment she removed the thick manila envelope her hands began to tremble and sweat beads formed on her upper lip.

The trembling had begun after Artie's accident and had grown steadily worse over the months. Beginning in her stomach, it inched its way over her entire body, and a tingling sensation, like pricking needles, began in the small of her back and spread across her shoulders and down her arms, so acute that she had to sit and force herself to breathe deeply until the tremor had passed. So far, she had managed to hide it from everybody but Molly. She sat down now, waiting, inhaling and exhaling slowly.

Once the earthquake inside her body had subsided, Autumn opened the envelope and pulled out a stack of papers that would stain the Osborne name so badly it would take several generations to remove it. From what she could learn, the fire at the mine had been an accident and not a cover-up. After Brian told her about the fire, she had given up on the records in the basement, but feeling drawn there, she had returned several times and pawed absently through the stockpile. The fire had destroyed all the records for the last five years the mine operated, save for the files Bob had found while rearranging the cabinets in John's office. Following orders, he had taken them to Douglas, who had placed them along with the others. In turn, Autumn had found them while picking idly through the cobweb-covered records. It was a report, or evaluation of the mine, and explained why Douglas had refused to close that night. He had wanted to squeeze every last cent he could from a dying mine.

Along with the narrowing vein, the coal had run from bituminous to sub-bituminous, a lower and less desirable grade of ore. Given the aged machinery and the expense of replacing it, Douglas had been advised to run full crews and strip the mine before the failing equipment forced him to shut down. The mine would have had to be closed, but the explosion had brought about the shutdown much sooner than planned. Possibly Douglas had believed the mine would be safe with the section of the blower system down; still, it didn't excuse his irresponsibility or bring back the fourteen men who had died because of his reckless decision.

The paper she had found explained why the mine was kept open, and why, after the explosion, Douglas had closed it permanently. The file actually proved nothing to anyone other than Autumn, but it would make interesting reading in the Edisonville *Times*.

She put aside the geology report and picked up the photocopies she had made of the second set of books. Douglas had kept them locked carefully away in the safe, but Brian was more trusting and left them lying on his desk. It was all there. Bootleg whiskey, gambling, prostitution, bribes, and payoffs. The name of every man involved was listed, along with dates and amounts paid. The most fascinating aspect was how Douglas had managed to incorporate the distillery into his bootleg operations.

Years before, he had bought control of a distribution company in Illinois. The liquor was sold legally and trucked out of the state, then returned in grain trucks and stored in the basement at the feed store until it was needed. He sold to himself, bought the liquor back at distributor's cost, which allowed him to sell the same booze twice, tax-free the third time around. If all else failed with the mine, the distillery provided an alternate way to ruin the Osborne name. But she would be ruining Brian at the same time. She had overheard enough to know Brian was getting out, but he had implicated himself by carrying on for his father for almost a year. She had also heard enough to know Brian was only a few days away from learning she was Sue Anne Corbett.

Autumn smiled when she thought of Fritz Jergenson and how much he would love to get his hands on the material spread out on her desk. She hadn't really given any thought to Fritz's paper until Artie's accident. Looking for new roads to travel, she had had Bob get next to Fritz and plant a few ideas in his head about a woman in San Francisco who was out to get the Osbornes. The paper seemed the perfect way to start, and bit by bit Bob had nudged Fritz into selling controlling interest. He had hedged for months, until his doctor had told him he would have to take it easier or his heart would do it for him. Fritz had wanted to be sure the people taking over weren't in league with the Osbornes, so he had come to Bob. It was her paper now, and she could publish what she wanted.

Autumn gathered the file on the Osbornes and arranged it in a neat stack. She picked up a cassette recording and rubbed her fingers against its smooth surface. Hearsay, inadmissible in court, charges can't be brought against a dead man—but again, it would make interesting reading in the Edisonville *Times*. If she couldn't get to them through the courts, she could get to them through her paper.

She removed a tape recorder from the desk drawer, inserted the cassette, and felt the trembling begin in her stomach again. She had hired a private detective and sent him to Edisonville with instructions to find out the names of the maintenance men who had worked the mine, one of whom had to have taken the call from Douglas the night of the explosion. The detective returned with four names. Three men had relocated in other states, but one man had opened a fair-sized machine-repair shop in Edisonville exactly a month after the explosion. It had been obvious to Autumn that the man had been paid off, but without big money behind her she had known it would be worthless to approach him, so she'd waited, perhaps too long. The man had died a few years ago, and she had more or less forgotten about him. He had left the shop to his brother Chester, and again grasping at straws, she had sent Bob to question him on the off chance that his brother had told him something before he died.

Autumn leaned forward and pressed the button on the recorder and the tape began to turn, spinning out Bob's and Chester's voices. At first Chester had been evasive; then, when Bob hinted that it might be worth money, his interest picked up. "All I can tell you, man, is what my brother told me. You can take it for what it's worth."

"That's good enough," Bob said. "Just tell me what you know."

"How much?" Chester asked.

"I think I can get you five thousand."

"You're on." There was a long hesitation, as if Chester was gathering his thoughts. "Well," he said, "according to my brother Paul, this Lonnie Norton was asking a lot of questions and stirring up a hornet's nest around town. He was claiming Osborne caused the explosion and he was threatening to go to the authorities. My brother went to Osborne and told him what Norton was doing. Osborne told my brother to bring Norton to the machine shop at the mine. He wanted to talk to Norton."

"Did your brother take Norton to Osborne?" Bob asked.

"Yeah, and Osborne tried to shut him up with money, but Norton told him to shove it up his ass. Osborne was so damned mad, he almost shit his pants. Insane, my brother said. According to Paul, he came at Norton then, swinging and swearing. This Norton fellow sidestepped and caught him a good one alongside the cheek with his fist. He knocked Osborne on his ass, then turned for the door to leave. This made Osborne even madder. He seemed to go crazy. Osborne picked up a heavy piece of pipe from the floor and went after Norton. This guy was a tall fellow and the pipe caught him along the shoulder and neck. I guess it scared the shit out of Paul when the man fell on the floor. He and Osborne tried to bring Norton around, but the man was dead. His neck was broken.''

"What did they do with the body?'' Bob asked.

"That's when Osborne offered Paul the money. He paid my brother to get rid of Norton and keep his mouth shut. Make it look like an accident, Osborne said. The man was dead, so Paul didn't think there was anything he could do, so he loaded the body in Norton's own car and drove it to the High Banks. After he had pushed the car over the edge, he thumbed a ride home.''

"Wasn't he afraid of being seen?'' Bob asked.

A chuckle. "My brother never was very smart.'' A short pause. "When do I get the money?''

"As soon as you sign this form releasing my client to use what you have just told me in any way she might see fit.''

"Sure, I'll sign the damned thing. It can't hurt my brother none now.''

When the tape ended, Autumn was crying. The tingling was back and she rubbed her arms, furiously—it felt as though bugs were crawling over her skin. She stared at the tape recorder as silent tears slipped down her cheeks, hugging herself and waiting for the tremor to pass. Slowly, as she regained control, Autumn replaced the files and the recorder in the desk drawer and locked it tight. She wiped away the tears and was rising from the chair when Molly entered the room, gazing at her critically. "What's this I hear about you leaving in the morning?''

Autumn nodded. "I'll probably be gone about a week.''

Molly frowned. "That's crazy,'' she said. "You got no

business leaving now. You're tired and you're half-sick. Nothing is so all-fired important that it can't wait a spell.''

"I don't have any choice, Aunt Molly. There is a very angry man waiting for me in San Francisco. If I don't go there, he could come here. I don't want that. Now now.''

45

Autumn watched as Lloyd paced his office, veins bulging in his neck from anger. Strange, she had always thought him taller. He was dressed immaculately in a pale green that matched his eyes. Lloyd wore his suits; Brian's suits wore him.

Autumn wore a white linen suit with black beading and a white fedora. She removed the hat and placed it on the sofa beside her. "I'm glad hats are coming back. I always feel so together when I'm wearing a hat. When I was a child, I had this little white bonnet with blue flowers on the brim. I really thought I was something when I got all dressed for church and wore that hat and my patent-leather shoes."

Lloyd paused in front of her, his face red with frustration. "You haven't listened to a word I've said, have you?"

"Every word. You're going to ruin Brian. You're going to bury him. You're going to pin his cock to the wall. By the time you get through with him, he won't have two nickels to rub together."

"I can do it, Autumn."

"Yes, I'm sure you could, but when you go up against Brian, you're going up against me too. You wouldn't want to do that, Lloyd. When a woman is fighting for the welfare of her child, she can be damned vicious."

Lloyd backed a step or two and gazed at her with an incredulous frown. "You're—"

"That's right. Pregnant as hell."

"How the fuck did you let that happen?"

Struck by the humor of it all, she burst into laughter. "The devious devil stole my pills."

Lloyd didn't see the humor and eyed her coolly. "You can abort."

Her face grew serious and she shook her head slowly. "I want this baby, Lloyd. It's only been a minute in my belly, but I love it dearly."

He gazed at her long and hard, analytically. When he spoke his voice was low and caustic. "You're a manipulator. You used us all. Everett. Me. Douglas and that young fool Brian."

Autumn stood then and faced him squarely. "Did I, now? I think we should go back a few years. Who called whom into this office and offered her the moon? You took a little girl from Turtle Ridge and offered her anything she might want, but at a price. You dangled your wealth in front of her hungry mouth. The only problem was, that little girl had already sold her body and she didn't like the feeling very much. You tried to use her innocence, Lloyd, but life had already taken too big a bite out of her. She wouldn't play your game."

"And what about the rest?" he said. "I made you what you are today. Without me, you'd be nothing."

"Yes, you invested in my business. I think you'll agree that your investment has more than tripled. Sex? I don't think you can complain there. You got as good as you gave." She crossed and gazed out the window at the scurrying people below. "Maybe I used Everett, but if I did, it allowed him to do the things he had wanted to do before and couldn't. He was all but broke when I married him. I worked two jobs to put the bar back on its feet, sometimes eighteen hours a day, while he sat upstairs with his writing. He died a rich man, and a fairly happy one. Douglas? Yes, we used each other. Brian?" She turned and looked back as Lloyd approached her. "I used Brian, coldly. Of all of you, he's the one that deserves it the least. He's given everything, and I've given nothing."

Lloyd gazed at her with searching eyes. "You're in love with him, aren't you?"

"Sadly, I love you both."

"But you love him more?"

"He's the father of my child, and tender."

"That's what you said about Everett."

"Everett was tender, and weak. Brian isn't weak, but he's tender. He's never been in love before. That makes him vulnerable."

"What about me? In all the years, didn't you think that I might have a soft spot too? That I might love you too?"

Autumn turned from him, nodding. "Yes, like a creator loves his creation. You set me up, dressed me up, and then pointed to me with pride. Look what I did. I took that cute little nothing from Turtle Ridge and made her what she is today. I'm a possession, your most successful protégée." She paused and looked at him. "Can you deny it?" When he remained silent, she crossed to the sofa, picked up her hat, and planted it on her mass of russet hair. Smiling at him, she turned toward the door. "How is your latest protégée, Lloyd? What is *her* greatest talent, business . . . or fucking?"

Lloyd smiled, a slow kind of smile that broke into quiet laughter. "There's never been one like you, Autumn. You're the best, and I'm going to get you back."

"You might at that. Once the truth comes out, Brian could very well run me out of town."

Still smiling, Lloyd folded his arms across his chest with self-satisfaction. "I'll be waiting."

Autumn smiled at Ed, then glanced at the window to the row of trees that lined the front of her office building. Heavy with leaves they swayed slightly in the breeze that was so much a part of the coast. The trees had grown amazingly in the years since she moved into the building but then, so had the company. She turned and half-sat on the window frame, gazing across at Ed. "Whether I want it or not, I'm going to have to take the time to be a woman. I'm going to need another year away from the office, Ed."

He removed gold-rimmed glasses and cleaned them with

a handkerchief. "It would help if I knew more, Sue Anne. There have been times when I needed to reach you and couldn't."

She hesitated a moment and glanced again at the trees below. "I won't bore you with a lot of details, but I can promise that things will be different this time. You'll know where I am at all times, and I'll give you full power to act in my absence." She turned and looked back at him, but remained seated on the window frame. "I'm married now. My name is Osborne, and I'm going to have a baby." She smiled when his eyes widened in surprise. "I know a lot of women carry on during pregnancy the same as before, but I lost a baby once, and I'm not going to take a chance on losing this one too. I want to have a few months of quiet without any strain. As much as I love this business, I love my baby more, and the work does get to me at times. Maybe because I do love it."

His eyes were full of questions. "Do you plan to come back after the baby is born?"

She shrugged. "I'll be able to tell you more in a couple of weeks." She left the window and slid onto the edge of her desk. "How would you feel about moving to Richmond, Virginia?"

He grinned. "I love the subtle way you give orders, Sue Anne. You'll come out with a long spiel of direct commands and then smile and ask, what do you think? as if we had a choice." He nodded "If you want me in Richmond, I'll go to Richmond."

"Good. I'd feel better if you were in charge of the east-coast offices there, at least for the next few months. I'll leave it up to you to choose your replacement, and you'll still be in full power. Everyone will report to you before making any major decision. I'll call a staff meeting in the morning and make the announcements."

"What about Murphy? Will he go along with this?"

"He won't have any choice. I still own controlling interest in this company. I'm closer to the staff than he's ever been, and he knows it. Lloyd is first and last a businessman. He won't do anything to jeopardize the company, or his share in what he believes it will be someday."

"How soon do you want me in Richmond?"

"When you feel it's right. I'll want you to work with your replacement until you feel secure about leaving." She paused and smiled a little. "Incidentally, how is Dale Osborne doing in Seattle?"

"Fine. He'll never make number one on the totem pole, but he carries his end very well."

"How would you feel about moving him to Richmond? There isn't much going on in Seattle right now, and there's not much chance for advancement. Richmond is bubbling. I'l like to see him catch one of the bubbles."

He smiled and shook his head in wonder. "I'm beginning to think this company is a refuge for old bar managers, fags, and whores."

"Have I brought you anyone that didn't work out?"

"No. Wally is handling his unit as well as any of the other managers. How is your venture with Ella doing?"

"It's coming along." She slid from the desk and picked up her briefcase. "I'm not asking you to carry Dale, but I'd like you to put him in a good spot. The rest is up to him." She turned and walked toward the door. "I think Dale is going to surprise everybody, namely my husband. Dale is his uncle—my uncle now." She grinned back at Ed, then ducked out the door.

The next few days passed quickly. She crowded shopping trips in between staff meetings, said all the right things, but Brian and Edisonville were always on the edge of her mind. When she and Lloyd met again, they avoided any mention of Brian or the baby, pretending neither existed. One of their meetings was on his yacht, and they had dinner several times. He tried various ways to draw her close, but she carefully skirted any personal contact. At least she could tell herself that she had been faithful to Brian.

Because Brian called her daily, she had checked into the Fairmont Hotel instead of her apartment. As prearranged, he sent the plane for her exactly a week from the day she had left him. Her flight home was smooth, the sky cloudless. She stared dreamily out the small window at the blue horizon until the sameness and the steady hum of the engines lulled her to sleep.

The plane was approaching their private airstrip when the pilot's voice roused her. She shook herself awake and fastened the seat belt as instructed for their landing. Resting her head against the back of the seat, she watched the familiar countryside glide past as the Lear gently touched down. Autumn unbuckled, but waited in her seat while the plane taxied slowly back to where the limousine waited.

She hadn't expected Brian to meet her, but he was waiting beside the Rolls. The moment she left the plane he strode toward her, laughed suddenly, and swept her high in the air. Easy laughter was something she hadn't felt lately, but when she gazed down at him it bubbled up and burst forth in a wave of silly giggles.

Before she could catch her breath, he called for James to collect her baggage and then hurried her into the car. He pulled her into a tight embrace, his face buried in the curve of her throat. "Damn, I've missed you. That four-poster has felt empty as hell."

"Ahh," she cooed. "Has your crooked thing been itching?"

"Like it was rolled in a patch of poison ivy."

She giggled again and drew him tightly against her. She thought back to her earlier meeting with Lloyd. Both men were strong, powerful, and stubborn. If Lloyd decided to be vindictive there could be one hell of a fight. Not an old-fashioned fistfight, but a humdinger of a power struggle.

Brian pulled away and glanced at her oddly. "You're trembling."

Autumn looked down at her hands, the long slender fingers that quivered. The trembling had become so much a part of her that she hardly noticed anymore. "I'm just excited," she said, slipping back into his arms. "It's so good to be home."

It wasn't until the car turned into the drive at Osborne House and the old mansion loomed among the oaks in all its grandeur that she realized with some surprise how very good it was to be back. She referred to Osborne House as home, because at some point it had become home. Over the months, she had unwittingly put down roots, and they were buried deep.

She waited with Brian while James carried her bags and packages into the house. After the chauffeur had made several trips in and out, Brian looked at her with a teasing grin. "You're going to be the best-dressed fat lady in town."

"Would you believe most of it is baby things?" She turned in the seat and looked at him with amazement. "It's hard to believe the little critters can need so much. Of course, I bought a few things simply because I couldn't resist."

"Of course." His voice was filled with pride and teasing laughter. He eased her from the car as if pregnancy had suddenly turned her into a delicate piece of china. "I have an appointment in fifteen minutes, but we'll catch up at dinner." He returned to the car, then gazed at her soberly. "I had a few bad moments while you were gone. I don't know why, but I kept remembering the man with the yacht. Did you see him?"

"Yes. I saw him and we talked. That's all."

"What is his name?"

"I'll tell you later." She turned and entered the house before he could question her further, climbed the stairs, and went to her room. Autumn hesitated on the threshold, her eyes drawn to the door next to hers. The room was cleaned periodically, but she had been inside only once. She felt a strange kind of pull, turned, and walked slowly toward the blue-and white nursery where Brian and so many other Osborne babies had slept.

The room was airy and cheerful. Near the window was a brasswork antique cradle with a skirting of blue and white ruffles. She picked up a pillow and held it against her breasts, rocking the cradle back and forth. The room looked ready and waiting with a crib for after the infant had grown, a chest of drawers, changing table, and a well-cushioned high-backed rocking chair. Toys and well-worn stuffed animals were lined on a sofa covered in blue chintz. A rocking horse grinned back at her from a corner. The headboard on the crib was rough, as if Brian had stood on wobbly legs while chewing the edge. For a moment she could see him there. He would have been chubby, no doubt, with a mass of golden hair and blue eyes that disarmed the household with their changing colors. Would her child have its father's beautiful blue eyes?

The room, the glimpse of Brian, was so good and right, so pure, that she felt black inside, hard and ugly. She felt the fast pounding of her heart, threw down the pillow, and raced from the blue-and-white room and all the innocence and purity it implied.

Autumn burst into her own room panting, went to the desk, and unlocked the drawer. She removed the manila envelope that held over ten years of planning and struggling, hate and despair, and knew it had all been for nothing. She couldn't use it, not against her own child.

She walked without hesitation to the fireplace and tossed the envelope onto the grate. Taking a match from the mantel, she drew the head against the brick, then touched the flame to a corner of the envelope. She sat down in a chair and watched as it slowly become ashes, the cassette a curled and melting ball of plastic.

46

The afternoon sun cast flickering patterns on the walls of the sunroom. At the open window, Autumn sat and listened to the sounds of Osborne House, the faint hum of a lawn mower, the birds nestling in the oaks, a soft whinny from one of the horses, a servant's occasional voice. She waited for Artie and turned over in her mind what she would say to him. Lonnie had been his twin and he had a right to his revenge, but she had destroyed all chance of that now.

Autumn had watched until the envelope was nothing but black ashes. When the last flame had flickered and died away, she had known Lonnie had finally been laid to rest. He would always be with her, a beautiful memory to cherish, but the dark shadows were gone. She felt an overwhelming sense of well-being, as if Lonnie had somehow reached out from his sleeping place and released her from a promise she had made so many years ago. "Love ya, sugar. Now, get the hell out of here and get on with your life." Crossing the room, she had picked up the music box, removed the plain gold band from her finger and placed it among the roses in the box.

Autumn looked up when Artie entered the sunroom. Such a handsome man. The years had taken nothing away. The slight graying at his temples only added charm. The scars and limp added mystique. Artie would always be a rogue, a fancy-free lover of women and excitement. She felt a special kind of love for Artie, but then, she had loved all the men in her life. There had been times when she had even felt a moment of affection for Douglas.

Waving him to a chair, she gazed at him thoughtfully. Where to start? she asked herself. A whinny from one of the horses drew her attention, and she turned toward the window, sat silently for a long moment before she spoke. "I have to stop," she said. "I have to end this ugly need for revenge that grew in me like a monster."

Artie didn't seem surprised. "I expected as much when you kept stalling. We would have moved on them months ago if you hadn't wanted to stick it to Brian."

She nodded in agreement. "I let things get out of perspective. I should have stopped when Douglas died, but because of a petty hurt when we were both kids, I pulled Brian in too. It isn't his fault Douglas was an ass. The irony of it is, Lonnie loved me, and you. He was full of love. Lonnie wasn't a vindictive man. He wouldn't have wanted this for me, or for you." She sank back in the chair and gazed at Artie intently. "What I did, I did for myself. What you did, you did partly for Lonnie and partly for the excitement of it all."

"Our reasons aren't important now. The thing is, we've put in a lot of time and money to stop cold."

"I know, but it isn't just you and me anymore. I have to consider my baby. I can't bring a child into a family black with scandal. Brian could face charges—go to jail. I don't want that for my child. I want it to have all the things the Osborne name can give it—not the wealth. I can give it money. The Osborne name is known and respected throughout the state. I can't destroy its birthright."

Artie pulled a pack of Pall Malls from his shirt pocket and lighted a cigarette with a gold lighter. He replaced the pack to his pocket, but toyed with the lighter. "Is it the baby, or Brian?"

"Both. I want my baby to have something I didn't, a mommy and a daddy. I want it to sleep in the cradle upstairs, cut its teeth on the same crib where its father slept, grow up in this house as firmly rooted as the oaks outside. I want it to have all the good things, Artie. Is that so wrong?" When he remained silent, she leaned forward and her glance locked with his. "You like Brian. You know you do. Would you really want to see him facing this mess his father made?"

He shook his head. "I wasn't thinking about that, Autumn. I was thinking about that man, Chester, and what he told Bob. You can stop, but he's out there and he can talk again. What if he decides to try for a little more money or to shoot his mouth off around town?"

"I've thought of that. Without me to back him up with Lonnie's story about the mine explosion, the people would only laugh at him. He doesn't know about me. He only talked to Bob. I think we're fairly safe."

"What about the stuff?"

"I burned it." She smiled mirthlessly. "Are you angry with me?"

He smiled too, leaned forward and crushed the cigarette out in the ashtray. "What the hell. I'm bored to shit with this one-horse town anyhow."

She rose along with him and walked into his arms. "I love you," she said simply.

He held her tightly, stroked her hair and back. "Yeah, little sister. I love you too. I guess you're the only woman I've ever loved. If not for Lonnie, we could have had a great time together. I bet you'd be terrific in the sack."

She smiled and drew away. "Want to go to Richmond? The gals are lovely there, and things are really stewing."

"No. I think I'll go to Australia."

"Australia? What are you going to do there?"

"Fuck Australians."

She laughed quietly and slipped her arm around his waist as they walked toward the door. "Need any money?"

"No, I have plenty. Besides, I'll work my way around. Money makes things too easy. I tend to get lazy and fall into a rut." He paused at the doorway and gazed down at her. "What are you going to do about Brian?"

"The question is, what is Brian going to do when he finds out his wife is Sue Anne Corbett?"

"You're going to tell him?"

"Everything. I think it would be wise if you were gone. I don't know what his reaction will be. He could come looking for you once he finds out you were in on this too." She patted his chest, his hips, his shoulders. "You're good, but he's good too. He might beat the hell out of you. You came through the accident without your pretty face being smashed. I don't think I would push my luck any further. Besides, it will be easier for me."

"I can pack and be gone in an hour."

She nodded, but her arms tightened around his waist and her eyes misted with tears. "I'll miss you."

"I'll miss you too."

"You'll keep in touch?"

"Always." He bent and kissed her on the mouth. "Keep your pretty chin up, little sister." He turned, looked back once, and then he was gone.

Autumn picked at her food during dinner and chattered distractedly. After dinner she and Brian had drinks on the terrace, and she chattered. When they played billiards in the game room, she chattered. She caught Brian looking at her with curious amusement, but she couldn't stop the nervous chattering. When she missed an easy shot because she was talking fast, Brian laughed and took the cue stick. "What's bothering you, Autumn?"

"What makes you think something is bothering me?"

"Because I know you."

"No," she said. "You don't really know me. You only think you do."

"I know all the important things. I know you're not given to chatter, and I know you don't slip out of your shoes unless you're nervous." He smiled and replaced the sticks in the rack. "You love children, bubble baths, books, music, cream of wheat, and the funny-looking hot dogs Molly makes for you. You hate waste, laziness, injustice against the little man, and maggots in the garbage cans. When you have gas, you run and hide in the other room for fear of letting off a little fart. You're warm and loving and lusty. You like me on top, and you like to be kissed when you come. What else is there?"

"You seem to have covered everything."

"Not quite. I still don't know the name of the man with the yacht."

He had opened the door, but she couldn't force herself

to walk through, not yet. "Why don't we go for a walk in the garden? We'll talk there." They left the house and walked silently past the oak and down the flagstone path to the fountain. The sun was low and dusk was approaching, the evening air filled with the scent of flowers. Brian sat on the bench, but Autumn stood and gazed down at the lily pond. Her inner reserves were wearing thin, but she drew on what was left and looked back at him. "The man's name is Lloyd Murphy." Her mouth felt dry and she licked her lips. "Autumn is a pet name Molly gave me when I was a baby. My real name is Sue Anne McAvan Norton Corbett Osborne . . . and Osborne. Molly is my aunt."

He stared at her, his eyes reflecting confusion as he sorted through the long list of names, then stunned disbelief for a moment, and then acceptance once his mind had articulated what she had said. "You're—"

"Please," she interjected. "Let me tell you in my own way. Then you can ask any question you want—do whatever you want. I won't ever lie to you again." She couldn't bear to face him, to watch as his eyes filled with hurt and disillusionment and turned away. She knelt beside the pool and dipped her fingers into the cool water. "I was born in Turtle Ridge, a little town in the hills about ninety miles from here. Molly raised me."

Quietly and without looking at him, she went back and retraced her life. She told him about Lonnie, and how he died, the loss of her child, and what she believed about Douglas. The words rushed from her when she spoke about the night at Rex's place when she had rolled him for three thousand dollars. Then: San Francisco, Everett, the bar, Lloyd Murphy, building the Corbett Corporation, Everett's death and her return to Edisonville, and why.

She paused, groping for words, and then she began again. Several times she heard him shift near her, then a quick indrawn breath when Lloyd's name was mentioned. But he remained silent. Telling him about Dale and how she had incited the fight between him and Douglas was the hardest. Then: Ginger, and arranging for George to meet her, and the fight between George and Douglas when the affair became known. Homer, and the card sharp she had hired to try to entice him into gambling. And buying the Edisonville *Times*.

The sun had dropped behind the trees and shadows were falling when she turned to look at him, grateful that his face was partially hidden by night. She had told him everything, almost. She had promised there would be no more lies, but there was one truth that could only bring more hurt. So she said, "I know now that Douglas was innocent of Lonnie's death, at least. Lonnie died in a car accident, nothing more. Your father was careless when he kept the mine open, but he didn't kill Lonnie."

Through the shadows his eyes gleamed as icy as his father's, his mouth set in a hard line. When he spoke, his voice was filled with scorn. "You were his mistress. While I sat in his office proudly telling him about you, the green-eyed son of a bitch was laughing his head off because he was fucking my wife."

"No," she said, and rose to her feet, went to him. "I was never his mistress in the true sense of the word. I never lived with him. He didn't keep me. He gave me gifts, but I always paid my own way. And he hasn't touched me since long before I became your wife."

Brian stood and towered over her. "Why the hell did you marry me, Autumn?"

"You called me a cheap little whore the night at Rex's. I wanted to hurt you as I had been hurt. It was a way to shove the words back down your throat. I thought it would be great fun to watch your face when you learned that cheap little whore was your wife."

"Well, you got it. Take a good look, honey." The muscles in his jaw tightened as he stared at her. "I worshiped you, woman. And the thing I worshiped the most was your honesty." He turned, his stride long and reaching as he walked toward the house. "So much for honesty."

Autumn chased after him and grabbed his arm. "Don't go, Brian. We have to talk. You can't just walk away."

"I can do any goddamned thing I want."

Her hand fell from his arm and she stepped away from him. "What do you want me to do? Do you want me to pack and leave, or wait?"

"I don't know. All I know right now is that I have to get away. I have to think."

She nodded. "While you're thinking, try to remember Lonnie was my husband."

"What the hell am I?"

"My husband." She held her hand up for him to see that the ring was gone. "I'll always love Lonnie, but that doesn't mean I can't love you too. I can't love you in the same way that eighteen-year-old girl loved Lonnie, but this twenty-nine-year-old woman thinks you're the greatest. Something good has come out of all this, Brian. You, me, and the baby. While you're away, try to think about these things, and not what happened before. I don't need your money, so ask yourself why I want to stay." The moonlight played against his face and gave it a haunted look. She touched his lips with a fingertip. "I'll wait. When you're ready to talk, I'll be here."

47

Autumn waited as one week slipped into two. Brian didn't call, and she didn't check to see if he had been in touch with his office. She tried to push all thoughts of Brian from her mind and think only of the one sure thing in her life: her baby.

She made a point of spending as much time as possible away from Osborne House. Turtle Ridge and her life there were set apart from Brian, or Lloyd, so she hid away at Molly's chalet. To kill the hours while she waited, she worked in the garden.

Molly had always kept a garden to help feed them while Autumn was growing up. To flee the tensions at Osborne House over the last few months, she had on impulse raked and spaded and seeded a patch of ground behind the chalet. It wasn't an ordinary garden. Autumn had planted the rows in swirls and flowing lines, bordered with flowers that bloomed a wide variety of colors among the vegetables. She had laughed to Molly that it was art drawn on earth rather than on canvas.

When she wasn't working in the garden, swimming in the river, or walking in the woods with Jerry and Gracie, she drove into town, parked her car, and went from store to store and talked with the simple, easygoing people who had helped to form her life. She sat on a keg at the hardware store and jawed with Jeb, winked wickedly when passing Mrs. Baker of the famous garbage cans, and had long talks with Preacher Anderson.

He made one remark that stuck in her mind long after she had returned to Edisonville. "All of us are sinners, Sue Anne. We must—or should—get down on our knees from time to time, but too much grievance against ourselves and repenting are bad for the soul. We must also stand tall, love and cherish this weak person God had seen fit to allow to spend time on his earth."

She felt as if his words had granted her absolution. She realized with surprise that the trembling that had racked her body for months was gone. Not only had she forgiven Douglas, but she had also forgiven herself. She woke each morning now with a feeling of well-being. Still, by the end of two weeks the days had begun to drag.

She spent more time than usual with the children at the home and with Ella, and often lunched with Bob. His practice had grown but he was still largely dependent on her. They were having lunch at the club when she brought up the subject of San Francisco. "I still need you here, but I don't know where I'll be a year from now. If you want to leave, I'll see what I can do about putting you in touch with some people I know in San Francisco."

"I don't know," he said. "I think I'd feel swallowed in a place like that."

"You do at first. After a while you build your own little place. I had the best of both worlds: the peace of Turtle Ridge and the excitement of San Francisco. I would have missed the city if not for going with Brian when he flew out of town on business. We usually managed to see a show regardless of how busy he was."

Bob glanced down at his half-eaten sandwich. "Have you heard from Brian, Autumn?"

"No," she replied, and stared across at him. His eyes were evasive and she reached a hand to him. "What is it? Is there something I should know?"

Bob was silent for a long moment and looked uncertain. "I don't know, Autumn." He threw up his hands. "What the hell. I'm probably an asshole for telling you this, but Brian is with Lisa."

"Lisa?" she said quietly. "Are you sure?"

He nodded. "Brian flew in a week ago and spent a couple of hours at his office. When he flew out in the Lear, Lisa was with him."

Nothing went unnoticed in Edisonville, and Brian knew it. It was his way of telling her he had made his decision. It was over. Autumn picked up her purse and pushed away from the table. "I have to go, Bob."

He grabbed her hand. "Get mad, Autumn. Scream and kick and call him a few dirty names. Don't be so docile. Fight back."

"No," she mumbled. "I'm too tired to fight anymore. I don't feel like screaming and kicking and calling him names. I just want to hide. I'm going home to pack my things. I'll be at Turtle Ridge if you need to reach me."

Home? Autumn walked throught the many rooms at Osborne House and realized that nothing belonged to her, save for clothes and a few jewels. She found Molly in the kitchen and led her upstairs. "Start packing your things, and have one of the women box up my stuff. I'll take only a couple of suitcases for now, and the pups. I'll send for the rest later."

Molly looked bewildered. "Ain't you gonna wait for Brian?"

"No, I'm not going to wait for Brian. There's no reason for me to stay any longer. There isn't anything more Brian can say. He said it all."

Molly shook her head and looked at Autumn with disapproval. "Don't do this, girl. Wait a spell longer. You got your baby to think about now."

"I can take care of my baby, and Bob can take care of anything that needs to be said to Brian." She turned toward the phone. "While you're packing, I think I'll take one last ride up to the lake."

Molly's face wrinkled in concern. "Do you think you oughta be riding a horse, you pregnant and all? You ain't the expert rider Mr. Brian is."

"I'll ride Penny. She's safe enough." Autumn turned from Molly, called the stable to have Penny saddled, then dressed in Levi's, boots, and her old floppy hat.

*   *   *

The climb to the lake was steep and Penny was lathered on the neck and breast by the time they reached the lake's edge. From the rise Autumn could see all of Edisonville, with its smokestacks, the huge sprawling distillery, the church steeple, even Miners' Row where it had all begun.

She tapped Penny lightly with her heel and reined her around the edge of the lake to the brush-hidden corner where she used to skinny-dip. After urging Penny through the thick undergrowth, Autumn slid from the saddle, loosened the girth, and tied her long so Penny could graze on the tall grass.

Penny whinnied quietly and looked at Autumn with her soft brown eyes. Autumn stroked her chestnut mane and buried her face in the mare's downy fur. "Oh, Penny," she whispered, "I hurt so inside. I've never been divorced before, and my little baby is going to have to settle for a part-time daddy." She slapped Penny on the neck. "Your master is a cheap-shot bastard." She turned from the horse and walked toward the lake. The surface was clear and calm and reflected the blue of the sky. She sat down on the bank, removed her boots and socks, and wiggled her toes in the cool water.

Her thoughts shot back and forth from Brian to Lloyd. "You'll die of boredom," Lloyd had said. He had called her again and again, and each time he had become more persistent. Everett and Douglas had never been a threat to Lloyd, but Brian and the baby were, so he had called repeatedly to remind her of her life in San Francisco, dangling what to Lloyd Murphy was the good life. "That town will suffocate you, Autumn."

"Nah," she had said, and forced laughter into her voice. "Not when I have all of Edisonville to rearrange."

"What about your company? Are you just going to walk away and leave it with managers?"

"No. I can run my company from here. I have the *Cart* for travel, and offices can be built. Douglas ran an empire from here and he seldom left town. He had gofers. I'll get gofers."

"What about Brian? Does he agree?"

"Brian isn't here. He's away thinking things over."

"You told him?"

"Yes, I told him."

"What was his reaction?"

"Very angry, very hurt. I really did a number on him. I'm going to try to make it up to him, if he will let me."

"How long has he been gone?"

"A week and a couple of days."

"Have you heard from him?"

"No, Lloyd. I haven't heard from him."

"Doesn't that tell you something?"

She sighed wearily. "What is it supposed to tell me, Lloyd?"

"That he doesn't want you anymore, or the child."

She frowned and her voice became taut with annoyance. "Why are you doing this, Lloyd? What do you want from me? You now have and have always had some classy mistress in some penthouse apartment. Why can't you let go?"

"We're a team. If the women bother you, I'll get rid of them."

"Bullshit. You couldn't be true to the Virgin Mary herself. There will always be a redhead or a blonde that shows promise."

"I'm not a monk," he snapped. "If you had been here, there wouldn't have been any other women. Pack up and leave, Autumn. I'll take care of you and the baby."

"I don't need anyone to take care of me or my baby, but I do need one thing from you. Right now I don't know what will happen, but if Brian and I stay together, I need to know that you and I will be able to work together in peace. Otherwise, I'll sell out. And I want you to promise that you won't do anything to hurt Brian financially. No wars, no power struggles."

Lloyd laughed. "I don't know why we're having this ridiculous conversation. I know you, Autumn. One year in that hick town with a screaming baby and you'll come flying back to me."

"You didn't promise."

"Okay, okay. I won't do anything to hurt your fair-haired boy. And business is business. We'll work together as we always have."

"Promise?"

"I promise. Let me know what's decided."

She sighed again. "Yes, Lloyd. You'll be the first to know."

Autumn stretched out on the grass with her feet in the lake, felt tears sliding down her cheeks, and kicked at the water angrily. It seemed to her that all she did these days was cry. Pregnancy, she thought. According to her book, pregnant women burst into tears at the slightest provocation.

She wiped at her cheeks, stared up at the cloudless sky, and tried to channel her thoughts in a direct line. It was over with Brian, so she would have to make plans to go it alone. Reno first, then Turtle Ridge until the baby was born, and then back to San Francisco and Lloyd.

She flung her arms wide and closed her eyes, felt the sun grow hot on her face, listened to the sound of Penny moving about—whinny. A sudden, louder whinny made Autumn sit upright with a start. Penny stood with her neck arched, her nostrils flared, her ears thrust forward as if listening to sounds that only she could hear.

Penny whinnied again and pranced in place, staring at the wall of undergrowth. Leaves rustled and branches snapped as Thunder broke through into the clearing with Brian straddling his back.

Brian dismounted and stood beside the horse, gazing at her soberly. "Hello, Autumn."

She looked back at him with a formal nod. "Hello, Brian. Did you do your thinking?"

"Yeah. I did my thinking."

"And what did you decide?"

"That any man who fucks around with my wife had better watch out." He smiled faintly. "You did something my father was never able to do. You kicked my uncles in the ass and made them take control of their lives."

Autumn chewed her lip for a moment. "Your father, and why I married him. Have you come to terms with that too?"

He nodded. "Did you know Dad was allergic to nuts?"

"No," she said. "I knew he hated nuts, but I didn't know he was allergic."

"His reaction to nuts was severe. His stomach content

showed he had eaten nuts the night he drowned. If I had thought somebody put them in his food deliberately, I would have done everything you did to learn the truth, and more.''

''How could he eat nuts without knowing? They crunch.''

''Stomach content showed apple, too. The nuts were probably grated or chopped. Mixed with spiced apples, the nuts wouldn't have been noticed.''

Autumn nodded. She had been afraid that Artie had had something to do with Douglas' death, so she had asked to see the autopsy report too. She hadn't known about the allergy, so the stomach content hadn't meant anything to her; for her the report had merely proved that Artie hadn't had anything to do with Douglas' death.

She sat with her legs crisscrossed, her hands resting on her lap. Brian's voice had been bland and noncommittal. She gazed at him for a moment, trying to read his expression. ''Lloyd,'' she said quietly. ''How do you feel about him now?''

''You're my wife. The baby you're carrying is mine. I'm not going to hand you over to that green-eyed motherfucker in San Francisco.''

''Is that your way of telling me you want to stay married?''

''Yeah. That's what I'm saying.''

He stood beside the horse, his hand resting on the saddle horn, wearing Levi's, boots, and a blue shirt that stretched tight across his wide shoulders. The sleeves were rolled and the collar was open, the coin glimmering in the afternoon sun. His blond hair was windblown, and if possible his skin had even deepened in color; a golden god that looked content and well-sated after his week with Lisa.

The thought of Lisa and Brian together twisted her stomach into a jealous knot. ''You asshole! After two weeks, you ride up on your trusty steed and expect me to fall into your arms because you've decided to forgive me. What makes you think I want to stay married to you anyhow?'' Autumn leapt to her feet, grabbed a good-sized rock, and aimed it at his head. ''You're as bad as Lloyd

Murphy. One woman is never enough.'' She reached for another rock.

Brian looked bewildered and stepped to one side. ''Knock it off, Autumn.''

''The hell I will.'' She picked up another rock, and another, and another. Brian ducked behind a tree to escape her bombardment of flying stones. She looked around, grabbed a broken limb, and heaved with all the force she could muster ''Rotten, cheap-shot bastard.''

The limb bounced off the tree and fell at his feet. Before she could grab another, he leapt the span between them, caught her by the waist, and tumbled her to the ground. She drew back her fist and cracked him on the jaw, bit him on the shoulder. He swore and grabbed her wrist, tufts of her hair, and held her hard against the ground. ''You vicious redheaded bitch. What the hell is the matter with you, anyhow?''

Pinned beneath him, she stared up and wanted to spit. ''When did you decide to stay married, Brian, before or after you screwed Lisa?''

He looked blank. ''I haven't been with Lisa.''

''The hell you haven't. You left with her a week ago in the Lear.''

He nodded. ''Lisa was going to Chicago to shop and visit with friends. I dropped her there, then flew to Seattle to see Uncle Dale.''

Autumn looked uncertain and her voice quivered. ''Truth?''

''Truth. Believe me, Autumn, the last thing I wanted after I left you was a woman, any woman.''

''And now?''

''I want my wife.''

''Even with all her sins?''

''Even with all her sins, and even if she was packing up to leave for San Francisco—and Lloyd Murphy—after telling me she would wait.''

''Are you still concerned about Lloyd?''

''No. If you wanted to be with Murphy, you would be in San Francisco instead of here with me.'' He smiled and rolled away slightly. ''I forgot.'' He reached in his shirt pocket and pulled out a limp rose with a two-inch stem. "It looks a little sick now."

Autumn took the crushed, bedraggled rose with its short, short stem. And then she burst into tears. "Oh, shit," she moaned. "I didn't want to cry again. I'm not normally like this, Brian. I'm a coolheaded businesswoman."

"I can see that." He grinned and wiped at her cheeks.

She smiled too. "We're going to spend our life fighting. You know that, don't you?"

"I wouldn't want it any other way."

She glanced at the rose and then at him. "Gosh, I love you."

"Me too."

She placed the rose carefully at the base of the tree to be added to the others later, then reached for the buttons on her blouse. "Let's be wicked and go skinny-dipping. I need time to wash away the tears."

He nodded, but grasped her by the hand. "I have one more question that's been driving me crazy for two weeks. The night at Rex's place, when you rolled me for three thousand dollars. Was I too drunk to get it up for the beautiful redhead?"

She grinned. "I'll never tell."

"Autumn!" He made a lunge for her.

She laughed, grabbed him by the ears, and kissed him on the mouth. "You'll be pleased to know your big thing performed admirably."

His face spread into a wide grin. "Good. I'd hate to think I missed out on such an expensive fuck." He stuck his booted foot out at her. "Pull, wife."

Autumn helped Brian off with his boots, then peeled off her own clothes and ran toward the lake's edge, arched, and dived into the water. She surfaced, looked back at Brian, and wondered if he knew the only apple dish Douglas would eat was Bea's Apple Betty pie.

She watched as Brian dived into the water and swam toward her. The tears were gone now and secret laughter bubbled in her throat. Dear, absentminded Bea had accidentally put nuts in her Apple Betty pie, which Douglas could not resist . . . or had it been an accident? Bea hated

Douglas and loved Homer. And Homer was being threatened. But Bea? Nah, not sweet, gentle Bea. She couldn't have . . . or could she?

Autumn lunged in the water, stroking, reaching out for her golden god. All things considered, she didn't give a damn.

About the Author

A native of Kentucky, Jonell Lawson has lived with her husband in Washington State for the last twenty-five years. She has four children and six grandchildren, and is currently working on her next novel.